M000194999

Yami-hara

Mizuki Tsujimura

YEN
ON

NEW YORK

Yami-hara

Mizuki Tsujimura

TRANSLATION BY STEPHEN PAUL • COVER ART BY KASHIMA

This book is a work of fiction. Names, characters, places, and incidents are the product of the author's imagination or are used fictitiously. Any resemblance to actual events, locales, or persons, living or dead, is coincidental.

YAMIHARA
©Mizuki Tsujimura 2021
First published in Japan in 2021 by KADOKAWA CORPORATION, Tokyo.
English translation rights arranged with KADOKAWA CORPORATION, Tokyo, through TUTTLE-MORI AGENCY, INC., Tokyo.

English translation © 2023 by Yen Press, LLC

Yen Press, LLC supports the right to free expression and the value of copyright. The purpose of copyright is to encourage writers and artists to produce the creative works that enrich our culture.

The scanning, uploading, and distribution of this book without permission is a theft of the author's intellectual property. If you would like permission to use material from the book (other than for review purposes), please contact the publisher. Thank you for your support of the author's rights.

Yen On
150 West 30th Street, 19th Floor
New York, NY 10001

Visit us at yenpress.com • facebook.com/yenpress • twitter.com/yenpress
yenpress.tumblr.com • instagram.com/yenpress

First Yen On Edition: June 2023
Edited by Yen On Editorial: Jordan Blanco
Designed by Yen Press Design: Liz Parlett

Yen On is an imprint of Yen Press, LLC.
The Yen On name and logo are trademarks of Yen Press, LLC.

The publisher is not responsible for websites (or their content) that are not owned by the publisher.

Library of Congress Cataloging-in-Publication Data
Names: Tsujimura, Mizuki, 1980- author. | Paul, Stephen (Translator), translator.
Title: Yami-hara / Mizuki Tsujimura ; translation by Stephen Paul.
Other titles: Yami-hara. English
Description: First Yen On edition. | New York : Yen On, 2023.
Identifiers: LCCN 2023007861 | ISBN 9781975367763 (hardcover)
Subjects: CYAC: Horror stories. | LCGFT: Horror fiction. | Light novels.
Classification: LCC PZ7.7.T836 Yam 2023 | DDC [Fic]—dc23
LC record available at https://lccn.loc.gov/2023007861

ISBNs: 978-1-9753-6776-3 (hardcover)
978-1-9753-6777-0 (ebook)

10 9 8 7 6 5 4 3 2 1

LSC-C

Printed in the United States of America

CONTENTS

yami-hara
An abbreviation of "yami-harassment."

yami-harassment
A compound of *yami* ("darkness") and *harassment*; unwelcome conduct toward a person stemming from darkness in one's own mind or heart. Applies to any action that threatens or violates the dignity of another person, regardless of intent or awareness.

CHAPTER ONE

New Student

"I'd like to introduce our newest student..."

She lifted her head, and their eyes met.

It was so sudden and unexpected that a thrill ran through her.

A boy in a collared shirt stood next to Mr. Minamino the teacher. His limbs were long and lanky. While he wasn't beautiful, his features were well-shaped and not particularly ugly. If anything, his eyelids were a little swollen and sleepy, giving him a hesitant look. Although perhaps hesitance was to be expected of a transfer student on his first day in class.

He was on the tall side. When he stood next to Mr. Minamino, who was a squat sort, they kind of looked like an odd-couple comedy duo. The one concerning point was his shaggy hair. This was his only chance to make a first impression, and it suggested he didn't much care about his appearance.

The stand collar shirt was a different look; maybe his uniform hadn't arrived in time. At this school, all students wore khaki jackets. Boys had neckties, and girls had ribbons.

Taken aback by the awkward moment of eye contact, Mio broke it off in a way she hoped wasn't unnatural. Mr. Minamino turned to the new student.

"Go on, Shiraishi."

"Yes, sir," the boy replied, recognizing the prompt to introduce himself. His voice a whisper, he said, "I've transferred here because of my father's work. It's nice to meet you all."

"Your name."

"Huh?"

"What's your name? Aren't you going to tell everyone?" the teacher teased.

"Oh," the new student muttered. Without raising the volume of his voice, he stated, "Kaname Shiraishi." Just his name. No other words.

Mr. Minamino wrote the kanji for *Kaname Shiraishi* on the blackboard.

"You all saw he can be a little scattered, but I'm sure we can all get along," the teacher said cordially in an attempt to smooth over the awkward situation. No one laughed.

Then Mio noticed something odd.

The boy was looking at her again. Maybe he just happened to glance over multiple times. Or perhaps Mio was mistaken, and he was watching something behind her...

"You'll sit in the second row, all the way at the back."

A new desk and chair were waiting at the rear of the classroom. The boy mumbled something in reply. His eyes weren't focused on the seat, but on Mio.

Shiraishi strode toward his desk, his school bag bobbing. Only then did he finally take his eyes off her.

Mio figured she was overthinking it. However, she wasn't the only one who noticed the new boy's gaze.

No sooner did she open her boxed lunch to eat with her usual crowd than her best friend, Hanaka Sawada, leaned in close and whispered, "Hey! Hey!" Her long hair dangled before Mio's face. "That gloomy-looking new kid was totally staring at you."

4

"What? No way. Really?"

There were three of them eating lunch together. They sat near the classroom windows—Mio faced away from the outside, while the other two faced her. This was how they always sat when they ate lunch.

At Hanaka's excited tone, Mio's other best friend Saho Imai turned back to peek at the transfer student's desk.

"No! Don't look!" Hanaka hissed. "He's going to know we're talking about him. Don't turn around."

"Wait, doesn't this mean he's, y'know, in love with Mio?"

"…It was probably just a coincidence," Mio insisted, smiling weakly. He'd only looked her way a little. "I haven't spoken a single word to him yet. He can't be in love with me."

"No, no, no," Hanaka and Saho said in unison. They waved their hands emphatically in front of their faces.

"Love at first sight is *totally* a thing. But it's kinda crazy, right? In a manga or a movie, love at first sight is so romantic, but the idea of it happening in real life, without even talking to the person, is creepy. Total stalker stuff."

"Stop it. Don't say it like that."

Saho had always been an avid reader of romance stories, and Mio knew from a lifetime of experience that she could get carried away. However, it didn't seem prudent to speculate so wildly about a person they'd barely spent minutes around.

"Sorry, sorry." Hanaka was the one who apologized. "Anyway, I'm sure Shiraishi's really smart. I heard the standards to transfer to our school are super high. Remember last year, when someone transferred into the grade above ours, and they immediately became the top student in the class?"

Mitsumine Academy was a private high school. It was a prestigious school for students who intended to go to college, one of the oldest in Chiba Prefecture. Transfer students were rare at private schools, but not unheard of. And rumors claimed that the transfer exam was far more difficult than the regular entrance exam.

"If they accepted his transfer, it means the school thinks he'll do well in college and win some prestige points for the school, right? So Shiraishi's probably really smart."

As a private institution for college-bound students, Mitsumine Academy was very picky in this regard. The college-test scores of the latest graduating class were always tacked up on bulletin boards and on the outside wall of the building. It was like how a major cram school showed off its successful track record.

"Probably. But he just transferred here, and it's not right to judge whether someone's smart or gloomy or whatever."

"Aww, c'mon," Saho protested, her medium-length hair draped over her ear.

A new voice suddenly called, "Harano." Somehow, Mr. Minamino was standing right there.

Hanaka and Saho went silent, looking guilty.

"Yes?" Mio asked very naturally.

"Would you help Shiraishi out for me? Show him around after school with some other kids. I would've asked Miyai, but he's not here today."

Miyai was the class's vice representative in the student body. Mio could feel Hanaka and Saho sending her meaningful looks, but she pretended not to notice them.

"All right," she agreed.

"Good. I've already given him a general rundown of what clubs and sports we offer and the special events we hold, so you can just focus on showing him where everything is."

"Yes, sir."

Once the homeroom teacher was gone, Hanaka and Saho smirked. "Look at you, class rep," they whispered.

Saho teased, "If you're nice to him, I bet he'll fall even harder for you."

"Don't be stupid. And if you don't eat quickly, you won't have time to go to the restroom before lunch ends," Mio shot back, playfully annoyed.

Hanaka said, "You're such a model student," and Saho added, "Mio gets all the guys."

She knew they weren't serious, and she turned away to brush off their teasing.

Huh? And that's when she noticed something.

Kaname Shiraishi was looking in her direction.

The boy with the collared shirt and different uniform stood out like a sore thumb. Mio looked down, afraid they might lock eyes again, and acted as though she were unaware of his staring.

"Ugh, I don't wanna go to class after lunch. I just wanna go home."

"Argh! I told Mom not to put cherry tomatoes in my lunch."

The other girls had already moved on to different topics, and they didn't notice Shiraishi's gaze or Mio's reaction. She played it cool and examined the boxed lunch her mother had made.

She still felt his eyes on her. If she looked up, she risked meeting those eyes. The only thing she could do now was stare at her desk. Out of the corner of her eye, Mio spied a navy-blue collared shirt, utterly still.

Her heartbeat grew louder, more out of discomfort than out of fear. Perhaps Shiraishi had overheard their earlier conversation about him. Mio wished Mr. Minamino hadn't asked her to help, at least not while Shiraishi was right there in the room.

Then something occurred to her.

It was the transfer student's first day of school. The boys in the class joked around a lot, but most of them were hardworking and good natured at heart. Had none of them invited lonely Shiraishi into their social circle? Had they left him to eat lunch alone?

The figure in the collared shirt sat in solitude. Mio didn't sense anyone near him, and from what she spied out of the corner of her eye, he never moved.

Later, Mio learned why Shiraishi ate by himself.

Before the end of school, she brought up the topic with a boy she was on good terms with, and he explained that some others had spoken with Shiraishi. They'd asked if he wanted to have lunch with them.

Shiraishi had replied, "Huh?" in total bafflement, like he'd heard a foreign language. When he saw the boxed lunches the other students had brought and the plastic-wrapped pastries from the convenience store, he'd exhaled sluggishly. "Ohhh… I didn't bring one."

Maybe he was planning to attend for only half the day. Or maybe his old school had a cafeteria system. That was common in middle school, but paid-for school lunches weren't really a thing for the high schools in this area. Perhaps they were more common elsewhere. A few people had asked Shiraishi about it, but he'd only answered, "No," to all their questions. He'd seemed annoyed.

The good-natured boys in the class were, understandably, a little put off by this, and decided to leave Shiraishi alone. They told him where to find the student store window and where he could buy some packaged pastries, too. However, he only bobbed his head, showing no inclination to go to either place. Eventually, he was abandoned at his desk.

After hearing this story, Mio found herself flustered as she walked with Shiraishi. The boys she talked to refused to take over the task of escorting him around the school. Their previous interactions with him must have left a sour impression. Hanaka and Saho had an important after-school club meeting and a prior engagement with a boyfriend, respectively.

"Sorry, Mio! Good luck," they said, smirking.

That was how a frustrated Mio found herself all alone with the sullen transfer student, taking him on a tour of the school.

Kaname Shiraishi was even quieter than she'd imagined.

"I'll be showing you around, Shiraishi. Mr. Minamino told you I'd help with this, didn't he?" Mio had said to the boy right after class ended.

He'd merely looked up at her and nodded. Not a single sound had escaped his throat. Feeling a bit taken aback, Mio had told him her name and that she was class representative, but his only response had been an inclination of the head so infinitesimal, it was hard to know if he meant to do it at all.

Where before, Shiraishi had watched Mio, now he refused to meet her eyes. He seemed to be quite shy.

"The third floor has all the special-use classrooms for things like music and art. Usually, when we leave the homeroom, it's for the third floor," Mio explained as they walked. However, the transfer student's expression never changed. He'd nodded silently at first, but now it was challenging to know if he was doing even that much.

"Aren't you hungry?" Mio asked with a smile, hoping to get some kind of response. Shiraishi seemed to turn his head the tiniest bit toward her. "I heard from the boys that you forgot your lunch at home. We're all worried that you might be hungry since you haven't eaten anything all day."

The last bit was an embellishment on Mio's part. The boys had said only that Shiraishi was creepy; they hadn't offered any further concerns. Under her close scrutiny, Shiraishi nodded. Just barely.

Having finally elicited a reaction, Mio followed up with "Did you bring lunch from home at your old school?" There was no response this time. His face was turned away, and he kept silent. Mio's words were left hanging in the air.

Her cheeks flushed.

If someone had seen that, it would've looked as though Mio was being ignored. She felt humiliated but recovered quickly and managed to say, "Well, next is the music room. Down at the end." She started walking, and Shiraishi followed mutely.

Shiraishi kept pace, but his total lack of reaction to anything made Mio feel like he was insulting her.

School clubs were already gathered in the third-floor rooms.

A brass section was practicing in the music room. Mio was on the track team. She'd asked another girl to tell the others that she'd be late to practice, but she worried the upperclassmen would think she'd ditched.

People often called Mio an honor student.

She realized it was probably true, yet she didn't consider it a compliment.

Ever since she was small, Mio had been good at looking out for others. She had a younger brother, which probably had something to do with it. By her early years in elementary school, the teachers and adults regularly praised her for being responsible. When kids were left out of the group in class, on group projects, or during practice, she spoke up about it. When someone who'd been sick for several days returned to school and felt excluded, she approached them and offered to play with them, even if the two weren't particularly good friends.

Before long, teachers and other adults latched on to a common phrase: "That's Mio for you."

She liked receiving such compliments but didn't try to get them.

Mio didn't help for the sake of looking good. She just thought it was what you were supposed to do. As a matter of fact, she'd heard the complaint that she was a Goody Two-shoes her entire life—even from friends. When Hanaka called her a "model student," it wasn't out of admiration. Mio could hear the unspoken second part of such comments: "I can't believe you do this stuff."

Unfortunately, once an idea wormed its way into her head, she couldn't let it be. She *had* to do it. When someone was alone, she figured they felt isolated. Even if they didn't, the impression of being friendless would hurt them socially.

School was a mysterious place. Elementary, middle, and high school—hierarchical layers existed at every level, in every class. Mio immediately understood when she learned about the concept of school castes.

Each class had an upper group and a lower one. Mio didn't enjoy the connotation of the words *upper* and *lower*. A mere difference in interests shouldn't dictate one side's superiority or inferiority. There *was* a difference between the sects, though. The assertive types, the submissive types. The flashy types, the plain types. The loud types, the quiet types.

The upper group in each class tended to be assertive, flashy, and loud, and they wielded influence. However, Mio thought that was owing to the group's insensitivity. Callous students claiming they belonged above the less confident ones didn't sit right with her.

In middle school, a quiet girl Mio spoke with told her, "You know, Mio, you're pretty nice for someone from the *other side*."

Mio didn't know what to make of that statement, and the girl continued, "I guess you're one of those rare ones. The kind who can have a conversation with anyone, regardless of their clique, upper or lower. A person in the middle."

It brought a pang to Mio's chest to hear that girl willingly call herself "lower." But at the same time, she understood. The upper kids spoke harshly to the lower kids, and the lower kids hardly ever spoke to the upper kids. They kept their distance.

Thus, Mio thought the idea of her being "in the middle" made a kind of sense. Maybe lots of people who made friends easily were in the middle. Mio's current friends Hanaka and Saho belonged there.

Even in a strict, prestigious feeder school, there were girls passionate about cosmetics and clothes and guys who liked wilder activities. The "upper" students arranged singles hangouts to meet and hook up with kids from other schools.

Hanaka and Saho were in athletic groups, and Saho had a boyfriend. From the perspective of plainer classmates, they probably appeared glamorous and popular. Yet both of them were kind, and while they liked to tease, they weren't insensitive.

They could be considerate.

Mio had to admit that, compared to her classmates, she was definitely on the empathetic side, too. She was always amiable to others, just as she was with Shiraishi.

People called her an honor student, but Mio knew the truth.

I'm just weak-willed.

Class rep and class chair. Mio often took on important roles at school, but not because she desired to be in control. She didn't think she wanted power or attention. Rather, Mio felt like it would be better if she took on those responsibilities. That was what caused her to keep volunteering.

It was no different this year, in Class 2-3. She hadn't volunteered, but she'd accepted the role of class representative when nominated. Everyone thought she was the best choice because she'd already done it as a first-year.

It was perfectly natural for the class representative to guide a new student around.

Being considerate of other people wasn't always worth the trouble, though. In fact, the other person typically never noticed and didn't repay the favor.

Mio walked down the long third-floor hallway with Shiraishi, silently lamenting. What would people think? Mio decided that if an acquaintance spotted her, she'd tell them she was only giving a transfer student a tour.

"The brass band is usually in the music room after school. Were you in an extracurricular club at your old school?" she asked, figuring that Shiraishi probably wouldn't respond. Unsurprisingly, he didn't. Going for broke, Mio said, "You're pretty tall. Did you play any sports? I bet you have good reflexes."

She didn't actually believe a word of this, but it was a habit of hers to lift up the people she talked to. She assumed he wouldn't give her a positive answer, if any. But to her surprise, there was a response.

"Miss Harano."

Mio was startled. It wasn't until a few moments later that she realized the voice had come from Shiraishi beside her. It was practically the first time she'd genuinely heard his voice. She looked up and met his eyes at very close range.

She thought to ask, "What?" with a smile.

However, Shiraishi's question caused her face to go stiff.

"Can I come to your house today?"

He was—his mouth was—grinning. The ends curled up slowly, revealing misaligned teeth, several of which were extremely sharp. It was a vicious, vicious smile.

Only after fleeing into a room did she feel ready to breathe again.

She couldn't remember how she'd escaped him.

Mio hadn't been able to answer. She'd screwed up her face, assuming she'd misheard Shiraishi or that it was a joke, and tried to smile amiably. However, she knew they didn't have the sort of rapport that allowed for humor like that. Smiling wasn't an option.

"Huh?" she'd said at last, waiting for Shiraishi to say more. She hoped her ears were playing tricks on her.

But the transfer student had said nothing else. He only stared at her with that grin plastered on his face. Her next thought was to run.

He's crazy.

She must have said something to him, a few words. Not out of consideration, but from instinct. Pushing him away or outright rejecting him could be dangerous. "I'm sorry. I need to get going." It was probably something like that.

Mio's heart raced. Now that she was rid of him, she realized how panicked she'd become. A moment later, she understood the feeling better—she was frightened.

Self-pity and shame flooded through her.

Mio remembered what Hanaka and Saho had said during lunch. *"Mio gets all the guys."*

A stalker, gloomy, love at first sight. Be nice to him, and he'll only get more obsessed…

Mio had gone through something like that before. She'd interacted with a boy who was not her type at all—an outcast in class, the unpopular type. Her treating him with her usual care and consideration had caused him to get a crush on her.

That's why Mio had understood when Saho claimed she got all the guys. It wasn't a compliment but an expression of exasperation. Mio was always kind to *those* sorts of boys.

Despite her being told she was popular with boys and knowing it wasn't praise, there was a part of her that enjoyed hearing it. Mio felt bad about that, and she always regretted getting involved because things like this occurred.

I got carried away and didn't think. I did it again.

Kaname Shiraishi was not normal. No typical person would ask what he had in that situation.

But she was the one who had given that abnormal boy the opportunity.

She could have delayed the tour to another day and waited for the vice class representative, a boy, to handle it. Could Mio claim absolutely that she hadn't wanted the out-of-place new student to think she was nice, though?

Not that she wanted him to be romantically interested in her. It wasn't like that. But Mio always did this. It always turned out this way.

"Is that you, Harano?"

Mio straightened up, alarmed.

She'd thought she was alone, but someone was sitting up in the corner of the room. The track-and-field team had separate changing rooms for boys and girls, but this was the all-purpose meeting room for both. Mio had figured everyone would be down in the quad by now. When she saw who sat up, she exhaled with relief.

"Kanbara-senpai..."

"Whew, that was a nice nap. Sorry, I didn't get much sleep last night. I told them I wanted to close my eyes for five minutes before practice. Did they abandon me?" He stretched lazily.

Itta Kanbara was Mio's senpai, an upperclassman member of the track team. Like Mio's, his event was the long jump. They often practiced together, making him one of the few third-years on the team she was close with. He rolled up his jacket sleeve to check his watch.

"Oh crap. It's gonna look like I ditched. Tagawa's gonna be pissed," he groused, somewhat more emphatically than was necessary.

The casual name-drop of the track team's faculty adviser was a note of levity that Mio really needed at the moment.

"What's the matter?" he asked.

"Huh?" Mio blurted out. The question took her by surprise.

"You're such a model student. You never show up late like this. That's for bad students like me."

"Oh, please..." Mio started to object to the usual "model student" praise, but she caught herself. She felt like she might cry; this reminded her of the conversation with the transfer student.

The look in Kanbara's eyes changed, and the sleepiness was gone, replaced with alert seriousness. "No, really, what's the matter?"

Kanbara wasn't very tall, but his features were pleasant. When he stared right at Mio, she found herself thinking he was attractive, as inappropriate as it was given the situation. He had crisp double eyelids, and his skin was tan yet clear, without a single blemish. Before she knew it, that clear, intense gaze had Mio talking.

About the transfer student who'd just shown up today.

About the way she'd felt his eyes on her twice, and the sudden request to visit her house.

Putting it all into words sent a chill down her spine. Kanbara looked more grave now than ever. He leaned forward. "That sounds crazy."

"It *is* crazy," Mio agreed. Mentioning it to someone else had helped alleviate some of the urgency. A hint of a smile formed on Mio's face. It was strange for someone so stressed.

"I don't know, maybe I did something that caused him to misunderstand...," she mused idly.

Because it truly was crazy.

Not just the new student, Kaname Shiraishi. Her train of thought was crazy, too. Telling someone else had turned it into a story. Now it was a piece of evidence, something she could point at to brag about her popularity with boys. Her inability to entirely deny she was a little glad for that worsened the guilt.

Kanbara briskly shook his head. "No, it's not your fault."

His vehemence was extremely heartening. He whispered, "I wonder if there's something we can do about this guy." Kanbara sat on top of a desk and crossed his legs. "It sounds like he's got a screw loose. Like he doesn't know how to communicate with other people properly."

"I guess you could say that..."

"Definitely. Who'd think what he said was cool?" Hearing it so firmly from a third party proved reassuring. "Maybe he likes you, but it's bizarre to make such a leap."

"Do you really think that's all it is? He's into me?" Mio asked.

"Why not? Attraction is attraction. I get it—you're cute and sweet."

Now Mio was speechless for an entirely different reason. It was the first time in her life a boy had called her cute. Right to her face, no less.

And he was older.

Mio already admired Kanbara-senpai.

"At any rate," he said to change the subject. Mio couldn't tell whether he realized his comment had rattled her. "If he tries this again or does something worse, tell me right away. Also, talk to your friends in class and make sure you don't spend any time alone with him."

"Good idea…," Mio replied while trying to control her stirred-up feelings.

"I'm worried about you." Kanbara's comment may not have been that deep, but it caused Mio's heart to stir.

◆

Mio dreaded school the next day.

The thought of returning to the same room as the new student was exhausting.

When her morning track practice was finished, she went to class. Kaname Shiraishi wasn't there yet.

"Morning."

Hanaka showed up a minute later, having completed her volleyball club drills. It was too bad that Saho wasn't there yet; Mio wanted to talk about what happened the day before. Both with the strange transfer student and between her and Kanbara.

Since meeting Kanbara last year, Mio had discussed him with her friends quite a lot. You could say she held a lasting interest in him.

Saho always showed up just in the nick of time, and today was no different. She entered class right at the bell, eyelids heavy from drowsiness. Mio didn't have a chance to chat with her friends during morning lessons.

Kaname Shiraishi's seat was empty.

For an instant, Mio hoped he'd be absent that day, but he entered right after the bell finished ringing.

He still didn't have a new uniform: He was wearing a navy-blue collared shirt again. He didn't seem in any hurry to avoid being late, sauntering slowly and unsteadily. He took his seat in silence. Some of the others near him offered, "Good morning, Shiraishi," but Mio didn't hear any reply. He might have nodded in response.

When he moved slowly, he shuffled like a zombie, perhaps because he was so tall. Mio recalled how he hadn't eaten lunch the previous day, and it struck her as more creepy than before.

This isn't good.

After what happened, minor things about Shiraishi that Mio hadn't thought much about previously now worried her, like his figure and gait. Mio fought the urge to turn and look at his seat. She sensed Shiraishi's eyes on her but ignored the feeling, chalking it up to imagination.

Until she had the chance to talk to Hanaka and Saho at lunch, Mio constantly felt like she was being watched.

Could stares apply physical pressure? The right side of her neck felt painful and cramped. Her body was tense.

Kaname Shiraishi disappeared during the lunch break. Did he not intend to eat today, either?

Well, he was gone now. Definitely gone.

After checking several times to be sure, Mio finally told her friends.

"So, listen to this…"

When she got to the part about him asking to come to her house, Hanaka and Saho were silent. Before that point, they'd smiled and teased her. *"Aww, he fell in love with you? We warned you!"* The amusement was gone now.

Hanaka stole a glance at Shiraishi's seat, still empty, then turned back to Mio.

"That's crazy."

Everyone kept using that word, and Mio agreed. It was the only descriptor that fit.

Hanaka and Saho lowered their voices. They'd been keeping the conversation quiet already, but now it felt more like people pressing their foreheads together to have a proper secret discussion.

"I don't know, it kind of sounds like Shiraishi's more than just a gloomy loner, right? Something's wrong with him. He's nuts."

"Yeah…"

Mio felt lost. Her friends scowled when she told them about feeling his stare this morning.

"But you were okay yesterday, right? He didn't follow you home?"

"I don't think so… When I told an upperclassman on the track team, he walked me home."

Recently it had become obvious that when Mio mentioned an upperclassman from the track team, she was usually talking about Kanbara, even if she didn't mention his name.

This newest wrinkle in the story caused Hanaka's and Saho's expressions to go slack. "Whaaat?!" they exclaimed.

"To your house? Holy shit! When did you get so bold?"

"It was a coincidence. I went to the clubroom, and there was an older student there. I told him about it because I was scared, and he was really worried for me."

Mio hadn't believed Shiraishi would follow her home, yet she'd felt emotional upon seeing Kanbara waiting for her at the school gate when practice ended.

"What? I'm fine! Is this necessary?" she'd questioned, despite the thrill running through her.

Kanbara had frowned and replied, "After what you told me, I can't let you walk back alone." Then he had taken her school bag right out of her hands.

Mio's heart had threatened to stop then and there from sheer nervousness and delight.

I wish I had a boyfriend like him, she'd thought.

"Whaaaaat?!" her friends squealed, all but shrieking.

Saho leaned forward in excitement and rubbed Mio's shoulder. "I'm so happy for you!"

"He wouldn't do that for an underclassman on the track team unless he cared about her. I know the thing with the transfer student sucks, but it's like…every cloud has a silver lining? Or the glass is half-full, or something? Maybe that upperclassman's feeling the pressure now that he has a rival? He was into you all along!"

"No, Senpai was just worried…"

Kanbara was nice to everyone on the team. He probably would've done the same for anyone else. That was part of why Mio was so drawn to him.

"Still, Shiraishi's concerning, for sure… Do you think he legitimately fell in love with you at first sight, even though you've barely said a word to each other?"

"It's probably because he's never said anything to a girl, *ever*. When someone shows him the tiniest bit of kindness, he gets the wrong idea."

Hanaka and Saho continued to chat for a bit.

"But you know," Saho said, "I can't say I don't understand the feeling."

"Huh? What do you mean?"

"I mean, love makes you feel like you're out of control." That came as a surprise. Saho normally hated guys like Shiraishi and spared no chance to make that clear. When Mio didn't say anything, Saho hastily added, "Of course, I feel bad for you! I'm just saying. When I fall in love, I can't trust myself. When I know I shouldn't text him, I get nervous and end up sending a ton of messages. And I keep telling people about my romantic problems, even when they don't want to hear them. I know I was unbearable with my old boyfriend last year."

Mio and Hanaka exchanged a surprised look. Saho was ordinarily extremely romantic, to the point that they hadn't realized she was this aware of her tendencies.

"You're not like Shiraishi," Mio insisted.

Saho grinned in her usual way. "Well, yeah, of course not. I'm only pointing out that I might look calm now, but I'm different when I'm in love."

"I don't know, your current boyfriend seems really nice," Hanaka remarked.

"Yes. Because we're so into each other!" Saho exclaimed, her response punctuated by a sappy smile.

"Mio," someone called, a classmate named Yanai. She was a plain and dedicated student in the literature club who wore braids and glasses. Her seat was next to Mio's.

Tuning out Hanaka and Saho's romantic discussion, Mio asked, "What is it? Did you already finish eating lunch?"

"Um, yes. I ate in the literature club room with the others… But I have something to tell you."

Mio noticed the girl looked a bit on edge and confused.

"Shiraishi just spoke to me in the hallway." Yanai tensed when she spoke his name. The eyes behind her glasses appeared troubled, and they blinked slowly in her attempt to regain control. "He asked me…he asked me to switch seats. Because he wants to sit by you."

Goose bumps formed on Mio's skin instantly.

Hanaka and Saho were holding their breath, watching wide-eyed and silent. Yanai seemed very distressed.

"I figured it was a joke, but I felt I should tell you anyway. Sorry."

Yanai left the classroom quickly, practically scampering.

The first thing to break through Mio's numb shock was *anger*.

Why? Why? The question repeated. She hadn't done anything to deserve this kind of attention. She'd met him only the day before, and there was nothing between them. Why was he doing this?

"I can't believe it," Saho and Hanaka said. They each put a hand on one of Mio's shoulders.

"You all right, Mio?"

"He can't do that just because he loves you."

"Because he loves you."

Saho's words sent a chill down Mio's spine. Love. Maybe that was how he saw it. Mio didn't feel that way at all. Forcing those feelings on her felt akin to violence.

"It's sexual harassment," said Hanaka. The strength of those words took Mio's breath away.

Sexual harassment. Maybe that's right, she thought dully. But it didn't feel right at all.

"It's not sexual harassment, though. It doesn't have anything to do with my gender..."

"Really? Well, it's *something* harassment. Whatever it is, it should have a name—being ignorant of your social distance with another person," Hanaka replied.

She had a good point. Something was going on: Shiraishi was making demands and upsetting Mio with no apparent realization that it was wrong. It wasn't normal behavior.

"Let's go tell him off," Hanaka suggested. Mio looked up, on the brink of tears, and her friend continued, "We'll go to the new kid and say, 'What do you think you're doing? Whether you like Mio or not, she doesn't like you.'"

"I don't...know if that's...," she replied, half on reflex.

"Why not?" Hanaka asked, one eyelid narrowed. "If you don't want to go in person, we'll do it for you."

"Thank you. But..."

More than anything, Mio didn't want to worsen the situation. To tell him off and speak her mind would be to declare antagonism. It would be best if she could ignore the issue until it passed.

"I'm afraid that just telling him to stop might make him worse."

"Yeah, I think I actually agree with you," Saho added, trying to calm an incensed Hanaka. "It kind of feels like giving him attention will feed the fire. Maybe not engaging is the best response."

"Really? But won't it feel terrible if you stay quiet and he escalates regardless? It'll be so humiliating."

"Hanaka, be quiet," Saho urged, leaning closer. Her eyes were trained on the doorway. Mio clamped her mouth shut along with her friends.

Shiraishi had returned to the class. Perhaps he had gone to eat lunch today. He returned to his seat. Mio avoided looking at him. If she saw him watching her, she might actually scream this time.

Saho and Hanaka likely watched him longer than Mio risked doing so. They didn't say anything, meaning he probably wasn't watching. Mio's heart raced. She was relieved that Shiraishi wasn't staring. Still, after what he'd said to Yanai, it was hard to believe he wasn't going to do anything more unless he was seriously messing with her.

"…Do you think Yanai actually said no to him?" asked Saho.

"Huh?"

Saho sounded hesitant to voice her question. "She came to tell you that he asked to switch seats with her, but what did she say back? I'm sure she turned him down."

Mio realized that Saho was right; she'd never heard Yanai's answer.

"…I'll go and check."

It was all right. It would be all right. But that didn't stop the uneasiness in Mio's chest.

Her appetite was gone, so she packed up her boxed lunch and hurried out into the hallway to find Yanai.

◆

"Was everything cool with him today?"

Mio was just softening up the sand before a long-jump attempt during after-school practice when someone approached from behind. She wanted to be alone and was crouched down with the rake.

Turning, she saw Kanbara in his tracksuit, and relief flooded through her. His tapping the toes of his sneakers against the ground, two touches with one foot and then two touches with the other, and windmilling his arms to stretch was a very mundane and reassuring sight.

"Kanbara-senpai..."

"I've been worried since I walked you home."

Some third-year girls speaking with first-years nearby were briefly distracted by this, Mio could tell. Kanbara was attractive, smart, and athletic, so girls in his grade liked him, too. It was pretty easy to discern that *everyone* on the team liked him.

Mio shook her head. "I'm fine. Thank you for yesterday."

"Just tell me if you ever need help. Technically, I am an upperclassman, so maybe that will convince that guy to back down."

Every word that came from Kanbara's mouth felt like a sweet temptation. Mio wished she could tell him everything that had happened today, but the other third-years were listening.

"I'm fine," she repeated.

Mio had tracked down Yanai and confirmed that she hadn't agreed to trade seats. However, her refusal had been based purely on the rules. "It's not entirely up to the students to decide their seats," she'd said. In other words, Yanai hadn't criticized the abnormality of Shiraishi's request. Mio felt a bit disappointed by that, although she didn't have much right to complain.

Nobody was telling him off directly. Mio even asked her friends not to antagonize him because she didn't want this to get worse.

"You sure? All right, then." Kanbara still sounded worried. The look on his face inclined Mio to accept his offer, but she held firm.

Practice continued as usual, and in the changing room afterward, Mio heard the third-year girls speaking about something in hushed tones behind her back.

"…said he walked her home…"

She quickly finished changing, feigning ignorance, and announced that she was leaving, as was customary. It was obvious that the older girls wanted to say something, but Mio took off before they could.

"Oh, I'm glad you're still here, Harano," said Kanbara, leaning against the wall at the end of the hallway. Mio was gauging whether or not to reply when he pulled out his phone. "Let's trade LINE accounts." Kanbara hit the button that called up a scannable QR code for adding friends and held out the screen.

"Okay, sure," Mio agreed, retrieving her phone. The act of linking messenger accounts had them leaning over their screens. Their faces felt very, very close.

Mio's heart skipped a beat.

"Drop me a message if anything happens. Later." Kanbara made to leave, and Mio thanked him loudly. Then he turned back. "That short hair looks good on you, Harano."

"Huh?"

"And it's good to hear your voice so clear when you say hi and stuff," he added casually.

The floor beneath Mio's feet turned light, and heat rose in her cheeks. Kanbara was walking away again.

"Th-thank you," she stammered, voice uneven from sheer happiness. Kanbara strolled off, waving a hand but not looking back.

Exchanging LINE accounts? It was like a dream. Mio clutched her phone to her chest.

I'm glad it didn't happen when the older girls on the team were watching.

Mio took a bus from the high school and got off at the seventh stop.

From there it was a roughly ten-minute walk to her home, a two-story building with a bamboo grove around back. It was her father's family house, and Mio's grandparents lived there, too. Her grandfather had passed away, though, leaving five: Grandmother, Mother, Father, Mio, and her younger brother.

A single bus ride to and from school was a big part of Mitsumine Academy's allure for Mio. However, the actual distance involved was anything but short. Mio was the only kid in her neighborhood attending Mitsumine. She hardly ever ran into fellow students around her place.

Evening was settling in after track practice, and a pale moon rose in the autumn sky. Mio liked this plaintive time of year, when summer was over and fall began. Lots of apartment buildings had popped up in recent years, but plenty of fields still dotted the area, and the gentle, quiet scenery helped ease the day's emotions. This had been a regular view since Mio's childhood.

That was what had made walking the route with Kanbara-senpai so thrilling. She'd insisted that he needed only to take her to the bus stop, yet he'd asked, *"Why? There's no point unless I take you home."*

Mio had walked with her crush through the neighborhood where she had been born and raised. He'd strolled right alongside her.

Actually thinking that word—*crush*—made it clear that her feelings had solidified since the day before. She'd hoped that someone would see her walking with him. The idea of the local women watching and assuming he was her boyfriend filled her with ticklish pride.

Imagining her family seeing them together was still too much, and she had no idea how her father would react. But if her brother Shizuku saw and asked, "Your boyfriend, Sis?" and she said, "Don't tell anyone," well… Mio's imagination was getting the better of her, filling her with a mix of elated excitement and embarrassment.

Saho, Hanaka, and Mio. The usual group.

Saho was always in relationships, and Hanaka claimed that she'd had a boyfriend in middle school. Mio was the only one who'd never been with a guy. She didn't know how it was supposed to go. Was this how relationships started?

He'd called her cute. He'd walked her home. They'd traded LINE contacts. Things were definitely getting closer. If this were one of those romance games, she would be locked on his path by now, right? Was it too selfish to hope that this was the case?

The moon hung in the pale sky, where the blues of evening and night mingled, while she walked beneath, indulging her imagination. Soon she was standing before the front gate of her house.

Someone emerged from the bamboo grove behind the house. He looked like a tall male student at first glance.

And then Mio realized something.

A male student.

She never saw kids from her school around here.

The boy approaching through the gloom wore a uniform. A familiar collared-shirt uniform. The one uniform in her class that was different from all the others.

The transfer student. Kaname Shiraishi.

"Ah." He noticed her. For some reason, his grunt sounded like "Oh, shoot," to Mio.

She'd spent all that effort avoiding him at school, yet he'd just emerged from behind her house.

Despite a resolution she'd made to scream the next time something happened with Shiraishi, she found herself strangely silent. Her eyes were wide, and her mouth hung half-agape. She wanted— she needed—to say something, but no words formed. She was too shocked.

Shiraishi's expression never changed.

Say something, Mio thought, but he kept quiet. He didn't look away awkwardly, or panic, or react in any way. It was like he had no emotions.

"What…are you doing?" Mio's voice trembled. It was up to her to speak first. "What are you doing here?"

This is my house.

She had to hold back the rest. An instinctual alarm blared, telling her not to reveal any information about herself. Confusion swirled like a storm in her mind.

Why does he know my address? The school doesn't distribute student home addresses. How did he find out? Did he follow us? When I walked home with Kanbara-senpai yesterday, proud and happy, was he lurking behind us…?

There was an eerie look in Shiraishi's eyes. It had been his decision to come here, it was his fault, yet he looked annoyed about it. He glared down at Mio lazily.

"I wondered what sort of place you live in."

That was when the scream emerged. But it was not with her full throat. It was thin and weak, like a high-pitched whistle releasing steam for a brief moment.

She felt the same kind of fear as when he'd asked, *"Can I come over to your house?"* the day before. The same alienness, the same creepiness.

But this time it was much, much worse.

This is my house. We're standing right out front.

Shiraishi stared at Mio. The ends of his mouth curved, revealing his jagged teeth.

He's smiling, she thought, and, at last, she could move.

Mio launched herself into the front yard, racing straight for the house. "Mom, Mom!"

She scrambled through the door and hastily locked it. Although she called desperately for her mother, there was no response. "Moooooom!" Mio cried, which finally got her brother Shizuku to pop his head out.

"Shut up already." He was in his first year of middle school. "Mom went out shopping," he explained.

"Shizuku…"

The scowl on his face turned to an expression of shock when he saw her. A graphic novel was in his hand; he'd been reading comics.

"What…?" she asked in response to his look.

"You look really pale, Sis."

Mio knew. Big goose bumps stood on her arms. She was scared, terrified. Despair gripped her, and she felt caught in the sights of something incomprehensible.

How could he be so obsessed with her when they'd met only the day before? It wasn't fair.

"I'm being followed…by this weird guy," Mio finally managed.

"What?!" Shizuku bolted to the door and rushed out. There was no time to stop him.

"Shizuku, no!"

Mio didn't want to antagonize Shiraishi or let him know about her brother. She didn't want him to see her family. However, she couldn't rush outside after Shizuku. The thought of facing Shiraishi again was too frightening.

Shizuku came back inside very quickly. "Nobody's out there."

"Oh," Mio muttered weakly.

Shizuku eyed his sister with concern. "Are you okay, Sis?"

"…I'm fine."

I'm not fine. I'm not fine.

But she said she was anyway. Mio was so scared that it brought tears to her eyes, which she carefully wiped away so Shizuku wouldn't see.

Back in her room, she felt a fresh wave of fear, but it was accompanied by tremendous relief. She'd made it back safely. She'd gotten away.

Mio cautiously approached the window and drew back the curtain to sneak a look below. From what she saw of the road in front of the house, there was no Shiraishi. However, she was still too frightened to turn on the room light.

Had she not added Kanbara-senpai on LINE, she would have gone crying to Shizuku or her parents for help. Instead, she found his name on her contact list, then typed, *It's Mio Harano. Do you have time right now?*

She clutched her phone and lowered her head while waiting for his response. Tears threatened to return. She was sick of all this. A sudden urge came over her to cry and bawl like a child having a tantrum.

A pale light bloomed in the dark room. Mio's phone vibrated. She wasn't receiving a text but a call. Mio heaved a tremendous sigh.

"What's wrong, Harano?"

"Senpai..."

She should have tried to figure out where to start. Instead, the moment she heard his voice, she lost her breath. Tears flooded her eyes.

"Senpai, please help me," she pleaded.

"Sure thing. What's up?"

He was trying to calm her down. The sobs in her voice didn't make him panic. He was perfectly strong and reassuring.

◆

I never expected things to start this way...

Kanbara was going to leave school with Mio every day and accompany her home. This time Mio didn't refuse the offer. She didn't have the strength to anymore.

After practice, Kanbara waited in the hallway for her to finish changing. The older girls were startled by this and asked what he was doing. Before Mio could answer for him, he cheerily replied, "Aw, c'mon, don't make me spell it out. We're going out, obviously."

Mio almost choked from astonishment. She thought her heart might stop. The other girls were stunned as well. Kanbara started walking off, as simple as that, and Mio had to rush to catch up. She turned to offer an apologetic bow to the stunned upperclassmen.

It was awkward, and she felt a bit bad for them, but she also felt incredible. When she caught up to Kanbara, he cut her off before she could ask him about what he'd said.

"Wanna get something to eat?"

The pair ate at a fast-food place near school. If only it could have lasted forever. Even if it was just defense against a stalker, Mio was delighted for the chance to play the role of girlfriend briefly. She even prayed that their little charade got fuzzy enough to become real.

Mio decided to completely ignore Shiraishi at school. Of course, she hated the idea of being in the same classroom as him—even the same building. He spoke directly to her only when she was alone, though. With others around, he'd never be able to say anything.

He was watching. Mio remained determined never to look in his direction when she felt those eyes. Glancing meant interacting. No matter how curious she got, she'd never check.

Shiraishi's new uniform hadn't arrived yet, apparently. Mio found that irritating. A certain vague, collared figure in the corner of her vision—not that she looked at him—stuck out like a sore thumb. She did her best not to think about it, yet he was always there, as though pursuing her.

But he couldn't do a thing. Hanaka and Saho helped ensure Mio was never truly alone, so she could ignore him.

Or so she thought.

During math class, Mio noticed something amiss.

An irregularity stood out. Mio looked down at her desk, where something caught her eye.

Unfamiliar writing sat below her textbook.

Mitsumine Academy was a private school for students who intended to go to college, and it had a reputation of being like a major cram school. Desks weren't typically vandalized because most students didn't fool around during lessons. Occasionally, there were marks or scribbles from someone who'd sat at the desk before, but it was rare.

nbara?

There was only the one small bit of text.

It was very clear handwriting, done in pencil, but the strokes and wings on the characters were the pristine sort left by a brush. But there was also something undeniably eerie about the uniform, almost mechanical script. For one thing, it was written on Mio's own desk. It hadn't been there the day before.

She slid her textbook aside to see the entire message and gasped.

Can you not be so close to Itta Kanbara?

Mio covered her mouth.

Had she not, she would've let out another whistling shriek. She collapsed against her desk. Thankfully, she didn't make any sounds. Mio's head rose reflexively, and it threatened to look at Shiraishi. She held firm, however, pressing her forehead back against the desk and staying put. Mio wanted to give herself a medal.

With trembling fingers, she pulled an eraser out of her pencil case and got to work. She had to remove the whole message.

The beautiful letters, almost sickeningly straight and orderly, had to belong to Shiraishi. What was his upbringing like for him to behave in such a bizarre and disrespectful manner? It was difficult to believe he had a home with parents and other family members.

Mio recalled Hanaka's words. *"It's sexual harassment."*

She also remembered saying that was wrong, and her other thoughts from that conversation. It wasn't sexual in nature, but this was definitely some kind of harassment.

Maybe I just don't know the right word. Trying to order someone not to be friends with someone else was like… What was the term used for abuse between couples? Moral harassment?

Mio rubbed the eraser against the desk, feeling ready to cry. She rubbed and rubbed. Even after the letters disappeared, she continued to work at the blank spot on the desk, hard.

The entire time, she keenly felt Shiraishi watching her. She couldn't shake the sensation.

"You already erased it?"

School was over.

All the other students—including Shiraishi—were gone, leaving only Mio, Hanaka, and Saho to discuss the writing on the desk. Hanaka's question caused Mio to realize something. Her friends stared at the clean desk.

"If it was still there, you could have shown the teachers."

"Yeah. That's a good point…"

Only now did Mio realize that she'd removed evidence to convince teachers and other students of her side of the story. That had never occurred to her in the moment. She was so disgusted that she couldn't help but run her eraser over the desk until it was warm from friction.

"…Do you believe me?" Mio asked.

"Of course, *we* believe you," her friends assured her, looking worried.

"But if you're getting harassed to this extent, you should really tell the teacher or the school. You need evidence, so the next time he tries something, save it," Hanaka added.

"…You're right. Sorry."

"C'mon, Hanaka, be nice. This is really hard for Mio," Saho urged.

That would undoubtedly soften Hanaka's tone. She'd say, "Sorry, I'm just worried about you…"

However, today Hanaka was hard as nails.

"Well, you don't really seem that nervous about it, Mio," she said, clearly irritated. "You talk about how scary it is and claim you hate it, but you don't seem interested in telling the teachers at all. You're going out with your senpai, so you've got a boyfriend, and it seems like you're kind of over this."

"That's not true!" Mio erupted. She was surprised Hanaka thought of her that way. Fresh anxiety gathered, and it had nothing to do with Shiraishi.

Hanaka's going to get sick of me.

"I'm sorry if you felt that way, Hanaka," Mio went on. "But I'm not officially going out with Senpai, and I really need your help. I'm not taking that for granted…"

Despite saying the words herself, Mio believed they sounded insincere, which heightened her panic. Hanaka was kind by nature, and she had a strong sense of right and wrong, but she was stubborn.

If I make her mad, I need to apologize. I need to apologize, Mio thought desperately.

Hanaka said nothing, and Saho was clearly uncomfortable being stuck in the middle.

While Mio searched for the right words to escape this situation, Hanaka's eyes drifted off.

"I'm sorry," she apologized. "I'm taking out my frustration on you, I think. Sorry. Maybe I'm just feeling left out, since both of you have boyfriends now."

It sounded as though she were talking to herself. Hanaka picked up her bag, and without looking either of her friends in the eye, she stated, "I'm just gonna go home. Sorry." Then she made to leave the classroom.

"I'm sorry, too," Mio echoed quietly, but Hanaka didn't reply. She hoped it was because her voice was too low to hear. Pain needled at her heart.

Saho looked upset. Mio hoped that whatever she was going to say, it wouldn't be an insult for their friend who had just left.

"She's so cute; she'll get a boyfriend in no time," Saho said, despite the absent person in question.

"Yeah," Mio agreed.

Kanbara was absent from the track team practice that day.

Mio was crestfallen, but couldn't ask anyone why he wasn't there, fearing what the other girls thought of her.

Everyone in the club, not just the long-jump group, seemed to be keeping her at a distance. Perhaps that was inevitable, considering Kanbara's popularity. Mio felt like she was being forced to sit on a bed of needles.

Hanaka and Kanbara were gone.

Mio walked past the school gate, fearing that she'd have to leave alone, when she heard a voice say, "Yo."

She looked up, and there was Kanbara. Realizing he'd waited for her again filled her with joy.

"But you weren't at practice…"

"Yeah, I got called to the faculty room for guidance counseling. The other seniors didn't tell you?"

I didn't have a chance to ask, Mio thought.

"Anyway, Mio. While I waited for you, I saw that girl you're friends with go by. The one with long hair."

Her ears got hot when he said her first name. It was the first time he'd ever done that.

"We had a fight," she admitted.

"What? No way!" Kanbara looked at her with concern. "Whose fault was it?"

"Mine, I think."

"Mmm." Kanbara exhaled, then said, "Oh, you'll be fine," in his casual way. "You'll be on good terms again in no time. You and Hanaka always look like you're having fun. All three of you. You're like the Three Amigas."

"I don't know…"

Kanbara took Mio's schoolbag from her hands and started walking. As she hurried after him, she felt heat in her cheeks.

He paid attention to me. He watched what I did and learned who I'm friends with.

Just as Kanbara had said, Hanaka's mood was better the next morning.

"Sorry about yesterday. I was really acting weird," she said in an especially bright and cheery voice. Mio sensed the other girl's willingness to put yesterday behind and be friends again, so she replied, "I'm sorry, too."

Saho was relieved.

"Nothing happened with Shiraishi later yesterday? All cool?"

"…Yeah." Mio couldn't mention that it was because her upperclassman had walked her home again.

"That's good," Hanaka said. "But you gotta speak up if something more happens." Her long hair was tied in a ponytail, revealing the nape of her neck and making her appear older. Mio reflected on how reliable and mature Hanaka was despite being the same age as her and on how much she truly loved her friend.

"But if that new kid really thinks he can compete with Kanbara-senpai, he's a total joke. They're barely even the same species, at *best*."

"Hanaka."

"It's true! Mio, it might be best not to show off how romantic you are with him. Kanbara-senpai's super hot, and he seems really dedicated. I'm jealous."

Hanaka's thoughts on Shiraishi were certainly caustic, but Mio was relieved to hear her friend speak so cheerily.

What made having a shared enemy so reassuring? Hanaka and Saho were beaming. The smile was infectious, and Mio joined them. "You think so?" she asked.

Hanaka chuckled through her nose. It felt good to hear her laugh.

When something truly upsetting happened, this kind of pleasantness vanished instantly. Yet when they could laugh and chat, Mio forgot all about her problems.

Something unpleasant and loathsome, but not so serious that she couldn't forget about it when it wasn't happening. Mio later came to regret speaking about it with her friends like a juicy bit of gossip.

During break time, Hanaka and Saho went to the faculty room for their class committee duties. Mio should have spoken up and gone with them. Instead, she let her guard down and did something else, telling herself that it was only a ten-minute break.

She was on her way back from the restroom when he spoke.

"Harano."

Mio's legs faltered, and she found herself suddenly paralyzed.

Kaname Shiraishi stood on the stairs to the next floor. The ones that faced the bathrooms.

There were many other students around this time. That's why she'd gotten careless and believed she was safe.

"This is your *fainull worening.*"

The words didn't sink in at first. They were just sounds.

It took a while for Mio's brain to convert the noises into the words *final warning.*

He spoke again, cutting through her panic. This time he didn't wear that hideous smile. It was almost comical how straight faced he was now.

"Don't be friends with Itta Kanbara."

◆

Mio fled the scene. Not since she was a little girl playing tag had she run this hard to get away from another.

She flew up the stairs, and in the blink of an eye, she was outside classroom 3-3—Kanbara-senpai's class.

"Is Kanbara-senpai here?" she asked a boy near the door, suddenly feeling awkward. The boy looked surprised. Perhaps it was strange for an underclassman to be here. However, he turned and called into the room, "Hey, Kanbara!"

He was slumped sleepily over his desk. Blearily, he lifted his head, and when he spotted her, he lit up.

"Mio!"

The mention of her name brought a profound change to the classroom. The girls buzzed and stared at Mio. Drawn by the shift in attention, the boys also took interest.

It was the first time anyone in school had called Mio by her given name in front of others.

Surely he did so because she was his "girlfriend."

After her flight in search of safety, the warm and gentle greeting nearly brought tears to her eyes. It had been so scary. So scary.

"What's up?" Kanbara came over to the door and examined her face.

"Senpai... Shiraishi, he..."

She couldn't imagine returning to her classroom.

Kanbara's face clouded over. "Huh?"

Mio continued, "He just started talking to me. I was alone during the break, and he said something about a final warning. That I shouldn't be friendly with you..."

"You were alone?"

Mio nodded. "I was only going to the restroom during the ten-minute break."

Kanbara's expression changed. He looked at the clock over the blackboard and whispered, "Class is gonna start." He seemed quite serious now. "I'll hear you out after school. Let's have a real talk."

"Okay."

Mio didn't think she could go back to the class with Shiraishi waiting. However, she felt better after seeing and speaking with Kanbara. She'd been careless. Being alone wasn't an option anymore.

She made it back to her homeroom just in time, right before the teacher for the next subject arrived. When she slipped into her seat, she felt the gazes again.

The gazes of Hanaka and Saho, quietly concerned—and one more. Kaname Shiraishi was staring at her. She never turned to see, yet she knew.

Shiraishi probably knew that Mio had gone to her senpai. She had a hunch. It was creepy, but her senpai was how she kept him at bay.

Senpai knows what you're doing. You won't get away with this, Mio thought, doing her very best to ignore Shiraishi.

After school, Mio left immediately and hurried down the hall. She wanted to see Kanbara as soon as possible.

He was in the corridor outside the track room. That he hadn't entered made it clear he was waiting for her.

Mio grinned at him, glad to have his concern. "Kanbara-senp—"

"Let's go."

"Huh? But we have practice."

He pushed off the wall and grabbed Mio's hand, leading her away from the clubroom. He shook off her protests and looked over his shoulder. "Is this really the time for that? We need to talk about what's going on."

"Oh. Then we should tell the teacher or other people that we're skipping practice."

Kanbara sounded sharp, agitated. He was going to tell off Shiraishi out of concern for Mio. What should she do if he said he'd confronted Shiraishi directly? It was nerve racking to consider.

Kanbara looked at Mio reproachfully.

She wasn't used to the feeling of his hand in hers. It made her self-conscious.

"W-wait. Please wait."

She felt bad about forcing him to stop for her, but skipping practice without telling anyone wasn't a good idea. Mio worked her hand free of his and went into the clubroom. Inside, she told a first-year girl, "I'm not feeling well, so I'm going to skip practice today. Please let the teacher and the others know."

"Okay, I'll do that," the girl replied. Mio could tell that she was curious about Kanbara behind her. Had he told the club he wasn't going to be at practice? Mio didn't enjoy that it looked like they were skipping practice together—never mind that they *were*. If they intended to be a couple on the team, it would be best to give their full efforts at practice and meets to ensure everyone was happy for them.

Mio felt guilty for leaving the club behind, but she took her personal shoes from the lockers by the front entrance anyway. She and Kanbara would have to pass by the track where the team practiced, which hurt. Mio crouched, trying to stay low and small, hoping no one would see.

However, Kanbara was bold about it. He showed no shame for leaving the others. When the third-years spotted him and said, "Huh? Itta!" he just smiled and waved.

"Yo!" He didn't go out of his way to explain anything. It was a sign of his popularity that he could stroll off like this without anyone realizing he was ditching. Mio felt very self-conscious about the meaningful way everyone who spoke to Kanbara eyed her, however.

Was Kaname Shiraishi watching from somewhere? He'd learned that Mio and Kanbara had grown closer in the last few days. What if he tried to attack Kanbara or something?

Kanbara walked a step ahead of Mio, saying nothing.

"Sorry I forced you to skip practice, Senpai."

He didn't answer right away. Maybe just saying "sorry" like that was a little too familiar. Before, she would have said, "I'm very sorry," or "I apologize."

"Listen," Kanbara began once they passed the school gate. "What's going on?"

"Huh?"

"I told you not to let yourself be caught alone. On the phone."

In the moment, Mio didn't know what he was talking about. It was too abrupt.

"I'm so sorry," she apologized hastily. Finally, she understood that Kanbara was angry with her.

"I told my friends to help ensure I'm never alone during the morning, at lunch, and after school. This time it happened during a break between periods. Other students were around, so I thought it would be safe."

"But it wasn't, was it?"

"You're right. I'm...I'm sorry," Mio repeated, stunned. Hanaka and Saho had warned her, but she hadn't thought Kanbara would scold her, too.

"Do you understand what you did wrong?"

Mio nodded. "Yes."

"Tell me."

"...I let myself be alone, even though you were worried for me."

Kanbara sighed, long and heavy. The rattle in his breath froze Mio's heart. *I don't want him to be fed up with me.*

"You're not serious about protecting yourself, are you?" he said. "It's occurred to me every time you've talked about this. If you were genuinely worried, you'd reject that guy, completely ignore him. Why are you talking with him?"

"B-but...," Mio stammered. *I wasn't.* "He just comes up and speaks to me. I don't say anything to him."

"Okay, then why are you letting him talk? If you're really ignoring him, just run away immediately. I keep telling you to do that."

Did he say that? Mio tried desperately to remember.

After each encounter with Shiraishi, Senpai always heard her out. When he said, "You're all right," or "I'm worried about you," she felt safe and reassured. Maybe he had cautioned her, too. But Mio was having difficulty recalling any warnings this strict.

Kanbara exhaled. "This is why he takes advantage of you."

"Huh…?"

"You're so nice. You don't tell him you don't like what he's doing, right? You're not mean. You're the class president, and you feel responsible. You can't break your honor-student persona."

It felt like Kanbara was saying this for Mio's sake. They were things she thought about herself already.

Kanbara's expression shifted. His eyes were narrow, searching her face.

"Those aren't positives," he stated coldly. "All that stuff you do just so other people think you're nice is a weakness. And people take advantage of it. You have to change."

Mio's pulse quickened.

Unlike the day before, when her heart had raced from being close to Kanbara, it now beat quickly from panic and anxiety.

I need to apologize, she thought. *He's angry.*

Mio didn't want to hear this.

She knew better than anyone that she was weak-willed and couldn't speak up when something troubled her. It was a downside to her personality she was intimately familiar with. It felt as though Kanbara had torn out a part of Mio to confront her with.

Shame flooded her every fiber.

Kanbara started walking again, stomping toward the bus stop. Mio wished to disappear, yet she managed to say, "Um, Senpai, you don't have to accompany me home today." He stared at her. She lowered her eyes. "I'm very sorry about this. I'll be fine on my own now."

"This is happening because you're *not* fine."

Oh, she thought.

Mio peered up into Kanbara's cold gaze.

"What gives you the right to make that decision?" he said. "You're feeling awkward because you got scolded a little, and now you're shutting me out? That's one of your bad qualities, Mio."

"I didn't mean it that way," she objected. She hadn't thought that she was shutting him out. "I just feel like I've been a burden on you."

"The only burden would be for you to go off alone so that new kid can mess with you more. All you ever think about is the easiest option that doesn't make you the bad guy. Stop going with your first instinct in every situation."

Mio didn't reply.

Kanbara was right. If she was alone, Shiraishi would bother her. That was the entire reason she'd come to Kanbara for help. Going it alone would undo all that.

"I'm taking you home," Kanbara insisted. His decision seemed final, regardless of Mio's feelings. "Because I'm worried about you," he added.

They got on the bus and sat side by side, and Mio still didn't say a word. Kanbara was right, of course. Mio felt sick at herself. She'd never be fine alone. What would she do if Shiraishi came after her again? She was afraid of that.

Every time Mio went through something frightening, she immediately reached out to Hanaka, Saho, and Kanbara, giving them a whole sob story.

Mio understood that it came off like she was milking the situation for attention. Kanbara's accusing her of not genuinely trying to protect herself cut deep.

"Mio," Kanbara said. She looked at him; he was searching for something on his phone. A few moments later, he said, "Here," and showed her the screen.

It was from their LINE text thread.

Whatever you do, don't act alone. You can't predict what he might do.

That's true. Thanks for worrying about me, Senpai.

The messages were from the day before. Mio didn't know why he was showing them to her, though.

"Guess you didn't take this very seriously." Kanbara stared at her—glared. "When you text this, you have to think of it like a signed contract. I said not to act alone, but you didn't listen. What am I supposed to do? I can give you all the advice and warnings in the world, but if you don't obey, there's nothing I can do for you. You broke the contract between us. Do you understand?"

"...Yes."

The bus shook Mio in her seat. She was taken aback, surprised this discussion was continuing. He'd even dug up old messages.

The words *Thanks for worrying about me, Senpai* seemed so distant. When they'd chatted the day before, Mio had had no idea this would happen. That had to be what he meant about not taking it seriously.

"I'm sorry."

Honestly, she didn't know what she was apologizing for at this point. Kanbara appeared to recognize that and asked, "Do you know what you did wrong? I don't *want* to talk about this. I'm doing it out of concern because I don't want you to be in danger."

Mio kept repeating that she was sorry, and she prayed that the bus would reach her stop soon. She wanted to tell Kanbara that he could let her go there and didn't have to walk to her house, but she realized that wasn't an option. Shiraishi knew her address. She had seen him outside her home. Kanbara was right: Mio didn't realize how ignorant she was. That was why he was upset. Mio felt sad.

They got off at her stop, and she walked shoulder to shoulder with

Kanbara back to her home. He was still angry. He didn't raise his voice, but he continued to berate her softly.

Right before they reached the house, Kanbara stopped talking to stare at the bamboo grove.

"Senpai?"

"Since it's such a problem, I think you should tell your family about the transfer student."

"What?!"

"Why is that so shocking?" Kanbara looked upset again. "Isn't that the obvious thing to do? He's come to your house. You've got your parents, your grandma, and your brother Shizuku, right? You should tell your family so they can protect you if need be."

"But I can't tell my parents yet…"

He hasn't actually done anything that bad to me.

"What do you mean, 'yet'?" Kanbara demanded. Mio was at a loss for words. "'Yet' means it's pushing toward that point, and you know it's coming, right? But you intend to ignore it until it gets worse. If you don't want it to be a big deal and would prefer not to make a fuss, why ask me for help? Am I meaningless to you?"

"I didn't…"

"You didn't think that far ahead? What did I tell you? Stop saying the first thought that pops into your head."

He was right, of course. Absolutely right.

"Also," he added, sounding disgusted. Mio trembled, worried what else he might say. Kanbara jabbed his chin toward the house. "What's with that bamboo grove?"

"Huh…?"

Mio's mind was blank for a moment, and she struggled to understand the question.

"It just feels really creepy, for some reason."

"Creepy…?"

The wind picked up, rustling the bamboo. The grove had been there since before her grandfather's generation. It had been a familiar, comforting sight to Mio since she was small.

There was no cause for Kanbara to say what he had. For the first time, something felt off to Mio. Yet before she could reply, Kanbara muttered, "Whatever. I'm leaving. I've walked you home. Whatever happens, don't get caught alone. Don't go outside. You don't know what might happen."

"I understand."

"Do you? Do you really?"

He sounded like her mother. Or a teacher.

It was the kind of cynical, bitter thing you'd say to a child when you knew the child didn't genuinely comprehend your point.

"Also, you should cut your hair shorter, Mio."

"...I should?"

"Yes. I thought it looked really good short. It hangs too low now, and I don't like that I can't see the back of your neck. Can't you trim it a bit?"

Mio was taken aback by the sudden change of topic. Did he usually say things like this? Despite her shock, she managed to give him a noncommittal answer and moved on to expressing her gratitude.

"Thank you for walking me home."

"It's cool. You don't have to make a big deal about it," Kanbara replied, turning on his heel. Although she liked him, there was relief in knowing she was finally free today. Then he delivered the final blow.

"Your gratitude's pretty hollow anyway."

Mio's feet—her body—froze.

He didn't look back to see that she was rigid. Mio watched him go until he was out of sight. Then she lowered her head and whispered, "Thank you," like a robot. Not because she wished he would stay, but because she was frightened. There was a sense that Kanbara would be angry if Mio wasn't there when he turned around, like he might scold Mio for fleeing into the house.

She waited for some time after Kanbara was gone. Eventually, she wanted to cry, and after a brief countdown in her head, she spun and headed for the house, then rushed through the front door.

"Your gratitude's pretty hollow anyway."

His last words echoed in her ears.

"Whoa! What's wrong, Sis?" Shizuku asked. Mio had dashed into the living room and dived face-first into the sofa cushions.

"Leave me alone," she said, fighting to think. Her mind was an awful mess. Amid the chaos, something new occurred to her.

"And your brother Shizuku, right?"

Did I tell Kanbara-senpai that I had a brother? Did I tell him Shizuku's name?

"You look really pale, Mio," Saho remarked the next day, obviously concerned.

It was lunchtime. Mio had opened her boxed lunch from home but found she had no appetite and made little progress on the meal. Her friends couldn't help but notice.

"Yeah. You seem out of it," Hanaka agreed.

"Is it about the new kid again?"

"Um, yeah…"

Mio had barely slept the night before. But she couldn't tell them the true reason.

After Kanbara left, Mio had checked her phone before bed and been shocked by what she saw.

He'd messaged her on LINE. Many, many times.

You heard the last thing I said today, right? Why didn't you deny it?

Why didn't you tell me it wasn't hollow gratitude? You basically admitted your thanks were totally empty.

That's fine, I guess. I don't care. It's just, I've been listening and helping you with this transfer student and walked you home because I feel responsible after getting involved. Maybe that's not what you really wanted, though.

It's normal for a boyfriend to worry about his girlfriend, but it feels unfair when you completely take it for granted.

You say sorry for making me miss practice, but it's just an indirect request for forgiveness. I have no choice but to tell you it's fine. Pressuring someone with apologies, especially on purpose, isn't kindness. It's cunning.

You probably seem nice and attractive to that new guy. But as someone who's known you a lot longer, I understand that your inability to reject someone isn't genuine kindness. You need to work on that. I get that this hurts to hear, but I'm telling you because you need to know.

And crying to your friends about this is part of the problem. You get that, don't you?

Mio didn't know how to respond. Her hands shook when she got a new message later that evening. She nearly shrieked, thinking it was from Kanbara. However, it was from a fellow second-year on the track team, Suzuka.

Hey, Mio. Why'd you skip practice today? The teacher and the third-years were super mad. Are you really going out with Kanbara-senpai? You've been weird lately. You should really apologize before people get the wrong idea. Everyone's worried.

Mio felt exhausted. The message claimed the others were worried, but Mio knew what that meant. Everyone was angry. They already hated her.

How was she supposed to attend practice? It made her dizzy.

She wasn't sure how to reply to Kanbara, but she had to say something or he'd criticize her for making the wrong choice.

And I already know I've been doing that.

Mio desperately wanted to ask Hanaka and Saho for advice. Her eyes drifted down to the text Kanbara had sent that warned her against doing so.

By making a big deal about the transfer student and asking for help so often, Mio had overindulged in sympathy. Kanbara-senpai's cold shoulder was a direct result of the bad side of her personality.

I'm sorry, Mio wrote back to Kanbara. It was the most she could do. *I'm sorry. I'll fix the bad parts.*

"And...something happened with Senpai."

Mio managed to verbalize it for Hanaka and Saho. They reacted with surprise. Realizing what she'd done, Mio shook her head.

"It's fine. We made up right away. He warned me that I was careless for letting myself be alone."

She didn't tell either of them about Shiraishi's "final warning."

"Awww," Saho sighed. "That's just love talking. I'm sure he's concerned about you."

"Yeah..."

Among the three of them, "Senpai" meant Kanbara. When he joined the track team's long-jump group, Mio talked about him to Hanaka and Saho nearly daily. He was so handsome, cool, nice, and so on. The days when she could gush about him so innocently seemed distant now.

"Hmmm." Hanaka brushed at the ponytail she'd been wearing for a while now and nodded.

Saho indulged talks about Kanbara, but Mio was worried about how Hanaka would react. They'd just fought over who did and didn't have a boyfriend, and she didn't want to make a big deal over Kanbara in front of her.

Mio glanced toward Shiraishi's desk. She didn't feel the gaze anymore. He'd left the room at some point.

Despite his final warning, she hadn't detected that heavy, oppressive gaze at all today.

"That new kid leaves every single lunch period. What does he eat? Bugs? Maybe he goes down to the quad to catch them." Hanaka smirked.

Mio replied, "Don't talk like that." Shiraishi was creepy, but fabricating insults about whoever you felt like turned the classroom into an alienating place. That could give way to real bullying, and Mio hated that notion.

Hanaka laughed. "You're too nice, Mio. He's the one terrifying you. Where does that endless charity come from?"

It was spoken like a joke, but Mio was in no mood to laugh. The words struck her too deeply for her to disregard them.

When she went to the track club's room after school and saw Kanbara standing against the hallway wall like the previous day, Mio held her breath unconsciously. His back came up off the wall when he noticed her.

"Let's go," he said. Goose bumps formed on Mio's arms.

I'm going to be isolated.

She was going to be even more alone on the team.

"Um, Senpai…"

"What?"

"I'm going to attend practice today. I already skipped yesterday, and I don't want to cause trouble for everyone else."

"Huh?"

A crease formed between his eyebrows. It was quite exaggerated, as though he couldn't believe the words he was hearing.

Mio was scared, but she did her very best to push on.

"It's my fault. When you helped me with the transfer student, I took you for granted…but I still need to go to practice."

"Listen." Kanbara scratched his head with open distaste. He shook his head, as if to question why Mio didn't understand. "That's the worst part. Don't you see? That whole 'It's my fault. I was bound to screw this up,' where you make it seem like you're blaming yourself. Then you raise the white flag and say, 'Hey, I give up, don't blame me.' It makes you look like you're owning up to your failure when you're not. Figure it out already."

"Uh…"

"Am I wrong?"

Mio couldn't respond.

"Let's go," Kanbara said. Mio nodded and walked with him as though drawn by invisible strings. If Mio wasn't allowed to think she was in the wrong, then she didn't know *whom* to blame for this.

"Today," Kanbara said, a while into the bus ride, "we're going to your house. Okay? We need to tell your parents and brother about this new guy."

Mio stared at him wordlessly. Her mother would definitely be home. Once his after-school activity was over, her brother would be there, too. But Mio wasn't ready to talk yet. She couldn't tell them a stalker was following her.

"By the time something happens, it's already too late," Kanbara stated. He offered no room for debate. No matter what Mio tried to say, he had her totally in check.

"Hey, Mio."

"Yes?" she replied timidly.

"Did you burn the grove?"

"Wha…?" she gasped. The question resembled a Japanese palindromic tongue twister: *ta-ke-ya-bu-ya-ke-ta*. Initially, that's what she'd thought he was referencing.

However, it wasn't quite the same sentence, and his eyes made it clear he wasn't joking. He was asking a serious question.

"It's still there? I told you to burn it, didn't I?"

"You..."

...*didn't tell me.* Mio knew she hadn't forgotten that. She would have absolutely remembered such a bizarre demand. Kanbara had only said that it felt creepy to him.

She knew that he'd never asked that of her, yet swallowed her response and offered only a "Sorry."

"Ah, geez," Kanbara muttered, glancing out the window. "That's just one of those things you do, Mio. You only half listen."

"I'm sorry," she apologized again.

"Whatever. I don't care," Kanbara replied, his tone suggesting he cared a lot.

How should I tell him not to bother coming to my house? Mio wondered. *Should I curl up and say I'm not feeling well? No, that'll just give him more reason to escort me.*

Mio clutched the phone in her pocket. Perhaps she could pretend to get a call and say that her mother had slipped and fallen? No, then he'd worry and insist on coming with her. It would only create more worry on her behalf.

I could get off the bus at the nearest stop.

Unfortunately, they were already at their destination.

"Let's go, Mio," Kanbara commanded, standing and disembarking. He'd taken her enough times that he knew the way by now.

Right when they got to Mio's house, Kanbara abruptly said, "That transfer student."

"Yes?"

"He should know his place. He just got here; he doesn't know the first thing about you, Mio. It's sickening. I've known you for a lot longer. He's mistaking your type of kindness for—"

"But you were a transfer student, too, Senpai," Mio replied, rather boldly. For some reason, she felt able to speak more freely now.

The wind blew. Kanbara faced her. The breeze rustled the bamboo behind the house from right to left.

She'd countered with a retort, the kind of thing he hated.

However, Mio couldn't hold back now. Something had been wrong this whole time.

When he said stuff like "I've known you longer" and "This is the Mio I know," she agreed here and there, blaming herself for things. Still, there was no refraining from speaking up here.

"You transferred into the school last year and only joined the track team this year. You haven't known me for ages or anything…"

Mio summoned all her strength. Once she took the first step and started speaking, the momentum grew, and she completed her thought firmly.

Kanbara pursed his lips. He wasn't smiling. His face was a blank mask.

Mio's mind raced. She realized this was the first time Kanbara had actually been critical of Shiraishi. Before, he'd always blamed Mio, the victim, not the stalker. He was swift to point out what she did wrong, and his anger was reserved for her alone. Shiraishi didn't seem to matter at all.

Kanbara acted as though it were all Mio's fault.

"What the hell?" He scratched his head with irritation.

Mio stared at him.

Was Kanbara-senpai always so insensitive? Was he always the type of guy who ditched practice without telling anyone?

The more she thought about it, the more Mio realized that she didn't actually know the answers.

The day Shiraishi transferred in, the girls had talked about Senpai. They'd discussed how hard the Mitsumine Academy transfer test was supposed to be.

"Anyway, I'm sure Shiraishi's really smart. I heard the standards to transfer to our school are really high. Remember last year, when someone transferred

into the grade above ours, and they immediately became the top student in the class?"

Kanbara-senpai was very smart. Mio admired him so much that any mention of a senpai between her and her friends referred exclusively to him.

But what kind of person was Itta Kanbara? She admired and was attracted to him, but on a personal level, she didn't know him at all. He certainly wasn't close enough with Mio to say things like "I know you" and "I understand you."

Kanbara lowered his hand and rolled his head as if to loosen a terrible shoulder ache. His eyes narrowed.

He stared at the house behind Mio—at the bamboo grove out back.

"It's all…this place's fault."

She was speechless, breathless. The voice had come from behind her.

"Give it up, Itta Kanbara."

Mio straightened up with a start and spun around.

A boy in a collared shirt emerged from behind the house. It was a familiar scene. This was the second time Mio had met him here.

"Shiraishi…"

It was Kaname Shiraishi. However, he wasn't watching Mio. His eyes were fixed on Kanbara.

Mio wasn't afraid. Despite how creepy Shiraishi had been before, his presence actually filled her with relief. Even realizing how conveniently her allegiance had switched, Mio felt saved.

Someone had finally directly intervened in this relationship of endless apologies that bound her to Kanbara.

Shiraishi stepped forward.

Kanbara stared at him with disgust. "This is the transfer student?" he spit. "You're Mio's stalker? Sickening. C'mon, Mio, let's go. Get inside, now…"

"Family massacre."

Huh...? The word stuck in Mio's throat. That ominous pronouncement had come from Shiraishi. Mio's feet were rooted in place. Kanbara didn't move, either. He watched Shiraishi with eyes wide.

"You slip in through a single family member, ensorcelling them while you wriggle your way in among the group. You browbeat them with your logic, convince the other party they're in the wrong, and impose your supposedly correct will upon them. Once you're in among the family, it's only a matter of time until they're all under your control. To think you'd try it again..."

Shiraishi chuckled to himself. Those sharp, fanglike teeth gleamed in a wicked grin. He pulled out something that looked like a silver bell.

It rang.

Kanbara's eyes went wide—even more so than before.

"I'm here to perform an exorcism. You won't kill this family."

"You...!"

The bell chimed again. The wind picked up, and the bamboo behind the house swayed.

The sound was clear and cleansing, but it was drowned out by a hideous scream that tore the air. Mio could hardly believe her ears.

Kanbara crumpled to the ground. He was cradling his head and rolling in agony. Mio put a hand to her mouth, shocked by the sight. She rushed to help him, grabbed his arm, and then recoiled with a shriek.

Kanbara's arm—his entire body—was hot. Not with fever. It burned like heated metal.

"I wouldn't touch him," said Shiraishi, still holding the bell. His tone was calm. For the first time today, he glanced at Mio. He sounded disinterested. "I told you it was my final warning."

Mio was speechless. Kanbara was in agony. His handsome face twisted, and his hands clawed at his face, throat, and head in anguish.

Senpai, Mio thought, yet her arms and legs were rooted in place now. His face was covered in blood from where he tore at it. The sight was so terrible it kept her from trying to help. Kanbara snapped his head back, jerking.

"I warned you multiple times," Shiraishi continued, seemingly bored by the sight of Kanbara's distress. His empty eyes fixed upon Mio instead. "I warned you not to get so close to Itta Kanbara. It's a good thing you have bamboo growing by your house."

The bamboo grove that Kanbara had called "creepy."

The wind blew, eliciting a bell-like sound from the bamboo. With each ring, Kanbara's body convulsed harder.

"Shiraishi...what *are* you?" Mio asked. For all the confusion in the situation, there was one thing she understood.

Shiraishi had probably—maybe—come to help her.

When he didn't reply, Mio pressed him, keeping an eye on the suffering Kanbara. "What happened to him? Why did you..."

Shiraishi clicked his tongue in annoyance. It seemed unnecessarily antagonistic, but at least it indicated emotion. This was preferable to when Mio had no idea how he felt at all.

"I knew from the moment I first saw you. I knew you were entranced."

Mio recalled how he'd stared intently at her on his first day in class.

Shiraishi directed his attention to Kanbara's writhing form at his feet. "I knew he was going to get you, so I asked if you'd let me come to your house."

The bamboo rustled.

"Can I come to your house today?"

His voice overlapped with the cleansing scent of the bamboo. She was stunned. So much of this didn't make sense to her, but one thing did.

The day that Shiraishi came walking out of the bamboo behind her home, he must have done something in the grove before he left.

"I wondered what sort of place you live in."

He was probably...

"But... But..." Mio's lips trembled as the fear of those moments returned to her. "When you just tell someone you want to see their house, it's not—"

"Not right? How's what I did any different from Itta Kanbara's actions? He tried to work his way into your home more persistently than I did—the only difference was the amount of time he spent and the order of events. He came to your house several times, Harano."

Shiraishi's tone was frank. Mio thought of him as so inscrutable that the simple act of calling her by name was surprising.

"They try to foist their darkness on others," Shiraishi said. He kept his gaze trained on Kanbara. "They move around from town to town, spreading their shadows and dragging others down with them. And we're the ones who sever the connections to their victims and exorcise them."

Mio's legs trembled terribly now that she'd heard him mention "family massacre." It was insane. Impossible. And yet Shiraishi's words were strangely persuasive.

Mio should have thought it was strange for Kanbara to say he was coming to her house, but she hadn't been able to defy him. She hadn't been able to resist him the way she had Shiraishi, all because of a difference in time and reason.

Normally, the order in which you do things makes all the difference. There's a proper sequence. Mio wished to tell Kanbara as much, but he'd saved her. As frustrating as it was, she understood.

"Speak," Shiraishi commanded Kanbara. The ringing continued. An odd light shone in Shiraishi's eyes, cold but not angry. His face was eerie and unreadable.

"Your family... Your father is..."

And then there was movement.

"Dammit!"

Kanbara was on his feet, covering his face.

It was hard to imagine where he'd found the speed and strength, considering the agony he'd suffered moments earlier. His forearms scrubbed over his face, his bloodied visage visible beneath them. He glared at Shiraishi silently—then pounced.

A sound like a wild beast's roar thundered. It struck like a physical blow. The rustling of the bamboo and the bell's chime vanished.

Kanbara fled. His agility was alarming. The way he rushed up the road defied reality, like a special effect from a movie.

Kaname Shiraishi held his breath. He chased after Kanbara, not bothering to tell Mio to stay put or anything else.

"No, wait!" Mio insisted. Her mind was pure chaos. She had been so terrified and creeped out by Shiraishi, but now she was pulling on his arm without realizing it.

He grimaced back at her. "What?"

"…I feel like this wouldn't have happened at all if you hadn't come."

Mio had gotten close to Kanbara only because she needed help with Shiraishi. Didn't that mean he was the cause?

Maybe *he* was the reason Senpai had gone crazy? Perhaps the kind and caring Senpai could come back…

"Doesn't matter," Shiraishi stated, cleaving through Mio's hopes. "This would have happened whether I was here or not. It was only a question of how soon."

"But…"

She had been through a terrifying experience, but not because of Shiraishi—because of Kanbara. Mio could admit that much. Recalling that long string of messages late at night made her spine freeze. How often had she apologized, thinking she was trapped with no escape?

Shiraishi narrowed his eyes, then sighed and gazed at Mio.

"I couldn't decide whether to ignore you or use you as bait. That's why I gave you that warning."

"That's what the message on my desk was?"

"…I wanted to startle you as little as possible," he muttered, looking awkward for the first time Mio could remember. She realized that it was true. He'd written that message with the extremely fine and menacing letters to warn her.

Mio was aghast. Shiraishi had no sociability at all. He didn't understand the proper social distance he ought to maintain with others. Now it was clear that was the simple truth behind his personality. He didn't appear sinister anymore. As strange as it was to consider, Kanbara filled her with much more revulsion. And she had liked him so much…

Shiraishi wasn't frightening.

"I said 'final warning' because it was genuinely your final warning. Admittedly, if you pulled away from him after that, I would've had to come up with another plan to deal with him." Shiraishi turned away, shaking Mio's hand off his arm. "I'm sorry for using you as a lure."

He took off running after Kanbara. Before he was out of sight, he looked back.

"Keep the bamboo grove like that for a while. He should give up on pursuing you."

"Bait." "Lure."

They were such rude things to say. It wasn't fair.

As Shiraishi hurried out of sight, Mio lost all the strength in her core. She dropped onto her backside, as though an invisible person had pushed her down. And she couldn't get back up on her feet.

The little scraps of a story Shiraishi had left her weren't enough for her to piece together the story. It was difficult to believe what had happened, but the image of Kanbara writhing in agony on the ground remained clear in her mind. The way he'd glared with such fury, face covered in blood, at Shiraishi, not Mio.

Kanbara-senpai never looked at me. He didn't make any excuses or give any explanations. He just ran. After all his criticisms and LINE messages, he hadn't cared about Mio at all when it counted most.

"*They try to foist their darkness on others.*"

"*And we're the ones who sever the connections to their victims and exorcise them.*"

Mio didn't understand or trust everything Shiraishi had said. However, she'd seen enough to believe.

Kanbara-senpai was not a normal person, and Kaname Shiraishi likely wasn't, either.

The neighborhood was quiet. The wind that had shaken the bamboo grove earlier was entirely gone. Kanbara had screamed at the top of his lungs, but no one had emerged from the nearby homes to inspect the commotion.

Mio dragged her weak legs to the front yard. A few moments later, she was through the front door.

"…I'm home."

"Welcome back, dear," her mother greeted her casually from farther inside. Instantly, Mio felt something hot surge into her chest. Sounds emanated from the kitchen.

"*He should give up on pursuing you.*"

She'd been saved.

◆

Mio was quite nervous about going to school the next day. Nervous, but also a bit eager to find out what might happen next.

For the first time in a while, she'd enjoyed a good night's sleep.

Everything with Kanbara had lasted only a few days, but she'd felt locked in tunnel vision the entire time. Now that her heart and mind were calm again, she finally recognized that she had become his slave, completely under his thrall. Everything felt different now, even the weight of the air around her. It was like she'd been hurled into a terrible storm and mutilated by it for a brief period. She'd come out alive, but could easily not have survived.

She wanted to have a proper conversation with Shiraishi.

He didn't frighten her anymore. And what about Kanbara? With Shiraishi around, Kanbara didn't frighten her as much as before. She felt ready to talk to her senpai without cowering.

"Morning, Mio," Saho greeted her. Mio responded in kind. She was very curious about the third-year class. What had happened to Kanbara? Was he in school today, pretending like yesterday hadn't happened? There was no way he could hide the injuries on his face.

Shiraishi wasn't in class yet. He always showed up right as the bell was ringing. Today, that felt agonizingly late to Mio.

What if he'd transferred schools again…?

The thought of him simply vanishing as abruptly as he'd come left her antsy. He still hadn't given her a satisfying explanation for all of this.

Mr. Minamino suddenly popped his head into the classroom and said, "You two. May I see you?"

This was strange. He always came into the classroom after the bell rang. Mio and Saho shared a confused look. Hanaka wasn't here yet.

Mr. Minamino's face, normally so genial, seemed stiff. Concerned, the girls asked, "What is it?" as they walked into the hallway. A woman stood behind the teacher.

She looked exhausted. Her eyes were dark and sunken. The pallor of her skin suggested that she hadn't slept or was ill. She stared at Mio and Saho, ready to burst into tears at the slightest provocation.

For some reason, her face looked familiar.

And then Mio recognized her, remembering this woman from parents' orientation day. She was Hanaka's mother.

"This way, please." Mr. Minamino ushered them to the student counseling office next to the faculty room. An ominous premonition came over Mio when they entered the small office.

"Have a seat," the teacher said, but Hanaka's mother didn't. She just stared at the girls. Since she refused to sit, they couldn't, either.

Clearly upset, Mr. Minamino got right down to business. "Hanaka did not come home last night."

Mio gasped.

"What?" Saho breathed.

"She did return home at one point, but then later slipped out of the house again without anyone realizing, and there's been no word from her since. She didn't come home in the morning, and no one's had any contact with her. She hasn't shown up at school, either," Mr. Minamino explained.

"...Does either of you know anything?" Hanaka's mother spoke for the first time. Her eyes were red. Perhaps it was from crying, or lack of sleep, or both. She leaned in toward Mio and Saho. "There was a note left on her desk. And the window was open, like she was spirited away by a vampire."

A vampire.

Hanaka's mother seemed very shaken by this. Mr. Minamino stared at her, uncertain how to respond to such a wild claim.

Mio felt the blood drain from her face. In addition, her body felt stiff and frozen, like her soles were stuck to the floor.

Her imagination was working overtime.

A wide-open window. Hanaka's empty room, with curtains swaying.

The vampire comment was just the first thing that popped into her mother's head. However, the absurd remark formed a clear image in the mind's eye.

"What was written on the note?" Mio asked. Her voice didn't sound like her own. She had a bad feeling.

Vampire.

Hanaka had started wearing a ponytail recently. When her slender neck was visible, it made her look more adult, and it suited her very well. That white back of the neck.

Hadn't someone recently told Mio to cut her hair because it covered her neck? He'd said he didn't like that, and she recalled how disappointed she'd felt after that comment.

Vampire.

A creature of the night, sinking fangs into a pale, exposed neck. Mio thought of Hanaka, yet felt a prickle on her neck. Her hair stood on end.

Kanbara smiled when she told him of the fight with her friend. He had given her a gentle, enveloping, forgiving smile and told her it was okay.

"You'll be on good terms again in no time. You and Hanaka always look like you're having fun. All three of you. You're like the Three Amigas."

She nearly screamed.

Mio had never introduced Hanaka and Kanbara. But he knew her name. The day he'd waited for Mio at the front gate of the school, he would have seen every student who walked past before she came by. That included Hanaka, who'd rushed out of the school before Mio and Saho.

"Here it is."

Hanaka's mother pulled a long, narrow piece of paper from her bag. Upon reading it, Mio opened her mouth in a silent scream, and she shut her eyes.

I'm with Kanbara-senpai, a senior at school. Don't worry about me.

It was Saho who cried, "Whaaat?!"

When Mio opened her eyes again, she saw Saho was so rattled and flustered by this that she didn't know whether to look at Mio, Hanaka's mother, or Mr. Minamino. It was almost sad. She was clearly most worried for Mio. Saho stared pleadingly, her question unspoken but obvious.

"What does it mean? What does it mean?" Hanaka's mother begged.

"Kanbara the third-year isn't here yet. I called his house, but nobody answered. Harano, you're on the track team with him, right? Have you heard anything?"

"...I don't know," she replied hoarsely. Saho eyed her with pity. "I didn't call or text Hanaka yesterday. The last time I saw her was when we said good-bye after school."

"Same for me," Saho added, shaking her head.

Hanaka's mother lifted her head and looked at both girls. "Is this older boy going out with her?"

Saho took a short, sharp breath. She glanced at her friend for help, but Mio avoided looking back, focusing on Hanaka's mother. Ultimately, Saho shook her head.

"I don't know."

It was doubtful Kanbara would ever show up at school again.

Mio might never see him again. It was devastatingly clear to her. Not on any logical basis; she just *knew*. After the sight of him writhing in agony yesterday, she knew.

It's my fault.

Shiraishi had saved her, that much was certain. Kanbara had given up on Mio. But what if more than one girl had been taken in by his charm and lured under his sway?

So soon?

Hanaka had switched to the ponytail only recently. Had it been enough time for her to get close with him? Mio sighed.

It wasn't about time.

Time didn't change the feeling of distance between people. Recently,

Kanbara had strung Mio along and manipulated her constantly. Her feelings for him had changed distinctly each day over the course of seventy-two hours. And with each shift, she was powerless to return to the way things had been before.

She recalled how Hanaka had laughed silently. *"Kanbara-senpai's super hot, and he seems really dedicated,"* she'd said, and Mio had joined in. *"You think so?"*

They were supposed to be friends.

What had Hanaka really been thinking at that moment?

"I'm going to visit Kanbara's home," said Mr. Minamino.

"I'll join you," Hanaka's mother added.

The teacher instructed the girls to go back to the classroom.

"Since there's a lot we still don't know about Hanaka, please don't go telling other people about this. She might return out of the blue, and it'd be a shame if there was a big controversy waiting to greet her." Mr. Minamino tried to be as cheerful as he could, but it made listening difficult. The hope in his voice caused Hanaka's mother to cover her face.

Between her fingers, she whimpered, "Hanaka…"

From the counseling room to the classroom, Saho kept her head down. It didn't seem like she was holding her silence for Mio's sake. Rather, she simply lacked the words to describe her feelings. The pair weren't ready to reenter class yet, so they wandered to a more out-of-the-way location, the emergency stairs.

There was a sniffle. Saho was tearing up. When she noticed Mio watching, she apologized. "I'm sorry, Mio. You're probably the one who really wants to cry, but I'm stealing your thunder."

"…It's all right."

Mio didn't know what was all right. She offered her handkerchief to Saho, who dabbed at her eyes.

"I wonder if Hanaka took not having a boyfriend a lot harder than we realized," Saho continued, almost to herself. "But it's still wrong." Her voice got stronger. There was audible anger. "You can't just go and take someone else's boyfriend. It's the lowest thing you can do. It's just not right."

Saho was so sweet and naive. Kanbara would probably call this righteous, truthful criticism hypocritical or self-serving or something. Mio grappled with the thought, but swept it out of her head before it controlled her.

I'm back in the normal world, where you can shed tears of frustration for your friend. I don't want anyone to speak ill of Saho's righteousness and kindness.

But no matter what either of them said, Hanaka was gone.

In the same way that Kanbara had repeatedly attacked and preyed on Mio's weakness of spirit, there was a darkness in Hanaka's mind that had served as a shortcut to her spirit, too.

Perhaps that shadow was a desire to get back at her friends and show them up.

What had gone through her mind the day she brushed at that long ponytail of hers?

Saho felt unwell, so Mio walked her to the nurse's office. Mio told her friend it might be best if she went home early, then returned to the classroom alone.

Shiraishi was already in his seat.

This came as a relief, because Mio had thought he might up and vanish along with Kanbara and Hanaka. His presence gave her confidence.

"...Kaname," she called. Why did she choose to call him by his first name? Even much later, she couldn't explain her decision. Whatever the reason, it came very naturally in the moment.

Because it was such an unfamiliar form of address and because no one in class had bothered to speak to him since the first day, Kaname Shirai-shi's head shot up. Mio's initial impression of him was unchanged: It was hard to tell what was happening behind those empty eyes.

However, they didn't frighten her anymore. If anything, their calm, unknowable manner was a source of strength she wanted to cling to.

Mr. Minamino didn't enter class after the bell. He was probably still talking with Hanaka's mother. He wouldn't be back for a while.

"They said Kanbara-senpai has disappeared," Mio told him, loud enough to make it clear she didn't care if the other students overheard. A tiny bit of life entered Kaname's eyes. It was so subtle that Mio would have missed it had she not been watching closely.

"If you're going to search for him, take me with you."

Kaname's eyes widened a bit. Previously, his expressions had always been of annoyance or exhaustion. This was different. He silently stared back at Mio with something reminiscent of interest.

He likely had already known that Hanaka had disappeared with Kan-bara. Mio's news elicited no visible surprise.

He watched her, and she gazed back.

It wasn't perfectly clear what Kaname was after, or what he was doing. Maybe he intended to leave this school now that Kanbara was gone. How-ever, he was the only connection Mio had to the prospect of finding Hanaka, no matter how slim. Losing Kaname would mean it was all over.

"It's sexual harassment." That was what Hanaka had said of Kaname's actions. Mio had claimed it wasn't sexual, but she had agreed it was *some* kind of harassment. A string of activities that demonstrated no respect for personal space, imposing personal circumstances and desires on a vic-tim with no regard for their needs. At this point, she realized that it wasn't Kaname but Itta Kanbara who had subjected her to that kind of harassment.

Kaname had said they tried to foist their darkness on others.

It was true that when Kanbara ordered Mio to do this and that, there was a darkness in his eyes. When she peered into that inky blackness, she'd found a world where common sense held no sway. That feeling had exuded from every inch of Kanbara's body like an aura.

A new word popped into Mio's mind.

Yami-hara.

"Dark harassment"—taking the darkness in one's heart and spreading it everywhere, forcing it on others and dragging them down with you. The shadow deep in his mind and eyes seeped out into the world. His actions could be called *yami-hara.*

"...sterday."

The whisper brought Mio back to the present. Kaname repeated himself.

"They say an unidentified male body was discovered in the mountains of Mie Prefecture yesterday."

Mio was taken aback. What was he talking about?

"I think it's Itta Kanbara," he added.

Mio gasped, her breath catching in her throat. She recalled Kanbara's bloodied, lacerated face.

Kaname stared right at her and asked, "Why do you want to come with me?"

Clearly, it was just a habit of his to reveal crucial information at the most abrupt and unexpected of times.

Mio replied, "Because I'm worried about Hanaka."

If that feeling was hypocritical, then so be it.

Call it altruism.

If kindness was a weakness, then Mio preferred to be weak. It was better than losing a part of herself. She wouldn't let anyone take that away. There was no need to change.

Concern, a feeling of responsibility, my fault—and thus, a preemptive apology.

If she was doing all this to protect herself rather than out of a true sense of kindness, then fine.

"I'm Hanaka's friend," Mio insisted.

Call me an honor student if you must. I do think she betrayed me, but my feelings are genuine.

"So take me with you."

There was a pause.

Several moments later, Kaname finally spoke.

"All right."

CHAPTER TWO
Neighbor

There was a loud *bang*, like something rupturing.

Ritsu was hanging up the laundry on the veranda of her apartment building when the sound caught her attention. She leaned over the balcony to look down, but what had happened wasn't immediately clear.

She thought she'd heard a scream.

But the sound before it had been so loud, her ears might have been ringing. It was a strange sensation. She remembered the shock of it, like a car horn blared right by her ear. However, it was somehow wet. Perhaps that was self-contradictory, yet it had sounded like a *splat*. Almost.

As Ritsu pondered the odd event, a stir rose from below. From the fifth floor, it wasn't possible to see the source of the noise. Feeling a bit uneasy, she quickly hung the rest of the laundry and returned to the living room.

She didn't learn the truth until her husband Yuuki returned from taking their son to elementary school.

"Welcome home, dear. How did Kanato do?"

Her husband's workplace offered flexible scheduling, so while he worked late, he had plenty of time in the morning before he needed to report to the office. It was his daily habit to walk their first-grade son Kanato to school, along with the dog. Since Kanato was often asleep by the time Yuuki got home at night, this was one of the few times of the day he could talk with his son.

Ritsu's question had no significant reason behind it. She asked it every time Yuuki got home. It was part of her greeting.

But there was something wrong with Yuuki this time. And Hatch, their mini Shiba Inu, was strangely agitated.

"Kanato's fine. But…"

Yuuki looked pale. He went to the bathroom to wash his hands, so Ritsu took Hatch from him and wiped the dog's feet off with a towel while waiting for her husband.

"I saw a jumper."

"What…?"

The sound from earlier played in Ritsu's mind. It must have been from…

Yuuki slumped into a chair at the table, exhausted. He was wearing his usual prework T-shirt and jeans. There were water stains on his shirt from his splashing his face at the sink.

"I took Kanato to the corner by the school before I let him go. Right when I reached the apartment complex's south entrance, I heard this big *wham!* I thought it was a traffic accident at first. There was a scream at the same time as the impact."

"Yeah."

"But then I realized there were no cars."

The sound he was talking about had to be the same one Ritsu had heard. It had sounded nearly like a loud car horn to her. Apparently, Yuuki had processed it in a similar way.

The south entrance faced a large road. It wasn't actually that busy, but the morning traffic was heavier now than it would be later in the day.

"There was a girl, maybe a college student, on the ground after falling off her bike. Then I noticed a woman wearing an apron lying in front of her."

"Was there blood?"

Yuuki shook his head. "Not much that I saw. But her hands and feet were pointing in impossible directions."

It was hard for Ritsu to envision it clearly, yet there was enough detail for her to sigh.

"When I got closer, I saw she was still breathing. Barely. I could tell she wouldn't last long." Yuuki chose his words carefully.

Ritsu asked, "Was there anyone else around aside from the girl on the bike and you?"

"Not at first, which was a big problem. The girl was completely in shock, and I was only walking Kanato to school, so I didn't bring my phone. The manager noticed and came over right away, though, so I asked them to call the ambulance. I've got to go to work, after all."

"Right."

It sounded like there hadn't been a huge crowd at the scene, unlike the way it often happened in movies and TV shows. However, that only made her husband's story more vivid and eerie.

"If she had an apron on, was she from the apartment complex?"

"Probably. Although I suppose she could have come here from somewhere else with the intent to jump." Yuuki sighed. "You can get into the emergency stairwell from outside the building."

There were many types of apartment complexes.

There were the so-called *danchi*, the large concrete public housing buildings that had sprung up everywhere in the 1960s. Their occupancy had slowly dropped over time as people left and long-term residents aged. Ritsu's family was living in a slightly different kind of place. This structure's near-complete remodel was done by a young, well-known local designer couple about a decade earlier, and everyone agreed it was great work. Where units were unused, the designers had knocked down walls to make apartments larger than the average ones in the area. The rent was low, too, making the complex popular with young people and families with kids.

The refitted buildings also had a new style that took advantage of their old-fashioned look. Even the vines that covered the exterior felt like an inspired touch rather than a sign of dilapidation.

Ritsu's family was one of those that had come to tour after hearing the rumors about the place. Previously, they'd lived in a cramped apartment in the middle of Tokyo, and it had felt smaller and smaller the more their son grew. Also, Kanato had started clamoring for a dog, so Ritsu and Yuuki had begun searching for a new place to live before their son began elementary school. That was how they'd come here, to Sawatari Apartments.

Because it was so popular, open units rarely became available. Yet the realtor they hired to find them a place had managed to get them a viewing appointment.

That was for 515, where they now lived.

The complex sat close to the city center, with three full-size rooms, unlike the one they'd had before. The buildings were old, yes, but the entrances and halls had been adequately updated. If anything, the fashionable retro look made the place feel chic, like a complex from another country.

However, what had pleased Ritsu most of all was a single piece of paper taped inside the elevator during their tour. Kanato spotted it and read it aloud.

"There's a festival. And a *mikoshi*."

The little poster read, *Sawatari Apartments Children's Festival*, and it featured smiling children dressed in traditional *happi* coats for a festival. Beneath, the text read: *There will be cotton candy! We'll go to the shrine and carry the* mikoshi *palanquin! Meet up at the center park at ten o'clock!*

That instantly made Ritsu want to raise Kanato here.

Ritsu had come to Tokyo for college, but she had grown up in Tokushima Prefecture, far to the west, on the island of Shikoku. There had been festivals and events for children all the time when she was a girl. Unfortunately, from the moment they got married, Ritsu and her husband realized their careers required they raise any children they had in Tokyo.

Ritsu knew that it would be impossible to give her children the same experience growing up that she'd had, but it still made her sad that she couldn't. The big city just didn't have the community cohesion of rural areas. At the old apartment, the best Ritsu had ever done was say hello to other parents with children the same age as Kanato. It never got any closer than that.

But here, in this apartment block, they could have a proper life. She wanted to raise her son here, within this local community. Yuuki had been born and raised outside of Tokyo, too, and he seemed to agree.

"Oh, this is great. It feels perfect," he'd said. That seemed to settle it. They'd made up their minds about moving into a new home. But then Yuuki added, "The only thing I'm worried about is the security, what with your job on top of mine. There's a building manager, sure, but the structure itself was only redesigned. It doesn't have autolocking doors like our current place."

"It'll be fine. I hardly ever pop my head into the office anyway."

"Yeah, but..."

Ritsu smiled and assured Yuuki it was okay. She appreciated his concern. "I think Sawatari Apartments is a great place."

Thus, the decision was made. That had been the winter before Kanato started elementary school, about one year before. They'd moved in March, just before the school year began in April. They'd lived here for about half a year already. Their first autumn in the new home had been very pleasant.

However, this incident made the lack of security apparent. The charm of old buildings and their openness also meant things like emergency staircases being accessible from the outside.

"I just hope it wasn't someone's mother from Kanato's school…"

Ritsu was concerned because the woman who jumped had been wearing an apron. The apartment block was a community unto itself, but naturally, she didn't know all two hundred or so families. Still, the idea of a young child's mother, a woman like herself, committing an act like that made Ritsu very uneasy.

"I couldn't tell you. She looked older than us, though. I didn't get a good look at her face, but I don't think it was anyone we know."

"…I'm glad the girl on the bike didn't get hit." Ritsu brought some barley tea out from the fridge for her husband, who still looked pale. "I've heard that people who commit suicide by jumping try to take other people down with them. They subconsciously wait until someone's walking below to jump."

Yuuki grimaced as he sipped the cold tea. "That's scary," he muttered. Ritsu nodded.

"It's supposed to be a totally unconscious thing, but it happens. That's what this neuroscientist said on the radio show."

Ritsu was a freelance broadcaster.

After getting married and having a child, she'd quit her position at the TV station to spend time with her family. She'd considered simply retiring from work to be a full-time stay-at-home mother, but her husband and others had strongly recommended that she keep working. She'd done her best to cut down on public appearances like TV shows and presentations. Her main work these days was recording voice-over narration at the studio.

Ritsu had considered retiring because of several health scares she'd had while pregnant. She hadn't been sure she'd have the strength to continue her job. Her condition improved after Kanato was born, though, and now she felt stable enough to keep working. Thankfully, many people remembered her from her time as a newscaster and singled her out for voice-over positions on TV programs and such. Last year, she'd become a regular on a radio program—a half-hour company-sponsored show. She chatted with a different guest on each segment.

After the recording, she would sometimes speak with the guests for a little longer. This nugget of information about suicide jumpers had come up during one of those discussions.

Yuuki furrowed his brow and set his empty cup on the table.

"At any rate," he said, "I'm glad it happened after I dropped Kanato off. I wouldn't want him to see that."

"Yes, thank goodness," Ritsu agreed. It had occurred just after school began. She shivered to think what might have been had the incident come earlier.

"Well, I've got to get to work now. There might be police downstairs and all kinds of trouble today, so take care when you leave, Ritsu."

"I will. I've got a school visit for some volunteer story time today, so I might go right past it," she replied.

Yuuki gave her a strange smile.

"What?" she asked.

"Oh, just thinking. You're taking this awfully well," he said. "I thought you'd be more creeped out and concerned that our home is the site of something like this."

His saying as much aloud suggested he felt that way himself.

"Isn't that sort of concern reserved for places where someone actually died inside? Does that include jumpers now?" Ritsu asked.

"I don't know. I think there's a website that lists homes where things like this occurred. Will our building be marked? Maybe the site determines whether the deceased was a resident of the property in question before putting the complex on the list," her husband remarked with a sigh. "It's depressing to think about. I mean, if I see our place on that list, I'll know for a fact that the woman I saw today is dead, right? I didn't think she'd make it when I saw her, but it's kinda tough to know concretely so soon after."

"Oh, I've heard of that website. I've checked it out before."

The famous site collected and compiled information about various homes and apartments where incidents and deaths had occurred. A coworker had told Ritsu about it while she still worked for the TV station, and she'd checked it out of curiosity.

"Really? You've seen it?" her husband asked, surprised. He shivered, which seemed like an exaggerated response. "I'm surprised you could stand it. Wouldn't it be upsetting to see your neighbor's house on there, or some other place we visit often?"

"Hmm. At first, I do remember wondering if I'd see spots in our area, or places within range of where I go for work, I guess."

Her morbid interest in it had been short-lived. She'd inspected the spread of dots on the map and thought, *Oh, look at all these places that have had incidents*—but then she'd concluded that it wasn't really that many at all.

"The more I looked, the more I realized there aren't very many people who die at home. The site includes people who pass alone and from disease, too. I'm sure it's not absolutely comprehensive, but given how many people live in this area, the idea that there are so few who die in the house made me realize that death is thoroughly hidden from daily life in the modern age. It's normal to die in a hospital, and anywhere else is the exception."

Ritsu recalled the website's map. There was a list that displayed numerical totals by area.

"So if this place gets added to the tally of homes with incidents, it might not really be that remarkable. It's just a fact of life."

"I guess you could think of it that way," Yuuki muttered. Jokingly, he added, "You've got such an intellectual way of looking at things, Ritsu. They don't call you Ritz the Rational for nothing."

"Oh, please don't bring that up."

That was the nickname the media had given Ritsu during her tenure as a newscaster. It was meant to be a point of comparison to her counterparts who were popular for their looks or glamour. Ritsu Morimoto was Ritz the Rational. They'd said she was better at interviewing authors and scholars than performing on variety shows, but to her, it sounded like people were calling her bland.

"All right, I've got to get ready for work now." Yuuki went to his room to change. When he came out, Hatch bounded around his feet, as usual.

"Oh, honey?" Ritsu called.

"What?"

"Be careful."

Ritsu looked into Yuuki's eyes. She thought he was just as rational and intelligent as she, albeit in a different way. It was a big part of why she'd chosen to marry him. Other people might have been more unsettled or panicked after witnessing such an event.

"You might think you're fine now, but you saw a death. The shock of it could still be with you. Don't push yourself too hard."

"Got it. I'll be fine." Yuuki grinned. As he left through the door, he called, "Thanks for worrying about me."

After seeing him off, Ritsu watered the plants, cleaned, did some minor chores, and prepared for her school volunteer appearance. For her outfit, she chose a tasteful slit dress she'd bought from the wardrobe department of an old job that had a stylist attached.

While getting ready, Ritsu found herself curious, and she checked the online news portal and turned on the TV. However, there were no reports about a jumper. Perhaps it was because suicides didn't get reported on unless

they were particularly newsworthy. It reminded Ritsu of her earlier remark—
death was hidden from daily life.

On the route to school, she passed through the south entrance, where
Yuuki had been when it happened.

She imagined the police would be there, maybe with one of those chalk
outlines on the ground you saw in police procedurals on TV, or yellow crime
scene tape. However, the reality of the aftermath was startlingly quiet. There
was no crowd, no tape, and no white outline.

There was only an unnaturally dark and wet section of the ground,
probably left over from when the stains had been washed away. To Ritsu, it
felt like a shadow cast by death.

This was her first time attending a school volunteer event.

Kusumichi Elementary, Kanato's school, had a very good reputation in
the neighborhood. There was housing for government officials within the
school district, and many of their children attended the school. Those families who sent their children here tended to be very focused on education.
Many of the kids had grown up out of the country, traveling with their parents for work before they reached school age. Some families were adamant
about moving to this district simply to get their children into this elementary school, where they would be influenced by other children from varied,
successful backgrounds.

Many of Ritsu's coworkers put their kids in private schools. When looking for places to live, Ritsu had also researched schools in this area, and the
allure of Kusumichi Elementary had been a big part of her choosing
Sawatari Apartments.

There was a healthy spirit of parent and guardian volunteering at
Kusumichi Elementary, with many positions beyond PTA appointments.

You could look after flower beds, prepare for the fall festival bazaar, hold flags for the crossing patrol on the streets around the school, and perform other duties.

Once Kanato was born, Ritsu wanted to spend as much of her time as possible doing things for her son.

She'd hoped to join the volunteer events once he started school, but her work had made it impossible to find the time. When she heard there was a group that did story time reading, however, she'd decided to participate, even if it was already the middle of the school year. After all, reading storybooks and novels was more or less part of her job already. Ritsu thought she could make a difference here. And naturally, there was a bit of professional pride at work, making her think others would be delighted to have a pro come in.

Yet as soon as Ritsu set foot in the school library, where the story time committee members were supposed to meet, she felt intensely out of place. She stopped and stood right inside the door.

The meeting time was one thirty, and Ritsu had arrived right on time. However, there were already many women sitting in chairs set up along three sides of a square table. They didn't seem to be discussing anything important yet. The group leader sat at the head of the table, but it was obvious that most of the women were simply chatting.

"By the way, did Tatsuya get home all right the other day? After the camping trip...?"

"Oh, you wouldn't believe it. He was better in no time. In fact, the very next day he rode his bike to the park with Mimi and their friends..."

"Well, that's not fair! We would have loved to go along."

The context was unclear.

Ritsu stopped at the entrance because it was immediately clear how close these people were. There were all intimately familiar with one another; there was no formality of any kind.

Maybe it wasn't a good idea to sign up partway through the year...

A glance around the library revealed something else. Nearly all the mothers here seemed to have children in older grades. Ritsu didn't see anyone she recognized from Kanato's year. Maybe this was the kind of organization where a specific group of mothers regularly connected, like an informal club.

Ritsu already regretted her choice to come. Feeling uncomfortable, she looked around, casting out a silent plea for help. However, all the mothers were so involved in their chat that none of them even seemed to notice her, much less glance in her direction.

Since Ritsu was already inside, it would be silly to walk right back out. She summoned her courage and took the empty chair closest to the corner, asking the woman next to her, "Do you mind if I sit here?"

"Huh? Sure."

The woman looked much older than Ritsu.

She was supposed to be the mother of an elementary school child, but her carelessly tied-up hair had many white strands among its waves. The fine wrinkles on her blouse weren't an intentional design, simply an indication that the garment hadn't been ironed in a long while.

The moment their eyes met, Ritsu felt startled.

Kusumichi Elementary—and the other schools in the area—was frequented by many trendy young mothers. Many of them followed fashions that concealed their motherhood, and they watched their figures. Yet the woman Ritsu had spoken to seemed so...*shabby*. Even her makeup, what little she wore, was an awkward mix of too-white foundation and overly red lipstick. It wasn't a contemporary cosmetic style. One might even think her a younger grandmother.

Without thinking, Ritsu looked at the woman's hands—and was even more shocked. The woman wasn't holding a smartphone, but an ancient flip phone. Ritsu worked with a few people who refused to carry a smartphone for one reason or another. It wasn't a big deal, but it still made her curious. She looked down, feeling guilty for staring.

The other volunteers still weren't getting down to business. The chatting continued.

"Hey, Yumiko. You said you were going to lend that thing to me."

"Oh nooo! I'm so sorry, Tomomi, I forgot."

Ritsu noticed that they were calling each other by their first names, an overly familiar thing to do. She felt even more like an outsider.

It wasn't clear if these were mothers from Ritsu's apartment complex. She didn't know every family. And which faces were recognizable depended on whether a person used the north or south exit more often.

The women gave no indication that they'd discussed the jumper Ritsu's husband had seen.

Ritsu had heard that school roles like those in the PTA involved a lot of foisting off responsibilities on others. Some committees were full of like-minded parents who conspired to snatch themselves a cushy little kingdom to control. That had seemed unlikely at Kusumichi Elementary, though. And this was a volunteer system. Anyone ought to be welcome to join...

She remembered the printout Kanato had brought home from school at the start of the year. It had read, *Volunteering at the school can teach you a lot about your child's education here,* and *You can meet and become friends with parents from other grades.* She hadn't realized that things had already moved on so much without her.

Maybe it had been foolish of her to assume that she could help read to the kids.

Suddenly, Ritsu felt eyes on her. It was the woman sitting next to her, the one who seemed quite old. She hadn't appeared particularly engrossed in the chat of the other parents, instead staring at her open phone. Now she was looking right at Ritsu.

"Has everyone here been on the reading committee for long?" Ritsu asked, going for broke. She smiled, feeling that it was natural to say something at this point. "Are you all mothers with children in the same grade? You seem so close to one another."

It was meant as a harmless question. Yet the moment she spoke, the other woman squeaked out, "What?" Eyeing Ritsu suspiciously, she sluggishly answered, "Ohhh. I could tell you, but do you have the time after this?"

Ritsu almost reacted with equal confusion. She lost track of the flow of conversation for a moment and sat stone-faced.

"I can tell you who has kids in which grade, and who's close with whom, but it's a lot to remember. Do you have a notebook or planner to write it all down?"

"Huh? Er, no, it's all right," Ritsu said abruptly. She inquired as a social nicety and wasn't that interested in the women. If anything, she hoped this was the last time she'd ever come here.

The woman glanced at Ritsu. "Well, I've been doing the story time committee for quite a while. The library—and the school—put me in the kids' section every week to read. I'm used to the deal, so if you want advice on good books, I can teach you later. Do you have time?"

"Um, actually, I'm sorry, but no. I have something after this."

Oh, darn, Ritsu thought. This kind of thing happened sometimes. It was fine now, but it would get uncomfortable later, when these women inevitably discovered what Ritsu did for work. She always felt bad when others found out she was a pro, as though she intended to embarrass them.

She had an idea of which books the woman might recommend. Ritsu had welcomed several authors of such books as guests on her radio show, and a few had become professional friends after their interviews.

The woman's eyes abruptly narrowed. "What's with your clothes?"

"Huh? What's that?"

"The bottom part with the lace attached is strange."

Ritsu's smile froze. It wasn't *strange*. It was *fashionable*. She'd bought the dress because of the lace. However, she held back what she really wanted to say and replied, "You think so?" instead.

"Oh my gosh, and is that a slit in the dress? But that's so odd, isn't it?"

"Er… My apologies. Is this outfit inappropriate?"

It wasn't an eye-catching dress by any means, but those in the know would recognize it as a fashion-forward design. Ritsu was starting to feel uncomfortable.

The woman shook her head. "No, no. I didn't mean it like that. You look like—like an actress."

She stared Ritsu full in the face. Ritsu wore a fake smile, wishing that she could disappear. After ogling her up and down, the woman said, "Earlier, I thought maybe I'd seen you before."

"Ah…yes."

Ritsu had been a TV newscaster for a time, and she also worked as a program host. That was probably it. No matter how many times this happened to her, she never quite knew how to react. Awkwardly, she answered, "I worked for a while, so that might be why."

"'Worked'?" the woman repeated.

Something cold trickled down Ritsu's back. She knew from experience that a certain kind of animosity existed between stay-at-home mothers and employed ones. Regret flitted through her breast for that careless comment.

"What do you do?" the woman inquired.

"I read the news…"

People occasionally questioned Ritsu about her job, but hardly any did it so bluntly. So Ritsu was equally honest in return.

"Wow!" the woman exclaimed, wide-eyed. "So you're a newscaster?"

"Well, yes," Ritsu admitted.

"You don't say," the woman whispered. She'd probably seen Ritsu on TV but didn't know her name.

A moment later, the woman said, in a hushed tone, "You know what?"

"Hmm?"

"Me too."

"Huh?"

Now it was Ritsu's turn to be shocked. "Oh, hush, hush," the woman whispered. "It's just between us! I'll bring it next time. I don't want the others to know."

"Oh…"

Bring it? Bring what? And when she said, *"Me too,"* did she mean she was also on a TV news program? Was that possible?

Ritsu's mind ran in circles. The woman looked much older than she, but Ritsu didn't recognize her face. Perhaps the woman had misheard something during their conversation.

Ritsu managed to smile through the bewilderment, and the woman asked, "Is your child in first grade? Did they start this year?"

"Oh, yes. I've wanted to join one of the volunteer groups since the spring, but I was too busy with work until now. I hoped that I could contribute by reading to the children."

"And are you still working?"

"Um, yes…"

"Do you have a son or a daughter? What's their name?"

"…We have a son."

Ritsu didn't give a name. *Why did I have to sit in this seat? Of all the people to sit next to, it had to be her.*

"Well, as for me," the woman went on, "I'm considering starting some work. My older child became a *hikikomori*, a shut-in, and refuses to go to school anymore. But at least my younger one is still doing well."

Ritsu could hardly believe her ears. The woman leaned in to chat more. Ritsu thought she would continue at a low volume, but apparently this part wasn't a secret.

"It's such a problem, you know?"

"Yes…it really is."

"Exactly. My older child is in high school, he was my son, but then he became a girl, and I'm not sure what to do now. It's like, What have you done to my life?"

Ritsu inhaled, and it made a hollow sound, like part of her throat was constricted. It was something like a little shocked shriek. Not at the truth, but at the rather indelicate way the woman had put it.

"'Became a girl'?" she parroted.

"Yes." The woman nodded. Ritsu really had no idea how to respond.

Gender identity was a very sensitive topic. Through her work, Ritsu met many different people, and the subject of gender arose numerous times on the radio show.

A child's most sensitive issues weren't necessarily worth treating like a dirty secret, but discussing this openly with so many people around didn't seem like the right sort of thing to do. That went for her kid's refusal to attend school or leave her room.

Suddenly, the woman's question about whether Kanato was a boy or a girl took on a different meaning.

I want to get out of here, Ritsu thought fervently. Goose bumps formed on her arms. The smiling older woman's face was so pale, and the way her dark-red lipstick stood out against the white was downright creepy.

They had only just met each other. If Ritsu extracted herself now, she could claim they weren't exactly acquaintances.

Just then, the woman opened up her planner and said, "Hey, write down your contact info."

"Excuse me?" It was such a blunt and, frankly, rude way of asking.

"Just your number is fine," the woman insisted. "And your name."

Ritsu prayed that the meeting would start soon. She glanced over, but found that the other parents were still absorbed in their chat and there was no sign of anything coming to order. *Please, help me*, she pleaded.

While she had cut down drastically on the number of on-screen jobs she took, Ritsu's profession was still one where her name was out there. She didn't want to give personal information if she could help it. In this era of ubiquitous internet, once your data was public, there was no telling what could happen. And this was Kanato's elementary school. If something befell Ritsu, that was one thing, but the idea of Kanato being singled out and victimized in some awful way made her blood run cold.

The woman kept staring at Ritsu, never looking away. Her pen and planner were outstretched.

I don't want to write it down. But I can't actually tell her that. If I refuse, they'll call me stuck-up. Rumors will dub me stuck-up. These fears had plagued Ritsu's mind since she'd had Kanato.

The meeting still wasn't starting. *Hurry it up!* she wanted to scream.

Ritsu Mikishima.

She wrote down her married name, not the one she used as a TV newscaster.

The woman clapped her hands and bounced in her seat. "Oh, I think I *have* seen your name before! That's amazing! Are you famous?"

"Oh…no, I'm really not."

She wanted to cry. This was her real name. The woman had definitely never seen it on TV. It felt like the woman was mocking her. Regret flooded through Ritsu for giving in. Normally, the other parents with kids in Kanato's grade didn't make a big deal of it if they learned her occupation. Everyone treated her with a certain level of courteous distance.

Why had she had to encounter someone like this today, of all days?

"We're starting now, Kaori," said a gentle voice that cut through the chatter. The woman next to Ritsu turned around, and so she looked over, too.

The speaker was a beautiful, slender woman. She wasn't very tall, but her face was petite, and her proportions were excellent. She wore a plain, color-coordinated outfit with a dress coat around her shoulders. It was a simple but unimpeachable look.

This woman is very sharp.

The speaker grinned. The woman next to Ritsu, whom she'd called Kaori, fell silent. Her expression vanished, and she silently put away her planner.

The new woman smiled at Ritsu. "Hello. This is your first time on the story time committee, isn't it? We're very glad to have you."

"That's right," said Ritsu. It was an enormous relief to have someone speak to her normally. Once again, she couldn't help but notice what a beautiful mother this woman was. Beautiful? No, she was perfect.

She seemed less like someone attending a meeting at Kanato's school and more like one of the notable types Ritsu met through work. One of those people whose makeup and clothes were impeccable, as though they'd stepped out of a magazine ad. The color choice of her wardrobe and the material of the dress coat were glorious.

"My name is Sawatari. I'm the mother of a boy in sixth grade," the speaker introduced.

Something clicked into place. Sawatari Apartments—the young designers who'd renovated the place where Ritsu lived. Upon reflection, her face looked familiar now, too.

"It's a pleasure to meet you," she said to Ritsu.

"Mrs. Sawatari, are you the designer of Sawatari Apartments?" Ritsu inquired, unable to help herself. The impeccably dressed woman gave her a searching look. Her long hair was done in a way that accentuated her compact features. Even her large earrings were stylish.

Feeling that she might have come on a little strong, Ritsu added, "I'm sorry. It's just that I live in Sawatari Apartments."

"Oh! You live in our development?" She beamed. "It's true. My husband was more involved in the renovation, and I did some work on the lobby interior and the art installations in the courtyard."

"I thought so," answered Ritsu brightly.

Sawatari graced her with an elegant smile and said, "I'm Hiromi Sawatari. What grade is your child in?"

"My son is in first grade."

"I see. Well, it's a pleasure to have you here." Hiromi moved toward the seats at the front of the group. Seemingly distracted by Hiromi's interruption, Kaori didn't speak to Ritsu again.

Thank goodness.

Ritsu assumed that Hiromi was the leader of the story time committee because of how she'd greeted her, but that turned out to be wrong. A different woman stood and announced, "Let's begin the fall planning meeting."

Hiromi took a nearby seat and watched the proceedings with a smile.

"We have an official reading month in the fall, which I will now go over. Those of you who've been through this before may be thinking, *Oh, I already know this*, but bear with me. Now, I'm not the best speaker, but I have been doing this the longest, so I'll handle orientation again today. I'm Yoko, mother of Mimi Wada, sixth grade. There's no official leader, but everyone else told me to step up, so here I am."

Yoko Wada's speech was met with smiles from the women familiar with her. Someone said softly, "You've got this," and others waved at her.

Ritsu found this speaker a little off-putting, much like Kaori. The way she kept including unnecessary asides like *"oh, I already know this"* and *"everyone else told me to step up"* was rather amateurish. It was only a parents' meeting, hardly the most formal thing in the world. Still, some level of public speaking skill was required. And as Yoko said, she wasn't the best at it. Judging by the way a few other mothers waved at her, it was clear this committee was a group of women who knew each other personally.

Yoko went on to explain the group's activities.

There would be daily sessions for the children after school during the reading month, and a parent presentation at the school's reading assembly. As Yoko went over the details, the other mothers who'd clearly known her for years offered remarks like, "Oh, that one really worked out well the last time," and, "Yoko, you're getting a bit carried away!" Again, it only accentuated the insularity.

All the while, Hiromi Sawatari sat and smiled, never offering any comments. She seemed all alone, quietly observing the situation.

"And with that, please take the rest of today's meeting to get to know each other better," Yoko concluded, gesturing toward the back of the room. There were bottled beverages and assorted packaged snacks. Everyone got to their feet and shuffled over to pick out drinks and food in a manner that suggested they were used to this.

Do they have time to sit around and drink tea at every meeting? Ritsu wondered.

Evidently, the school committee volunteers were mothers with more time on their hands than Ritsu had realized, and this was a way for them to keep themselves occupied. Secretly disappointed, she stood like the others. Ritsu could have chosen to leave, but since she was there, she resolved to have a little chat with a few others first.

"Hey, so is this you?" Kaori asked, picking up where she'd left off when the meeting began. Ritsu turned to see the woman holding up her flip phone, screen on, for her to see. "I searched, and this showed up."

The instant she saw the screen, Ritsu felt dizzy. She nearly toppled to the floor.

There were pictures of Ritsu from back when she'd appeared on TV programs. She saw promotional photos from her talent agency and her profile, too. At the top, "ritsu mikishima" was entered in the search bar.

Kaori had searched for her online. Right here. In her presence. And she was showing off the results to the person in question.

It was so beyond the standards of decency that Ritsu didn't know how to react. The internet was not some utopian place of positivity. In fact, it was more common to be met with malicious statements from an undetermined number of anonymous parties. That's why Ritsu never searched for her own name. After getting married and changing her last name, she felt secure that her work name and her private one were separate.

She'd known—because the management at her agency had told her—that her real name had leaked onto the net somehow. It didn't feel good to hear that, but she managed her anxiety by simply not going out of her way to search for herself. And yet...

"My goodness, this picture is so nice! And your eyeliner is perfect. Was this professionally done?"

The promotional headshots agencies used were important for crafting one's image, and they got a lot of use over time. Naturally, they were taken by professional photographers. And when one was working with professionals, it was important to project the right expression and attitude. To see such a serious, stoic picture in this relatively private place went completely beyond embarrassing and straight into downright unbearable.

"Er, yes..."

Ritsu tried to put on a pleasant facade, but her cheeks were too stiff to manage. Meanwhile, Kaori muttered comments to herself as she scrolled through the pictures. "Hmm. Ooh, this one's pretty. Is that a dress? Did you really wear that?"

Just then, a different voice called out, "Oh, Ritsu!"

She looked up and saw Hiromi standing by the drinks in the back with a hand raised. Once again feeling spared, Ritsu returned the greeting. She excused herself from Kaori and moved away from the seats. She took her bag and jacket with her so she wouldn't need to come back for them.

As Ritsu approached, Hiromi gestured to the plastic bottles. "Would you like something to drink? They have juice and tea. Which would you prefer?"

"Uh, I'll have tea..."

"Of course."

They spoke like old friends, despite having just met. Ritsu felt no uneasiness now, unlike with Kaori. Hiromi was very well socialized, and seemed to know exactly the right social distance to maintain for another person to feel comfortable in this situation.

Ritsu took the cup of tea that Hiromi poured for her and glanced over her shoulder at Kaori. The older woman was still in her seat, fiddling with her phone by herself. No one spoke to her, and it seemed to Ritsu that she might have always been the odd one out.

Hiromi looked Ritsu over. "Were you one of the first to move in after the renovation? When did you come to the complex?"

"Only half a year ago. We timed it with our son starting elementary school."

"Ah, I see. Well, I'm happy to meet you. Hopefully, it won't be the last time. Are you on the south side of the complex or the north?"

"South."

"Ah. Then you're closer to the school. We live near the north entrance."

Ritsu knew that already. She'd learned via the grapevine just after moving in that, as part of their renovation work, the Sawataris gave themselves a much larger apartment on the top floor on the north side.

Hiromi spoke so casually and comfortably that it immediately felt like they were equals. Unlike Kaori, who was blunt and forward, Hiromi had a fond, familiar way. It was a practiced style that reminded Ritsu of the TV and radio world. Although they were in different lines of work, they shared a certain kind of glamorous allure. Hiromi just seemed comfortable around people.

"You and your husband made many media appearances for Sawatari

Apartments, right?" Ritsu asked, a bit awkwardly. Magazine pictures showed their penthouse furnished tastefully, with plants and abundant light. It was clear from a glance that the couple coordinated their home carefully, down to the wallpaper and floor color.

"Oh, you saw all of that?"

"I had no idea your child attended this school."

"And already in sixth grade. My husband and I are hardened veterans of this place. Anything you need to know, just ask. Do you take part in the apartment complex's festivals and events?"

"Yes, often."

"Oh, that's wonderful. At the start of the remodeling, we were so focused on doing all of those things as a family, but once we got older, we got so busy with cram schools and the like."

"Yes, it seems like the kids in earlier grades are the focus of the festivals. Or even those too young for school."

"That's right. Getting to know other parents with kids at this school isn't easy, especially if the child's in a different grade. Unless you live in the same housing complex, that is."

Hiromi's eyes briefly grew distant, as though she had spotted someone behind Ritsu. "Let's get together again sometime," she said, smiling. "You'll have to visit our place. I'll send you an invitation."

"Thank you so much."

Hiromi walked off to one of the other parents, drink in hand. "Hello. Thanks for your work the other day. That must have been hard," she said to a mother she was likely already acquainted with.

"Oh! The same to you, Hiromi. Thanks again," the woman replied with a grin.

She wasn't kidding about being a veteran. Hiromi was apparently on good terms with everyone here.

"Excuse me," called a quiet, timid voice. Ritsu turned and saw two rather reserved-looking women. One wore an elegantly colored blouse, the other a similar one-piece dress. Both had undyed, perfectly black hair. They looked very straitlaced.

"Yes?"

"You're Ritsu Morimoto, aren't you?" said the one in the blouse, who appeared to have been working herself up to ask. Ritsu was about to reply when the other woman hastily added, "We've seen you at all the other parent events since the spring. We'd say, 'Oh, there's Ritsu again.'"

"I've always admired how beautiful you are. Are you really joining the story time committee? Even though you already do this sort of thing professionally?"

Familiarity and nervousness colored her voice in equal measure. There were times when Ritsu felt a bit conflicted about her face and occupation spreading through the school, but hearing these women speak of her positively was a tremendous relief. Especially after Kaori's rude treatment.

Ritsu beamed. "Thank you. I'm flattered that you consider me a professional, but really, I'm only trying to help my son's school, that's all. You'll have to teach me about the job."

"Oh, no, we wouldn't dare! We're just happy you're here with us, Ritsu."

"Yes, we have nothing to teach you. We were hoping you could show us."

They fawned over her. Frankly, it didn't feel bad.

"I'm Kinosaki. My child's in fourth grade."

"And I'm Takahashi. My daughter's also in fourth grade."

Grateful that they'd both properly introduced themselves, Ritsu replied, "I'm Mikishima. Morimoto was my maiden name."

"Oh, of course. I'm sorry. We only know you by that name."

"It's incredible that you can raise your child while still working."

Based on their statements, they seemed to be stay-at-home mothers.

"If there's anything we can help with, just say the word," Kinosaki said. "We have lots of time. If anything happens with your child, Mrs. Mikishima, or you want to switch spots with someone else on the committee, I can help get it done."

"Yes. It's not like we have anything better to do."

"Oh, no, no," Ritsu insisted. "I'm sure you're too busy for that."

Ritsu had received offers like this from housewives before. Each time, it seemed to her like the women felt inferior about not working, and it made Ritsu uncomfortable. With all the housework and child-rearing involved, they couldn't possibly be as available as they claimed.

Ritsu wasn't certain how to respond. Thankfully, Takahashi saved her the trouble.

"This really is an amazing school, when you think about it. We have Hiromi and you, Mrs. Mikishima."

"Oh, just Ritsu is fine," she said. The women shared a delighted look, then repeated, "And you, Ritsu."

Kinosaki and Takahashi watched Hiromi Sawatari, who was speaking with another group of mothers at the moment.

"Isn't Hiromi great? She's so talented and wonderful. Yet she's still very friendly with everyone, and she's always smiling. Despite the prestige of her job, she's so humble. And her kid is just as sweet."

"How do you get to be as warm and welcoming as her? I really idolize that quality."

"Mrs. Sawatari's really nice, isn't she?"

"Yes, very much so," Ritsu agreed.

"Did you know?" the women said. "Hiromi designed the famous Sawatari Apartments near here."

"Oh, I was just talking to her about that. I live in Sawatari Apartments."

"What? You do? So do we!" Kinosaki exclaimed, pressing her hands together in front of her chin. Her face lit up, as did Takahashi's.

"I had no idea. I knew that you had a child in this school because we've seen you a few times, but that's all. Wow! At the same apartment complex, too."

"It's a large place, so I suppose we never ran into each other. We only moved there in the spring," Ritsu explained. "Well, I hope I see you again sometime."

Both women nodded. "Yes, us too!"

Ritsu followed Hiromi with her eyes while the other women talked. Hiromi had been speaking with a group earlier, but had since moved seats to speak with someone else. She didn't have especially eye-catching clothes on, but fashionable people had a way of drawing the eye regardless.

Hiromi bowed and moved on again. Ritsu suddenly realized that she seemed to be staying on the move to ensure that she spoke with everyone present. She kept a lively tone with all the women, never faltering.

Takahashi noticed Ritsu's gaze and whispered, "Impressive, isn't she? She's very attentive, calm, and relaxing. It makes you feel good when you talk with her."

"I noticed," Ritsu replied.

Kinosaki added, "That's right. Hiromi's amazing. When I'm feeling down, she sends over a text or a LINE message right when I need it. Once I wondered how she knew I was down, and she explained that she noticed I wasn't uploading as often on Instagram and got worried about me."

"Her husband is great, too. There was this one time when my husband might have been sent on a long-term work transfer, and Hiromi's husband said he'd take him out for a drink and give him some advice. They weren't even that close, but my husband was delighted that he was so considerate and helpful."

"Yes, they're both so perfect."

"Wow…"

Perfect. The word took Ritsu aback. She had been thinking the same thing about Hiromi. Ritsu didn't really know the woman, but she'd already saved her from Kaori twice. However, Ritsu wasn't sure about the way Takahashi called her *"perfect."*

Did speaking on friendly terms with everyone really make her that wonderful?

Ritsu also had misgivings about Hiromi being called "*calm.*" Yes, she was very attentive in the way she interacted with everyone, but her friendliness resembled her fashion sense—too flawless to be real. It seemed familiar, somehow...

And then she realized why.

The way Hiromi moved seats continuously, talking with every person present. It was the same thing a National Diet member did years before at a work event, some kind of reception. It was less that the woman found people she knew and caught up with them and more that she intentionally circled the tables to create evidence she'd spoken with everyone. Hiromi had never met Ritsu before, yet during their talk, she made sure to mention "I see you on TV all the time." It was flattering, but looking back, that was how a person acted when they knew the power of their presence. No one was this universally friendly unless they were confident they could bypass anyone's defenses.

Ritsu thought Hiromi or her husband could definitely run for office in the future. Their local recognition was high after the striking remodel of Sawatari Apartments. It made sense that they'd take time to help fellow school parents with problems and emotional issues if that was their goal.

When viewed any other way, it seemed like extreme behavior, almost as though Hiromi and her husband were intentionally seeking out troubled people and trying to get involved...

"Kaori," Hiromi called, pulling Ritsu back to herself. Hiromi approached Kaori, still fiddling with her phone by herself. No one else bothered to chat with the odd woman, yet Hiromi strolled up to her and peered at her phone screen, asking what she was up to like a close friend.

Ritsu couldn't tell if Kaori's search history was still displayed. However, there was an obvious note of surprise on Hiromi's face. She pointed at the screen, then chuckled. Unsurprisingly, Kaori didn't smile, but she nodded in response, and they started talking.

"Isn't she wonderful? Even spending time with *her*," Kinosaki muttered. Perhaps she didn't mean for Ritsu to hear, though she did. That made it clear that Kaori was indeed an outcast among this group.

That realization brought another one to mind: Hiromi had never asked Ritsu's occupation. Perhaps she'd thought it wasn't the right time or place for a more personal inquiry. But hadn't Hiromi addressed her by name?

"Oh, Ritsu!"

That's what she'd said. However, did Ritsu give her name in their brief conversation before that?

Ritsu never introduced herself, which meant Hiromi already knew her as the newscaster Ritsu Morimoto, like Kinosaki and Takahashi. So why didn't she say as much specifically?

"All right, until next time. It was good to talk to you, Kaori." Hiromi smiled as she left the odd woman. Ritsu hastily tore her eyes away from the two.

When the story time committee meeting concluded, Ritsu felt exhausted.

There were a few people Ritsu thought she could be on good terms with, but as she walked home, she realized she'd never traded contact information with them. It was probably better not to give away that information until necessary, though. She was especially glad she hadn't given Kaori a way to reach her. Did she live at Sawatari Apartments, too?

Ritsu was curious, but didn't want to interact with that woman again. Thinking it would be awkward to walk with the other mothers returning to the complex, Ritsu decided to run an errand, heading the opposite way from home.

Despite having written her name on the story time volunteer sheet, she felt it was better not to take part in the group anymore.

* * *

The day after the story time committee meeting, Kanato brought home a brown envelope and said, "Here."

"Hmm?" Ritsu answered.

The boy tossed his book bag onto the living room couch. "They gave it to me. It's for you."

Ritsu was making hamburgers in the kitchen for dinner, so she washed her hands and walked to the dining table to pick up the envelope. It read, *To Ritsu*. Below that were the words *Tea Party Invitation*. Ritsu turned it over and saw the words *From Hiromi Sawatari*, written in the Western alphabet beneath the neatly sealed fold. The beauty of the script was amazing. The letters were printed in what was presumably an original, personalized font. It was like receiving a private piece of mail from a famous brand.

The envelope exuded a faint scent of bergamot.

"Is this…?"

"Asahi Sawatari gave it to me. He's a sixth grader. He said I could come, too."

"Asahi Sawatari…"

That had to be Hiromi's boy. Until now, Ritsu had never heard Kanato speak the name of a child from a different grade at school.

"Have you met him before? Are you close?" Ritsu asked.

Kanato shook his head. "Not really. I never talked to him before. But he's the student chairman. That's how I know him."

Hiromi's son was the student chairman. "Wow," Ritsu hummed.

"Right?" Kanato replied, and his face lit up. "Hey, can I go to Asahi's? Can we bring Hatch?"

"Hmm, I don't know about Hatch. Some families like dogs, but others don't. We don't know how Asahi's family might feel about it, so we'll leave Hatch home."

Kanato was already familiar enough with Asahi as a person to look forward to visiting. Ritsu opened the envelope and removed the paper inside. The bergamot scent grew stronger.

Dear Ritsu,

It was lovely to speak with you yesterday.

The Kusumichi Elementary mothers who live in the complex will be meeting for tea Wednesday evening. Please come by if you have time.

Here is my contact information.

At the end were Hiromi's name, LINE ID, and cell phone number, and the words *Sawatari Apartments Unit 701.*

◆

On the trip over to the north side of the complex, where the Sawatari residence was located, Ritsu saw a light-blue tarp placed in the hallway.

It was a sanitary cover for movers to walk on.

"Oh, it's the movers with the doggy mark," Kanato remarked from Ritsu's side. It was the same mover they'd hired when coming here, which was why he remembered it.

"You're right," Ritsu said. "I wonder if someone new is moving in."

Sawatari Apartments was a hot-ticket destination with scarce vacancies. That's what Ritsu and her husband had been told back when they changed apartments. But things might be different this time of year compared to the high-traffic spring season. In recent weeks, these moving sheets had become a little more commonplace.

When Ritsu was searching for apartments, a realtor told her, "You'll really regret passing up this opportunity," in reference to Sawatari. However, she might have gotten a slightly better price if she'd waited. That was unfortunate, but when it came to finding a living space, everything was in the hands of fate.

"Let's hope it's a family with children. Maybe you'll have a new classmate, Kanato."

"Awww. I like having a small class."

Since starting grade school, Kanato had noticeably become a bit of a contrarian. That seemed like a kind of growth in its own way, though, so Ritsu just exhaled and rubbed her son's head. The movers passed the mother and child in the hall, wearing their company uniforms. Two of them hauled a large refrigerator toward the elevator.

Ritsu pulled her son over to the wall so that they weren't in the way.

"Hey, Mom? How late will the moms' meeting go today?"

"Well, everyone's got dinner to make, so I'd guess five at the latest."

"Aww! Make it six, Mom."

"Why?"

"Because I want to play in the courtyard park longer. It's my first time playing with Asahi."

Kanato seemed obsessed with the opportunity to play with the older boy.

Earlier, Ritsu had added Hiromi to her friends list on LINE and sent a message. Hiromi had immediately responded with, *Yes, please come!* Then she'd given the details of the time and place, adding *You may bring Kanato with you, too. My son Asahi will be playing down in the park during the tea party. That's usually what the children do when we meet.*

The party was on Wednesday, Kanato's piano lesson day. Initially, Ritsu had intended to decline the invitation, but before she had the chance, Hiromi had texted her again.

I just spoke with Asahi, and he's very excited about playing with Kanato. He says that Kanato is very good at soccer. Apparently, he's seen him play with friends during recess.

Hiromi added a smiling emoji. After all that, it was difficult to refuse. Kanato seemed excited to play with Asahi, and most importantly, it was Ritsu's first offer to visit Hiromi's home. She didn't want to come off as ungrateful for the generosity.

The place where Kanato took piano lessons took requests for makeup days. So, after some consideration, Ritsu typed, *We'd love to. Kanato seems quite eager to play with Asahi, too.*

Ritsu would just have to call to reschedule the piano class later. "You're looking forward to this, aren't you?" she asked, recalling how Kanato had spoken about the games he wanted to try and comics he wanted to read with Asahi while loading up his backpack.

"Yeah! It's my first time playing with a sixth grader."

Although she felt bad, Ritsu had to stop Kanato from bringing his portable game console and manga over. Every family had their own standards when it came to allowing their children such recreational material.

In Ritsu's experience, the "better" a mother was, the more concerned she was over the addictive potential and negative mental effects of such diversions. She could just allow her children to have them whenever. Ritsu and her husband Yuuki thought that games and manga were fine in moderation, and limited Kanato's access to them to certain times of day. However, some families didn't let their children touch video games at all. Ritsu's experience had taught her that children who were completely denied such activities became raving addicts after their first experience at a friend's house. That made stopping difficult. Even when the other children got bored and moved on to something else, that one deprived child remained glued to the little screen. Ritsu had seen it happen many times with Kanato's classmates.

Hiromi was probably a "good mother." The kind with a keen interest in education, who spared no effort in child-rearing and housework. Ritsu had a feeling that Asahi was a boy who never played video games.

"Aww! I want to play games with Asahi!" Kanato protested. There were play fixtures in the complex's park, though, and today was just a test to see how things would go. In all likelihood, there would be more children besides Asahi. If they brought games, Ritsu would permit Kanato to do the same next time. Instead, she gave him a big bag of snacks that he could share with the others, which Kanato grudgingly accepted.

When Ritsu and her son arrived at Unit 701 on the north side of Sawatari Apartments, they saw a large wreath hanging on the door. It was a tremendous decoration, with amber vines and flowers of blue and yellow.

Ritsu rang the doorbell. Naturally, the chime was identical to her own apartment's.

"Be right there!" Hiromi's voice called from behind the door. A few moments later, it opened.

"Hello. Thank you so much for—"

—*your invitation.* That's what Ritsu meant to finish with, but the words caught in her throat. Hiromi wasn't the one who opened the door. It was someone else—an unfamiliar man. When their eyes met, Ritsu realized who he was.

Kyohei Sawatari—the main renovation designer and Hiromi's husband. She'd seen his face in the media before. His eyes were round, large, and friendly, and he sported a short goatee. He was taller and broader across the shoulders than the magazine and TV appearances suggested, with an all-around solid frame.

"Oh, it's a pleasure to meet you. I'm—," Ritsu began.

However, Kyohei Sawatari just nodded and interjected, "Ah, yes!" Beaming, he said, "You must be Ritsu. Hiromi told me to expect you. I'm sorry, you probably have other things you'd normally be doing at this time."

"No, no. It's no trouble."

Leaning back into the apartment, he called out, "Hey, Hiromi!"

He wore an expensive-looking sweater his wife had likely picked out for him, plus a pair of nicely faded jeans. In the magazines and TV shows, Kyohei Sawatari looked commanding and stately despite his youth, but in person, he appeared surprisingly personable and charming.

The sound of hurrying children came surging from the back of the apartment.

"Is Kanato here?"

"Let's go down to the park, then!"

Three boys notably larger than Kanato came to the door. Kanato peeked from behind his mother nervously. One of kids raised a hand and said, "Hey, Kanato!" Kanato suddenly burst into a smile. Two of the boys had buzzed heads, but the one who greeted Ritsu's son had longer hair and was paler. The intelligent look in his eyes matched Hiromi's, making it clear that he was Asahi Sawatari.

"We're going now, Dad," Asahi said, putting on his shoes, then bowing to Ritsu. "Good afternoon."

As a sixth grader, Asahi had certainly matured a bit, but considering how the other two boys ran by Ritsu without a word, his courtesy was obviously more than an age thing.

"Let's go, Kanato."

"Okay!"

"I'll come to pick you up in a bit! If anything happens, come back here," Ritsu told her son as he bounded off excitedly. Kanato gave her a perfunctory "Okaaay!" without looking back. She realized too late that the extralarge bag of snacks was a bit too much for only four boys.

"I'm so sorry, I don't mean to turn him into a babysitter..."

"Oh, no. We have guests over all the time, so Asahi's used to it. Please, come in," Kyohei replied. Ritsu was right on time, but there were already several guests inside. At Kyohei's ushering, Ritsu entered and removed her shoes, at which point Hiromi arrived.

"Right this way, Ritsu. Sorry for sending the hubby to get you. That must have been a surprise."

Hiromi looked perfect today, too. Her makeup was flawless for a simple home gathering, and despite the chill outside, she wore a sleeveless dress in the warm apartment. A simple silver brooch glinted from its spot on the right side of her chest, and her upper arms were slender and beautiful.

Simply magnificent, Ritsu thought, admiring the sight of her.

"Oh, no," she said, "we're the ones who have the privilege of living in your complex. It's an honor to be invited, er…"

"Just Kyohei is fine," said Hiromi's husband, already heading to the living room after bringing indoor slippers for Ritsu. "Both my wife and I go by Sawatari, so it helps reduce confusion."

"Kyohei, then," Ritsu replied. "It's an honor to meet you. We were very happy to get approval to move into Sawatari Apartments. We thought the renovation was wonderful."

The Sawataris shared a look, and Hiromi shrugged. "People here say that to us often, but really, we didn't do much. We just happened to know some good contractors, and they redid the interiors the way we like. Please don't feel that you have to put us on a pedestal."

"That's right. We're only neighbors."

"Ah, yes. Thank you," Ritsu said, agreeing despite her instinct not to be so casual.

Hiromi looked sidelong at her husband and smiled awkwardly. "It just so happens he has a work meeting at home today. I forgot about it when I put together the tea party plans. Sorry there's a dad at this mothers' meetup."

"Oh, that's all right… Does Kyohei often work from home?"

"I have an actual office, but many clients feel better seeing homes that I actually worked on when we talk."

Hiromi beamed. "And he still gets magazine and TV offers."

In the center of the hallway wall was a row of Arabic mosaic tiles with a very heavy, antique-looking set of hooks. Several coats and jackets were already hanging from them, and the combination of colors stood out in the carefully coordinated interior. Any crew that came here for an interview undoubtedly had a field day shooting the place.

"It must be a lot of work to deal with," Ritsu commented, referencing the media attention. "It's gone down in recent years, but I had people trying to get pictures inside my home or ones of my private life all the time."

Ritsu could only guess how much Hiromi and her husband knew about her professional career. She hadn't had the chance to bring it up, but Kyohei called her Ritsu when they met. That plus the way Hiromi conducted herself around Ritsu convinced her to speak with the Sawataris under the assumption that they knew who she was and her profession.

"It meant several days of cleaning with my family every time. Honestly, it was such a hassle," Ritsu added.

She meant only to sympathize, yet she sensed an abrupt chill from the Sawataris. It was puzzling to her until Kyohei replied, "Actually, it happens all the time, because of the nature of our jobs."

He wasn't smiling. Ritsu panicked. Had she said something wrong?

Hiromi and Kyohei showed off their home because it was a demonstration of what they could do in their professional capacity. Ritsu understood that, of course, but there was an elementary school boy living here, too. Her remark had been about the difficulty of erasing all the lived-in traces a child would leave before having your home professionally photographed. She hadn't meant it to be a slight in any way.

Hiromi was walking away, as though she hadn't heard that exchange at all.

"Listen up, everyone. Ritsu is here!" she announced, cheerily opening the door to the living room. The women who'd arrived before Ritsu looked her way together. There were three of them, and two were familiar faces from the story time committee: Mrs. Kinosaki and Mrs. Takahashi. They smiled and said, "Good afternoon."

The other woman wasn't from the meeting. She looked younger than Ritsu. Her bobbed hair was dyed a lighter shade of brown. In contrast to the other two, who again wore subdued outfits, she had on a bright-green dress with a frilly silhouette.

"Oh, you're right, it *is* Ritsu. It's nice to meet you—I'm Yuzuki, from Unit 601." She grinned, revealing large front teeth. Her weak chin made them appear even bigger, like a squirrel's or some other rodent's. She seemed very adorable.

"That's directly underneath us," Hiromi commented serenely. "I'll hang up your coat," she added, taking Ritsu's jacket away. "We've known her since she came by for a visit after moving in. Her son goes to the same school as ours, and they've been over a few times now. Her son's name is Michiya Yuzuki. He's in fifth grade."

"He's one of the boys you saw at the door."

Ritsu bobbed her head. "My son is still only in first grade. His name is Kanato Mikishima."

With introductions finished, Ritsu took a longer look at the living room. She couldn't help but sigh in wonder.

The first thing to catch her eye was a large vase in the corner. It was short but translucent, like a large fish tank, with several full maple branches stuck inside. Mentally, Ritsu likened it to an entire portion of a tree brought inside for display. The sheer power of it made her gasp.

"Do you do flower arranging as well, Hiromi?"

"Oh, I wouldn't call it anything so fancy. I got the branches for cheap from a friend who's a florist."

"You used real flowers for the wreath on the door, too. I thought it was lovely."

"Oh, you noticed? Thank you. I knew you would, Ritsu."

Wreaths hung for long periods typically used fake or dried blossoms. Real ones wilted quickly, and they'd have to be exchanged and rear-ranged. Dried flowers helped with that, but Ritsu got the sense that Hiromi went to the trouble of redoing her wreath with new blossoms each time. Ritsu could never do that. And even if she'd had the space for the maple branch display, she couldn't put together something so incredible. It all felt...

"Just like a business, isn't it?" Kinosaki said, taking the words right out of Ritsu's mind. Takahashi and Yuzuki nodded in agreement.

"It's been carefully arranged, just like a nice restaurant or hotel. Every detail is right. It's incredible. I could never pull this off."

"We have frequent guests—restaurateurs and artists—and they say, 'This is better than our place,'" Kyohei stated matter-of-factly. Ritsu was mildly alarmed by this comment. It was a totally transparent boast. However, the other women just nodded along. Despite the brief, odd sensation in her chest, Ritsu looked past the flower display and noticed that a very familiar painting was hanging on the wall behind it.

"That painting..."

"Oh, are you a fan?" Kyohei asked, watching Ritsu closely. "You like that artist?"

"Er... Yes," Ritsu answered, swallowing what she'd meant to say.

"Great, great." Kyohei grinned. "Every woman the same age as you and Hiromi loves that one. I guess it's a generational thing? The floral motif is very feminine friendly, of course. It was a limited run, but Hiromi just *had* to have it."

Oh no, Ritsu thought.

Maybe she was the one being unfair and cynical, assuming that Kyohei was boasting. Perhaps she was just jealous because it was all so incredible. Ritsu kept her queued comment to herself and turned to Hiromi instead.

"Um, if you don't mind, I brought these for the tea party." She presented the paper bag she'd brought. There were a container of strawberry jam and some homemade scones inside.

A housewives' tea party was surely the sort of gathering where people brought things to share. Hiromi was so very sensible and thoughtful that Ritsu had known she had to bring something respectable. A friend of hers had made wonderful fresh scones when she visited once. The jam had been homemade, too, with plenty of real fruit texture. When Ritsu complimented her friend on how good it was, she'd replied, "It's actually quite easy." She'd taught Ritsu the recipe.

"I'm hardly an expert baker, but I thought this would be a nice way to introduce myself to you. The scones and jam are homemade," Ritsu explained, presenting the bag.

For an instant—just an instant—Hiromi's face went blank, like time itself stopped. A moment later, she was smiling and thanking Ritsu. "We'll enjoy them together."

"Oh, and there's clotted cream, too, if you like."

"Of course."

Had she been offered a plate, Ritsu would have gladly served the scones herself. However, Hiromi took the bag to the kitchen. From what Ritsu saw from the living room, the open kitchen was done up in Hiromi's signature style.

It was flawless in that movie-set way, and Ritsu quickly understood why. There were no labels or displays of any kind. Bottles of seasonings and containers with ingredients from the supermarket and convenience store all had labels with logos and information. Bottles of drinking water, sacks of flour, soy sauce, rice cooker screens…

There were none of those in Hiromi's kitchen. It was nearly shocking. Rows of nice-looking bottles and cans had been laid out here and there. Presumably they held flour, spices, and everything else. On close inspection, a few bottles did appear store-bought, but they all sported striking designs or logos in foreign languages. Nothing in that kitchen could be bought at the local corner store.

There was no rice cooker, either. Ritsu had a few friends who were dedicated cooks, so she thought she knew why. The Sawatari family cooked rice in a pot.

Ritsu was stunned. Her friends who loved cooking rice in a pot were either single foodies, housewives good in the kitchen, or culinary researchers and coordinators. She couldn't imagine a mother with a growing boy and a demanding job not using a rice cooker.

It was at this point that Ritsu felt a pang of regret. *Perhaps I made a mistake.*

She had come prepared to see a Hiromi who was a "good mother," dedicated to both education and housework, and for the Sawataris to live in a very "good home." However, she'd never expected this. Homemade scones might have been a poor choice.

In fact, none of the other women had brought anything. Yuzuki, whom Ritsu had met moments earlier, thanked her for the gift. "That's really nice of you to bring scones. And homemade? Fantastic."

"Were we not supposed to bring our own items today?" Ritsu inquired. "I hope I didn't overstep my boundaries."

"Oh, we always leave everything to Hiromi at these events. We've gotten very spoiled."

"Don't let it bother you! I do this because I like to," Hiromi replied from the kitchen while heating water for tea.

Ritsu felt oddly uncomfortable inside the perfectly designed home. It was almost as though guests were meant to gather and gawk at the astounding and wonderful Hiromi. Uncertain of what to say, Ritsu asked Hiromi, "Is this everyone? Are there any others coming?"

"There are two more. There's Yoko, the leader of the story time committee, and Mamiko, the mother of a girl in Asahi's class."

No sooner had Hiromi replied than the doorbell rang.

"Coming!" said Kyohei, getting to his feet again. "Now who will this be, Yoko or Mamiko?" he said to himself while heading for the entryway. Ritsu found it surprising he referred to the mothers by their first names. As he walked off, she wondered, *Does he intend to stay for this whole thing?*

"Sorry there's a dad at this mothers' meetup."

Ritsu had assumed that Hiromi was only saying that, and that Kyohei would either leave the apartment or retire to another room. Yet he remained present the whole time, showing no sign of removing himself from the gathering.

A man in the midst of a group of women could be helpful at times, yet Ritsu felt quite alienated by it in this instance.

"Thank you for waiting," Hiromi said as she returned to the table. The tray she carried held a scone for everyone, each on its own tiny plate. When the fragrant, buttery smell hit her nose, Ritsu realized that Hiromi must have popped them into the oven for a minute to warm them back up. The strawberry jam was garnished with mint leaves, which Ritsu definitely hadn't brought. This was a reflection of Hiromi's perfectionist artistic streak. Anything she did needed to have her personal touch applied.

From the entryway came a loud, "Wow, the place looks just as amazing as ever!"

It was the same overly familiar speaking voice Ritsu had heard at the story time committee meeting. As Yoko continued to talk, her voice grew nearer and nearer.

"Makes you wonder if this is really the same complex we all live in. You're leaving the rest of us in the dust, Hiromi! I bet you took the day off when revamping our place, Kyohei!"

Ritsu found this blunt jocularity rather distasteful, but the Sawataris didn't seem upset in the slightest. Kyohei shook his head and said, "Oh come, now!" as he followed Yoko into the living room. "We did everything equally and fairly. If your place feels cramped or unsatisfactory, that's between you and Goro, Yoko."

"Ahhh, I should've known. Guess we just don't have your refined taste. How disappointing," Yoko replied.

Goro was clearly the name of Yoko's husband. It was stunning to hear two Japanese couples referring to each other by first names simply because their children were classmates. This level of intimacy was nearly unheard of. It was as though they'd been close friends for decades.

"Well, since you're all here, I might as well put on the special playlist I whipped up for today."

"Ooh, that'd be great. You've always got the best taste in music, Kyohei."

Kyohei used his smartphone to operate the little music speaker on the counter between the kitchen and the living room. It played a song from some Western artist Ritsu didn't recognize.

Just like Hiromi, Kyohei was comfortable being around people. He was almost unbearably personal with the loud and blunt Yoko, but with the more reserved Kinosaki and Takahashi, he maintained a genteel manner. His demeanor with Yuzuki fell at neither extreme, but she nevertheless listened to him happily.

Hiromi attended to the tea preparations, smiling as she watched her husband and friends converse. The bergamot scent that had wafted from the party invitation envelope now emanated from the Earl Grey she poured into Ritsu's cup.

"Ooh, scones! Did you bake these, Hiromi?"

"No. Ritsu made them for us. And the jam. It's homemade. Very delicious," she replied to Yoko with a smile. Ritsu's heart ached.

She'd made more than enough scones for everyone, but Hiromi did not have a little plate with a serving like all the others—meaning that she didn't intend to eat. Her husband Kyohei had a scone and jam, and he tried them with a little, "Ahh," but did not even bother with the passive social nicety of saying they tasted good.

Everyone else marveled over the flavor and asked Ritsu, "You really made the jam, too?" She could only respond with a fake, pained smile.

The recipe Ritsu had followed was good, and she used it often at home. Although Kanato and Yuuki enjoyed the results, it was ultimately amateur cooking.

Between the busywork of preparing and refilling the tea and the need for "something like a nice salty cracker for variety," Hiromi was constantly flitting back and forth, more often in the kitchen than at the living room table.

Suddenly, from the kitchen came a loud, high-pitched cry. "Oh! This clotted cream!"

It was Hiromi. She always maintained the most elegant and practiced demeanor; this was the first time Ritsu had ever heard her in a state of high excitement. She came out of the kitchen with Ritsu's paper bag in hand.

"I'm so sorry, I forgot to serve this with the rest. This clotted cream is the organic kind from Lyla, isn't it? Forgive me, I'll bring it out at once. Thank you, this is great!"

"Er, I…"

Ritsu had brought the clotted cream to go with the scones. It came from an organic foods company overseas and couldn't be purchased in Japanese stores. Ritsu had hoped to make the cream, too, but she'd still had a leftover unopened container from her friend and brought that instead.

Kyohei chuckled, "Oh, my wife is a sucker for anything organic. She says you never know what they put in other stuff on the market."

The smile that teased the corners of his mouth contorted and vanished.

"It's a real problem, sadly," he added, eyes on Ritsu. She smiled back awkwardly to hide her real feelings from Kyohei.

"You never know what they put in."

She knew what that meant.

The issue wasn't whether food tasted good or was well prepared. It was that Hiromi didn't know what Ritsu might have put in the food.

"Ooh, this clotted cream is so delicious. I've got to put some on the crackers," Hiromi sang, spreading the cream on a brown whole wheat cracker, presumably one from a brand she trusted. Next to the cream was another garnish, leaves of some of unfamiliar seasoning.

◆

"By the way, what are we going to do about the issue?"

The tea party had already gone on for a while when Yoko raised this topic. Ritsu didn't know what it meant, but based on the quiet sighs and reactions from Kinosaki and Takahashi, everyone else did.

"You mean about Mr. Nirei."

"Yes, of course. How unlucky that we have him as the homeroom teacher again."

"Ahh, Mr. Nirei." Kyohei smirked, although it was more like a grimace.

Ritsu recognized the name. He was the teacher of Class 6-1 at the school, a young man in his midtwenties.

"It's plain wrong to deal with such an unreliable teacher, especially when our kids have to take middle school entrance exams this year. It might be too late for second trimester, but we've *got* to get him exchanged by the third. Let's sign a petition!" Yoko exclaimed.

Ritsu squeaked with surprise at the vehemence of the statement. Kyohei tried to calm down the fervor. "Now, now," he said to Yoko, "Nirei is doing his best, I'm sure. It just happens to not be very good, that's all."

"But Class 6-2 has Arakawa, so they're sitting pretty. It's not fair that we're stuck with Nirei. Don't you agree, Hiromi?" Yoko looked to the woman.

Like her husband, Hiromi wasn't enthusiastic about lambasting the teacher. Suddenly, someone's phone went off—Hiromi's. She jumped at the vibration.

"I'm sorry, I've got to take this," she said before walking into the hall.

"Maybe I should go see about the mail," Kyohei added lightly, rising from the table. He seemed eager to escape the topic.

Once the Sawataris were gone, Yoko crossed her arms and sighed heavily. "The problem is, Hiromi and Kyohei are just too nice! I don't know about you, but I'm collecting signatures and issuing a complaint with the principal. Did you hear? The staff liaison for the story time committee might be Mr. Nirei next year, too."

"Oh, really?" Takahashi replied, looking worried now that it actually concerned her.

Kinosaki quietly asked, "Does that mean it won't be Ms. Tada anymore?"

"Yes. So you see, it affects everyone here, not just us. Our kids are graduating soon, and I don't want to see our years of activity ruined by that teacher. You'll help, won't you, Yuzuki?"

"I will. It sounds bad. I wonder if I can get some signatures from the other mothers and fathers with fifth graders," Yuzuki said.

This came as a surprise to Ritsu. She would have thought that someone involved with a different grade and not on the same committee would abstain, or at least be a little weirded out by the whole thing. Yet Yuzuki matched Yoko's enthusiasm perfectly.

"Um…excuse me," Ritsu said without thinking. Only afterward did she realize this was something she ought not to have gotten involved with. However, she couldn't stop herself. "My son is only in first grade, so I don't know much about this Mr. Nirei, but has he done anything to deserve this?"

"Oh, nothing really that major, but he's really, really young. Maybe half as old as some of us. For your final year of school, you really want an excellent veteran teacher handling your child."

"So he's still young. Is that it?"

"Yes. How old is he, about twenty-five?"

"In that case…"

Ritsu felt a bit dizzy from all this. These women had a concerning lack of decorum. Suppressing her irritation, she explained, "Why don't we wait before demanding a new teacher or collecting signatures? At my job…I often have the chance to speak on the radio with someone involved in education."

Ritsu regularly compared stories she heard with her own experiences raising Kanato.

"These days, there are a lot of teachers who lack confidence. Younger ones feel they can't object to senior coworkers and parents, and they wind up leaving their careers because they can't find a sense of belonging or pride in their work."

Ritsu didn't know Mr. Nirei, or what kind of teacher he was, but these women believed he was ineffective with no evidence. She didn't know how the children felt, but learning with a teacher for two trimesters only to be forced to adapt to a different one at the end of the year seemed like it would work against what the mothers wanted.

"Voicing concerns to the principal is an option, but it seems rather cruel to gather signatures and make a big deal about this, don't you think?"

"Oh… Maybe you're right."

Yoko's confident bluster faded immediately. Maybe she wasn't gung ho on the idea but had talked herself into it over time.

Ritsu added, "If something really problematic *does* happen, we can get together and discuss it again. And seeing a sixth-grade class off at graduation is a major accomplishment and an important experience for a teacher. Why don't we try supporting this new teacher like we do our children?"

"You want us to help the teacher? Isn't that backward?"

"Well, you're nearly twice his age, aren't you? Mr. Nirei's a teacher, but as adults, we're more experienced," Ritsu said. Her professional voice had crept in. She tried to avoid that when off the clock.

Yoko and the others exchanged sheepish looks. They muttered things like, "Hmm, really?" and "I wouldn't call myself a *veteran*, exactly…," yet they didn't seem particularly upset.

"That person in education you mentioned, Ritsu… Is it Mr. Kojima the educational critic?" Yuzuki inquired hesitantly. It sounded like she'd been waffling on whether to speak up. "I actually listen to your show all the time."

"Um, me too," said Takahashi, raising her hand. "It comes on right after I send my kid off to school and have a bit of time for myself. I usually tune in while I'm doing household chores or cleaning up after breakfast."

"Yes, it's a really great show."

Yuzuki and Takahashi's agreement warmed up the mood in the room. For the first time since her arrival at the Sawataris', Ritsu's job was a topic of conversation. Everyone's eyes lit up with interest as she became the focal point.

"Oh, wasn't the artist of that painting over there a guest on your program, too?" Takahashi pointed at the interesting painting on the living room wall, the one with abstract flowers and a photorealistic background. Ritsu had been eyeing it since entering the room.

"That's right," she answered.

The women squealed, "I knew it!" and "That's amazing!"

The artist was a painter named Nagaishi. Ritsu had known him since her days in TV work and maintained a personal friendship with him. He'd even visited when Kanato was born. A painting of Kanato as a baby hung on a wall in Ritsu's home.

When Kyohei mentioned artists visited often, Ritsu had seen the painting and wondered if he and Hiromi knew Nagaishi, too. Perhaps theirs was an original like hers. Ritsu had nearly asked, but when Kyohei said it was *"limited,"* she'd held her tongue. Sure enough, *2098/10000* was printed on the edge of the painting. It was a numbered replica—a lithograph.

"Oh wow! Well, I'm not super knowledgeable about that world, but does this mean you've met famous people in show business?" Yoko asked, without a shred of tact.

"Slow down!" Yuzuki and the others chided, laughing while giving Ritsu apologetic looks.

"Sorry about Yoko. She can be a bit of a star chaser. You can't just ask that, Yoko!"

"Oh, come on," Yoko protested. "You all want to know, too! Have you met Ryota Shizuki before?"

"I have," Ritsu admitted. Sure, Yoko might be celeb obsessed, but it felt much better to have people ask questions out of curiosity than try to remain overly respectful and avoid Ritsu altogether. The women chatted excitedly.

"How long ago did you meet him? His big break was on a show this season. Was it before that?"

"Oh, yes. He played a student in a show shortly after his acting debut. He was a guest right around then."

"Wow, you mean *Sayonara Academy*! He was my favorite of the entire class!" Yuzuki squealed and clapped her hands, no longer pretending to be the tactful one. "Oh, what about the other boy? The one in the morning show—"

Before she could say the actor's name, the living room door opened and Hiromi returned. "So sorry about that. I didn't mean to leave while you were in the middle of an important discussion."

She had her phone in hand, business concluded. Immediately, everyone's mouths clamped shut. They turned to Hiromi as one, stopping the conversation in its tracks.

"That's all right. You must be so busy. Was that a work call?" Yuzuki asked demurely. A slight wrinkle formed between Hiromi's brows. It made for quite a picturesque image.

"No. It was from Kaori."

Ritsu sensed everyone holding their breath, although she wasn't sure what gave her that feeling.

Hiromi shrugged slightly. "She wanted to know if we were having a tea party. I didn't invite her today, purely out of happenstance. Why would she ask that? Kaori has a way of finding things out and getting into your business, doesn't she?"

Though Hiromi's mannerisms suggested this was troublesome, the smile never left her face. Inclining her head a bit, she turned to Yoko. "So, did you talk about Mr. Nirei? What's the plan?"

"Oh... Yes. We decided that maybe we should hold off. Wait and see," Yoko answered clumsily. That topic was long behind the group.

Hiromi seemed taken aback by this answer, but recovered and smiled again. "Well, that's good. I agree. That reminds me, Mamiko was supposed to be our last guest today, but she's late. I'll go call her." With that, she stepped into the hallway again.

An eerie tension settled over the room after she left. No one was bold enough to return to the conversation about Ritsu's job.

At last, Ritsu understood what felt so uncomfortable about this house.

It was the odd, strained feeling that followed Hiromi everywhere. No one was permitted to speak about anything that threatened to overshadow her. This situation was meant solely to prop up the image of the Sawataris.

It wasn't by force, and Hiromi didn't demand it, of course, yet it felt like no one was able to speak with Ritsu while Hiromi was present. Ritsu herself got the same feeling. She couldn't bring up a single topic about her work in Hiromi's presence. Instinct told her it was best she didn't.

"How did Kaori find out about today?" Takahashi wondered, making an awkward attempt to change the subject.

Kinosaki replied just as awkwardly, "Yeah, good question. I wonder if that call was..."

"Are we talking about the same Kaori from the story time committee meeting?" Ritsu asked.

From the way Takahashi and Kinosaki acted that day, Ritsu could tell that the rest of the group tried to avoid Kaori. Takahashi and Kinosaki had mentioned how great Hiromi was for making the effort to speak with everyone, even Kaori.

And Kaori had called to ask if they were having a tea party today.

That was an unsettling thing to call and inquire about, not to mention prying. However, Ritsu was more concerned with Hiromi. Her and her husband.

They'd made every effort to avoid direct disrespect against Mr. Nirei the teacher and Kaori. They were both absent right now, for example.

Hiromi had remarked that Kaori had a way of *getting into your business*," a carefully selected phrase that skirted being an insult. If Hiromi hadn't invited Kaori today purely because of "*happenstance*," did that mean she'd asked her to come for previous get-togethers? Probably not.

But between the casual references to the teachers at school and exclusions from the party, it was clear that the Sawataris chose their guests carefully. They were cautious to treat everyone equally and play the part of kind, good hosts, but they were strict about whom they allowed in their home and treated as special.

The group leaned over the fashionable tea set on the table in the room without the party hosts.

"That's right. Kaori lives in our complex. On my floor, in fact, so I see her often. She does have a way of getting into your business."

"She's very personable, though. She'll talk to just about anyone."

Unconsciously, the group adopted Hiromi's softened choice of words to avoid being blunt.

"…And she'll always say, 'Oh, me too,'" Yuzuki said, wearing a plaintive expression, much like Hiromi, to insist that she didn't mean it in a bad way. Not at all. Ritsu was startled, for she'd heard that one herself.

"The high school I went to, my work details," Yuzuki continued, "all these things you would never expect her to share, she replies, 'Oh, me too.' It's like she read some conversation manual that told her saying that would win people over, so she repeats it endlessly. She's done it to me, and other people, too."

"That's right," Takahashi agreed. "She's done that to me, too. I mentioned I was from Sendai, and she replied, 'Me too.' But it was obvious that she didn't know anything about the place. She had no idea what I was talking about."

"Oh...I see."

That had happened to Ritsu as well. When she'd revealed she was a newscaster, Kaori responded, "*Me too.*" However, Ritsu wasn't sure if adding her story to the pile was the best decision.

"She just can't take a hint," Yuzuki stated. Now that someone had finally voiced an outright negative comment, the dam burst.

"Yes, exactly," Yoko agreed. "That's absolutely true."

Kinosaki timidly chimed in. "Isn't she *really* aggressive about it, too? I'm afraid to ignore or dismiss her, so I can never just run by her. I'm always locked into pointless small talk until I find a chance to escape..."

Yuzuki nodded at Kinosaki. "Exactly! For some reason, you just can't say no. Like, if you actually mention anything real to her, she latches on even harder."

A smartphone buzzed.

The group looked up with a start and saw that Hiromi had returned through the kitchen at some point. The music had probably covered up the sound of her walking. She must have circled around and come into the kitchen from the other side.

Yoko, Yuzuki, and the other women went silent. They hadn't been uncomfortable talking before. What was it about Hiromi that made everyone hesitant to speak ill of others? How long had she been listening? Had she stood there and eavesdropped despite her refusal to be rude?

Hiromi beamed at the group with phone in hand. Her fine, shapely lips parted. "I'm so sorry. This one must be from Mamiko. She didn't answer when I called, so she's calling back now."

And with that, she departed the living room yet again. The mothers all watched her go, frozen with nervousness. They could only manage pleasantries like, "Oh, okay," and "See you soon."

In the awkward quiet that followed, there was a soft "Hello?" from Hiromi out in the hall.

The women glanced at one another, waiting. Suddenly, there was a much louder "What?!" from beyond the living room. "Oh, no, I had no idea… Yes, yes. No. It's all right. Don't worry about us, please."

Something had happened, that much was obvious. It sounded like Hiromi was finished with her call. She was back a moment later.

"This is awful," she announced, yet her expression didn't seem the least bit troubled. It was as though her beautiful face were tasked with pretending to look concerned. "Mamiko's been in a traffic accident."

A wave of shock ran through the room.

"A car hit her on a crosswalk. Kazuomi noticed my call coming in on her phone and returned it."

"What?!"

Now the group found its voice. Even Ritsu, who'd never met Mamiko, was astonished. "I'm so worried," Hiromi whispered, her brows furrowed.

"She was crossing the street…and a car ran the light and struck her?"

"No, apparently Mamiko ignored the light. The pedestrian signal was red, but she went ahead anyway. The driver and a witness said as much."

"Why would she ignore the signal…?"

"Which intersection was it?"

"You know the bakery near the train station? Between there and the bank."

"Right there...?"

Everyone who lived in this area walked that intersection. Ritsu was stunned, just like the others.

"Is she all right?"

"They're operating on her now."

"Operating?"

The room was silent.

Kyohei's special playlist switched styles often to suit his tastes, starting with Western rock, then transitioning to old J-pop from Ritsu's generation, jazz, and classical. The current track was a piano concerto. A cymbal crashed.

It reminded Ritsu of another sound. She'd hoped to ask the others about it if the topic came up.

The sound of someone hitting the ground.

Ritsu realized that she just lost the opportunity to inquire about the suicide jumper the week before.

Given the Sawataris' preference for trustworthy organic food, Ritsu felt bad about the idea of leaving the scones and jam. She didn't want to make any trouble for Hiromi. If possible, Ritsu would take the scones and jam home with her.

Yet to her surprise, when it was time to leave, Hiromi handed Ritsu the empty container. "Here." Hiromi had washed it at some point during the party.

She beamed at Ritsu. "I cleaned it for you. They were very delicious. Thank you."

"You're welcome..."

Hiromi had never taken a single bite. Maybe she'd tossed out the leftovers. If she'd returned them, Ritsu could've had them with Kanato. She tried not to be resentful and did her best to smile back.

I just don't understand.

Ritsu considered herself a shrewd judge of character because of her work experience.

But she couldn't see the purpose behind Hiromi Sawatari's actions. The woman refused to let on, keeping herself closed to all outsiders.

She was picky with her guests, looked down on others, and spoke about the parents of her child's classmates in overly casual terms, and she and her husband were brazenly proud of their trophies, even rubbing others' noses in them. However, they refused to use insults. They avoided direct hostility.

I've never met anyone like them, Ritsu decided. *What exactly are they getting out of inviting people to their home, hearing what they have to say, and simply being nice and kind to all?*

When Ritsu had admitted that she lived in Sawatari Apartments, too, Hiromi responded, *"Oh! You live in our development?"*

The Sawataris were only in charge of the renovation; they didn't own the complex. Yet it was *"our development."* The same thing had happened today, when Ritsu mentioned her family was glad to move in.

"Really, we didn't do much."

"Please don't feel that you have to put us on a pedestal."

"That's right. We're only neighbors."

Did they make statements like that because they believed that people ought to fawn over them?

Perhaps they wanted to be the king and queen of the complex.

Ritsu took the empty container from Hiromi and said, "See you."

Before she could go, Hiromi called, "Oh, that's right, I meant to ask." She was grinning. "Aren't you going to talk more about your radio show?"

Ritsu thought she'd misheard.

She stared at Hiromi, forgetting to blink. The large eyes set in Hiromi's shapely face narrowed. Menacingly.

"You'll have to tell me more about the famous people you've met some other time."

But she wasn't there.

Ritsu spoke of her work when Hiromi left the room. It was the only reason she felt comfortable enough to talk about it with the others. It seemed easier for everyone to ask Ritsu questions without Hiromi's imposing presence.

Yet she heard somehow.

The phrase "famous people" stuck like a barb under Ritsu's skin. A helpless anger flooded into her.

Ultimately, she didn't know why Hiromi had chosen to say that at this moment. All she could do was stare at her in silence. Hiromi donned her perfectly beautiful smile once more and added, "Your stories seem like they would be very fun to hear."

At that point, Ritsu realized her exact occupation never came up before with Hiromi or Kyohei.

Good people. So attentive to others. Wonderful.

These things were true of Hiromi Sawatari, sure. But she certainly wasn't as aloof and demure as others believed. Maybe Ritsu was overthinking it. However, based on personal experience, the people who knew she was a newscaster and didn't bring it up fell into two camps. One was formed of people who chose to give her some privacy, while the other was composed of those who meant to use her career as bragging rights for themselves.

Ritsu's name was formed from two uncommon kanji, yet Hiromi knew them and wrote them on the tea party invitation.

To Ritsu.

Was Hiromi aware of the unusual kanji combination because she knew who Ritsu was and what she did for a living?

Perhaps she didn't bring it up during their first social function together to be polite. Ritsu's experience had taught her that when people didn't mention her job for reasons other than consideration, the results were unpleasant.

Many people who refused to touch on the topic of Ritsu's career were jealous. On several occasions, she'd been met with preemptive remarks about how famous people weren't special and shouldn't be given extra attention. Statements and actions meant to establish superiority were a kind of dominant behavior, and when Ritsu discussed her professional life, some people reacted defensively, believing she was attempting to place herself above them.

The name Ritz the Rational often carried a little note of malice, and Ritsu was sensitive to it. Her tendency to get lost in thought, as she was now, probably didn't help. Compared to some of her fellow newscasters with thicker skin, she'd always had trouble keeping cool.

The Sawataris did not display their malice in any kind of obvious way. If anything, they were extra-nice, and they found insults and backhanded remarks distasteful. But while their home appeared nice and friendly, the party struck Ritsu as a display of dominance.

Or was she just being petty and mean?

Still, it felt off. Ritsu's mere presence there seemed to have been taken as a display of superiority, when that wasn't her intention in the least.

There was never a single word uttered about it, yet Ritsu sensed an unspoken competition happening beneath the surface.

It was very upsetting.

The sun was already going down, and the hallway outside the Sawatari residence was darkening. The autumn sunset as viewed from the top floor of the building looked gloomy and forlorn.

"Poor Mamiko."

"I hope she's all right. I wonder what Yukari's doing today."

Yukari.

That was probably the name of Mamiko's daughter. Ritsu had never met them, but hearing their names in this context made her heart ache.

The gentle, warm feeling that had been present right at the start of the tea party was nowhere to be found. The last thing Ritsu did before saying good-bye to the other guests was join the LINE group for the mothers regularly invited to the tea parties.

◆

Ritsu went down to the courtyard to find the boys. The park sat directly in the middle of the complex, visible from every unit, making it the perfect play place for parents who wanted to keep an eye on their children.

"Kanato!"

He and the other boys had been playing tirelessly in the park, even as night loomed. A soccer ball bounced left and right. Evidently, they'd been using it and the jungle gym. No one had any handheld game consoles or manga. Not letting Kanato bring his was the right choice.

"Oh, Mama!"

Kanato turned around when she called him. The other boys were old enough to go home on their own, so only Ritsu came to pick up her son.

She was about to tell the other boys that it was time to head home, too, but stopped when she realized that Asahi—the Sawataris' son—was not among the group in the sandbox with Kanato. The other boys were right there, but Asahi was sitting on a bench alone.

"Asahi, the tea party is over now. You should get back to your par—"

As Ritsu walked toward the bench, she stepped on something near the sandbox that made a crinkling sound, a wrapper. It was a Golden Chocolate bar, one of those Ritsu gave to Kanato as a consolation prize after he threw a tantrum because he couldn't bring his handheld console. Ritsu hadn't known how many children there would be, so she'd given him a large bag from the wholesale store. Now she regretted that decision.

"Hey, you know the trash is supposed to go in…"

Ritsu crouched down to pick up the wrapper, then gasped. There were many more discarded wrappers. Some were even half-buried in the sand.

What's going on?

The bag had had nearly thirty individually wrapped little chocolate bars. Had they eaten them all? Just the four of them?

"Kanato. I gave you those chocolates so that each person could have one or two. I can't believe you ate them all."

Naturally, children were prone to eating as much as you gave them. It was shocking that they could consume so many of the richly flavored candy bars, but ultimately Ritsu was at fault for giving her son so many.

Kanato just gave his mother a confused look. "I didn't."

"Huh?"

The other boys shared a look with Kanato, then peered up at Ritsu.

"We all had, like, two of them."

"Yeah. I had one. I don't really like chocolate that much."

"Asahi ate all the rest."

"What?!"

The mention of Asahi's name made Ritsu's jaw drop. She could feel the blood draining from her face.

A family that preferred organic food. Hiromi's preferences surely meant she was strict with Asahi in that regard, too. She would definitely object to someone bringing a whole bag of preservative-heavy chocolate to her carefully managed event. This was even worse than Ritsu's careless gift of homemade scones.

"I'm sorry, Asahi! I shouldn't have let you eat…"

The rest of the sentence crumbled in her mouth.

Faint smacking sounds—*shlurk, shlurk*—came from Asahi, who sat hunched over on the park bench. Lights over the park flickered twice in the gloom, like blinking eyes casting yellow beams that illuminated the boy.

Asahi Sawatari's pale, handsome mouth and cheeks were covered in chocolate. It was melted and smeared on his fingers. Undoubtedly, he'd eaten all the chocolate he could stomach, but there was a piece of brown plastic in his hands. He was licking the melted chocolate off the wrapper.

"Asahi…" Ritsu gasped.

The boy kept lapping, his eyes vacant. When he recognized someone calling him, his gaze shifted to Ritsu. He never let go of the wrapper, though. He just kept licking. As he did so, he said, "Oh, Kanato's mother. All right, I'll go home now."

He beamed, but his mouth and hands were still locked on the wrapper. His actions were totally at odds with his expression and words. His smile was so beautiful, on those features that so resembled Hiromi's.

"Oh, excuse me, but can you keep it a secret from my mother and father that I ate the chocolate?" he asked, so daintily and politely, as he stared into Ritsu's eyes. Still, he never released the wrapper. There was nothing left on it for him to taste.

He's starved.

The thought came over Ritsu like a sudden chill. She remembered why she didn't give Kanato his game system today. Once you opened that door for children who didn't normally get the privilege, their feeling of deprivation, of starvation, caused them to cling to the new pleasure and forget everything else.

The other boys were satisfied with one or two candy bars, but Asahi didn't let go until he finished every last one.

On the other side of the park, more lights turned on. All at once, the Sawatari Apartments complex lit up. The many windows of the surrounding homes suddenly came into view. One color in particular flooded Ritsu's vision from above.

Blue.

There was so much blue. Moving tarps covered the outdoor hallways. The moving companies were different, but oddly enough, they all used the same blue tarps.

The movers lugged furniture and items lined up in the hallways to the elevators. They weren't going to just one unit. Many pieces were going to apartments on different floors simultaneously.

Sawatari Apartments was a popular destination with rare vacancies. It wasn't until very recently that anyone had a decent chance to move in. Ritsu had felt resentful that there were more openings now when she struggled for her spot not long before.

However, she had it backward.

The movers weren't bringing new tenants in. Furniture wasn't being carried into units, but out and to the elevators. Dark, curtainless windows stood out in their number, exposed by the glow from the streetlamps.

They're leaving. The realization caused Ritsu's eyes to go wide. People were vanishing from the complex. The lights from the homes were vanishing.

The sound of Asahi crinkling and licking the plastic wrapper persisted.

Shlurk, shlurk, shlurk.

The next day, word got around that Mamiko never regained consciousness after the traffic accident and that she died in the hospital.

I wish I could see her face one last time...

Ritsu thought she misread the text message.

She actually said, "What?" out loud, with the phone in her hand.

"What is it?" her husband, Yuuki, asked.

Ritsu was in the kitchen, looking at her phone after putting Kanato to bed. Unsure how to explain, she replied, "Oh, it's nothing…"

Mamiko, the woman who was supposed to be at Hiromi Sawatari's tea party but hadn't shown up, had perished after a traffic accident.

Once the news was made public to the members of the tea party chat group, the LINE thread went crazy.

All the members expressed their shock and sadness at the sudden death of one of their own, lamenting the unthinkable accident. They commented that it seemed like such tragedies were on the rise lately, and how they felt crushed for Mamiko's husband and poor little Yukari.

Ritsu understood their feelings. For the mother of a child in elementary school, it hurt to imagine the pain of passing away and leaving a young child behind.

However, she was also keenly aware of the poor timing of her joining the LINE group. Mamiko was everyone else's friend, but Ritsu had never met her. Perhaps they had both been present at some school event, but given that they'd never formally met, Ritsu felt it would be wrong to mourn like the other mothers. The best she could do was type, *It's too shocking to know what to say, so I'll pray for her and her family.* The outpouring of grief from the others intensified, and Ritsu's simple message was swiftly buried.

I have to contact so-and-so's mother from Yukari's class… I know that so-and-so was really close with her. She must be so shocked…

More and more names that Ritsu didn't recognize appeared. Eventually, she felt guilty, like she was snooping on a tightly knit community. After a while, she started skimming the messages, checking only once in a while.

When Kanato came back from school the day after the news broke, Ritsu asked him, "Did you hear anything from the teachers about somebody's mother?"

Kanato asked, "'Anything'? Like what?"

Ritsu had thought that the teachers might tell the kids about the accident, but apparently, that wasn't the case. The school had likely decided something that befell a particular family wasn't meant to be news for the entire school.

In which case, when incidents occurred, only those directly involved would be aware of them. When Ritsu was a girl, her local community had been very close, so word would spread right away. But in this place, where many of the residents were nuclear families who had moved from different areas, information was shared only among select groups. It made Ritsu realize she was probably ignorant of many things that transpired in the complex.

Such as the suicide Yuuki had witnessed.

The person who'd jumped off the building could've had children. Ritsu didn't know the circumstances of every family who lived in the apartment development.

After the recent tea party, she'd told Yuuki that it seemed like many families had been leaving Sawatari Apartments recently. He'd replied, "Oh, really? But if they're moving out, that just means different families come in, right?" and hadn't seemed interested enough to continue the conversation.

However, Ritsu's careful observation since that night suggested no one was replacing the tenants who left. She regularly saw moving teams, but all of them were for departing families.

"Did something happen?" Yuuki inquired again, looking toward the kitchen from the sofa in the living room.

This time, Ritsu answered, "Yeah," and walked over to her husband. "Remember that mother I told you about? The one who died crossing the street? She was supposed to be at Hiromi's tea party."

"Oh. The one with the sixth grader…"

"That's right. Her funeral's being held behind her husband's family home. Relatives only."

"Really? Relatives only?"

"Yes. Maybe because it was an untimely accident."

"Oh, that makes sense…"

The details of the funeral had made their way onto the LINE chat group. The service would be held at the widower's parents' house, which was far away. And only relatives were permitted.

Ritsu thought that was because the family didn't wish for people to see Mamiko's body after it had been struck by a car. She didn't give the service much consideration beyond that, since she wasn't Mamiko's friend.

The rest of the mothers, however…

"The women in the group chat were saying this morning that they have to do something for her. They were talking about putting out incense at her home. I think it's a little insensitive when the family wants the funeral to be private."

"Well, it was very sudden. Her relatives probably haven't had time to process everything."

"I know. I think the others in the group should wait until things have settled down. Barging in on the bereaved before the funeral is crazy, right? There must be a better way to express condolences, like sending a telegram or a flower delivery."

"Are these people all housewives? Maybe they don't understand these things. You could try explaining it to them, Ritsu."

She understood what Yuuki wanted to say. Since the other women lacked experience with professional courtesy, they didn't know how to act during a tragedy. Of course, not all housewives were the same. Some of them could have been office workers before they got married and started their families, and perhaps they'd always lacked common sense. Whatever the reason, the emotional outpouring happening in the chat thread went beyond good reason.

This can't just be the end of it.

I still can't believe what happened to Mamiko.

I want to see her.

Don't you want to at least offer some incense to her memory?

Yes. Who knows her husband's contact info?

Yoko, the one who'd been openly derisive about her son's homeroom teacher, had stirred up the maelstrom. When she got insistent about offering incense, the others gave their approval.

"Yes, they're mostly housewives, but I didn't think I'd have to keep the peace. Mrs. Sawatari is the center of the group, after all."

Hiromi was the one who learned of the funeral details and put them in the chat. However, she'd kept silent since. Ritsu had hoped Hiromi would keep the others in line upon seeing them get so worked up. Surely she would say the right thing to defuse the situation.

She didn't.

"But Hiromi just sent another message. I thought she'd calm everyone down, yet instead she wrote, 'I wish I could see her face one last time.'"

Yuuki scowled a little from his spot on the sofa. Ritsu felt the same way. "'I wish I could see her face…'?" he repeated.

"I think she means it literally. She wants to offer incense and see the body for herself."

"To what end?"

It was very like Yuuki to ask that. He was always the rational type.

Ritsu shook her head, at a loss. "I think it just means they want to say good-bye in person."

Mamiko's death was the result of a sudden and violent accident. Her family had elected to hold a closed funeral because they were still processing the grief. Why didn't the other women understand? They seemed concerned less about Mamiko and more about maximizing their mourning potential. At first glance, it looked like an act of sympathy, but it was actually turning a death into an event about themselves.

And Hiromi wasn't stopping it.

In fact, depending on how you interpreted it, the statement, *I wish I could see her face one last time*, within the context of the group chat, could be viewed as being in poor taste. That's why Ritsu couldn't initially believe Hiromi had typed it. Did no one else recognize this?

A little later, Hiromi sent another message.

My son Asahi is close with Yukari, and he said he'd like to give her mother a proper good-bye. If that can't happen, then it'd be nice if our little group could give Mamiko a real send-off.

Responses came nearly instantly.

Of course. We all want to see her one more time.

Maybe there's still time to do something.

My daughter is close with Yukari, too.

If we contact her husband early enough…

Texts barraged the screen.

Ritsu couldn't bear to watch anymore. She turned off the LINE app's notifications, then set her phone on the table. With a hand on her chest, she took deep breaths.

"Are you all right?" Yuuki asked. "You don't have to go along with them if you don't want to."

"Thanks. I don't have any personal connection with the woman who passed away, so I'm not obligated. I'm fine." That was a supreme relief. Mamiko died in an accident. Her face could be terribly disfigured.

Were the mothers in the LINE group so close to Mamiko that they were genuinely distraught? Did they love the deceased?

"I need a bath," Ritsu said to Yuuki before standing.

After bathing and returning to the living room, she checked the chat thread again. The women had devised a plan in the meantime, and Hiromi reported that she'd contacted Kazuomi, the husband.

Mamiko will be in her home at Sawatari Apartments from midday to evening tomorrow. All gifts at the family service will be refused, but flowers for the deceased will be accepted tomorrow. And maybe letters? Can you spread the message to as many people who want to see Mamiko as possible?

Ritsu's skin crawled.

Her breath felt tight, and her eyes were locked on the screen. *And maybe letters? Mamiko will be in her home at Sawatari Apartments. Can you spread the message?* Every little word from Hiromi was pleasant and in character, but felt chilling. Ritsu found the last bit the most shocking. *Can you spread the message to as many people who want to see Mamiko as possible?* What was the point of the private, family-only funeral, then?

She must have used her delicate words and that friendliness she and Kyohei shared to get ahold of the deceased's husband. By presenting herself in the right way, Hiromi might have convinced the man that refusing would make him heartless, thus winning herself the right to visit and offer incense. Ritsu was certain that was how it happened.

A splash of color in the chat abruptly caught Ritsu's eye.

Yoko had sent a stamp of a rabbit giving a thumbs-up and saying *GOOD JOB.*

Hiromi's actions and attitude were bad enough, but Yoko's choice to send a goofy cartoon stamp during such a serious situation was unbelievable. Others used little emoji here and there while they discussed this tragedy. It was so insensitive that Ritsu felt like she was going crazy. Or maybe she was too stuck-up?

"What's up, Ritsu?" Yuuki inquired. He'd taken a bath after her, and just now returned wearing his pajamas.

"Look." She handed him her phone. Yuuki took it and looked over the screen. "Who sends silly stamps during a discussion like this?" Ritsu said.

"I don't know, but perhaps this is normal for them. It seems unacceptable to you, and honestly, I agree. But it could simply be how they do things.

If another in their group passed away, they might do the same thing without thinking twice."

"You think so?"

Imagining they were talking about Ritsu herself made her shiver. Ritsu's death would belong to her, and the sadness would belong to her and her family. The last thing she wanted was for it to become a big event run by the sort of people who traded emoji while discussing it.

"I'm kind of surprised, actually," Yuuki said while handing the phone back to his wife.

"What about?" she questioned.

"Hiromi Sawatari. I thought she was more sensible. She seemed like she ought to get along well with Ritz the Rational."

"Don't—"

Ritsu meant to say, "Don't compare us," but she held off. There was something about being associated with Hiromi that rubbed Ritsu the wrong way.

"…She's had a lot of career success, so I think she's smart. But I guess intelligence and character don't always align. This whole thing lacks dignity."

Hiromi undoubtedly knew Ritsu would see everything that happened in the LINE chat. Yet she didn't consider how her actions came off as appalling. As Yuuki had stated, this was *"normal"* to her.

"This is Hiromi Sawatari, right?" Yuuki had pulled something up on his smartphone.

"Huh?"

"When we moved into this place, I followed her husband's Instagram account. And because they're linked, I peek into hers, too, from time to time."

He showed Ritsu the screen, which displayed Hiromi's Instagram account, before handing her the phone. In true fall fashion, there was a perfect picture of a dish decorated with pumpkin tarts atop a pristinely designed table. Everything was set at the right angle.

Homemade tarts prepared with the succulent pumpkins sent to me every

*year. My family loves them, and my son says they smell like the rich soil of
the fields! It seems my family's got its own sommelier of sweets. (Or is he just
a poet?)*

The post resembled a picture and caption from a magazine. Ritsu sighed.
The tart was probably entirely organic, like everything else Hiromi made.

Ritsu's eyes fixed on the word *son*. Asahi. The image of a smiling boy
sitting on the bench in the darkened park, face slathered in chocolate, popped
into her head.

"And she keeps up a steady rate of posts. That's impressive," Yuuki
remarked.

"It is," Ritsu agreed. She had nearly handed the phone back to her husband when she noticed the time of the upload and went rigid.

This is from today.

Hiromi had prepared the tarts today. She'd baked them, garnished
them, staged a photo, and posted it to Instagram. With the same phone
she'd used to chat with the mothers in the LINE group, wailing about
Mamiko and lamenting that they wouldn't have one last chance to see
her. Some of the mothers from the tea party group had to follow Hiromi's account.

On the same day that Hiromi typed that Asahi would like to give
Mamiko a proper farewell, she uploaded a picture with the caption *My son
says they smell like the rich soil of the fields! It seems my family's got its own sommelier of sweets. (Or is he just a poet?)* It felt insincere in the extreme.

It'd be nice if our little group could give Mamiko a real send-off.

Even that phrase, *give Mamiko a real send-off*, had a whiff of arrogance
behind its seemingly well-meaning exterior. Why didn't anyone else notice?

"Hey…"

"What?" Yuuki asked, hand still outstretched to take his phone.

"Do you think we should move?"

"Huh?"

Yuuki looked stunned. His reaction brought Ritsu back to her senses.

She quickly smiled and said, "I'm only kidding," hoping he didn't realize how serious she'd been. "I'm sorry. It's, well, between the jumping suicide and the traffic accident, there's been so much tragedy, and it's upsetting me. I've noticed that lots of families are leaving the complex, too."

"I'm fine with moving again someday, but what's gotten into you? We just got here. We can't move right back out. There aren't any places with the same kind of space in the area."

"Yeah, you're right."

Realistically, it was a very unlikely thing to go through with. Still, Ritsu had voiced her impulsive thought, and there was no pretending it hadn't happened. She apologized and returned her husband's phone.

◆

The next day, Ritsu saw Hiromi, Yoko, and the others on the north side of the complex, where Mamiko lived.

She was heading out for some afternoon shopping to buy groceries for dinner and turned in a different direction upon seeing the group of women. They were probably going to Mamiko's apartment to offer incense. At a glance, Ritsu recognized that Hiromi, Kinosaki, Takahashi, and Yuzuki wore black or otherwise dark clothing. Yoko was in her usual sweatshirt, but she held a flower arrangement obviously meant for the deceased.

Ritsu didn't need to avoid them, yet felt guilty and hid behind the corner of the building. She waited there, holding her breath, praying the women would pass by.

Saying nothing to acquaintances was tantamount to the cold shoulder, and that gave Ritsu pause. *But it has nothing to do with me. I never met Mamiko*, she reasoned, and she took the long way from the south entrance to do her errand.

Ritsu's mood remained heavy even while she picked out items at the supermarket. No matter how often she repeated that it didn't concern her, she found herself snared by the constraints of the group.

"They say she was being chased by someone."

The words caused Ritsu to look up.

She'd finished checking out moments before and was bagging her items when she heard. Two women, older than Ritsu but clearly locals, were chatting near the door with bags in hand.

"Chased? By whom?"

"I don't know, but she shouted, 'Stay away from me,' and that was when she jumped out."

"How scary. Was it a crazy person?"

"Who knows. The people who were there all claim they heard her say it."

"*She jumped out.*"

Ritsu's heart thumped. The phrase brought Mamiko's traffic accident to mind. "*She was being chased by someone. She shouted, 'Stay away from me.'*" Was this story about Mamiko?

She wanted to hear more, but the women were already done with their shopping and were leaving. Ritsu rushed to finish her bagging and follow, but once outside, she couldn't find them. There was no way to tell which direction they had gone.

Ritsu came back to herself with a start.

I'm going crazy.

It was entirely possible they hadn't even been discussing Mamiko. Why was she trying to pursue them? Even if they had been talking about her, it had nothing to do with Ritsu.

Perhaps Ritsu was tired. She thought it best to go home and rest until Kanato got back. She had another radio recording session in two days, and there were background materials about her guest she needed to study. She started off in the direction of the apartment complex.

"Ritsu-chan?"

Someone called her name and she stopped short, bag clutched tightly. She looked around for the speaker but didn't see anyone.

"Hey there, Ritsu-chan! Sorry, did I startle you?"

Ritsu's eyes went wide. The window of a red Audi parked on the curb next to the supermarket rolled down. The driver's seat was on the left-hand side, contrary to domestic custom, and a man wearing sunglasses sat inside. She couldn't tell who he was at first, and it took a few moments for her to recognize Kyohei Sawatari, Hiromi's husband.

"Mr. Sawatari."

"I told you, 'Kyohei' is fine. Are you shopping? I thought my wife was meeting up with the ladies today. You didn't go with them?"

Something about what he said struck Ritsu as wrong, but she couldn't identify what. She only replied, "No," and shook her head.

"You weren't supposed to be with them?" he asked from the car. "My wife said they were going to say good-bye to Mamiko."

"…I didn't know Mamiko before she died. That's why."

"Ahh, I see. Yes, I suppose Hiromi did say that she asked you, but you declined to join."

Ritsu smiled awkwardly in reply. She had gotten a message like that, although not in the group thread. It came from Hiromi privately.

We're going to say our good-byes to Mamiko today. What about you, Ritsu? You were with us when we found out. I'm sure that Mamiko and Kazuomi would be delighted if you came, too.

What is she talking about? Ritsu had thought.

Mamiko and Kazuomi would be delighted? Because of Ritsu's profession? Because she was famous?

Maybe Hiromi wanted the credit for bringing Ritsu to the event. She hoped to turn Ritsu into another powerful card for her hand.

It had felt like an extension of the hysterics from the night before, so all Ritsu said in response was, *I'll decline, thank you*. She didn't think much of people who got overly involved in the deaths of others. In fact, the idea sickened her. Hiromi hadn't texted her since.

Kyohei hummed. "Say, Ritsu-chan."

"Yes?"

"Are you all right?" He took off his sunglasses. "You aren't holding in your feelings on account of Mamiko, are you, Ritsu-chan? You seem like you're really having a tough time. You sure you're okay?"

Goose bumps formed on her skin.

"I can give you a ride," Kyohei offered. "You've got some heavy stuff to carry. Want me to take you back to the apartments?"

Ritsu understood what felt wrong now.

He was calling her Ritsu-chan. She'd met him only the one time, at Hiromi's tea party, yet he was blatantly acting as though they were close by adding *-chan*. It was like how he addressed all the school mothers by name: Yoko, Mamiko, and so on.

He wouldn't even rein in his overfamiliarity out of respect for the dead, referring to the poor woman as just Mamiko instead of Mamiko-san. Ritsu felt repulsed.

"…I'm fine. It's not that heavy." She gave Kyohei the friendliest smile she could manage. The apartment complex and the supermarket were almost right next to each other. It wasn't worth the ride, and Ritsu didn't want to be seen getting in a car with a man who wasn't her husband so close to home. Careless actions like that bred mistaken assumptions and confusion.

Alarms blared in Ritsu's head. She didn't think she was being stuck-up. Ritsu knew better because men had approached her like this several times in the past, when she was single. With enough confidence, those sorts of men assumed their targets wouldn't resist, and they showered their prey with affection and lust…

Ritsu's arms were fraught with goose bumps now. She smiled to hide her discomfort.

"Please give Hiromi my best." She made sure to use the woman's given name, then walked off. Kyohei looked like he still had something to say, but Ritsu beat a quick retreat. Quick enough that she hoped he interpreted her speed as a pointed rejection.

She didn't turn back once on the way home. When Ritsu finally inhaled, she realized that she'd been holding her breath nearly the entire time. Her body and mind were extremely tense. It wasn't fair; why did she have to go through this torment?

A figure moved outside the south entrance.

Ritsu blinked and stared as a feminine shape that had been leaning on the wall next to the gate approached. Once again, Ritsu held her breath as the person drew near.

It was Kaori.

She was staring right at Ritsu.

"Hel…hello."

Ritsu's expression was awkward and uncomfortable. She hadn't seen this woman since the story time volunteer meeting. At Hiromi's tea party, Ritsu heard that Kaori lived here, too. It was fortunate she hadn't run into her until now, and this was a warning to be more careful in the future…

"So, um… You live at this apartment complex, too, Kaori. I'm on—"

Ritsu had to clamp her mouth shut to keep from reflexively telling what floor she lived on as part of a habitual introduction. This was the woman she didn't want to give any personal information to.

"Me?" Kaori gazed at Ritsu dully. Had she not heard? Talking with this woman was so off-putting.

Ritsu nodded awkwardly. "You live in Sawatari Apartments, right?"

"Oh… Live here? Well, lately."

"Uh-huh."

So she'd just moved in, then. Ritsu didn't feel comfortable addressing her as "Kaori," but she didn't know the woman's last name, so it was the only option.

"They were talking about going to Mamiko's today. What floor?"

"Huh?"

Ritsu was taken aback, the question was so sudden. When she didn't respond, Kaori leaned closer.

"Hey, what floor?"

"I didn't know her, so I'm not…"

How many times would she have to explain? To Hiromi, to Kyohei, to Kaori. Why did an incident of inopportune tragedy demand such sorrow and mourning from her?

Kaori's eyes bulged so far, it was almost comical. "What? No way!" she mumbled, childishly. "Didn't you get invited? To the tea party, I mean. I didn't get an invitation, so I didn't know where it was, and I had to ask and follow people, but you got an official invite, didn't you? My kid saw it."

Ritsu's breath stopped. It felt like something had punched her in the chest.

She was speechless from astonishment, but even more than that, she felt something cold slide down her spine because of the word *kid*. Kanato had received Hiromi's invitation from her son, Asahi.

Was Kaori sending her own child to keep tabs on Kanato?

"Hey."

Kaori openly stared at Ritsu without a hint of shame. She still looked so much older than the other mothers, like she couldn't possibly have a child in elementary school. Even her white dress, puffy and buoyant, appeared anachronistic. The color made it easy to see the yellowing lace around her collar and the brown stains that made it seem like the garment had sat in storage for years.

"Hey, just a question, but are you seeing Sawatari-san? Is that what you two are up to?" Kaori asked.

A gasp stuck in Ritsu's throat. At first, she was taken aback, but then true confusion set in. Was she talking about Hiromi? That wasn't who spoke with Ritsu earlier. It was her husband—the *other* Sawatari-san.

"Are you seeing him? Is that what you're up to?"

A shiver ran through Ritsu. Did Kaori see that? When? Ritsu didn't see her on the route here at any point.

"What do you mean?" she questioned, anxious.

Kaori was still staring right at her. Then she broke into a smile. An impish, knowing grin.

"Oh, it's fine, it's fine."

What was fine? Kaori seemed to be operating under some mistaken assumption. Or at least, that was what Ritsu intended to argue before the next unbelievable statement escaped the woman's mouth.

"Me too. So you're fine, you're fine. A lot of different people are, so don't worry about it. Like Yuzuki."

"Huh?" Ritsu breathed. But Kaori was unperturbed, and she continued talking and nodding.

"I've been warning Yuzuki, you know. Her time should be just about up. Don't worry about it."

"Er, I…"

"Oh, y'know, I thought about picking her as a replacement, but I just don't know who to choose… Still, the choice has to be made. It's about time to wrap up."

"Um… What…?"

"Don't worry about it. You're okay. Me too."

Everyone did mention how she says, "Me too" to everything.

Even when it made no sense. Even when it didn't line up with other details. Kaori claimed to be a newscaster like Ritsu, and said that she was from the same area as someone else, as though mindlessly following a manual for how to get along with others.

Ritsu's cheek spasmed.

"Ah, I see," she grunted. "Well, good-bye."

She smiled and tried to get past the other woman, and suddenly she felt every bit of herself freeze with panic. A mysterious, unseen fear gripped her, robbing her of speech.

A manual for how to commune with the hearts of others by agreeing with them. It sounded like something that didn't belong to a human, but to something else entirely...

Ritsu's notion wasn't entirely serious, but it made her shiver all the same. Just as she passed Kaori, Ritsu noticed that she was holding something white. A bag.

She must have brought flowers for Mamiko. But no, Ritsu saw a package of candy in the white bag. A large one, wholesale size. Yet it seemed flimsy, like it was already empty.

Why is she carrying garbage around? Is she not going to join the other women in mourning?

"Ooh." Kaori noticed that Ritsu's eyes had landed on her bag. "Want a bite?"

Cold air escaped Ritsu's nose. "If you'll pardon me," she said, refusing to deal with Kaori's nonsense. She took off, but felt Kaori's eyes on her back, and she couldn't just walk straight home.

Ritsu wanted to pull her hair out. *What is going on today?* She had her groceries but didn't want to return to the apartment. Kaori couldn't know which door was Ritsu's.

Ritsu hurried down the hallway, then walked from the south side to the north, where the Sawataris and Mamiko lived. Along the way, she passed another apartment with a tarp set out. She didn't even want to look at it.

That was when Ritsu realized her phone was vibrating. She could feel the tremors coming through the handbag slung over her shoulder.

Ritsu could tell that she was in danger of hyperventilating.

The group of mothers, dressed in a mix of mourning and regular clothes, carrying flowers on their way to grieve; housewives at the supermarket gossiping about the accident; Kyohei Sawatari offering her a ride with an intense, overbearing gaze; Kaori creepily accosting her at the south entrance, like she'd been lying in wait. *"Me too." "About time to wrap up." "Want a bite?"*

Ritsu couldn't go home. She wanted to, but she couldn't.

Feeling trapped in some large, elaborate nightmare, she reached for her buzzing smartphone. It felt like the vibration was an alarm bell, something that would wake her up from this bad dream.

But it wasn't.

The name on the screen was *Hiromi Sawatari.*

Ritsu held her breath. She answered because she couldn't take it anymore. *What in the world does she want from me?*

"...Hello?"

"Hello, Ritsu? Do you have a moment? I'd like to ask you about something."

Her heartbeat got louder. She already regretted answering the phone.

What if someone witnessed Kyohei call to her from his Audi? What if someone saw? It wasn't Ritsu's fault. She turned down his offer to ride. But...

"Me too."

What did Kaori mean? I have nothing to do with Kyohei.

"You're fine, you're fine, a lot of different people are, so don't worry about it. Like Yuzuki."

Why did Yuzuki's name pop up? Of all of Hiromi's younger friends living on the north side who attended the tea party, Yuzuki was indeed the youngest and prettiest. Kyohei referred to the mothers by their first names—Yoko, Mamiko—in an overly friendly way, and he spoke very intently with Kinosaki and Takahashi, too. Maybe he didn't pay much attention to Yuzuki to hide something between them. Now that Ritsu thought on it, that seemed to track.

He had no right to call me Ritsu-chan and act like we're close. I'm sure that he'll start just calling me Ritsu eventually, informal as can be. I hate men like him.

If Hiromi inquired, Ritsu planned to be honest. She'd say, "I'm tired of this." She was ready for it now. But that was not what Hiromi inquired about.

"Did you give chocolate to Asahi?"

This was a line of questioning she wasn't prepared for. The air in her lungs turned cold. The slurping, smacking sound came to mind. *Shlurk, shlurk.* Plastic wrappers all over the sandbox. His angelic smile as he asked, *"Can you keep it a secret from my mother and father that I ate the chocolate?"*

Hiromi's voice was quiet and muffled.

"Please, answer me. Did you give Asahi Woodcutter's Waltz?"

"Woodcutter's…Waltz?"

The tension drained out of Ritsu's shoulders after she heard the actual product name. Woodcutter's Waltz was a popular children's treat, a tree-shaped cookie shell with a chocolate filling. On the day of the tea party, Ritsu gave Kanato a bag of Golden Chocolate bars, not Woodcutter's Waltz. Hiromi was asking about an incident from a different day.

Hiromi's voice was tense, desperate. "I'm asking everyone. Asahi had these things when he came home today. I asked where they came from, and he said someone gave them to him."

She sounded shaken, but more than that, she was irritated.

"This has happened before. These packaged chocolate products are so heavily flavored, and once kids get a taste of them, they never enjoy natural food again. So we've been very careful to keep them away from him. I don't know what I'll do if he's already eaten them. Asahi insists someone gave them to him and that he hasn't tried any, but what if he has?"

Ritsu thought back to Hiromi's Instagram post from the previous day.

Pumpkin tarts made from a yearly gift from a farm. A perfectly staged photograph. A son who claims "They smell like the rich soil of the fields!" The family's own sommelier of sweets...

Are you crazy, lady?

Your friend just died, and you talked up being so sad and wishing you could see her one final time. Now you're getting upset over your son eating some processed chocolate? It's not going to kill him, you know.

He ate bar after bar of the stuff. Completely stuffing himself with chocolate. And I know he did the same today. You're the one who put that starved desire in him.

Ritsu's impulses screamed at her to rub it all in Hiromi's face, but it was so ridiculous she couldn't bring herself to speak. *I want to go home, but I can't. Kaori might be lurking around, so I'm stuck here, farther away from home, carrying this heavy grocery bag and having this stupid conversation.*

No wonder your husband is cheating on you, she thought.

"Did you hear me, Ritsu?"

Ritsu answered in the affirmative, but Hiromi clearly recognized her heart wasn't in the reply. Hiromi was clearly affronted.

"What's the matter with you? You think I'm some kind of idiot, don't you?"

Her voice lashed at Ritsu. She was furious.

"You are so self-centered," she spit, voice trembling. "You think other people are jealous of you just because you exist, don't you? Everyone's thinking about you, envious of you, and your presence and job are so impressive that everyone feels inferior. I bet you think, 'I'm act normal, so why does everyone treat me differently?' Don't you? But that's exactly what you want. You're not that pretty, and you're not that special."

Hiromi wouldn't stop. Her voice was so relentless that Ritsu couldn't tell if it was real or if she was hearing things. The wind was in her ears, howling. She didn't remember boarding the elevator, she'd only walked across the ground floor. Yet the wind beat in her ears as though she were on a higher level.

"But that's exactly what you want."

Hiromi was repeating things now. "You only imagine that you're so incredible in comparison to everyone else. You think you're special. You want them to notice you, to think about you, to compete with you, to try to prove their superiority. It's all your self-centered wish. No one—*none of us*—cares about you. We don't even give you a thought. That smug superiority you feel for me is laughable. You wish I cared that much about you."

I don't think that way.

I don't know what you mean.

But the sound of the wind was so powerful that Ritsu couldn't reply. *Flap-flap-flap-fwup-fwup-fwup-fwup.* Her clothes beat against her skin. Her hair whipped back. It was so strong that Ritsu feared she might lose control of the grocery bag.

Flap-flap-flap-flap, flap-flap, fwup-fwup-fwup-fwup.

The wind didn't let up.

The bag of groceries was about to slip loose.

Wait. I know that name. Woodcutter's Waltz.

The one with that bag was…

"You really think I'm an idiot, don't you?" Hiromi said.

Her voice was frustrated, yet it seemed like music to Ritsu's ears.

She felt almost tranquil.

She's thinking. About me.

We don't care. Off-base. What you want. All in your head. Despite Hiromi's many acerbic claims, each new word was greater evidence that Hiromi *did* think about Ritsu—quite a lot. Being inferior made her upset, jealous—it sounded like praise.

Say more, Ritsu thought.

◆

When Ritsu woke up, she was on her back in a dark room, alone.

For a moment, she wasn't sure where this was. Her head ached when she sat up. In her twenties, when Ritsu suffered from insomnia as a result of work stress and relied on sleeping pills, she'd always had a headache when she woke up. This sensation was similar—that of emerging from the foggy effect of a powerful drug.

Ritsu was in her bedroom.

When had she gotten home? She still had on the outfit she'd worn out. Kanato's rocket-shaped alarm clock near her pillow informed her that it was seven o'clock.

Seven? Ritsu gasped when the number sank into her head. It was dark outside already. The curtains were pulled closed. How long had she been asleep? Kanato ought to be home by now. Panic at the thought that her son might be locked out jolted through her mind, clearing any lingering drowsiness instantly.

"Kanato!"

"*Hyip!*"

The sound came from beside her ear. Hatch was licking her outstretched hand. He looked up at her with excitement, tongue lolling.

"Hatch…"

His wet nose twitched. Even in the dark, he was a very cute dog. The sensation of his smooth tongue on her fingers brought a sense of reality back. Ritsu could tell that he was worried.

The door slowly opened, letting in light from the hallway.

Yuuki poked his head through.

"Awake now? You okay?"

"Honey..."

Ritsu's head ached. The light from the hallway stung her eyes.

"Wait, where's Hatch?" asked Kanato's voice from behind Yuuki. Hatch reacted, trotting out of the bedroom. Moments later, Kanato exclaimed, "Hatch!" with delight, much to Ritsu's relief. He had gotten home safely after all.

"I'm sorry. I fell asleep. When did you..."

"It's all right. If you're not feeling well, go back to sleep. I'll whip up something for dinner. Are you hungry? You aren't feeling sick, are you...?"

"You came home early. I'm sorry... I don't even recall when I actually got home."

"Huh?" Yuuki's look of concern turned to one of skepticism. He looked her in the eyes. "You don't remember?"

"Remember what?"

"You called me. You were practically screaming."

"What..."

"You really don't remember?"

Her husband looked even more worried now. Ritsu was stunned. "I called you?"

Yuuki was the one wearing a doubtful look, yet it was Ritsu who felt like her husband was lying. She truly didn't remember. Her recollection simply ended. She had gone out shopping in the afternoon, seen Hiromi's group out in front of the complex, gone to the supermarket, and come back to find Kaori. From there, her sense of time got fuzzy.

Ritsu felt that somewhere in there, Kyohei Sawatari had hit on her, and there was a nightmarish phone call from Hiromi...

Yuuki approached the bed and hunched down so he was at eye level with Ritsu, sitting up in bed. After a hesitant silence, he asked, "Do you not remember this, either?"

"Remember what...?"

"That Hiromi Sawatari fell from her veranda to her death."

A tiny shriek escaped Ritsu's throat.

Her eyes went wide, as wide as they could go. What was Yuuki talking about? Her lips pursed, and her cheeks tensed.

"Fell…to her death?"

"I don't know the exact details, but people around the complex say her son Asahi might have pushed her. People saw her chasing her son around the veranda with a ferocious look on her face. Then they grappled, and she fell off."

"Are you serious?" Ritsu's voice sounded distant and faint. There was pity in Yuuki's eyes.

"You called to tell me about it," he replied. "You said, 'Hiromi fell. She's dead.' By the time I got home, there were police cars and media vans all over the place."

Perhaps that was because there was more at play here than in a simple suicide. But what happened to Asahi? Hiromi chased him around the veranda with a ferocious look on her face. Ritsu never saw Hiromi look anything but pleasant and beautiful, yet the image came to her easily. And she knew why Hiromi was upset.

Because her son ate chocolate.

"Is Asahi…?"

"I don't know. Probably with the police. I think they're asking him about what happened."

"With his father?"

"Actually…from what I've heard, he was taken away in an ambulance."

"What?!"

Yuuki's expression darkened.

Ritsu frantically asked, "Did her husband get hurt, too? Did he fall with her, or…?"

"No, he's in critical condition after being stabbed. For some reason, he was in an apartment a floor below his family's. People said the wife in that unit might have done it... Do you know her, Ritsu? I think it's the Yuzuki family."

Ritsu sucked in a breath and couldn't let it out. Kyohei was on the floor below his, in another unit, as though that was ordinary for him. Something he did when Mr. Yuzuki wasn't home.

Ritsu didn't know how to feel. What was that man doing while his wife and son were going through that awful event? And why did Yuzuki, today of all days, decided to let another woman's husband into her home? She went to mourn a dead friend with that man's wife hours before.

Something very, very heavy settled in Ritsu's lungs.

She was less worried about Kyohei Sawatari than about his son, Asahi. Neither of his parents was around at the moment.

"Phone."

"Huh?"

"Where's my phone?"

"Isn't that it by your pillow?"

Ritsu brought up her call history.

There were entries of calls from Ritsu to Yuuki. She didn't remember making them at all, but she evidently had. At the top of the list was a call from Yuuki to Ritsu. At the very bottom was a call from Hiromi Sawatari.

That wasn't a dream. It was real.

But how much of it?

Hiromi had claimed she was asking everyone if Asahi ate chocolate. So maybe Ritsu wasn't the only person she'd called.

Death from a fall.

She didn't just take a spill. She was dead.

Ritsu recalled that bang, the bursting sound she heard once before. This was beyond belief.

They hadn't known each other very well or for very long, but the shock of someone Ritsu knew passing away, and so soon after speaking with her, was tremendous. The headache that had faded was returning.

The smartphone in her hands buzzed, and a little light activated on the front. She caught a glimpse of the word *LINE*, and thought, *Ah, right*.

Yuuki had summed it up last night.

"Perhaps this is normal for them. If another in their group passed away, they might do the same thing without thinking twice."

Someone had posted a stamp in the chat—a goofy-looking rabbit character with tears streaming from its eyes.

Along with the message, *Hiromi... I can't believe it.*

"Is everything all right?" Yuuki asked. Ritsu lacked the willpower to say, "I'm fine" at this point. Her breathing was shallow and her chest hurt.

Hatch barked, and Ritsu heard Kanato approach. Through the sliver of the open door, she saw her son's face.

"Are you okay, Mom? I'm getting hungry."

"Kanato."

"Are the police cars still outside? Did something happen? Did somebody get hurt?"

Ritsu noticed Yuuki's shoulders tense. That was enough to tell her that the boy didn't know what had happened. He didn't know about the Sawataris yet.

Kanato was quite fond of Asahi, the child who pushed Hiromi to her death. The elementary school kept details of parents' and guardians' misfortunes private. However, Asahi was an active student and the student chairman. Sooner or later, Kanato would learn the truth. What kind of shock would that be, when he found out?

It was horrifying to consider. Ritsu pushed the feeling aside and managed to reply, "Why don't you two go and get some dinner for yourselves? I don't have much of an appetite yet."

"You sure?" Yuuki pressed, watching his wife with concern.

She nodded. "Yes. I think I could use a little alone time."

Ritsu wanted Kanato as far from this apartment complex as possible.

Once he was in bed, she'd give Yuuki a proper pitch on moving out. She just needed to collect her thoughts first.

"All right. But don't get too deep inside your own head."

"I won't."

"I want to get burgers at Treeland!" Kanato exclaimed. He was enrapt at the thought of his favorite local restaurant. Yuuki smiled at him, though it was clearly a little stiff. Ritsu's husband and son left the bedroom. As she listened to them prepare to go, she thought, *I bet Hiromi wouldn't let her son eat a hamburger at a family restaurant*, despite the recent tragedy. *She'd claim she didn't know what was in it.*

Oddly, the notion brought tears to Ritsu's eyes. She didn't know what they were for.

Ritsu clenched her eyes tight and turned on her side. Her wits were razor sharp, and her mind was amped up and reeling from the news of Hiromi's death, but she was also utterly exhausted and sleepy.

Her phone vibrated.

It was a light, easy buzz, like a pulse.

It happened again, telling her that she was receiving messages.

Ritsu lifted a heavy arm and grabbed her phone. She didn't know how much time had passed. She needed to check the time, but first, she opened LINE.

The group had lost its queen, Hiromi.

You want to see her, don't you?

Ritsu could scarcely believe her eyes.

She thought time had somehow rewound.

But that wasn't the case. The sender's icon wasn't Hiromi's. Instead of her profile shot with her large earrings and smug, dignified smile, this icon was of a crappy-looking quilted doll. A doll with braids and a white dress.

An unfamiliar icon. However, the name below it gave Ritsu chills.

Kaorikanbara-WhiteQUEEN.

Huh? A lot had happened in the chat thread since the stamp from Yoko and Ritsu's long nap. When did Kaori become a member of this group? Then the unsettling answer occurred to her.

Maybe she had always been there.

Maybe she was a member of the group and simply never said anything, content to watch everyone else message. That would make her no different from Ritsu, who sent a text at the start, then found herself unable to add anything more and so observed going forward.

With just an old flip phone?

The confusion compounded itself. Was this Kaorikanbara-WhiteQUEEN not the Kaori Ritsu knew?

Yoko, Yuzuki, and the others sent many texts after Kaorikanbara-WhiteQUEEN entered the feed, suggesting this was totally normal. Expected, even.

Oh, I know. It turned into a big incident, so I doubt we'll get to say good-bye at a normal funeral. If we want to see her, it has to be now.

This just can't be the end.

Yuzuki, can you get in touch with her husband? You two were close.

Why do you have to say it like that? LOL.

A stamp of a guffawing character.

Look, everyone knows already. LOL.

Yeah, we all know. You're so obvious about it ROFL. Is it true that you did that to him today, Yuzuki?

I'll leave that to your imagination! LMAO.

Stamp,

stamp,

stamp,

stamp,

stamp,

stamp.

You're there, aren't you, Ritsu?

That was the latest message.

Come in, Ritsu, come in. No leaving us on read. LOL.

Let's go say good-bye to Hiromi together. I'm sure everyone will be happy if you come.

Ritsu?

You can't say you didn't know her this time, Ritsu.

Ding-dong! The doorbell rang.

Ritsu shrieked. Her shoulders hunched up, bouncing much harder than she would have expected.

"Yuuki... Kanato..."

She couldn't imagine who else would be at the door this late.

They must have returned from dinner. But if that was true, why didn't Yuuki just unlock the door? Sawatari Apartments was a very chic and fashionable old place, but its security was dated and poor. There were no building entrances with autolocking doors. Anyone could just walk up to an apartment door.

Argh!

Ritsu could scream with frustration. They should have updated the security systems before redecorating the interiors and refinishing the exterior! Those two appearance-obsessed idiots!

Ritsu left the bedroom and timidly approached the intercom screen on the living room wall. Before she got there, she heard the voice.

"Mrs. Ritsu Mikishimaaa?"

It came from a distance.

She clamped her hands over her ears, praying she was hearing things.

A woman stood in the center of the screen, wearing a very white, unfashionable, old dress, with caked-on foundation and red lipstick.

It was Kaori, the woman Ritsu wasn't particularly close with, whom she'd only spoken to at the volunteer event.

Ding-dong.

The elongated ringing sound repeated. For everything that was different, the chime was identical to the one in the Sawataris' apartment.

"Oh, Ritsuuu. Let's go and see the dead."

Bam-bam-bam, bam-bam-bam, bam-bam-bam, bam-bam-bam, ding-dong, bam-bam-bam, bam-bam-bam, ding-dong, bam-bam, "Riiitsuuu," *bam-bam-bam-bam,* "you can't say you didn't know her this tiiime," *ding-donnng…*

"Hyip!"

Hatch barked at the door. For a moment, the banging stopped.

But it swiftly resumed. The doorbell rang constantly.

"Hyip! Hyip!"

Hatch kept barking. It was all the terrified Ritsu could do to simply cling to the little dog.

"*Ohhh, Riiitsuuuu,*" the voice called from the other side of the door.

Maybe this was how it went for everyone else, Ritsu thought. *I don't know. I don't know, but maybe this is how each one was stalked, cornered, and trapped. Chased around, families harassed, as she worked herself closer in bizarre, uncomfortable ways.*

Hiromi wasn't the queen at all. She just wanted to be. It's clear what she sought to be to the group, how she longed to be seen. It wasn't apparent at first, but now it's so obvious that it seems unmistakable. She and her husband wanted to sit on the throne, ruling over the apartment complex.

But I don't understand this woman. She must exist beyond the limits of common sense.

"Ohhh, Riiitsuuu…"

"Just stop it!" Ritsu screamed.

That was when she realized her mistake. She had given away her presence, not that it would have stopped Kaori anyhow. The banging on the door seeped into her ears. Her head was pounding, threatening to burst.

"I'll call the police!"

Ritsu could sense that she was trapped. However, there was still time. Maybe the family next door would realize that something was wrong.

Just after she shouted about the police, the banging on the door stopped, as did the voice calling her name.

It was so anticlimactic that it left Ritsu baffled. She glanced at the intercom screen. All she saw was...the top of a head. It was Kaori's downcast head and her hair, streaked with white.

Suddenly, she snapped her head back up straight.

"Boo!"

She laughed long and loud. There was a huge smile on her face, plastered on like part of a mask. As always, her red lipstick stood out, hovering above her other features.

"Let's go, Ritsu." Kaori's voice dripped with glee. "Let's go see Hiromi. You knew *her*, didn't you? You have a right to see her face. Hiromi's still around. She'll be happy. Just go visit her. Let's write a letter, too. Tell as many people as possible."

Ritsu put her hands over her head. The air was too thin to breathe.

Kaori leered at her through the screen. Her face pushed closer to the camera at the door.

"We need to tell Kanato, too. Asahi's mother's dead, after all. He'll be very sad, and he'll want to say good-bye. I can tell him about it. Let's go, Ritsu. Shall I go to him?"

Stop...

She only recognized the wail at the mention of her son's name as being her own when the pain built in her exhausted lungs. She was going to open the door. Open it and jump out, into the hallway...

Pressure squeezed her chest.

Kaori wasn't there. Then she looked to the side with a gasp.

Her body tilted, hard.

Her legs felt weightless.

Bang. The sound of something bursting.

The sound of a fall.

Yuuki had described it as a *wham*. The noise instantly grew dim. She was engulfed in silence.

Well, that's that.

Flap-flap, fwup-fwup. Something was billowing in her ears. Through fading wits, Ritsu realized what the sound was—blue sheets.

The movers' tarps that covered Sawatari Apartments beat in the wind, all at once. A gigantic creature breathing in and out.

The last thing she heard before tumbling into the dark was Hatch barking, *"Hyip!"*

CHAPTER THREE
Coworker

"That's what I mean. I'm asking why you couldn't bother to send a word of explanation my way. I'm not requesting an apology."

Toshiya Suzui tried to focus on his computer monitor and wait out the voice coming from the hallway.

An in-progress reminder email for a business partner who'd made an appointment for the next day sat on the screen. It was the kind of message he sent to every partner before each appointment, so the contents were mostly a standardized template; he could write them with his eyes closed. But with that voice in his ear, he found it difficult to get through it, as though he was more likely to make a mistake.

"I mean, how many times has this happened? You always apologize and claim you'll be careful in the future, but you don't improve in any meaningful way, so it's totally pointless to say sorry. What are your thoughts about this? Tell me."

"I'm sorry," replied a tiny, meek voice. It was painful to hear, and Suzui could only pretend to concentrate on his screen. *I'm not hearing this, I'm not noticing this*, he told himself.

There was a loud sigh, which said more than any of the previous words. It sounded louder than the last admonishment, too.

"How did you even handle the work at your last job? What have you been doing with your life?"

"I'm sorry."

"I just told you..."

My heart hurts.

Suzui likely wasn't the only one who felt that way. Nearly everyone in this section heard the berating, yet they continued their work in silence. It made Suzui feel like he was taking part in a pattern of bullying.

He looked up and saw his senior coworker, Mutsumi Maruyama, stand from her seat. She crossed the open office and left, not through the door near the desk where the shouting came from, but through the one on the opposite side.

"And didn't this happen when you took the appointment with Midorimura Market last week? I just warned you the last time, and I didn't want to have to tell you again. Given the route, you had Akaya before that, so obvious order dictated you hit Miyata Liquor in the same neighborhood, *then* Midorimura in the adjacent one. That would decrease the travel time. Did that not occur to you when you reviewed this trip in your head? It didn't even need to be in your head, in fact. You put it down in writing when emailing me, didn't you? So if you couldn't have imagined it then—well, at that point, it's not even imagination, it's just a lack of consideration, isn't it? You're making someone go from one train station to a different one, then back. Personally, I think the power of imagination is no different than kindness and consideration. Am I wrong?"

Suzui caught himself before saying, "There's no point to rehashing all of that now, is there?" Plus, the order of company visits could be affected by things other than distance, such as when a liaison or manager was available. One station's travel time wasn't really worth making such a big deal about.

Suzui glanced over and met the eyes of Hamada, the coworker who occupied the seat ahead of him. His features twisted; he clearly shared the same idea.

"I'm sorry, I'm sorry," the apologetic voice repeated in a lifeless tone. That only made the angry voice louder.

"I'm not asking for apologies. I'm asking for answers. Help me out here. How have you survived to this point?"

Suzui couldn't take it anymore. He stood, and, like the woman before him, headed for the door farther from his seat and out of the room.

As Suzui suspected, Mutsumi was at the vending machine. She had a can of sweetened milk tea and smiled at Suzui when he approached. "Hi there."

"Hello," he answered. She pointed to the machine and asked, "What's your poison?"

"Oh, it's okay. I'll get it myself…"

"Don't be stubborn. This is about the only chance I get to play the work senior role."

Mutsumi was forty-three. She had a child in elementary school, so she rarely took part in bar outings and drinking parties with her coworkers. Indeed, she had very few chances to buy Suzui a drink.

Unlike Suzui, who was in his third year at the company, Mutsumi was a longtime veteran, the lead salesperson in Sales Section Two. That made her the number two person after the section chief, but she looked young for her age, and Suzui had been stunned when he learned how old she was. Mutsumi was friendly and generous with new employees, so everyone new to the company treated her warmly and with respect.

Buying Suzui a drink was definitely not the only thing she could do for him. Everyone relied on Mutsumi and looked up to her. She'd helped Suzui on many occasions, and he knew he owed her a great debt.

"Then I'll have something carbonated. Um, if you don't mind."

"Sure thing. This one it is."

Mutsumi put a coin in the slot and pressed the upper right button on the machine. She even crouched down to get the bottle from the slot.

"Thanks so much," Suzui said while accepting the drink.

"Guess you couldn't take much more of Chief Sato, either?" she asked.

Finally, Suzui thought. He was dying to talk about it.

"Nope."

"I've told him so many times that scolding Jin in front of the others is bad for Jin and the rest of us who are forced to listen."

"Yeah." Mutsumi fixed Suzui in her gaze. He twisted off the bottle cap and continued, "I heard from Hamada and the others. You warned the chief about it, and he stopped doing it on the floor. But he just moved to the hallway outside. But everyone can still hear him."

"It's hilarious that he thinks this is more considerate." Mutsumi smirked sadly. The remark was obviously meant to be ironic, but it sounded mournful rather than acerbic coming from her.

Suzui didn't feel like going back to the sales section, because the berating was likely to still be going on. So he went with Mutsumi to a small guest reception space beside the lobby. Fortunately, no one was there, so they sat down together.

He felt depressed.

Had he known that the section chief would tell people off, he would have scheduled some outside meetings for this morning to get out of the office. Now he was stuck here.

"Sometimes I wonder why he doesn't talk back. But I guess there's no point. If he makes excuses for himself, it'll just make the chief angrier."

"And given his position, Jin can't really talk back. I think it's really painful. I want to help somehow; I'll look for a chance to talk to the chief later. If necessary, I'll have the department chief talk to him."

Their employer, Yotsumiya Foods, was a midsize food company. Suzui was a member of Sales Section Two and primarily handled frozen goods.

He had been in the planning division until last year. He had been a science major in college and had applied at the food company hoping to take part in planning and research, which had made his transfer to sales this year an unpleasant shock. The older members at the planning division had told him, "It's good experience to take part in different sections while you're young." However, Suzui wasn't happy about it. Even worse, his boss in Sales Section Two was Section Chief Sato.

Unlike Suzui, Sato had worked for the company in sales from the start, and he was only forty-one. The company had many longtime employees, but Sato was extremely young for a manager. His shoulders were broad and his voice was loud, giving him the air of an intense athlete. As someone who had come up in the crucible of sales, he probably saw Suzui's planning background and thought him a weak, useless salesman. Suzui always felt intimidated by him.

Still, he hadn't outright disliked Sato until he witnessed the way he berated subordinates.

Of all of them, Sato was definitely the hardest on the man he was scolding today, Jin.

Jin had been a part of Sales Section Two since before Suzui transferred in. He had been a midcareer hire at the end of the year before, and he was most likely in his fifties. That meant he was older than the section chief. Maybe such things were common these days, now that the era of absolute by-age seniority had passed. In fact, Suzui had seen many situations like this one in other company divisions. But none of the older subordinates seemed so obviously *aged* as Jin, in terms of both looks and attitude.

When Suzui first came to Sales Section Two and stepped onto the floor, he saw Jin sitting next to him, closest to the door, where the newest people sat, and done a double take, rude as that was. Jin was a man with plenty of white in his hair and black-rimmed glasses on his nose. His straight-backed posture reminded Suzui of a principal at the morning address in elementary school, and he was stunned to learn that Jin wasn't a senior manager.

Chief Sato had been the first to call him by the nickname Jin. He'd instructed everyone else to do the same, to help the older man blend in with the rest of the section. Suzui found that rather disconcerting. The idea that you could change how people felt about others with a nickname seemed so old-fashioned and out of date.

He'd even inquired with Jin about that once. Everyone else used the nickname, so Suzui naturally found himself doing the same, yet he felt bad about it. So one time, when they were both working overtime, he asked, "Don't you mind? I'm sorry, I feel bad about it. Like, it feels presumptuous for younger people to give you a nickname."

Jin's eyes bulged with surprise at the question. Then he broke into a gentle smile. "You were worried about that? That's very kind of you, Suzui."

"Uh, I mean…"

"I'm glad to have people call me by a nickname."

"The section chief started it, right?"

"Yes."

Jin's white hairs were translucent silver beneath the fluorescent lights. Suzui recognized that color—it was the same as his dad's hair had been the last time Suzui went home.

Oh, so he must be about Dad's age. That led Suzui to another notion. *What if my dad were getting chewed out by a younger boss at work? When Chief Sato goes off on Jin, does he think of his own father?*

"The chief is a very good man. I'm grateful to him," Jin said, entirely too easily. Suzui couldn't help but stammer a "Wh-what?"

Jin smiled. "Are you surprised?" he asked, staring at Suzui.

Up close, it was easy to see that Jin's features were very distinct. Heavy eyelids hung over his beak of a nose, which, combined with his tall, thin profile, gave the man a particular kind of dignity. It just didn't feel right that he was someone else's underling.

Suzui nodded awkwardly, and Jin continued. "I was brought on as a new hire, and I was sure my age would make certain things uncomfortable. Also, he asked me about the nickname before he told everyone. He said, 'I was thinking of calling you Jin, do you mind?'"

"The section chief did that?"

Was Sato really the sort who paid attention to those little details? Suzui was skeptical, but Jin assured him, "Yes." He claimed the chief was a *"good man,"* but it only convinced Suzui that Jin was a much better man.

"I think he's creating an environment where I can fit in with the others."

Suzui didn't know much about Jin's previous job. He didn't offer a lot about himself, and Suzui took it as a sign not to inquire. Still, he had to wonder if Jin had previously been in a senior position. Perhaps as a manager. Maybe he was a talented worker who got unlucky during a round of layoffs.

While Jin was in the sales department now, Suzui had heard that his wage structure and health benefits were different from a standard employee's. He didn't go out on calls, either, mostly talking on the phone and managing schedules like an aide. If he had held a senior position at his old job, then it was remarkable that he could endure this menial drudgery.

Every time Chief Sato berated Jin, he used the same phrases. *"How did you even handle the work at your last job? What have you been doing with your life?"*

"Help me out here. How have you survived to this point?"

"I can't stand hearing the way he talks. It's like he's tearing down Jin's personality. What decade does he think we're living in?"

It was workplace abuse. A picture-perfect example of worker harassment, the sort of thing anyone should be ashamed of. Suzui wanted to bemoan the company's old-fashioned structure for enabling this. He felt miserable that it happened to be at *his* company.

"I get it," Mutsumi said, lifting the tab on her can of tea. Suzui's leg started bouncing restlessly. It was a habit of his when he was on edge, something he'd tried to fix many times without success.

"For one thing, what did he do to get chewed out so hard today? Did Jin screw up that badly?"

"I think he was only addressing some minor mistakes initially. But somehow, that got the section chief really worked up, and once he's revved up, there's no stopping him. By the latter half, Chief Sato was talking about a different topic entirely."

"It really sucks. What if that were me?"

Fortunately, Suzui had never been picked on or lectured by the section chief. However, that was part of why it felt so bad. Jin was a target for Chief Sato, like he knew the man was in a weak position and couldn't say no, and he used that opportunity to vent all his frustration.

"It seems like Jin's work is no worse than anyone else's. He's not some total failure, is he?"

"No. If anything, he's pretty good at his job. Remember how we shared the client list the section chief made last month? The one the department chief asked him to make?"

"Oh yeah."

It was a list of carefully updated client information, well crafted and detailed, almost surprisingly so. Despite his youth, Chief Sato favored the analog—he was good at interacting with business clients but bad at the nuts and bolts of office work. His emails that went out to the section were in a format that made them difficult to read, with almost no line breaks. Suzui wondered if he was hunting and pecking at the keyboard with two fingers, too.

"Jin made that list."

"Huh?"

"The section chief acts like it was him, but Jin did everything, working overtime to get it done. I watched Chief Sato while everyone praised the list, wondering if he'd admit the truth, but he never did."

"What a small, petty man," Suzui grumbled.

Mutsumi nodded, frowning. "He wasn't always like that, though. I remember when the section chief fought back against the boss to protect coworkers. He used to hate corruption and was a generally reliable guy."

"So he had the stones to talk back as a worker, but his attitude shifted into a horrible disaster when he became the boss."

"You're really bitter about this, Suzui," Mutsumi remarked, chuckling. "You might be right, though. He got mad and defended me when we were the same rank."

"Huh?"

"He argued that it didn't make sense that I couldn't be management, just because I had a period of maternity leave."

"Oh…"

That reminded Suzui that Jin wasn't the only one with a younger boss. It was the same for Mutsumi. She'd been working two years longer than Chief Sato.

She undid the barrette that collected her long, silky hair, placed her milk tea on the low table, and started to tie back her locks.

"But then," she said, "we had a chance to talk recently, and he told me, 'It's hard for women because they have to get pregnant. It's too bad for you, but that's just a woman's job, socially speaking. It's just the way it is.'"

"That sounds like…"

Sexual harassment. Or maybe pregnancy harassment. Mutsumi lowered her eyes. The shadow that crossed her features made her look terribly sad.

"He claimed that it's better to have at least one woman in upper management; it helps the company image to appear like it has some kind of gender balance. I remember he hoped Chief Osada from accounting would quit soon. Then I could move to accounting and be section chief there. 'Maybe you should submit an application to transfer,' he said. It's almost like he didn't want me in sales."

"He's a petty man, so he doesn't want someone who can do everything better than him around," Suzui remarked. It probably wasn't the best thing to mention at work, but it was how he felt. He was heated. "I've heard partners trust Chief Sato, but that's only because he has personal connections with people he's known for years, right? He hasn't built a relationship with any of the newer business contacts, and he doesn't leave the office to go visit them. I know I probably shouldn't say this, but all the contacts he's tight with are older men with ancient ideas. His only skill is sucking up to more powerful guys like himself. You're way better at staying on top of all the little things around the office."

"I'm sorry, Suzui, I'm sorry. I got you all riled up," Mutsumi apologized. She bowed, too, and it was obviously sincere, not just a formality. "I felt a bit sad, that's all. Someone going from fighting the boss to being the boss and doing a one-eighty is just how it goes, isn't it? Maybe that's just life. The passage of time can be a cruel thing."

"If I get married and have a baby, I'm definitely the type who will go and demand paternity leave. He'll probably turn me down if he's still my boss, though."

"What?! That's your plan, Suzui?"

"No. But it's a potential option I could look forward to." Suzui leaned his head back and groaned. "At the college classes and seminars, they told us those kinds of rights are guaranteed and commonsense. And I was stupid enough to believe it, until I actually got hired," he spat.

Mutsumi gave him a weak smile. "This company's so backward. And we bear some responsibility for not improving things before the next generation came along. I'm sorry for that."

Mutsumi and Jin—who was probably still being lectured on the sales floor—were just too nice. That was the problem. There were people out there who took advantage of kindness, and the unfairness made Suzui livid.

"I'll get going now," Mutsumi said casually. She picked up her tea and walked off, hair tied up. Her steps were light and breezy, and Suzui likened the gait to a survival tactic. Without it, maybe Mutsumi wouldn't have made it this far.

◆

It wasn't until later that evening that Suzui finally headed home.

Following the afternoon rounds of sales, he had a business dinner with his final appointment, a chief purchasing contact, then took the train home. Suzui clung to a hanging strap and stared out the window. It was before ten o'clock, so the train wasn't packed. The crowding after nine o'clock and after ten o'clock were completely different. Because Suzui's dinner partner wasn't a drinker, he hadn't had to worry about being held late into the busy nightlife hours.

Suzui wasn't much of a drinker, either. He could barely hold his liquor. In fact, he seemed to have almost no alcohol-metabolizing enzymes; even the disinfectant alcohol wipes before a vaccine shot made his skin puffy and red. He'd tried getting hammered a few times as a student, hoping the old wives' tale about building tolerance the more you drink was true. However, it only made him sick and forced other people to look after him. The silver lining was that he knew his limits before becoming a working adult.

Suzui heard that companies didn't force their employees to drink like they had in the past. In fact, during his tenure in the planning division, no one gave him a hard time about liquor.

But since coming to sales, he'd learned that you didn't always get that ideal treatment.

"You can't drink? What were you doing in college, man?"

Unsurprisingly, that's what Chief Sato said. He'd eyed Suzui with a mixture of annoyance and snide mockery.

"You never took part in a sports team, did you? I didn't think so; that's *why you don't know how to get along with people. Look, you only have to join in for the first sip or two. If you're not drinking, don't come to the bar meetups."*

That would have been fine with Suzui. He didn't want to go out drinking after work if he could avoid it. But he knew that if he didn't attend, it would put him on the outs with the section chief, so he forced himself to go. Although Suzui's sales job meant occasional solo meetings, like the one today, there were plenty where he assisted the chief. Sato never wasted any time insulting Suzui in front of the client.

"Can you believe this guy? Can't drink a drop. I want to complain to personnel for sending him to sales. I apologize on his behalf for being so boring and not having a good time with us."

Sato believed that mocking people on his side helped him maintain a harmonious relationship with the client. It was a mindset that made Suzui sick to his stomach, but even worse was the way Sato gave him a condescending smile as soon as the outing was over.

"If I didn't address that one right off the bat, you'd end up feeling like a real asshole when they found out you couldn't drink later, right? I did you a favor by bringing it up first."

Suzui had learned through personal experience that there were methods of getting through social drinking functions. There were plenty of ways he could have handled the situation without a big fuss. It was irritating that the chief made the choice for him. Unfortunately, the contacts Sato wanted to personally meet were always the sort who got along with him. By turning Suzui into the butt of a joke, he defined their relationship in a certain light.

Suzui saw Chief Sato and those like him as old-fashioned, but he knew they saw him as the one at fault. He couldn't drink, yet still called himself a man? No, he was a boring drudge who couldn't get along with others. They often asked him what he had done in college. Did they think Suzui wasn't mocked like this in school? College was unbearable, too. Why was Suzui forced to endure this attitude in the workplace?

These days, the accounts Suzui managed all belonged to customers who were moderate drinkers, even at big gatherings. He'd learned that Mutsumi, his section leader, had arranged that. Naturally, she never pressured Suzui to return the favor.

The stations that flew by beyond the window steadily got closer to the one by Suzui's place, where he lived alone.

At one station that Suzui never got off at, the train's stop took longer than usual. Before long, a voice came over the speakers.

"We're receiving a stop request from the train ahead of us. Please bear with us. The wait will be an extra two minutes."

Suzui wasn't in any particular rush to get home, so he took out his phone to pass the time by browsing the internet or looking at social media. However, something caught his attention in the blurry background past his phone, out through the train doors. Suzui looked up, and his eyes locked on to someone.

There was a familiar face at this station he'd never visited—Jin. Despite his height and usual good posture, the man was hunched. He carried a large document briefcase and had a cellphone to his ear.

On the phone? Suzui thought, confused. A train platform, with all the trains coming and going and various other noises, was a terrible place for a call.

Suzui couldn't make out Jin's voice, but he saw him. Phone in one hand and heavy briefcase in the other, Jin hunched over even more than before, as though apologizing to the person on the other end of the call, who wouldn't be able to see.

"We're sorry for the ongoing delay. It should be one additional minute," the voice over the train loudspeaker said. Suzui didn't care about the delay, although maybe enough other people did to warrant the announcement.

Then again, he might have felt differently were he in a rush. Thinking about it got Suzui in a bad mood, and he jumped off the train on an impulse. The coworker around his father's age, a very capable employee in his own right, was apologizing to someone over the phone. Suzui's body moved unconsciously.

"Jin!" he called while stepping off the train. Jin flinched at the sound, but he didn't remove the phone from his ear. His eyes found Suzui, and his mouth made a shape like "Oh." He continued speaking solely to the person on the other end of the call, however.

"Oh, er, it's nothing. Yes, it's fine. Yes, yes, that sounds very bad. I know, Section Chief. I agree, I think you're correct."

Section Chief.

The words made Suzui's head feel numb from the center outward. Jin was clearly troubled. There were weak wrinkles around his eyes. His eyebrows hung low as he stared in Suzui's direction apologetically. It was the kind of expression someone made when they were crying and smiling at the same time.

"Hang up the call," Suzui said.

"Huh?" Jin replied, shocked.

Even Suzui didn't know why he suggested such a brazen act. Maybe he felt emboldened now that he was off work. Regardless, the anger coursing through his chest was honest and direct. Maybe reflecting on the chief's alcohol-related bullying had left him in a foul temper.

"C'mon, let's hang up."

He wrested the phone away from Jin's grasp. As he did so, he caught a glimpse of the screen. The section chief's name was displayed. But it was what he saw below that locked his eyes to the phone.

3:12:14.

As Suzui watched, the second counter increased to *15*, then *16*. He heard a faint voice through the speaker.

"So I don't think Mutsumi's making any sense. The department chief takes her side, but that's just cowardice, if you ask me. He thinks no one can argue if he says the woman is right. I don't think that makes sense. If anything, it's reverse sexism."

19, 20, 21… The count continued. The section chief's voice seemed to dig into Suzui's ears deeper via the phone speaker than in the hallway at the office. It felt like his heart and mind were being ground by a rough file.

This had been going on for three hours…

Suzui shivered, so intimidated that he couldn't even press the end call button. He knew how to, of course, but for a moment, he forgot. He panicked and started hitting buttons at random. The section chief's name left the screen.

The man was in the middle of a sentence when his voice vanished.

Suzui's train emitted a chime to warn that it was leaving. It was very loud. *Three hours.* He repeated the thought, just to grapple with it. For over three hours, Jin had endured this phone call, trapped here in this noisy environment.

"Um… I'm sorry, Suzui," Jin apologized, perhaps because Suzui was too shocked to actually speak.

"Was that from the chief?" Suzui finally asked. It felt stupid to ask a question with such an obvious answer. However, the voice over the phone had wrapped itself around him, dulling his mind and body.

The train doors closed. Suzui heard the sound of a train rolling by and felt wind on his face.

Once the train had left the station, Jin inclined his head awkwardly. "Yes."

"But you can barely hear anything here. Why would you stay in a place like this?"

"I was on the train when I got the call. If I didn't pick up, it would just keep ringing, so I thought to answer just long enough to explain and then call back later. But he never stopped talking."

Suzui didn't know where Jin lived. However, based on his story, this wasn't the station closest to his home. Jin had meant to be on the phone for only a minute, and the call lasted for over three hours…

Suzui was stunned and rooted to the spot. Just then, Jin's phone buzzed in Suzui's hand, the vibration of an incoming call. He almost yelped at the surprise.

"Oh, I've got to take that," Jin said. The section chief's name was on the screen again.

On sheer impulse, Suzui snapped, "Don't do it. You don't have to answer!"

He was shouting because he was scared. Jin's eyes went wide, and he stared with concern at the phone in Suzui's hand.

Suzui shook his head. "You don't have to answer. You talked plenty already, didn't you? It didn't sound very urgent anyway." He felt guilty for overhearing, but admitted to it all the same.

It wasn't just the length of the phone call that unnerved Suzui; it was the content as well. *Mutsumi. Not making sense. No one can argue if he says the woman is right. Reverse sexism…*

He didn't want to hear it. It was all so tiresome. There was no reason to call an employee after work hours and subject them to commentary like that for hours.

The buzzing continued. Sato should give up, yet he didn't.

"All right," Jin said at last, staring Suzui in the eyes. After several long moments, he said, "I won't answer. Will you give back my phone if I don't pick up?"

"…Okay." Suzui handed the phone back, and immediately his body felt lighter. They walked over to a bench on the station platform and sat down. Jin looked utterly exhausted, as though he were about to crumble into nothing. No wonder; he'd probably been on his feet the entire call.

"Does this sort of thing happen often?" Suzui asked.

"Yes," Jin admitted. Suzui was stunned, despite having expected that reply. Jin wasn't even a full employee. There was no reason for him to deal with all this.

The overturned phone kept buzzing on Jin's lap. Having a conversation with that noise in the background felt bizarre, like some kind of poorly performed comedy skit. Suzui got the sense he was seeing something he ought not to.

He nearly suggested they file a complaint.

Admittedly, he didn't know where, but he wanted to try. To human resources, to the department chief, to the labor board—somewhere.

But the ceaseless vibrations from Jin's phone made it challenging to voice the words.

"He must be really bored."

The noise stopped at last. Suzui stared at Jin's silent phone.

"Chief Sato's married, isn't he? He probably has children, right? Doesn't he have anything better to do? Or does his family ignore him?" Suzui joked. However, it lacked the same zest as when he complained with Mutsumi at work. The phone call had been mostly Sato griping about Mutsumi. He wasn't even scolding Jin. Who went around forcing their employee to listen to an endless stream of grievances for three hours?

Just then, the quiet phone erupted again. *Vnn-vnn-vnn-vnn…* Fear welled up in Suzui like before, but this time it was colored by a streak of anger.

"Just turn the phone off, Jin. This is ridiculous."

Jin wasn't looking at him.

His eyes were resting on the shaking phone on his lap. It made Suzui worry. If these calls were commonplace for him, then he might be completely broken and traumatized…

Jin mumbled something. It coincided with an announcement about a train coming in on the opposite platform, so Suzui couldn't hear.

"Huh?" he said, and Jin lifted his head to look at him.

"...I think it's because I might hear him out."

"Pardon?"

"That's why the section chief acts this way."

His lips were curled in his usual weak smile. It wasn't self-derisive, but serene and contemplative, as though Jin was full of more emotion than he could suppress.

"Thank you for your concern, Suzui."

"But I didn't..."

Jin's courteousness, even when speaking with someone young enough to be his son, wounded Suzui.

"Shall we go?" Jin asked. "My family's waiting."

He stood from the bench.

Vnn-vnn-vnn-vnn, vnn-vnn-vnn-vnn.

All the while, the cellphone vibrated in his hand. Suzui got the sinking feeling that as soon as they parted ways, he was going to answer the call.

He wanted to say something before he left, but no words would have sufficed.

◆

"What did you want to talk about, Suzui?"

Mutsumi took a seat across from him at the soba restaurant he'd told her about.

"Maybe I'll have grated daikon over my soba noodles," she whispered to herself, scanning the menu briefly before turning her attention back to him. "Did something happen at work?"

"Well, it's related to work, but technically, it didn't happen to me..."

Right after parting ways with Jin at the station the previous night, Suzui messaged Mutsumi on LINE. He wanted to let the emotion of the moment take him, to write everything he saw, but he held back. Explaining in person would be easier, and Suzui had an odd feeling he shouldn't leave a record of this in writing. That wasn't born of a concern for Chief Sato's or Jin's privacy; Suzui just really didn't want the text to be on his phone.

The soba restaurant was near the office, but because it was more expensive than other restaurants in the area, Suzui almost never saw coworkers there. He'd asked Mutsumi here for lunch to be considerate of her schedule. She always went home promptly at quitting time to take care of her family.

A waiter came out with tea. Suzui ordered, wiped his hands with the wet towel, and then broached the subject.

"Last night, I saw Jin on a train platform on the way home. He was talking to someone on the phone. But the train platform is really noisy, you know? And he was in this long conversation, so I started to worry, and I called out to him."

"Uh-huh." The mention of Jin's name made Mutsumi straighten up.

"Then I heard him say 'Chief' into the phone. So I told him, 'Let's hang up,' and I ended the call. It was outside of work hours, and Jin was just going to keep apologizing for something or other."

When Suzui had seen Jin at the office this morning, he seemed his usual self. When he walked by, Jin offered his characteristic weak smile and said, "Sorry to have worried you yesterday, Suzui."

Suzui replied, "Uh, it's fine." The chief was out at a meeting with another division in the company. It was a small relief that they didn't have to see him for a bit.

I bet he comes into work looking perfectly pleased with himself after subjecting his employees to ridiculous after-hours rants, Suzui thought. Anger was building in him again. The feeling practically caught in his throat, forcing him to breathe deeply to clear it.

"When I hung up the call, I saw it had been going for over three hours."

Mutsumi's eyes went wide, a very understandable reaction.

"I was shocked. And before I hit the button, I heard a little bit of what Chief Sato said."

"So I don't think Mutsumi's making any sense." Suzui thought about letting Mutsumi know her name had come up, but decided he couldn't.

"It seemed like he was just complaining about someone and forcing Jin to listen for hours."

Mutsumi would obviously feel terrible knowing that someone was talking about her behind her back, even if it was just their pushy boss.

"At first I thought Jin was being yelled at, like he always is at work. But this was more like he'd been forced to listen to a bunch of whining."

"When was this?"

"Close to ten, I think. He probably got the call as soon as he left work, and then he was on the line the whole time. And I doubt this was the first instance."

After Suzui hung up, the phone had kept ringing. Would Jin have been able to resist answering without someone else there?

"Jin told me, 'I think the section chief acts this way because I might hear him out.' That's evidence that he's under a lot of mental strain. I mean, it's just wrong, isn't it?"

"That's what Jin told you?" Mutsumi asked, concerned.

Suzui nodded. "Yeah."

"Then you're right. It does sound pretty bad. Almost like a habit."

"A habit?"

"Yes."

The waiter came to the table with their soba orders. Suzui had soba with duck, while Mutsumi's noodles came with grated daikon. Suzui gazed at the steam rising from the dipping broth and brought his hands together in the typical expression of gratitude before eating. Mutsumi did the same. They broke their wooden chopsticks apart, and after a period of silence, she finally spoke.

"Obviously, the section chief is the problem, but I also feel like Jin is so used to this unfair treatment that he's numb to it. By just passively allowing it to happen, even when he doesn't need to, Jin's learned to accept being scolded, and it's become a kind of routine that he slips into…"

"Yeah."

"The department chief's been concerned about Sato's actions lately. His attitude with his superiors has been bad, too. He says all the right things about wages and offering support to the staff, but he's too vehement and clashes with others. The department chief even asked me about the morale in our section."

Mitsumi called him "Sato" instead of "the section chief," perhaps because they used to be coworkers of the same rank. Suzui didn't think there was any value in worrying for his boss. However, Mutsumi had known the section chief for years and had a different perspective, so her concern was a bit understandable.

"Should I try talking to Sato?" she wondered aloud. "Maybe he's just on edge because of poor section performance. Something else might be weighing on his mind."

"Um, I…don't know about that…," Suzui replied clumsily.

Mutsumi stared him right in the eyes. "Why not?" He really couldn't find the words to respond.

Chief Sato clearly had it out for Mutsumi. If she chided him for his actions, he'd undoubtedly explode at her. This was all because she was a woman who got the job done better than Chief Sato and was respected for it.

It felt so ridiculous.

Suzui didn't want to explain it out loud, so he shook his head. "I'm worried he'll make you his next target if you speak out. I understand your concerns, but I suspect it's best for him to hear it from above. I don't think he listens to anyone below him."

"'Below him,'" Mutsumi repeated.

Uh-oh, thought Suzui. Sato had become section chief over her, despite her seniority with the company.

Suzui worried that he'd touched a sore spot, but Mutsumi just sighed and said, "Maybe you're right. In the past, he didn't get hung up on hierarchy. He was enjoyable to talk to. But it seems like he's getting worse and worse. I don't remember him being such a stereotypical bad boss."

"Maybe it's because he liked you. And when you didn't give him the time of day, it made him angry."

"Oh, please," Mutsumi replied, her expression finally softening. The two slurped their noodles for a bit before she said, "All right. I'll talk to the department head. I'm sorry you have to worry about this."

"No, I'm fine."

Mutsumi really didn't need to apologize just because she was the team lead and felt responsible for the section. Still, Suzui knew he could count on her to do the right thing at times like this.

Their lunch break was short, so they needed to eat quickly and get back to the office. Mutsumi put her head down and slurped her noodles rapidly. Suzui found himself staring and bit his lip.

I can only imagine how hard it is to be a woman and a mother fighting to earn your place in the sales department. Unlike for Mutsumi's colleagues, her short lunch break was the only free time she had, and she always spent it listening to younger workers like Suzui. That someone as talented and capable as she was subject to the whims of more incompetent men meant the company was truly unfair.

"Mutsumi-san."

"Yes?"

"If there's anything I can do, please say the word."

She looked up to confirm if Suzui was joking, and once she was satisfied, grinned and answered, "I know. I'm counting on you. Thanks, Suzui."

Although Suzui had invited Mutsumi to lunch, she paid the bill. "This is the only time I get to play the work senior role," she said, repeating a phrase she'd used recently. Suzui thought things like this were why she was so respected.

If only she had been made section chief instead.

◆

About three days later, Suzui had a slate of away meetings on his schedule. His plan was to pop into the office for some materials and go. However, he noticed that Jin wasn't on the sales floor.

Jin was a very dedicated worker and showed up at Sales Section Two earlier than anyone else. It had become second nature for Suzui to expect his presence by the entrance when he arrived. This absence was unusual.

Maybe he'd fallen ill.

Jin's desk was the cleanest in the area. His PC was turned off. Suzui kept an eye on Jin as he got ready, and before he left, an incoming call hit the section's reception line.

"Yotsumiya Foods, Sales Section Two," said Hamada, the man who sat in front of Suzui. There was a bit of back and forth, and then Hamada exclaimed, "What!" at a much higher pitch. "That's terrible! Uh-huh. And then?"

Others on the floor stopped what they were doing to listen. The expression on Hamada's face turned intense as he listened.

"All right, then. We'll manage over here. I'll tell them. The section chief? Sure thing."

Hamada pressed the hold button, turned toward the section chief's desk, which was up against the window, and called out, "Chief, Jin's on line two."

The section chief looked up from his computer. "Hmm?" Then he reached for the phone on his desk.

Hamada must have sensed Suzui looking at him, because once he patched the call through, he whispered, "Jin's wife was in an accident."

"What?!" Suzui cried in time with the section chief, who had undoubtedly just heard the same thing from Jin himself.

The others in the section took notice of the disturbance, and hushed words spread across the floor. Suzui hastened to ask, "A traffic accident?"

"No. He said she fell from the outside hallway of their apartment building," Hamada replied in a hushed tone. It was so shocking that Suzui didn't know what else to say.

"When?" he pressed.

"Last night."

"Meaning..."

The first thing that popped into his head was whether the fall was genuinely an accident. Suzui didn't know anything about Jin's family, but the recent event at the train platform surfaced in his mind. He remembered the way Jin had smiled weakly as they parted ways, and how he said, *Shall we go? My family's waiting.*

The memory clawed at Suzui's chest.

Was there something more to the situation with Jin's family? Perhaps there was a specific reason he had taken an entry-level job at his age.

"I wonder what floor she fell from," Suzui muttered, praying that it was just the second, or even closer to the ground. *Danchi*-style apartment buildings could go pretty high—the thought caused Suzui to shiver.

Hamada shook his head. "I don't know. But she's in the hospital. Jin won't be coming to work for a while, that's why he asked to speak to the section chief."

Sure enough, at that moment a crisp, clear voice rang out across the floor.

"Please don't worry about it. Of course you can take the time off. Please stay with your wife," the chief said. He leaned over his desk as he spoke to Jin. "Rest up and stay at her side."

Suzui was rattled over the sudden news, but that came as a small relief. Sato was a real asshole of a boss, but at least he still had a heart in his chest.

Perhaps that thought was why Suzui was so shaken that afternoon when Mutsumi accosted Sato.

After finishing his meetings and returning to the office, Suzui immediately noticed something strange about the vibe.

The lights were on, yet it felt dark inside.

Nobody was welcoming him back or paying attention. They were all focused on a single spot, whether subtly, from a distance, or by staring outright.

Suzui returned to his desk with his briefcase in hand. Hamada and the others in his area were either at their desks or standing by the copier, but almost all of them had eyes on the section chief's desk.

When Suzui turned to look at last, he nearly gasped.

"Tell me," demanded a trembling voice. Someone was on the brink of exploding, barely holding their emotions back.

Mutsumi stood before Chief Sato's desk. She stared at him, her face pale, almost openly furious.

"Talk to me. You weren't actually calling Jin, were you?"

Calling. The word sent a shiver down Suzui's back.

He recalled the phone, and the screen that showed a call of three hours, twelve minutes, and fourteen seconds. He thought of how it vibrated again and again…

The section chief didn't answer Mutsumi's question. He was as silent as a sulking child, and he looked away.

It was astonishingly immature. Everyone else in the room was speechless.

"I heard you from the meeting room," she continued, each word trembling. She no longer gave Chief Sato the benefit of deferential courtesy. "'This is what the department chief told me, what do you think? What do you think he meant by this word? That's how the company president valued me in the past, what do you think in light of that? I can do my job, and people expect good results from me, so this is clearly jealousy from smaller people, right? Our retail partners tell me Yotsumiya Foods equals Sato, so if I'm not around, the majority of those partners will lose confidence in the company. People complaining about my methods are just whiners. Yeah, that's right, they're all just idiots.' And on, and on, and on."

Mutsumi repeated quite the list of statements, as though reading them from an invisible script. There was a real momentum to her speech. Anger pushed her to go faster and faster.

However, the section chief had no reaction. He refused to look at the woman.

"That's fine. You can talk on the phone. Talk about whomever you want, even me. Although I don't think highly of doing so during work hours."

She took a deep breath.

"But," she continued, "I thought I heard you mention Jin's name. And when one subject was just about over, you'd say, 'Oh, that reminds me,' and continue on about another thing. If I hadn't forced you to stop from outside the room, you'd still be on that call, wouldn't you?"

Everyone held their breath, even Suzui. He swallowed audibly.

"Answer me," Mutsumi insisted. She sounded ready to cry. "How can you do this? Jin's in the hospital because his wife's in critical condition. How can you waste his time by filling his ears with this stream of one-sided nonsense?"

"It's not one sided," the section chief replied at last. You could hear a pin drop in the office, the room's attention was so laser focused.

As impossible as it was to understand the section chief's side, he seemed to take offense. His eyes were narrowed, as though the concept of Mutsumi scolding him was in itself insulting. "I wasn't just yelling at him. We were having a conversation. It's rude to insinuate otherwise," he snapped.

"No. It was entirely one sided."

Mutsumi didn't back down. She wasn't crying, but the look on her face betrayed grief equal to her outrage.

"You're the boss. When you're the one in charge, your subordinates don't have the right to refuse you. You took advantage of that. All you wanted from Jin was someone to listen and say, 'Uh-huh.' You constantly demand his approval, forcing him to agree so you can keep hurling every negative thought you have at him. Jin doesn't exist solely to exorcise your frustrations."

"You were standing there, eavesdropping on me the entire time? That's despicable." The chief grimaced with distaste. He glanced out at the floor, looking for support from the others.

Suzui had no idea where the chief found the guts to entreat them with that ridiculous expression. However, it was clear the section chief didn't feel an ounce of regret.

Say she's wrong, Suzui thought. *Please, tell us she's mistaken. Yeah, you were on the phone, but maybe you were talking to someone other than Jin. I mean, no sane person would have a conversation like that with someone tending to a family member in the hospital. Say she's wrong. Say it, damn you.*

But what Suzui got instead was a heavy sigh.

"Jin will be fine. When I talked to him this morning, he said that it wasn't serious. If something happened to his wife during the call, he'd hang up on me, wouldn't he? He could've told me as much, and I would've ended our call right there. It was only going to be a brief talk anyway. If he was too busy for it, he should've said so."

"You can't—!"

Chief Sato's blithe attitude caused Mutsumi's face to rapidly pale from shock. She looked ready to keel over.

The chief's snarl twisted into a grin. "I knew it was you, though. I've been getting called out by the department chief and the personnel department for things that weren't my fault. Almost like someone who had it out for me spread a bunch of lies... Aren't you ashamed of yourself? It was your fault you didn't get the promotion, and you choose to take it out on me by dragging your boss down with you?"

Mutsumi's face froze.

Her eyes were wide, and it seemed like she didn't know what to say. Everyone else on the floor was similarly speechless. This went beyond annoyance or anger—it was just mute astonishment.

Such was Chief Sato's devastating lack of rational logic. Getting through to him was impossible. He didn't even try to avoid blame out of a sense of guilt; he honestly believed he'd done nothing wrong. In his mind, he was correct. This man lived in a world where his every action was utterly righteous.

"I can't believe you...," Mutsumi managed at last, although she struggled to get the words out. There was nothing more. When your conversation partner refused to listen to reason, there was nothing else you could say.

A phone ring broke the silence.

"Yotsumiya Foods, Sales Section Two," said Tamiya, the youngest in the section. He seemed grateful for an escape from the uncomfortable scene. The chief and Mutsumi continued glaring at each other. The heavy quiet made it easy to hear Tamiya's nervous stammer.

"Ch-Chief?"

Tamiya gripped the receiver and looked ready to cry. The section chief tore his eyes away from Mutsumi and grunted, "Yeah?"

"External call on line three. It's from Jin."

The call was to inform them that Jin's wife failed to regain consciousness and passed away in the hospital.

Chief Sato was transferred the following month.

He was removed from company operations altogether and placed at a management firm that oversaw the company's warehouse space. However, his workplace harassment wasn't the reason for this change.

Sato was kicked out because he got into a fistfight with a senior member of a partner company and injured the man. He was at a reception with the executive director of Midorimura Market, the largest grocery store in the Kanto region, disagreed with the man over something trivial, and attacked him.

Suzui and the other employees weren't told what the "trivial" cause of the argument had been. But Hamada, who attended the event and helped step in to stop the fight, claimed that Sato screamed, "Are you saying I'm wrong?" with bloodshot eyes. "I'm not trying to antagonize you. I want a peaceful resolution. But objectively speaking, I'm obviously correct. Why don't you understand? Don't you realize you're the one talking nonsense? You should realize your mistake."

Suzui wasn't there to hear it, but he could easily envision the scene. He could imagine Sato, his tone confidently righteous, expecting everyone to believe he was correct.

Hamada quietly told Suzui that after Sato attacked the other man he ranted in his usual way, saying, "I knew he was incompetent. I go so far out of my way for him and he has no idea. He's where he is today because I made things easier in my capacity as section chief."

Unable to bear any more of that, Hamada had pleaded, "Sir, we should go back and apologize."

Chief Sato had glared at Hamada and spit, "Oh, so you're incompetent, too! You're a waste of my time. You just don't get it!"

And then he'd promptly made a phone call, right on the spot.

After his wife's passing, Jin took time off from the company. The funeral was held privately, so the company only sent an offering gift. While Jin was away, the department chief and Mutsumi acted swiftly, ordering him not to answer any calls from Chief Sato. Mutsumi said Jin seemed troubled at first, but being told to refuse all contact also made him look very, very relieved.

"Shit!" the chief had raged after making his call. According to Hamada, he'd even slammed his smartphone against the ground. It was pretty clear whom he'd tried to reach.

"Chief," Hamada had said.

Sure enough, Sato had replied, "Why isn't he picking up? That's not supposed to happen."

Sirens had approached quickly. The act of violence had caused the staff at the restaurant hosting the reception to call the police. When Hamada noticed the red police lights nearing, he'd gone pale. The chief had kicked his phone and continued screaming, "Shit! Shit!"

Maybe it's better that it happened this way, Suzui thought.

Relations with Midorimura Market had worsened, and the higher-ups were desperately trying to restore faith. Fortunately, the two sides were able to settle the assault out of court. And best of all, the section chief had clearly crossed a line in a way that would cost him.

Maybe he let his early appointment to a senior position go to his head and went mad from the power. If so, then he was unfit for any sort of management job, just as Suzui believed. Perhaps a move from sales to a place with less personal interaction would be good for him in the long run.

Fortunately for Section Two, the sudden vacuum left by Chief Sato's personnel shift meant that the lead salesperson, Mutsumi, was made the new section chief. The choice might have been made to minimize upheaval and reduce friction with other departments, but it didn't matter. The entire team was delighted to bear witness to the first female sales section chief in Yotsumiya Foods history.

"Um, excuse me… Are you Dr. Shiraishi?"

Suzui whirled around at the unexpected greeting. An elegant-looking woman in her midsixties stood before him. She was rather fashionable, wearing a scarf and tinted glasses. Her dog was on a green leather leash. Perhaps they were on a walk.

Suzui didn't recognize her. Initially, he assumed he'd overheard this woman's conversation with someone else. Then Suzui noticed she was looking at Jin, who stood beside him.

"Huh?" Jin stared at her, taken aback.

Suzui and Jin were returning from the headquarters of a major drugstore chain after delivering a presentation on new frozen goods.

Once Jin returned to work after his wife's funeral, the new section chief, Mutsumi, suggested he go out on location instead of solely being an in-office aide.

"I'm sure he has plenty of experience from his prior workplace, so it will be great to take him along," she'd told Suzui, and he'd agreed. Jin always seemed capable, but he was held in check by Chief Sato. It was a shame that Jin's passivity held him back and deprived the sales team of a good employee.

Thus, in the new regime, Suzui and Jin took many trips out for meetings and presentations as a team, and Suzui was grateful for it. Having an older man like Jin along gave clients a feeling they were being treated with respect and care. Jin's calm, reserved outlines of products attracted senior management to meetings—people who had never attended before.

The little dog circling around the older woman's ankles yapped at Suzui and Jin. "Oh, stop," she scolded quietly before resuming her examination of Jin.

"I knew it!" she exclaimed, patting her palms together with delight. "It's been so many years. Goodness, I was worried for ages after you suddenly quit, wondering where you went. How have you been? I just moved to this area, and I never expected to see you here."

"Umm..."

Jin looked perplexed. His very uncertain reaction caused the excited woman to turn skeptical. She tilted her head in a gesture of confusion.

"Um...*are* you Dr. Shiraishi?"

"No..."

"Oh..."

Doubt became evident on the woman's face. She'd started to avert her eyes in awkward embarrassment when the dog at her feet erupted into barking.

"*Growf!*" it growled. "*Grau! Grau! Grau-grau-grau!*"

Jin gave the old woman an apologetic bow and walked away as she scolded her dog. "Hey! Chiko! Stop that, Chiko!"

Suzui wanted to hurry after Jin, who was removing himself from the situation, but he also felt uncomfortable about ignoring the woman. "I'm sorry," she told him. "Chiko's usually so well-behaved, but she's all worked up about something. I'm sorry to have startled you."

"Er, it's all right," Suzui reassured her. He wondered if Jin was afraid of dogs. "I'm sorry about that. He's a coworker of mine—do you know him from his old job?"

Maybe Jin had pretended he didn't recognize her. He didn't speak about anything before his time at the company. Suzui assumed he'd been in senior management at a large firm and that he chose not to discuss his experiences for a reason.

Once the woman reined in her dog and got it to sit, she replied, "Yes. At least, I thought so, but maybe I was wrong. Do excuse me."

"Was he the president of a company?"

"Pardon? No, a doctor," she said, a bit surprised. "A well-respected practitioner in my area, but the office closed down at some point. It was very disappointing."

The dog was no longer barking, but it wasn't entirely calm, either. It growled lightly, issuing muffled grunts and glaring in Jin's direction.

◆

Suzui eventually found Jin sitting on a park bench a short distance away.

"Jin?" he called.

"Oh." The man looked up. "I'm sorry, Suzui. I'm not very fond of dogs."

"I'm surprised." Suzui chuckled and sat down next to him.

Jin sighed. "I'm sorry for embarrassing us. You were really great, though. The section chief from the other company was really amazed by your presentation. They didn't agree to stock our products, but still, I wish everyone at the company could learn sales pitches from you."

"Huh? Really?" This came as a surprise.

Suzui hadn't gotten any positive feedback during the meeting. The potential client's section chief had looked bored by the presentation. Jin didn't seem at all surprised when the man promptly handed back the details and said, "I don't think we'll be taking this one." Suzui convinced him to keep the sheet, but it could hardly be called a success.

"'Huh? Really,'" Jin parroted, surprised in return. "When you left momentarily with your contact, the clerk said to me, 'With a presentation that clear, you get all the information you need without looking at the sheet. We can't accept an offer now, but I'm sure that when the time comes, we'll be in touch.'"

"Oh, is that why..."

Is that why they didn't need the materials? Suzui had to think on it.

"It helps that you have a very nice voice. I'm sure it makes your presentations clear and memorable," Jin added.

"No way..."

If anything, Jin was the one with the pleasing voice. He cut a fine figure, and he had an actor's gravitas. It was nice to receive compliments from him. However, Suzui wasn't used to this sort of praise, and he could only mumble back, "Thank you."

Jin had met lots of people in his life. The old woman called him by a different name. It was probably just a case of mistaken identity, but it did raise a question: What did Jin do before joining the company?

He's probably led a much richer life than I have and been through a lot, Suzui thought. "I appreciate you saying that...but I already know the truth. I know why they didn't buy that item from us."

Jin watched the younger man carefully and quietly. Suzui pictured the info sheet in his briefcase and admitted the truth.

"I was involved in developing the product we presented today. I worked on it back when I was in the planning department. A spring roll that would stay crispy even at room temperature, specifically for boxed lunches—it was the first item I ever got approved. I would've liked to see it go from planning to development to retail, but..."

A sudden personnel shake-up had sent Suzui to sales instead, cutting off that career path. The product he helped devise was like his baby, the very first thing Suzui ever worked on. He'd hoped that whoever replaced him had seen the project through as he envisioned.

Unfortunately, when he had a chance to taste-test the finished spring roll, Suzui was disappointed. He couldn't tell what made it different from the ones that had come before. When he learned that his suggested manufacturing method wasn't being used, he lost almost all personal attachment, even as a salesman tasked with selling the product.

"It just didn't taste good to me. And when I hear other people claim, 'It's better than before,' I have to assume they're basing that off of nothing but the new packaging. It hurts. I can't in good conscience pitch the qualities of something I don't truly believe is good."

"Suzui," said Jin. Suzui looked up and met Jin's clear gaze. "You poor thing." His voice penetrated deep into Suzui's mind, sonorous and crisp. "You really cared about this item, didn't you? When you say it tastes bad, it tells me that the ordeal must have really hurt you."

Oh, Suzui thought. Jin stared him right in the eyes.

"You thought really, really hard about this product. I'm sure that came across to our clients during the sales pitch."

"You...think so?"

"Yes. I do," Jin replied.

Something warm spread through Suzui's chest. It felt like a part of his true thoughts, a piece even he'd never noticed, was being recognized and affirmed.

Jin stood from the bench. "We should get moving. The section chief will scold us again if we're not back at the office on time."

"Good idea," Suzui said, grimacing.

A little time had passed since Suzui went from calling her "Mutsumi" to "Section Chief." Initially, she'd said that people could use whatever name they were used to, but everyone was so pleased with her promotion that they intentionally called her "Chief" to help make it official. Suzui wasn't accustomed to it yet. He was still adapting to the new chief's regulations as well, particularly the observance of work hours.

Mutsumi had a child and a family, and she always left on time. If you wanted to tell her something, you had to do it during regular work hours. She even begged employees to cut down on overtime and business meals with client companies. None of it was mandatory, she simply expressed a vague displeasure about it all, which Suzui found irksome.

At some point, he began to think, *It's easy for you, since you always go home right on time.* Most work time in a sales position was spent out of the office. Mutsumi had been in this division long enough to know that clerical tasks could only be finished once you returned from meetings. However, she felt bad for leaving early despite being the boss, so she forced her schedule on everyone else.

She used her child as an excuse to escape, but as a leader, her job was to stick around after hours while others completed their responsibilities.

"Um, Jin," Suzui called hesitantly. He'd been wondering if he ought to say anything for the last few days. Now that they were safe outside the office, it seemed as good a time as any. "Is it just me, or has the chief been kind of hard on you recently?"

"Jin? Excuse me, Jin? What do you think of this? This should be fine, right?"

Recently, it had become obvious that the section chief relied on Jin, the oldest employee, more than anyone else. That was standard to a degree, but her demands had become excessive.

What concerned Suzui most of all was a comment he heard in passing out in the hallway recently.

"I was counting on you! I only told you because I thought you could handle it!"

The comment gave Suzui déjà vu. It was very concerning. But he trusted that Mutsumi would handle it better than someone else had.

"It's nothing to worry about," Jin assured him, grinning and shaking his head. His voice was as gentle and kind as could be.

"But...," Suzui protested.

"It's just the nature of our relationship."

"Huh?"

"It's not really her fault. She acts that way because of how things are between us. Really, it's fine."

"It is?"

Jin had no obligation to defend the chief, and Suzui told him as much, yet the older man remained adamant.

"It's not her fault."

"Maybe it's because you're too nice to her."

"You think so...?" Jin stared down at Suzui.

Dusk was coming.

The setting sun was more orange than before, and Jin's face became too dark to make out when rimmed by the glow. A long, narrow shadow extended from his feet.

"Everyone has words they long to hear," Jin began abruptly. His voice was so gentle.

"Huh?"

"They want people to say things to them like 'It's not your fault.' They hunger for others to tell them, 'You did the right thing.' And when you satisfy that for them, they'll relinquish anything you want to know. They place themselves in your hands."

Yes. He was right.

That's why everyone relied on Jin—the current chief and the previous one.

The current chief said the previous one had had a dependency problem with Jin. She was right. Other than Jin, the last boss had no one to accept and support him. Sato indulged in Jin's approval, telling his superiors, subordinates, and even partner companies that he was always right. He became incapable of acting any way but superior.

It was wrong.

I want Jin to hear what I have to say, they'd think. And whatever it was, no matter how selfish or abusive, Jin took it all in like a black hole. He never criticized anyone. He never pushed people away or told them they were being repulsive.

Telling the previous chief those things might have been better for him. But Jin couldn't because he was too kind.

It's their fault. They don't speak to him like an equal, Suzui reasoned. *When Jin listens to me, we're on an equal footing; it's an actual conversation. But the section chiefs just blab at him nonstop. How can they keep talking about the most inconsequential things?*

Mutsumi had raised this same complaint to Sato, so she ought to understand. Her falling into the same kind of relationship with Jin would be terribly ironic.

Mutsumi and Sato probably operated under the same mistaken assumption that Jin actually liked them. All he did was agree. In that sense, the section chiefs were kind of pitiful.

"Let's go. We need to hurry," Jin said. His face was still dark from the sun at his back. Suzui could discern only the frames of Jin's glasses.

As he examined what little detail there was, Suzui couldn't help but wonder, *Did his face always look like that? What does he actually look like, again?*

"Speaking of presentations and explanations, I think Section Chief Maruyama is quite capable at them, too. Her skills differ from yours, of course, but she can instantly recognize when people have trouble understanding, then addresses it with pinpoint accuracy."

"Oh... Really?"

Something clicked into place in Suzui's mind.

Aha. I see. Jin's never been in the planning department, so he doesn't know. Frustration surfaced in Suzui, and he had to dispel it.

"Sure, she seems capable of explaining things, but it's only because she doesn't understand the products. For example, knowing all the ingredients in an item means I know what not to say. Someone with a sales-only background might say anything to close the deal, which could cause issues later down the line."

"What? Is that true?"

"Yes, it's true. There are things I never say, specifically because I know them to be true."

"I see, I see." Jin nodded deeply. Although the sun behind him still masked his features, Suzui could tell he was smiling. "That must be why your presentations are so honest and forthright. Well, I can't wait to see where you wind up. Whether you get sent back to planning or continue to rise in sales, I'm positive you'll become one of the company's elite workers."

"Oh, I'm really not that special..."

Behind Suzui's protest, his heart grew soft and warm. He regretted speaking ill of the section chief in Jin's presence, though.

Jin was amazing. He hadn't agreed with the insult or completely taken Suzui's side, and he'd still managed to move the conversation forward without criticizing or contradicting anyone.

"Let's go, Jin— Oh!" Suzui stopped as he got to his feet. Looking sheepish, he said, "The chief's going to scold me if I keep calling you Jin all the time."

It was Chief Sato who'd started calling him Jin around the office, claiming that it would help the much older man fit in with the rest of the team. Suzui thought it was stupid. A single nickname wasn't going to make someone popular automatically. And Chief Maruyama had already made her opinion on the matter known.

"It's not good for us to call him Jin forever."

It seemed silly to try removing the nickname long after it had stuck, and Suzui was annoyed with the chief's micromanagement. *You've got the same values as the last guy. You're just as old-fashioned as he was.*

"Come on, Mr. Kanbara, let's go," Suzui said. Kanbara turned slowly, pointing his back away from the setting sun, which restored contour to his profile. His expression was visible again.

"It's fine, you can continue calling me Jin," he replied.

"Kan just sounds a bit awkward. What if we call you Jin instead?" the previous section chief had suggested with a laugh. That was how he'd come up with the nickname, by changing the reading of the first kanji in *Kanbara* to its alternate form. The memory of that moment made Suzui feel strange. He never liked Sato's laugh, but considering how nasty and snide he became, the idea that he could chuckle at all felt distant. It nearly seemed fake. How was that ever the case?

Kanbara took a step in front of Suzui. "I'm very, very lucky to have the chance to work with you, Suzui," he stated. "I don't know anything about the planning division, so I'm sure I'll learn a lot from you. You're good at sales presentations and teaching people."

If only he were the section chief instead, Suzui mused. *Rather than a chief who goes home right on the hour, we could have someone who's the proper age for the position and pays attention to my strengths. It should be him.*

The setting sun was such a beautiful color. Suzui peered down at his feet and the shadow that extended sharply behind him. Then he took a step forward while watching his own shadow.

Beside him, Kanbara's silhouette stretched, growing longer and longer still. It wavered, too, yet no one around them noticed.

CHAPTER FOUR

Group Leader

It all started when he came to the class, Sota thought.

Before he showed up, Class 5-2 at Kusumichi Elementary had revolved around Toranosuke Nakao. Both of Toranosuke's parents were lawyers, and he'd maintained excellent grades and fulfilled every expectation set by adults since the first grade.

"*Just what I'd expect from the son of two lawyers.*"

"*Just what I'd expect from such an education-focused mother.*"

Toranosuke's mom was famous at the school for being extremely dedicated to her boy's tutelage. She was proactive around the school, a PTA committee member every year, and she acted as a sort of leader for whatever grade Toranosuke was in. The other moms always contacted her. Sota's mom often remarked how amazing it was that the woman did so much for her child despite having a job.

Toranosuke was an unquestionably excellent student. He was also tall, large, strong, and good at sports.

However, Sota didn't care much for Toranosuke. And many classmates who got along with Toranosuke shared that sentiment, even if they refused to admit it.

He was a bossy, violent braggart.

Since he was better in class and outside, he assumed he was the most important kid of all.

"I've already done all of this stuff at cram school, so things here feel really dumb to me," he repeated constantly. He often didn't finish his homework and forgot to bring textbooks and other supplies. "There's no point in reading my textbook," he'd say. If someone in class forgot their book, the person sitting next to them had to share, meaning Toranosuke constantly made things harder for kids near him. Sure, he did excellently on tests, but he was a real slob in terms of personal habits.

On top of that, he was a fickle sort, given to unpredictable moods. He would hit and kick people out of nowhere. It didn't matter if you had done nothing to deserve it.

Sota had been kicked several times himself.

It was a frequent occurrence; usually, there was nothing to do but suck it up. Last year, however, Toranosuke had been angry over something and punted a chair that was on top of a desk during floor cleaning. Sota happened to be passing by, and the chair landed on top of him. It banged against his knee, which turned an ugly shade of red.

That became an actual issue. Sota's mom came to the school and had a lengthy discussion with his teacher. Apparently, the teacher apologized for the injury.

But Toranosuke had never said sorry to Sota for hurting him. He was clearly grumpy as the teacher scolded him, pouting magnificently while silently leaning against the wall.

The teacher had talked to Toranosuke for a long while, yet the boy had never apologized. He'd just stuck to his guns, insisting, "It wasn't on purpose."

The teacher had promised Sota and his mom that she would visit Toranosuke's mom and have a discussion at her home.

The morning after the incident, Toranosuke held up a smartphone and told Sota, "Hey, did you know your mom sent my mom this?" All the other kids had special children's cell phones. Toranosuke, who had a smartphone of his own, liked to boast, "What, you guys are still using those baby things?" No one was allowed to bring a smartphone to school, but that didn't stop him.

Sota's knee had recovered after a day, but it was still tender enough that it hurt when pressed hard. The parts that had been red were starting to bruise up.

Toranosuke kept the screen pointed at Sota. Unable to resist the silent pressure to look, he finally took it and saw the LINE app on the screen. Sota didn't have his own phone, but he'd seen his mom use LINE a few times before.

At the top were the words *Sota's Mom (Sachiko)*. The body contained a screenshot of a message Sota's mom had sent to Toranosuke's mom.

To Toranosuke's Mom:

I'm sorry to contact you out of the blue. I'm sure you're busy.

The school just called me to pick up Sota. They said that Toranosuke kicked a chair in the classroom, and it hit my son's leg. He wasn't hurt very badly, and Sota seems to be doing fine, but you should hear from the school soon, and I thought to let you know first so it wouldn't be a surprise.

When I went to the school, I saw Toranosuke, too. I know he wouldn't do something like that for no reason, and that he's a very smart boy, so I asked him, "Why did you kick the chair?" And he said, "I don't know."

I asked, "Really? Well, I care about Sota, and I care about you. I don't want either of you to get hurt, so please be careful." I wonder what happened with Toranosuke? Sota cares about Toranosuke, too. I hope they remain good friends. Thank you.

Below that was the reply from Toranosuke's mom. It was much shorter than Sota's mom's text, just two brief messages.

* * *

No way! I'm sooo sorry. Did Toranosuke really do that, Sachiko?

Thanks for letting me know. I just got word from the school, so I'll head over.

That was all that was on the screen.

Sota felt at a total loss. He returned the phone to Toranosuke, totally uncertain how he was supposed to react. Toranosuke just smirked at him.

"Your mom's kinda freaky, huh?" He grinned even larger than before. "My mom showed this to my dad last night. She was like, 'Look what Toranosuke did,' and I got yelled at. But they also said, 'Who sends an essay like this out of nowhere? What a freak. It's scary.'"

Sota envisioned his mother's face.

She'd examined his reddened knee the day before and asked, "Are you all right, Sota?" Again and again, she said, "Are you sure you don't need to see the doctor?" to which he replied that he was fine. She took a cold pack from the fridge and wrapped it in a towel to place on his knee. Sota recalled the feeling of her hand on his skin, and his ears went red.

His mom had written that message for Toranosuke's mom. He remembered her fiddling with her phone on the way back home, but he'd assumed at the time that she was telling his dad about what had happened.

Sota was too young to be familiar with the word *essay*, but he understood the implication. A message that was too long. *"Freak." "Scary."*

What was he supposed to say? To feel? One thing was very clear: Toranosuke would never apologize, and his parents had made fun of Sota's mom. And him.

The very long and polite *"essay"* that Sota's mom had typed out had earned nothing but a line or two of text in answer.

Now it sounded like his mom was the one with the problem. What did this mean? *Mom must have known that I don't like Toranosuke. She wrote "Sota cares about Toranosuke, too," just to make his mom feel better. So why did they say that about her? It hurts.*

Why? Because Toranosuke's mom was on the PTA, and that kind of made her the boss of all the other moms? That didn't give her the right.

And why had Toranosuke shown this to him? It was as if he were bragging. Had Toranosuke's mom let him take that picture from her screen?

It hurts, it hurts, it hurts.

When the teacher showed up that day, Toranosuke hid his phone and gave Sota a very hollow, "I'm sorry for yesterday."

The teacher was pleased, and told Sota, "There. Toranosuke spoke with his parents and has learned his lesson. It's time for you to forgive him, Sota."

After that, they had to turn in papers about friendship for Japanese class. Toranosuke wrote, *I hate people who pick on their friends. People who pick on their friends are evil. I've heard that people who stop bullying get targeted by the evil bullies. But I want to be the one who stops the bullying. I want to help my classmates.*

Despite the pain and frustration, Sota couldn't say a thing about that ridiculous paper. All he could do was remind himself to keep far away from Toranosuke.

Not long after that, Niko Kanbara joined the class.

The name Niko sounded like a girl's, but the child introduced up by the blackboard next to the teacher's desk was a small, skinny boy with glasses.

"My mother and father gave me the name Niko as a shortened version of *nikkori*, or 'smile.' You can just call me Niko. It's nice to meet you all," he said, bowing politely.

Maybe he was teased for the name at his old school. The boy with glasses proved to be a diligent student who got good grades and an avid reader who often visited the library during lunch break and after school. Sota's mom told him that his mother enjoyed books, too. She was a member of the school's story time committee.

"Niko's mother is rather strange, giving her son that distinct name. I wonder if that family has a lot of quirks," she said.

Sota's mom wasn't part of the story time committee, but she'd heard about Niko's mom from an acquaintance who was. She didn't explain what exactly made Niko's mom *"strange,"* though. Instead, she asked Sota, "Is Niko a little odd sometimes?"

"Umm. Well, he's smart and responsible, and sometimes he talks a little funny, I guess."

All those books he read gave him a more grown-up vocabulary.

Sota's mom hummed. "Has anything happened between you and Toranosuke?"

"Not really."

"You're in the same group in class, right?"

"Yeah. So is Niko. Niko's the group leader," Sota replied.

His mom made it sound incidental, but he felt she was more concerned about Toranosuke than Niko. She'd never admit it, but she clearly didn't want Toranosuke involved with her son.

"I see," she said breezily, conveying that she wasn't concerned. And then, truly incidentally this time, she added, "I hope you get to be good friends with Niko."

The next day, Niko stopped before the chart of flower-circle stickers at the back of the classroom.

"What are these, Sota?" he questioned.

Sota was on cleaning duty, sweeping the floor nearby with a broom. "Oh, those are flower-circle stickers. If nobody in your group forgets anything, or you answer lots of the teacher's questions during class, the teacher will give your team one."

There were rows for each group, one through six, with stickers lined up next to them. Despite being called "flower circles," they were just regular red dots. Everyone did their best to get as many as possible, but there wasn't any prize for having them. The first-place group didn't get a special award. However, the competition got everyone fired up, and the kids did their best to win, if only to avoid losing to the other groups.

"Our group doesn't have many stickers," Niko noted, eyeing Group Five's standing.

Sota nodded. Of course they didn't. "It's because we have Toranosuke."

"Is having him a problem of some kind?" asked Niko. If anything about this boy was strange, it was his precise way of speaking.

Sota looked around to make sure Toranosuke and his buddies weren't around. "Toranosuke forgets stuff all the time. And he never does his homework. He's smart, so he answers a lot of questions in class and wins points that way. But there was a time when he raised his hand, and the teacher asked someone else. He whined, 'It's favoritism!' and caused a fuss. Since then, he's been sulking and refuses to raise his hand in class."

"Huh," Niko remarked. He pushed his glasses up. "So you're saying this is a system designed to incentivize following the rules, healthy expression during lessons, and general improvement among the entire class?"

"Y-yes. I think so."

Sota replied in the affirmative, but the truth was, he hadn't known all that. *Oh, okay, I guess that's what these stickers are supposed to do.* Sota had been so focused on the competition that he never considered there was a point to it.

"Interesting, interesting." Niko bobbed his head. He stared at the sheet on the wall. "This has been most informative. Thank you."

Soon after, Sota realized just how strange Niko was.

Everyone either became one of Toranosuke's entourage and did whatever he said or did their best to avoid him, like Sota. However, Niko started policing him instead.

For example, when Toranosuke forgot his eraser or ruler, he would turn to Niko to borrow it because they sat beside each other. Sota and others would have thought *Ugh* or *Not again* before reluctantly lending the item. Niko was different, though. When Toranosuke reached for the other boy's eraser in the middle of class, Niko stated, "You can't have it," in a loud voice that carried. "That won't do you any good. And I don't like people repeatedly borrowing my things."

It startled Toranosuke. He wasn't used to being told off right to his face, and it proved so stunning he forgot to sulk.

The teacher was surprised, too, but soon looked relieved. "That's right, Toranosuke. You need to remember to bring your own."

Niko didn't stop there, though. At the class meeting before the end of the day, he suggested, "We shouldn't lend things to anyone who forgets them. Today I refused to give Toranosuke my eraser, but it doesn't just have to be him. Lending people objects when they forget them doesn't help. They need to regret their actions to learn they're better off remembering next time."

Everyone applauded him. The kids were sick of Toranosuke's slovenly nature.

Toranosuke grinned like he always did, despite the clapping. "Well, I don't really mind that sort of thing," he muttered. "I don't need to borrow your stuff, because I can still study just fine. You guys and the teacher are the ones with the real problem."

Toranosuke's forgetfulness never improved, but he stopped asking to borrow stuff from his seat neighbors. When the teacher grew concerned that Toranosuke wasn't reading his textbook and said, "Please follow along using your neighbor's," Toranosuke loudly replied, "Nobody will let me see. It's for my own good." He made it sound extra snotty. It was an obvious jab at Niko.

When the class split up for group projects, he announced, "Nobody will lend me their scissors, so it's okay if I don't do this, right?" and started scribbling on his own for fun.

Niko just watched the entire time.

*   *   *

Sometime after that, Toranosuke's mother messaged the other moms with kids in the class.

"Hey, Sota, I heard that new transfer student is going to Toranosuke's house every day. Do you know anything about that?" his mother asked.

"Huh?"

He didn't know what she was talking about. Niko was going...to Toranosuke's place?

"He walks home with Toranosuke every single day and won't leave until Toranosuke's finished his homework and packed for school the next day. If Toranosuke tries to leave alone, Niko manages to find him."

"Every single day?"

"That's what it sounds like."

If Sota's mom was surprised by this, so was Sota.

He realized that Toranosuke had been doing his homework for the last few days. And he hadn't been scolded for forgetting things, either. Group Five's total flower-circle stickers were increasing.

Sota's mom looked confused. "She said that on days Toranosuke has cram school, Niko comes over right when Toranosuke returns. She warned him that it was too late for a boy to be out, but I guess Niko told her, 'It's fine. I came with a parent.' He must be getting a ride from his mother or father."

"Well, Toranosuke does forget stuff all the time. And Niko's the group leader," Sota explained. He told his mom about what had happened at school—the flower-circle stickers and Niko's refusal to lend Toranosuke anything. But even after his explanation, his mom looked troubled.

"But... Why would he go so far?"

"Uh, because Toranosuke forgets stuff all the time and causes problems for everyone."

"Yes, I get that, but this is a little much, don't you think? Going to his house every day to make sure he fulfills his responsibilities? And getting a ride from his parents? I can't imagine Toranosuke's family is thrilled about it."

"But..."

Sota agreed, but it was Toranosuke's fault. Sure, Niko was a bit excessive, but he was doing the right thing.

"Toranosuke's mom called it scary."

Scary...

That word pricked at Sota's memory.

"Who sends an essay like this out of nowhere? What a freak. It's scary."

"He's not scary," Sato found himself saying. "Toranosuke's doing his homework and remembering everything. Before, our group wasn't getting any stickers, but now we're doing much better."

It wasn't Niko's fault.

The boy had a strong drive to set things right. That was all. Nobody stood up to Toranosuke before, and Niko was laudable for doing so.

"Is that right? It makes me wonder what Niko's parents are like, though. Their son goes out late at night, and they encourage it."

"Didn't you say Niko's mom's kind of weird?"

"According to Toranosuke's mom, more than a little. She even told Niko's mother off. She said, 'This is a real problem for us.' But Niko's mom just smiled and answered, 'That's right. Me too.' When she yelled at his dad, he apologized and said, 'I see. I'm sorry,' without scolding his son. It sounds like both of his parents are total weirdos."

At some point, "more than a little strange" had become "total weirdos." Sota hummed to himself and nodded.

The next day at school, Sota asked Niko, "Do you go over to Toranosuke's house?"

Without an ounce of hesitation, he replied, "Yep. It's not good for the class to be sloppy."

Sota looked over at Toranosuke's seat. The boy was silent, and he never looked in their direction. He carved nicks in his desk with a razor, evidently irritated. His usual smirk had vanished.

There was an unannounced group change that day.

"We're starting first period with a change of plans. It's time to switch groups," the teacher announced, to the class's surprise. It was right in the middle of the school term.

Sota happened to be watching Toranosuke when the news broke. He leaned disinterestedly over his desk, but there was a faint hint of a smile on his lips.

Maybe Toranosuke's parents asked for this to get him away from Niko.

After the change, Niko and Toranosuke were in different groups, and Sota wasn't with either of them. The chart with all the flower-circle stickers was taken down, but a new one was not put up in its place.

It seems kind of babyish, but that's that, Sota thought. *Maybe Toranosuke's learned his lesson, and he'll be better from now on.*

However, all was not well.

One day, Sota's mom said to him, "Listen, sweetie, can you do something for me?"

"What?"

"Toranosuke's mom asked me if you would give Niko a warning for them. Can you do that?"

"A warning about what?"

"Remember what I said before? About how Niko visits Toranosuke's house like he's on guard duty, making sure Toranosuke does his homework and brings all of his things to school?"

"Wow, really? He's still doing that? They're in different groups now."

The term *"guard duty"* was new, but it was understandable that Toranosuke's family felt like they were being watched.

Initially, it seemed that Niko was doing this because he was the group leader and wanted more stickers. However, Niko had also claimed it was for the good of the class. Maybe he had never cared about the competition.

"But why's she asking you to do that, Mom? I thought Toranosuke's mom was closer to Yuichiro's and Go's moms."

Yuichiro and Go were good friends of Toranosuke's and acted as his henchmen. The three had been in the same group since the switch, and Sota suspected that Toranosuke's mom had requested the teacher set it up that way. All three of their mothers were close friends, regularly attending school events together. Sota's mom seemed very careful about how she interacted with them, as exemplified by the message she'd sent. The one Toranosuke had shown Sota.

His mother shook her head.

"Actually, Niko's not the only one standing watch anymore. Yuichiro and Go are doing it as well. It's like they have a system for who goes each day."

"What?!" Sota exclaimed. This was a real shock.

"There are girls helping, too—Yuki and Rinko. Toranosuke's mom asked their parents to get them to stop, but they all say, 'This is how it works,' or 'It's for the good of the class.' They won't listen."

All those names were from Group Two, Toranosuke's group. Sota wasn't involved with him anymore, so he hadn't realized this was going on.

His mom sighed. "Toranosuke's mother thinks Niko's ordering the children to do it. So will you tell him he's going too far, Sota?"

Sota could definitely imagine Niko doing that. He'd probably said, "You're all in the group together, so you guys have to help keep an eye on him."

Before Sota could reply, the phone on the table buzzed. Sota saw *Toranosuke's Mom* on the screen.

Originally, Sota's and Toranosuke's mothers had only traded messages on LINE, but it had since escalated to phone calls, frequent ones at that. Sometimes they came late at night or during dinner, and Sota's mom often tried to wrap them up quickly. His dad seemed worried, too.

On several occasions, he'd grumbled, *Is it from that lady again? Can't you just hang up on her?*

Sota had wondered what was so important that they had to talk about it all the time. Now he had the answer.

His mother pulled the phone close to hide it, like a dirty secret, and sighed again.

"Do you understand, Sota? Please, I'm asking you."

If she was asking Sota for help, she must have already tried speaking with the other kids' mothers. Maybe Sota's mom wasn't the only one Toranosuke's mom regularly called for help. When his mother pressed the phone to her ear, Sota heard the voice on the other side say, "Do you have a moment?"

Sota was watching TV in the living room with the volume set low, but Toranosuke's mom's voice was so loud that he heard everything perfectly.

"I think I'm going neurotic! No one's on my side!"

Each hysterical statement sent bolts of horror through him. In between two such panicked utterings, Sota's mom managed to interrupt with "I'm sorry, but I've got to start working on dinner" and end the call.

Even when she took the phone away from her face to press the button on the screen, the voice continued squawking from the speaker.

Sota's dad got home after that. From when Sota got out of the bath to when he went to bed, his mom's phone kept buzzing. She never answered, though, only exhaled and watched it.

"You're not going to pick up?" Sota inquired while drying his hair.

"Mm," his mother responded uncomfortably. "It's time for bed now."

She pulled the vibrating phone close to her chest so Sota wouldn't see.

* * *

Toranosuke did his homework every day.

He stopped forgetting to bring things. If he kicked something for no reason, or got violent against his friends, there was a class meeting after school, and someone raised their hand to call out his transgression.

"Toranosuke, you kicked the wall in the hallway today. Why did you do that?"

"When you were on cleaning duty, you threw the broom. Why did you do that?"

They all spoke with Niko's mature tone.

At first, Toranosuke gave mocking or silly answers, like "Because I was angry" or "I didn't do nothin'," but they wouldn't let up.

"Being angry doesn't change what's right and wrong."

"You can't say you didn't do it. We all saw you."

They didn't just accuse him or point out bad behavior. They all pressed him on the why and demanded answers. No one accepted a facetious "Yeah, yeah, I'm sorry," as good enough.

"If you're sorry, what do you think you should have done?" they asked, cornering him. When he fell silent, looking thoroughly displeased, a different person raised their hand to speak.

"If you're feeling angry, I think you should hit your own head. How about if you punch and kick yourself instead?"

Toranosuke didn't know what to say. His eyes shot wide.

The girl who offered the suggestion, Yuki—a fellow member of his group—was not being snide or sarcastic. It sounded as though she was giving a very straightforward opinion.

And then the room erupted.

The class burst into cheers. "Yeah! Yeah!" Sota was stunned. Toranosuke looked to the blackboard, mouth agape. Sota glanced at Niko. Things had gotten weird after he showed up. Sota expected Niko to look smug and pleased with the influence he wielded, yet what he actually saw caused him to gasp.

Niko was totally expressionless. He observed the scene quietly.

The class was in a swell of excitement all around him, but he stood placidly, as though uninvolved. He was totally disinterested.

The kids wrote on the blackboard, *If you get angry, punch your own head.* They treated this very seriously.

It was at that point that an old paragraph popped into Sota's head.

"People who pick on their friends are evil. I've heard that people who stop bullying get targeted by the evil bullies. But I want to be the one who stops the bullying. I want to help my classmates."

For a moment, he wasn't sure how he knew the words, but then he remembered they came from Toranosuke's paper. It was the one that had been so frustrating to listen to because Toranosuke clearly didn't believe a word of it.

What had brought it to mind now? Sota couldn't get that paragraph out of his head for whatever reason.

Toranosuke hung his head, and his classmates cheered and shouted all around him. Sota was rooted to the spot.

"I can't believe it," his mother said to Rinko's mom while they were on the way home.

Sota and his mother had finished grocery shopping and run into his classmate Rinko's mom on the way back. While the two women stood and chatted, Sota pretended to play in the nearby park alone, all the while actually listening to the conversation.

"I can't believe it. Did you know that the Nakaos are actually really close to Niko's mom now? I was shocked when I heard."

Nakao was Toranosuke's last name. They were talking about his parents.

"That's right. I saw them together, but I didn't know it was Niko's mother. I didn't even realize she was someone's parent at first. She seems, I don't know, a little too old? Like a grandma, or a housekeeper. But then Niko followed her. What a shock it was to realize she's his mother."

Toranosuke remembered everything these days. He did his homework, took his classes seriously, and never hit his classmates. But it was all because whenever he snapped and started to swing a fist, the entire class turned to him and shouted, "You're going to hit your own head!"

Sota heard that phrase many times after the class meeting, and then he didn't hear it at all. Toranosuke mended his ways and stopped causing problems. He was like a different person altogether. He no longer spoke to anyone in class.

"You know what Mrs. Nakao said to me when we met at the last parents' meeting?" Sota's mom whispered. "She said, 'Since none of you will listen to me, the only people I can rely on anymore are the Kanbaras!' I was kind of worried. She didn't seem right."

"I know what you mean. She's gotten really thin. When I saw her, she had no makeup on, and her hair was all scraggly. Before, you could tell she was a working woman, because she had everything perfectly in line. Last time I saw her, she wore this dirty apron, and standing next to Niko's mom, they nearly looked identical. I was like, 'What happened to you?' I'm concerned."

For all their talk about worries, the two moms chatted for a while. To Sota, it sounded as though they enjoyed themselves. Perhaps it was his imagination, but it seemed like they could have gone on even longer.

Orange sunset fell upon the street around them, making the shadows coming from the two women's feet darker, longer, wavering.

Things felt different in class.

"Hey, Sota. Kana's been forgetting her things lately. Since you're in her group, could you help her out?" Niko said to him one day. Sota felt something cold trickle down his back, and he knew why.

Kana was Sota's seat neighbor and group partner. She hadn't been doing her homework recently. Her concentration was poor, and she forgot to bring things to school. When Sota had asked her what was wrong, she'd explained that her mother was in the hospital, and she was really busy taking care of her little brother and sister and getting them ready for kindergarten. It kept her up late, meaning she was exhausted in class. Sota didn't think it was a lie.

For some reason, Sota had found himself thinking, *This is bad*. He'd recalled the toothless version of Toranosuke after the class defanged him, and the way they'd cheered at that class meeting after berating him.

"Do you want to see mine?" he'd offered, showing Kana his homework. After that, Sota let her copy from him every morning before Niko showed up.

When Sota replied to Niko, his voice came out a bit hoarse. "Kana's mom is in the hospital. Her brother and sister are too little to take care of themselves, so she has to help."

"Uh-huh."

"It's only her dad at home, so it's tough. She has to pitch in around the house and goes to bed really late."

"I see. I lost my older brother while at my previous school, and that was really challenging."

Sota almost gasped at that remark. The way Niko spoke of the event with so little inflection and interest was hard to believe. Did *lost my brother* mean that his brother died? In an accident or at the hospital? Did that have something to do with Niko transferring here?

So many questions popped into Sota's head, but he didn't know which, if any, were safe to ask. Instead, he just stared at Niko, who added, "But so what?"

His eyes were as clear as marbles, without a speck of cloudiness in them.

"What does that have to do with failing to finish her homework and forgetting to bring things to school? If Kana's having trouble, why don't you go to her house to help her?"

"Help…?"

"Yes, help. I'll go with you, if you want."

"Umm…"

"The sticker chart's coming back, after all."

"Huh?"

Sota glanced toward the back of the room. There was a new chart where the old flower-circle sticker one had been, fresh and blank.

Sota looked uncertainly at Niko. The other boy said, "It's such a helpful system for the good of the class. It would be a shame to lose out on it forever."

His gaze was impossible to read.

And that was when Sota had a major realization.

Despite being named after the word for *smile*, Niko never actually smiled, as far as Sota could tell.

Unsure of whether to go to Kana's house—or of what his mom would say if he told her—Sota walked the route back home in an uncertain daze, and he spotted Toranosuke sitting on a park bench along the way.

He was no longer larger than life, as he had been. In fact, he literally appeared smaller now. He was hunched, shoulders drooped, on the bench all alone. Sota couldn't help but call to him.

"Toranosuke?"

Toranosuke's reaction was muted. He looked up slowly, his recognition delayed, then scooted over a bit without a word. Sota took that as a sign that he could sit down.

They were both silent for a while.

Sota was unsure what to say, but he felt there was something he ought to ask. "Are Niko and the others still showing up at your house?"

Toranosuke glared at him with baleful eyes. "They're not," he said. "They don't come. They're probably not worried that I'll forget anything anymore. My mom's lonely now that they don't visit, though."

"Lonely?"

"She thinks the rest of the class abandoned me, that ignoring me is a form of bullying, and that none of the parents will listen to her problems. Niko doesn't come, but sometimes his parents do. They say things like, 'We're so jealous of you, Mrs. Nakao,' and, 'Mrs. Sawatari is nothing compared to you,' and stuff like that."

"Sawatari?"

"The mom of the sixth-grade student chairman. She's the owner or designer or whatever of that huge apartment complex near the school. Hilarious, right?"

Toranosuke laughed. It didn't sound convincing.

"My mom's always felt like his mom's her rival. She tells my dad, 'Oh, she's in a magazine. She thinks she's so special, but I never liked her.' Now my mom's obsessed with talking to Niko's mom and repeating all of the same insults to her. She's on the phone all the time."

"I hate it when moms do that," Sota offered. He wasn't sure what he could give in reply to Toranosuke, but the way his mother talked with other women on the way home from the grocery store seemed like a common annoyance they could bond over.

However, Toranosuke seemed taken aback by this. Sota had only meant that he understood the feeling, yet Toranosuke responded, "No, it's not just my mom."

"Huh?"

"My dad does, too. My dad talks to Niko's dad about all kinds of stuff, like his useless employees at work, and sometimes he says the same stuff as Mom, about how much he hates the dad who designed Sawatari Apartments. On and on and on."

His dad, too? Sota had nothing to add there. He was at a loss.

Toranosuke grew weary as he explained. "He said someone should die at that apartment complex. Then there would be all kinds of bad rumors, and the real estate value would drop."

Sota didn't know what "*real estate value*" meant, and he assumed Toranosuke didn't, either. When adults used strange words, it made you curious, and you wanted to use them in front of your classmates, even if you had only a vague idea of their meaning.

But what about Niko?

The way Niko spoke, it didn't sound like he was mimicking someone else. He chose every word carefully. What kind of childhood did he have to have turned out that way?

"…Want to hang out the next day off school?" Sota asked before he realized what he was doing. Toranosuke seemed surprised, and he regarded Sota in a way he hadn't before.

Sota grinned a little. "I still can't do a handstand. You could do that in first grade, right? Can you teach me how?"

"…Okay."

Toranosuke's reply almost sounded like he was asking, "Is that okay?" He'd been behaving himself ever since that class meeting, but no one played with him anymore. Even Yuichiro and Go, his best buddies, acted like they'd never been friends with him.

Sota recalled Toranosuke's paper once again.

"*I've heard that people who stop bullying get targeted by the evil bullies. But I want to be the one who stops the bullying. I want to help my classmates.*"

Toranosuke was a real jerk, and Sota hated him—but he agreed with that.

They were supposed to play together on the next day off school.

However, Sota and Toranosuke never got to fulfill that promise.

The following morning, Toranosuke's mom jumped from Sawatari Apartments.

The apartment complex that her rival, the mother of the student chairman, had designed. Toranosuke's mom didn't live there, but the stairwell was accessible to anyone, so she climbed to a high floor, jumped off, and died.

Toranosuke was pulled out of school by the vice principal that day, and he didn't come back.

The homeroom teacher followed him, so Sota's class was tasked with self-study for the rest of the period.

Normally, kids descended into chaos and mischief without adults around, yet they all sensed the wrongness in the air, and no one misbehaved. They worked on the printouts they were given in obedient silence.

Even without what had happened with Toranosuke, no one in the class was likely to get into trouble anyway.

Niko was there.

Not a single student did anything childish or unworthy of a flower-circle sticker anymore.

After that, many things happened in Class 5-2. Almost too many to count.

Toranosuke was dead.

From what the moms were saying, after his mother's suicide, Toranosuke went to be with his grandma. Then, suddenly, his dad went to get him. It was difficult for Sota to understand what this meant, but the police had questioned Toranosuke's father about what had happened to his mother. Supposedly there was possible "foul play" involved in her death.

After picking up Toranosuke from his grandma's house, his dad drove back to this area and got into a traffic accident. He went straight through the red light, as though he were trying to hit the other car.

Toranosuke and his dad both perished.

The police investigated the accident, too, but nothing was confirmed yet, so the teacher told everyone not to talk about it with anyone.

Nobody in the class could speak up. The only exception was a group of girls who asked if there would be a funeral, but the teacher only replied, "I don't know." Her voice was frail. Perhaps this experience had weakened her spirit.

Toranosuke was gone.

He'd never come back.

It sounded like a story from some far-off place Sota would never visit. He couldn't believe it was real.

Niko's suggestions continued. He said kids should take turns going to Kana's house to "help" her stop being so forgetful.

Sota thought they were done doing that sort of thing, so he was shocked when Niko asked him, "Aren't you going?"

"Um, but after what happened to Toranosuke…," he protested weakly.

Niko looked nonplussed. His expression suggested he didn't understand what Sota was getting at.

"What does that have to do with anything?"

Sota couldn't muster any further comment.

The same thing happened in the other groups in the class.

Ryohei, who slacked off on his cleaning duties.

Akane, who was suspected of cheating on her tests.

Keito, who faked being sick to get out of school.

"We should make them stop," Niko stated to the others. "Let's all help them act right."

After a beat, he added, "For the good of the class."

Sota didn't want to go to Kana's house. He spent time every day practically praying that Kana's mother would be discharged from the hospital, and he watched with helpless concern as the other kids in the group went to "help" at Kana's house. Still, he never went himself.

This wasn't contained to just Sota's class anymore, either.

The mood at the entire school had become twisted and ugly. Secretly, Sota believed that it all started after Niko showed up. He was too terrified to say it to anyone, though.

But when he thought about why he couldn't, he realized it was because Niko was *right*. He was so right that you couldn't argue back. The moment you did, you outed yourself as the bad guy.

Not long after, the teachers told them that the student chairman had caused an "incident."

He'd pushed his mother off their apartment's veranda. Unlike what befell Toranosuke, this occurred at the apartment complex near the school and concerned the student chairman, so there was an assembly to address it. A teacher explained that something very tragic had happened. There was no class for a while, only consecutive days of parent meetings. So much went by in quick succession that Sota had difficulty processing that it was all going on at his school.

There was so much confusion, but there was one thing Sota felt sure of.

He was glad that the school was on a break. It meant no monitoring classmates and going to their houses. That, at the very least, was a good thing.

After the incident the student chairman caused, Niko was the next one to stop attending school.

No one said he transferred or got sick—he just stopped coming. There weren't even any rumors, like there were with Toranosuke. He had a seat in the classroom, but didn't show up.

Suddenly, children stopped watching each other, as though waking from a collective dream. It really was like they hadn't been fully aware; everyone wondered why they had done all that in the first place. Only Toranosuke's and Niko's empty seats proved that the events of the past few months were genuine.

What happened to Niko?

One day, Sota was home alone while his mother was out on an errand. The doorbell rang, and, assuming it was a package delivery, Sota opened the front door without much thought.

There was Niko. All alone.

"Hello," he greeted, in his usual grown-up manner, much to Sota's shock. Sota blinked rapidly until he could find his voice again.

"What…happened?"

Niko looked leaner than before, and his shirt was absolutely filthy. Sota had so many questions to ask.

"You haven't been at school. I wondered what happened to you."

"I'm going now," Niko stated abruptly. He stared at Sota. "I came to tell you that. You've got potential, so I kept my eye on you. It's a shame. I've got to go now."

"Go where? Are you transferring again?"

"Yes. I'm getting a new mom."

"Uh…"

Did that mean his parents were divorcing, and his father was remarrying a different woman?

That sounded really tough. Sota stared at Niko, trying to glean something more from his expression. However, the odd boy just shook his head. "It's nothing, really."

Maybe Niko had major issues to deal with at home himself. The thought squeezed at Sota's heart.

"You were showing Kana your homework every morning, weren't you, Sota?" said Niko.

"Huh?"

"That's cheating. It won't do Kana any good."

Sota felt a pang of guilt, but Niko was grinning.

It was the first time Sota ever saw the boy's namesake smile.

"Umm…"

Goose bumps formed on his skin, and shivers ran through his limbs. Somewhere in the center of Niko's smile was a core that instantly chilled the air around him.

"Did you make the class act that way because of Toranosuke?" Sota asked. He'd hated Toranosuke. But now he would never get to see him again. Sota recalled how Toranosuke looked the last time they met—his hunched shoulders while he sat shriveled on the park bench. "Was it because you didn't like what Toranosuke did?"

"No. Frankly, children like him are everywhere. People like Torano-suke, and the residents of Sawatari Apartments."

"Huh…?"

"I truly hoped you would take over for me."

Take over? Sota was confused.

Niko sighed but never let the smile leave his lips. "I see kids like you every now and then," he said. "I pondered what it was about you. You're protected by bamboo, aren't you?"

"Huh…?"

Bamboo? Like, *bamboo* bamboo? It was a truly puzzling statement.

The only time Sota had anything to do with bamboo was during his family's yearly trip to his grandma's house in the countryside every spring. They went digging for new shoots. That was the only bamboo Sota was familiar with…

"It's always the people around things we need to avoid, like bamboo and dogs, that we're the most drawn to. It's one of our downsides."

What does that mean? Sota wondered idly.

"Good-bye," Niko announced.

His face looked absolutely white. A frigid, icy shade, the color of frozen air. The smile drained from his features. His face and body—Niko's entire form—faded away, losing color and melting into space. And at his feet, a long shadow stretched into the distance.

It was the evening, and the sun wasn't shining anymore. Yet somehow, Niko had disappeared, leaving his shadow behind.

FINAL CHAPTER
Family

"There's no one left around here," Kaname Shiraishi said out of the blue while he stared up at the ceiling in the middle of the empty library.

He spread his long arms as a bird might its wings and closed his eyes, feeling and sensing, like he was in the midst of some prayer. It resembled a cool pose a manga character would strike on a book cover. If another boy his age did this, people would laugh and mock him. There was nothing funny when Kaname did it, however.

Maybe it was because she had witnessed his agility—the way he wielded that silver bell and chased after his fleeing opponent. She'd seen him defeat his enemy in battle like a comic book character might.

"No one left?" Mio Harano questioned.

As usual, Kaname's explanation left something to be desired. He had a tendency to speak directly about the core of a topic without any transition or introduction. Mio was entirely used to it by now and understood it as a quirk of the boy's personality.

He slowly retracted his extended hands. "Yes. They were here—but not any longer."

This library was part of Kusumichi Elementary. Mio had read the name on the school gate when Kaname brought her here.

An elementary school? Mio had wondered. Kaname had made his way through the school grounds without clarifying. She'd called to him, uncertain if they were allowed to be here, but Kaname hadn't responded. He'd headed directly to the library without a single detour.

"Are we allowed to be in here? I don't think strangers are permitted to walk on school grounds…"

There were no children now, after hours, and the school was silent. The orange of the sunset cut across the building, creating that strange, fantastical period between afternoon and night during which no souls could be felt. The front door was unlocked, and there were probably some teachers lingering around. The building couldn't be totally empty, yet it felt mysteriously lifeless.

"It's fine. Places tend to be desolate after they've been there. People stop caring about outsiders and strangers," Kaname stated without turning around. As usual, he spoke with a one-sided tone.

"Do you mean Hanaka isn't here?" Mio asked.

"No, all of them."

To Mio's mild frustration, it didn't feel like the answer was relevant to the question. Kaname slowly shook his head. The high-collared uniform shirt beneath his light coat seemed strangely appropriate. This was an elementary school, but a school nonetheless.

Kaname lowered his gaze from the ceiling to a level plane, then exited the library without comment. He stopped at odd points, looking left and right, but always narrowed his eyes and returned to staring toward the end of the corridor. Then he would resume walking, as though following invisible arrows marking the path.

Mio didn't understand what it meant. There had to be something that only he understood—that only he could see. The same had been true back in their second year of high school. Something had occurred that day that surpassed Mio's understanding, and only Kaname Shiraishi could see it.

He was drawn to a particular classroom.

"Here. They were here, but not anymore."

"Huh?"

The sign over the room read *Class 5-2*. Sure enough, the desks and chairs were a lot smaller than those meant for adults. Each seat featured a handmade cushion and drawstring bag. Student drawings and calligraphy covered the walls. It seemed like a perfectly ordinary elementary school classroom to Mio. Nothing appeared out of place.

Kaname paced toward the back end of the room. He held up his skinny arms to the far wall and eyed a particular spot.

What could it be?

Mio followed his gaze to some kind of chart. *Flower-Circle Stickers.* Next to each group's number was a very long list of red stickers stuck to the sheet.

◆

"Miss Harano."

Last week, a familiar voice stopped Mio in her tracks.

She wondered how she'd ever recognized it, given the crowd and noise. It was a familiar voice, unforgettable even. Mio had to chalk it up to her ears remembering the sound of it.

She was helping out at a pop-up shop for the spring festival at her college.

Mio was in an educational volunteer club, which was selling crepes today. She'd finished her shift at the register and switched places with an older sophomore. The stand was quite active, and it was just after Mio stepped away from the line of customers and walked to a nearby tent to remove her apron and hat that she heard him.

Mio looked up with a start and saw Kaname Shiraishi right in front of her.

She held her breath. The young woman's eyes went so still they forgot to blink.

However, she wasn't surprised. The timing was startling, but she'd long since lost the ability to be surprised when it came to him. The concept of surprise meant nothing to her anymore.

"Kana...me..."

Kaname Shiraishi.

The transfer student who came to her high school out of season.

Nearly two years had passed since she last saw him. The time they spent in the same class totaled less than a month.

Yet when Mio saw his face, the memories came roaring back in her ears—the sound of the wind rustling through the bamboo grove behind her family home accompanied the sight of Kaname's face.

The senpai from her track team whom Mio had had a crush on, the delight of her first boyfriend, the girls she'd enjoyed chatting with. Saho and Hanaka. Hanaka, the one who'd disappeared.

I'm with Kanbara-senpai, a senior at school. Don't worry about me.

The shock Mio had felt when she saw the message Hanaka had left behind. The pain.

The words Kaname had said to Itta Kanbara in front of the bamboo. The way her senpai's face had become lacerated and bloodied in the blink of an eye. Itta Kanbara, grimacing with pain, running away...

"An unidentified male body was discovered in the mountains of Mie Prefecture yesterday. I think it's Itta Kanbara," Kaname had told her.

She'd said, *"Take me with you."* If he meant to search for them, she wanted to be there. Mio was Hanaka's friend.

Several beats later, Kaname had nodded firmly. *"All right."*

The next month, Kaname Shiraishi vanished from Mio's high school.

He hadn't spoken with Mio during the weeks leading up to his disappearance, but the two had remained aware of each other's presence. A while before he left for good, Kaname had given Mio a piece of advice.

"No matter where you go, take a piece of bamboo from the grove behind your house with you. Even a leaf will do."

Mio had been taken aback.

"That bamboo is really, really good. It's seeped into you," Kaname had explained. He hadn't exactly smiled, but it was the first time she had seen real emotion on his face, the sort she might expect to see when someone *did* grin. Mio had nodded, encouraged by that show of friendliness.

The next week, Kaname had left. He'd just stopped showing up to school. On the first day, Mio had thought he was sick, but when he didn't show up the following day, or the one after, she went to Mr. Minamino to inquire about it.

"Shiraishi transferred again," he explained, leaving Mio numb. She felt like he'd abandoned her. However, some deep part of her was convinced of the opposite.

Kaname would come back to get her.

Mio still kept a bamboo leaf in the bill compartment of her wallet. So when Kaname showed up out of nowhere at her college pop-up shop, she wasn't particularly astonished.

In the almost-two-year interim, Mio had graduated from high school, left home in Chiba, and started attending a college in Kanazawa. And that's where he'd appeared without warning. Somehow, Mio had suspected it might happen this way.

In the past, she'd thought Kaname's abrupt movements and way of conversing were scary and creepy, but her opinion had since changed. In fact, she was delighted he'd kept his promise.

Kaname stared at her.

"I'm here for you. I found out where they are."

"...You remembered."

"Yeah." That was all Kaname said before going silent. The two years hadn't made him any better of a conversationalist.

He still had swollen, sleepy eyelids and scruffy hair.

Mio had never noticed until Kaname rescued her that he had long limbs and a nice figure. He was too thin and delicate, but that unbalanced quality gave him a certain kind of dangerous allure. In fact, it even looked like his facial features had grown more gentle and pleasing, including his sloping eyebrows.

"Did you find Hanaka?" Mio asked. Immediately, there was a firm pinch in her chest.

Hanaka—a girl Mio counted among her best friends. How many times had Mio thought about her in the past two years? On multiple occasions, she'd seen Hanaka's mother at the train station and at school, handing out flyers about her daughter's disappearance and asking everyone who passed for information. People said that Hanaka vanished of her own accord, but her mother tearfully stood in public and protested that Hanaka was not the type to run away without another word.

Mio realized at some point that she'd selected a distant college to escape her childhood town. When Mio and Saho had walked to the train station after classes, or waited for the bus near the school gate, they saw Hanaka's mother handing out her flyers. She greeted them with empty eyes every time, saying something like, "You'll be taking college entrance exams soon. That's great," and Mio felt her heart coming undone.

It was hard to believe so much time had passed since.

"I think I found her," Kaname replied. He squinted the way nearsighted people often did. His eyes were just as inscrutable as they had been when he stared down Itta Kanbara.

"Are you still interested in coming?"

"Yes."

Mio didn't hesitate, undoing her apron while her mind raced. It was the school festival period. There were no classes for a while.

Her lips formed a smile. Kaname's priorities seemed bizarre. He came all the way to see her in Kanazawa, yet if she claimed she wasn't interested, he probably would've accepted it at face value. He made her a promise, so he came. Even though they'd spent so little time together in class, Kaname's strange, unconventional way of thinking felt fond and familiar to Mio.

"Huh? You leaving, Harano?" someone asked while Mio folded up her apron and put away her hat. It was a senpai, a college third year, who had just gotten off his shift, too. He seemed mildly alarmed. Soon after Mio joined the club, she had gotten some unsubtle hints from him on several occasions. He never said anything directly, but he seemed to have a pushy, subconsciously possessive demeanor. Mio always managed to lightly brush him off. He started at the unfamiliar Kaname, clearly suspicious.

"Hey, who's this guy? Oh, I get it," he said, the displeasure in his eyes promptly turning to delight. "Is this your little brother? You said you have one, didn't you? It's Shizuku, yeah? You came to hang out?"

"No, he's my boyfriend from high school," Mio replied. She wondered why guys like this one always remembered her brother's name and liked to use it in their pickup schemes.

As soon as she muttered the word *boyfriend*, her senpai—and, surprisingly, Kaname as well—looked shocked. Kaname's eyes were as round as a startled cat's. Mio had never seen him like that before.

Feeling a little odd, she continued, "He came to see me—sorry about that. My shift's done for today, and I'm not coming to the festival tomorrow, so best of luck with everything else. Oh, and I'm taking one of these."

Mio grabbed one of the crepes on display out in front of the sales stand. Club members were each permitted to have one for themselves. The crepe was stuffed with a chocolate-dipped banana and whipped cream, and she thrust it into Kaname's hand.

"Here. I'm assuming you don't mind chocolate and banana."

"...I don't."

They walked off, leaving the stunned upperclassman behind. Kaname gave the crepe a tentative bite. Mio took note of that and remarked, "You eat stuff, Kaname?"

"Yes, I do eat food. Also, the whipped cream was about to spill off. I didn't want to get it on my hands."

Mio chuckled internally. The corners of her lips quirked up, which Kaname recognized.

"What?"

"Oh, just surprised that you talk about normal things."

"I do."

That he was responding to her comments told her that he had enough sense to know what a normal conversation was, so she kept going.

"Can I ask you something?"

"What?"

"Why are you still wearing that uniform?"

Mio wasn't surprised at Kaname's sudden appearance, but that still felt weird to her. They weren't in high school anymore, but under his lightweight beige coat, Kaname still wore the same collared uniform he had when they first met. He'd transferred into her school and left before he got a new uniform, so he'd had that same high-collared shirt on the entire time he was in class.

"Oh..."

Kaname shook his head languidly. For an instant, Mio got the idea that Kaname had popped into existence two years later without any time passing for him—an eternally youthful presence. Mio didn't think she'd be surprised if that turned out to be true.

He stated, "This is all I have."

And then he smiled. At least, it felt like he did.

He has the emotions necessary to smile? Mio stared at him, stunned.

"You've gotten stronger, Miss Harano."

◆

Mio took the bullet train from Kanazawa to Tokyo Station the next day. From there, she switched to the subway and continued toward her destination, a neighborhood in Tokyo she'd never been to before.

It seemed peaceful enough. There was a large park and a big supermarket, and neatly manicured trees beautifully lined the boulevard. It seemed like a wonderful place for families with children to live.

However...there was something else.

Something was *dark* about the place. Even when the sun shone, a shadow remained over the neighborhood, as though a roof or lid covered the area.

Of course, when Mio looked up, there wasn't actually anything there.

After leaving Kusumichi Elementary, Kaname took Mio to an apartment high-rise development near the school.

It's buildings were very large and stylish. Unlike the usual *danchi* complexes, flavorless drab structures in rows, these edifices had just the right amount of novelty to their design. A few glassed-in terraces were combined with the concrete texture tastefully. The lettering on the entrances, gates, and buildings was chic, giving the complex the appearance of a fashionable foreign hotel from a movie.

The rent was undoubtedly high. Curiously, Mio found herself hesitating when she and Kaname reached the entrance. She didn't know why. The place seemed very nice, but she wouldn't want to live here. Mio knew that she'd never allow herself to stay in this place.

The side of the building was bright with the afternoon sun, but somehow, it seemed *dark*, just like the neighborhood at large.

"Wait over there for a bit." Kaname pointed at a park in the middle of the complex. Mio did as instructed, sitting on a bench while Kaname ventured off toward the south side. When Mio saw what he returned with a short while later, she gasped.

It was a carrier for a dog or cat. She stood up and rushed over to him.

"I borrowed this," he said. "We might need it."

"Borrowed it? A dog?"

It could've been a cat, but she guessed dog based on the size. Sure enough, a little *"Hyip!"* issued from inside the case. Mio promptly squealed with delight. Her family kept a dog during her elementary school years. The memory of its fluffy fur and excited panting sent a twinge through her chest.

"I think the poor thing's agitated. Maybe it's not used to being in the carrier. I feel like this is unfamiliar to it," Mio said.

"You might be right," Kaname replied quietly. The constant tapping of nails from within the carrier, like the dog was scrabbling, was concerning.

"Can't we let it out?" Mio asked.

Kaname hummed to himself. After a moment of consideration, he said, "We can let it out, but there'll be trouble if it runs away. What about later? Once we get back to the place I'm renting. It's an indoor dog."

"The place you're renting?"

"Yeah. I have a place here. There are lots of rooms, so you can stay, too, if you want."

Mio had wondered where she'd stay if they were going to be in this area for a while. Kaname had never given Mio the details, and she hadn't bothered inquiring because she was used to how he did things.

"You're renting an apartment in this complex? You went to all that trouble for this?"

He must have done it to find "them," the people he was searching for. Kaname nodded very matter-of-factly. "I'm renting a couple. I asked Misumi Estates, the company that owns it, and they said I can use whichever ones I want."

"Misumi Estates...?"

That was a major real estate company. Mio saw the name all the time on apartment ads, shopping mall commercials on TV, and so on.

"A couple of them? Like, multiple apartments? When you say 'lots of rooms,' you don't just mean in a single unit? As in, we would stay in separate residences?"

Mio was hesitant to stay in the same unit with a boy her age, even in separate rooms.

"Yes. There are a bunch of empty apartments, so we can use any we like," Kaname confirmed.

"What's going on with this place?"

"One of the local wives has gone missing."

Tap-tap-tap-tap, tap-tap-tap. The sounds of little dog feet continued from the carrier.

"There's a couple more people who have died here. I assumed that if I followed their tracks, they'd lead me here," Kaname stated without batting an eye.

◆

"All right, you can come on out now!"

Mio set the carrier down on the floor and opened it. A dog with a brown tail burst out of the case, free at last.

The mere sight of the roll of neck fat around the red collar was enough to charm Mio. It reminded her of Roku, the Shiba Inu her family had kept when she was a little girl. Her mother had been distraught after they lost Roku, and she swore never to go through that kind of sadness again, so they didn't get another pet. Mio had always hoped to have a dog of her own again once she was a working adult.

Of course, this dog was entirely ignorant of all this, but it remained notably calm for a meeting with two strangers, not wary of Mio or Kaname at all.

It was a very friendly-looking mini Shiba with big round eyes.

"What's its name?" Mio asked.

"Hatch," said Kaname.

If the family he'd borrowed the dog from was in the complex, then perhaps the smell of similar building materials put Hatch at ease, even if the actual surroundings were different. To Mio's surprise, Kaname seemed knowledgeable about handling a dog and treated it very naturally. Hatch trotted over to his hand and buried its snout in the palm. It did not seem concerned about him at all.

While Mio wasn't exactly beaming, there was something about the way Kaname interacted with Hatch that made her feel warm inside. When they'd reunited at her college in Kanazawa, he'd worn that same collared shirt, and Mio had been prepared to believe he was immortal. However, close inspection revealed that Kaname had aged since their high school days. He still looked totally at home in the uniform, but there was something more reassuring and confident about him now.

Where did he come from, and who was he really?

Unsurprisingly, the apartment Kaname rented was sparse to the extreme. The only signs that someone lived here were the bedding, and a toothbrush and facial cleanser by the sink. There wasn't even a refrigerator in the kitchen. Thankfully, Kaname had made preparations for Hatch: He'd gotten the dog's food from the owner and set up a potty area, too.

Seeing the toothbrush and facial foam in front of the mirror gave Mio a strange feeling. She was strangely impressed that someone who seemed so unalive had basic biological habits. This glow of admiration filled her as she stared around the empty room.

"I had the movers bring in a bed and curtains for the apartment I thought you might use, Miss Harano. Though you could also use one of the units that's still furnished."

"Still furnished?"

"Yeah. A bunch of the families here basically got up and left in the middle of the night. But I wasn't sure you'd want to sleep in the bed a stranger left behind."

This situation was growing more unsettling, and Mio refrained from comment. Kaname stood, holding the puppy. Hatch licked at his fingers. Having determined that the dog wouldn't run away, he headed for the door with the dog in his hands, no longer bothering with the carrier.

"Let's take a look at one more place for today."

Kaname led Mio to the top floor of north building.

A placard that read *Sawatari* and a wreath of dry flowers hung on the door. Dead petals and leaves littered the floor beneath.

Kaname already had the key, and he opened the door to the Sawatari residence.

The moment Mio set foot inside, she gasped reflexively.

It was an incredibly tasteful and fashionable home, like something out of a magazine photo shoot. The art on the walls, the beautiful wooden coat rack, table, and chairs. A refrigerator with a pristine, unmarked surface. And the rooms were so spacious. Clearly, this was a special unit with a different layout and specifications from the others.

Kaname let Hatch down. The dog yipped.

What was it about this place? The picture-perfect interior only made it creepier that no one was around, particularly because Mio normally wouldn't enter a stranger's house without permission.

"Where are the people who live here?"

"Either dead or gone. They're saying the missing wife might have something to do with it."

Kaname spread his arms like bird wings, closed his eyes, and took a deep, slow breath, just as he had in the elementary school library.

"They've been here, too. I can't be sure if the rumor is accurate or not, but they worked their way into the school committees and housewife cliques, slowly foisting their darkness on others."

The phrase *foisting their darkness* stimulated Mio's memories.

Her phone, back in high school. All the frightening LINE messages. The harassing words that never stopped. The waves of guilt because she unhealthily agreed that she bore some fault for what he said…

"*They try to foist their darkness on others,*" Kaname had told her while his eyes remained fixed on Kanbara. "*Family massacre. You slip in through a single family member, ensorcelling them while you wriggle your way in among the group. You browbeat them with your logic, convince the other party they're in the wrong, and impose your supposedly correct will upon them. Once you're in among the family, it's only a matter of time until they're all under your control…*"

At the time, the phrase "*family massacre*" sounded preposterous, unbelievable even. However, hearing Kaname talk about it again in this empty, recently lived-in apartment gave them an eerily realistic weight. Had this family suffered the way Mio had under Kanbara's pressure?

"What do you mean, 'foist their darkness'? Are you saying that wife did the same things Itta Kanbara did to me?"

It was getting dark outside. This probably wasn't Kaname's first time in this apartment. He opened a door by the entryway, revealing a shoe rack with a breaker box above it. Kaname opened the breaker box while Mio noticed there were children's sneakers on the rack. *So this family had a child.* It made her heart hurt.

After Kaname pressed a switch on the wall, the lights came on. And now that everything was illuminated, Mio finally got her answers.

"The ones I'm looking for foist their darkness on others to bring out the others' darkness and drag them down to their level. They pressure and trap their prey, sap their ability to think and fight back, and make them lose track of what's right. By limiting their perception, they can breed their darkness inside their targets and make them unpleasant."

"Unpleasant?"

"Yes. They become aggressive, attacking other people and inflicting their darkness upon them. In this way, they spread death and darkness to those around the original targets, and the damage continues to spread. I'm guessing it's already happened and played out here at this complex."

"And 'they' did this?"

"Yes. Kaori Kanbara."

Mio gasped. Kanbara—the same last name as her track and field club senpai. Kaname was staring Mio right in the eyes. She summoned her courage and asked, "That was Itta-senpai's last name."

"Yes. They're a family."

She forgot how to blink.

"Want to see?" Kaname took out his smartphone, searched for an image, and showed it to Mio. "You know that site that collects info on every home that's had an incident? Houses where people died from accidents or suicide, all collated so you can see the causes and times of death in one place?"

"...I've heard of it. Never actually looked at it, though."

"This is the site's map of the area before the Kanbara family moved here."

Apparently, the site was designed to display a slice of time. There were several candle icons across the map. Each one represented a person's death. The many rows of candles conjured a mental image of the departed. Tapping on an icon brought up the details of that death.

"And this is the area after they were here."

Kaname changed a setting. Suddenly, a vast wave of candles appeared on-screen. An especially large one hung over this apartment complex, and when Kaname touched a finger to it, a pop-up listed many entries.

South Bldg, Unit 515. Subject jumped to death from hallway.

Subject fell to death from roof.

North Bldg, Unit 601. Subject was murdered.

North Bldg, Unit 701. Subject was murdered on veranda...

Mio remembered the placard on the door to this apartment. Was this the Unit 701 on the list? Mio almost turned to look at the veranda. The word *murder* made her feel very uncomfortable.

However, it didn't stop at this complex.

Smaller candles were all over the map. The arrangement resembled a ritual at a shrine or temple.

Candle after candle, fresh and new, where there hadn't been any before.

"When that family shows up, people die. That's the kind of family they are," Kaname stated.

Toshiya Suzui was in a good mood.

The management structure at his company had changed recently; those who did the grunt work now had a greater say in things. Before, this had been an old-fashioned, abusive business. Bosses could say things like, "Shots before thoughts," and demand you go to the bar with them after work hours. Or you might later wind up with a useless boss who attempted to shorten work hours so she could focus on her children. It was a difficult workplace, and very stressful.

But not anymore.

Suzui strolled along, humming to himself and reflecting on the last several months. *Maybe having a woman as a sales section chief was asking a bit too much of her after all.*

She was the first female sales department section chief in the history of Yotsumiya Foods. Sales Section Two had been very excited about the event and had high hopes for her, but Mutsumi Maruyama turned out to be a disappointment. Maybe the pressure of being the first woman in her position was too much for her. In any case, she developed a fierce rivalry with Sales Section One.

"We have to do this and that to ensure Section One doesn't beat us."

"All this work you're doing will benefit Section One! Am I wrong?"

"Are you close with the chief of Section One, Mr. Kanbara? Listen up, everyone! Mr. Kanbara is a spy for Section One, so keep your guard up around him!"

It was stunning. A spy? Yet Mutsumi had seemed totally serious. She actually thought that Mr. Kanbara and Section One caused her section's poor performance.

For one thing, Section One and Section Two handled different products. The former peddled raw and fresh products, while the latter sold processed goods like frozen meals. When Section Two employees negotiated with stores, they sometimes introduced associates from Sales One or other parts of the company and vice versa, depending on the client's needs. Accusations about "spies" and "stealing credit" were really inappropriate of Mutsumi.

"I trusted you, Mr. Kanbara. You said I would be fine here!" she'd cried, clinging to a disturbed Kanbara in an empty meeting room. She was quite beside herself. Kanbara was tall and possessed a gentlemanly sort of appearance. Watching the spectacle had made Suzui feel like he was witnessing a scene of uncovered infidelity between a romantic couple.

Despite feeling awkward about it, Suzui had still interrupted. "Chief, you shouldn't talk that way. We're at work. Please calm down…"

Kanbara had looked relieved for the interjection. "Ahh, I'm so glad you're here, Suzui. Let's help the section chief get some rest…"

The look on his face had reminded Suzui of when the company instructed Kanbara to stop taking calls from Section Chief Sato, back when that was still a problem. Suzui had heard that Kanbara was very glad about that change.

"It must be difficult, the way people keep doing this to you again and again," Suzui had remarked.

"Yes, I was so thankful the last time," Kanbara had said with a grin. "When they told me I didn't need to answer the phone anymore, I thought, *Oh, my duty is complete. It's all okay.* I was quite relieved."

Chief Sato was later involved in a second assault, this time at the affiliate company warehouse he was reassigned to. His touchy personality got him into an argument over work, and he punched a subordinate. This time, the company fired him. However, he returned to the office enraged, caused a scene, and roared that he had been unfairly dismissed. Security had to toss him out.

He then returned home and committed suicide, but not before killing his wife. In the lengthy message he left behind, he detailed his great enmity for Yotsumiya Foods.

Suzui and his coworkers were shaken by the news of Chief Sato's end. Mutsumi was especially affected, and cried, "Did I push him to it?" while everyone was in the office. "That's what you all think, isn't it? You think I killed him."

Senior management was informed of her condition and recommended that she take some time off work. She wouldn't have it, though, screaming, "You're just trying to gaslight me into thinking I'm depressed!"

Perhaps she really was exhausted, because after leaving work, she slipped on the stairs at the train station and hit her head. She was taken to the hospital, where she remained unconscious and in critical condition.

"I wonder if the company's cursed," Hamada mused gloomily.

Suzui replied, "Right?" But in truth, a part of him was relieved about this turn of events. He'd grown sick of Mutsumi griping around the office.

It would've been nice if Kanbara were made the new section chief, but he was a special hire, and sadly, the company was still rather traditional regarding promotions. There was a bit of irony to that, because Section Two's recent success was all thanks to Kanbara charming the retail clients, not Mutsumi's stewardship.

Before Suzui knew it, Kanbara had become a very trusted individual to many business partners. A lot of them acted like Chief Sato, and a few started using that familiar old nickname, Jin. They'd say, "Jin, about that place we talked about earlier—about my daughter—about my husband—about my boyfriend…"

Somehow every secret or rumor came to him. Suzui thought Kanbara's ability to win the trust of others was remarkable.

Even Suzui found himself revealing things to Kanbara on occasion and seeking his advice. Complaints about his current boss, the changes he wanted to see in the company structure, his sickly grandmother back in the country, his inability to get over his ex-girlfriend from back in school, his insistence that she shouldn't have dumped him…

"Yes, I understand. I understand," Mr. Kanbara would say, offering encouragement. "It's really a terrible shame that she chose to break up with you."

Suzui knew he was repeating the same things over and over, yet Kanbara was so patient and supportive. He was just so *nice*.

"Do you have troubles on your mind, Mr. Kanbara?" Suzui asked. It was only a moment later that he realized his mistake. The man recently lost his wife. Suzui had posed a very insensitive question. However, Kanbara's gentle smile never wavered.

"My oldest has turned into a bit of a shut-in. I suppose that weighs on me a bit. I'd like to help when they're ready to come out of their shell. I'm not in any rush, though."

I bet he's an ideal father, Suzui thought.

As a matter of fact, that *"ideal"* man had recently achieved a most remarkable promotion.

Kanbara had finished his service as a rank-and-file employee, and he was elevated to business consultant and executive director of Yotsumiya Foods. It was a stunning development for Suzui and the rest of the company, made possible by the company president's firm insistence.

"After what happened with my wife, I planned to quit, but the president was very keen on keeping me around," he explained bashfully. The thought that he'd intended to quit—without telling Suzui—left Suzui strangely bothered. He wouldn't be going, though, and that was ultimately a great relief.

Apparently, the president heard that Kanbara was a business consultant for another company prior to this and had personally offered him an executive position.

"I'm so glad you accepted the executive director offer," the president said to Kanbara in the office. Suzui had hardly ever interacted with the president since joining the company, but somehow, Kanbara had come to know him very well.

Suzui hadn't been aware that Kanbara possessed experience in business consulting. As time went on, the fact that he'd kept that from Suzui formed smoldering discontent in the man. Suzui knew that he shouldn't care that much, but he didn't like that it felt as though someone had stolen Kanbara from him. It was a good thing that Kanbara was in a senior position, but it was bad because he was farther away now. Suzui wished that Kanbara would listen and help more with his problems.

Didn't someone say that he was a doctor or something?

Suzui tried to recall, but he couldn't remember who said that or when.

A woman came to visit Kanbara one day after he became an executive. She was there to deliver his lunch. When she saw Suzui, she asked, "Excuse me, are you Suzui?"

"Uh, yes. That's right."

"Oh, I've heard all about you. Mr. Kanbara mentioned he had an excellent coworker, someone very talented for being so young. Here, please take this. Share it with everyone."

The woman handed him a wrapped package, inside of which was a beautiful pumpkin tart topped with whipped cream. It was expertly prepared to the point of appearing store bought.

After the woman left, Suzui ran into Kanbara on the office floor and asked, "Um, Mr. Kanbara, who was that? She gave me a piece of cake."

He chuckled and simply replied, "Oh, she's my wife."

Niko Kanbara stood before the blackboard and introduced himself to his new class.

"My mother and father gave me the name Niko as a shortened version of *nikkori*, or 'smile.' You can just call me Niko. It's nice to meet you all." He looked into the faces of all his classmates.

He also peered beyond them, to the papers displayed on the back wall—six groups in total. Good, that was enough spots on the chart.

"Teacher, I'd like to propose something."

"Oh? What is it, Niko?"

"What if we make a chart with all the groups on it, and each group that does a good deed or behaves well gets a sticker?"

He pushed his silver-framed glasses up and showed the teacher the flower-circle sticker sheet he'd brought to class.

Shoko Miyajima stood before her dresser, at a loss for what to wear.

Not this. It was too formal, something for parent-teacher day. This dress was cute, but it would look like she was trying too hard to doll herself up. This skirt was a little frumpy…

She hadn't had this much trouble deciding what to wear since going out on dates with boys she liked as a teen. However, it was like this every week now. Before the tea parties, she pulled so many clothes out of her dresser there was nowhere left to step.

It was already one thirty. She really needed to focus on preparing the tea.

The smell of banana cake wafted from the oven. Yet here Shoko was, alone in her sweet-swelling room, on the verge of tears.

She wanted to cry, "Why is this happening to me?" but she already knew the answer.

It was that woman: Kaori Kanbara.

"Quite a few mothers with children in the same class live in this development. Why don't we get together and have a tea party?"

After that, all the moms in the complex started having get-togethers with Shoko at their center.

Shoko's husband was a doctor at the university hospital. She never intended to show off, but she felt that when in a new place, it was essential to be honest with everyone at the earliest possible moment. Otherwise, she might embarrass other women if they tried to boast about husbands and careers that weren't actually impressive.

Before, she'd been around other wives with doctor husbands, but those men either had small private practices or worked at general hospitals that were far below where Shoko's husband was employed. Her husband didn't work for any old place. He was a surgeon for C. University Hospital. Plus, he was up for a management position next term. The man was anything but your average doctor.

Shoko knew that she'd always had a competitive personality. However, she couldn't help it because she'd never actually lost at anything. It was in her nature at this point. When she entered a new environment or group of people, she let everyone know that she was now the best of them. That helped resolve things smoothly and prevented anyone else from being unpleasantly upstaged down the line.

So when the woman named Kaori Kanbara arrived, Shoko assumed she was ignorant like the others.

She doesn't know who I am. It's the only thing that explains why she invited me to tea. She doesn't know that I'm on another level.

To counter, Shoko had turned the invitation back at the woman.

"Oh, if you want to have a tea party, we do that at my place rather often. Feel free to come by if you like."

"Oh, really? Thank you for the invitation."

Shoko didn't like that everyone talked about how that woman resembled someone from TV. From Shoko's perspective, Kaori's clothes were worn out, and she looked tired and just plain old. Her hair was unkempt, and she did a poor job taking care of herself.

While Kaori Kanbara was at the tea party, Shoko told her the truth.

"It's not just my husband; I'm a doctor, too. I'm taking a break from work because of our new baby."

It always felt good to play that ace. *My husband is special, but I'm someone, too. You common housewives could never imagine being this elite.* However, Kaori didn't even bat an eye.

"Oh, me too," she replied with a grin. "It's a secret, so I don't go telling anyone, but I am, too."

Huh? Shoko thought. *That can't be right.* She examined Kaori closely, but the woman just sipped her tea and didn't elaborate.

"What hospital did you work at? What university did you go to?" Shoko questioned, but Kaori only gave nonanswers like, "Oh, you know." Kaori acted like Shoko was the weird one for demanding answers, and it was infuriating.

There's no way you are a doctor. Do you know how much hard work it takes? Do you really think you can just lie through your teeth and not get called out on it?

It was irritating, but what angered Shoko even more was that Kaori didn't take a single bite of her homemade treats.

"They look good," she praised, yet she never touched them. Despite this, much of what Kaori talked about gave the impression that she loved cooking and made her own sweets at home all the time. It felt like a prank on Shoko.

Shoko didn't like this woman, and it should have been a simple matter of not inviting her anymore. But for some reason, she found herself repeatedly calling her over.

They barely traded any words—the woman just sat there and smiled—but it threw Shoko completely off her game. *Why doesn't she mention how incredible I am? Why aren't things going the way I want?* Maybe that was why she kept inviting Kaori to her events—an intense desire to see her break and acknowledge Shoko's excellence.

The doorbell rang.

The sound surprised Shoko.

The tea party guests were already here. Even that horrible Kaori had arrived, giving Shoko pumpkin tarts she claimed to have made herself.

"I made them with the pumpkins I get sent every year. Try one if you like."

Shoko had made a banana cake for today. Did Kaori not care that bringing the same category of sweet to the host's party was insulting?

Shoko didn't know what to make of it when the other moms all squealed, "Ooh! They look so yummy!" Irritated, she served both the banana cake and the pumpkin tarts. It seemed the tarts were disappearing off her guests' plates faster than her own handiwork, which irked her even more.

Kaori smugly refused to eat Shoko's cake. She never ate anything Shoko prepared.

"By the way, what does your husband do, Kaori?" Shoko asked, determined to get an answer out of her today. Kaori didn't reply. Instead, one of the other mothers responded, "It's some kind of food company, right?"

Oh, just a salaryman, then. Shoko glared at Kaori.

The woman continued, "He's an executive at Yotsumiya Foods, isn't he? That's amazing."

"Oh, you know." Kaori grinned. Shoko grew angry at the mention of *"executive,"* but Yotsumiya Foods was just a small, midlevel company, hardly some grand conglomerate. *Plus, if you're going to let other people talk about how "amazing" you are, you ought to return the favor once or twice,* she groused to herself.

"Kaori, your little Niko has an older brother, doesn't he?"

"Yes."

"How old is his brother? I heard he's grown up; has he already left home to go to college?"

"Oh, I suppose you could say that," Kaori replied enigmatically. She had her phone out, evidently typing a text. That, too, was irritating. She shouldn't be playing with her phone at someone else's tea party.

It was constantly aggravating that the topic of discussion always seemed to revolve around Kaori when she was present. The topic nearly turned to what a great college this "big brother" attended. He probably wasn't a medical student, though.

I'm going to make sure my child goes to medical school…

Kaori set down her teacup. For once, she looked Shoko right in the eyes.

"I've always meant to ask you…"

"Yes?"

"Is that painting authentic?"

"Huh?"

Kaori was pointing at a poster hung on the living room wall. It was on the cover of a bestselling book that had gone on sale during Shoko's school days, a painting of a seaside town done by an English artist. The image was very famous.

Huh? The picture was very well known. No one would believe a poster was *"authentic."* Whatever original existed, it was either in the author's possession or in some museum. Shoko had only a printed copy on the wall.

"No, it's not… It's a poster."

"Oh. I see. So it's not the genuine article."

This one really irked Shoko. Before she could think better of it, she snapped, "That's rather rude to say, isn't it?"

"Oh, it's just, I know the painter, so I thought maybe you did, too."

"Huh…?"

Shoko's throat, her very features, seized up. However, some part of her deep down jumped with excitement.

I've been waiting for this.

I've been waiting for you to try acting better than me. You've foolishly challenged me, and now I can smack you down. You're bragging. They all saw it. They all saw you try to one-up me.

She started it, so I have the right to answer. I've never liked you, and you're going to know it now.

But Shoko didn't have the chance to talk back before Kaori said, "It's this painting, right?"

She had taken out her phone again, an old flip one. *Really? In this day and age?* Worse yet, the screen was cracked.

The image on the screen was of the picture hanging on Shoko's wall.

"Oh, and I found this, too." Kaori switched to a different image: the very flower-print skirt that Shoko had on. Although not too expensive, it was a new item from one of Shoko's favorite brands. Kaori had the official website open. A model displayed the same skirt, and underneath the picture was the tag showing the price: 37,000 yen.

This is what she was doing with her phone earlier? Looking these things up?

"That's a pretty expensive skirt. I was just thinking of changing my style. Maybe I should copy you."

The rest of the group had gone very quiet. Shoko was openly staring at the other woman.

Is she actually insane…?

The doorbell rang.

Shoko jumped a little, surprised.

The tea party guests were already here. Shoko wasn't expecting anyone else. Who could it be?

Shoko got up and pressed a button on the intercom. "Hello?" She expected the camera to show her who had come by, but again, she was surprised.

There was no one there.

Not a soul was visible on the screen.

"Oh, that's strange," she remarked aloud. And then something happened.

All the women in the room sucked in a sharp breath. There was an unfamiliar person present.

A young man wearing a uniform with a tall collar. From the look of him, he was in high school. Somehow, he'd entered the home without a sound.

"Huh?" Shoko's eyes went wide.

The young man stood before the table and raised his right hand. Then there was a clear, crisp ringing. Wholly befuddled and frozen in place, Shoko could only listen to the chime.

Ding…

There appeared to be a silver bell in his hand.

A faint scent wafted through the room, too. Something different from the rose-based fragrance that Shoko used. It was fresher and greener—like bamboo, almost.

No one quite knew what to do. The tea party guests were trapped between looking at the uninvited guest and looking at Shoko, the host.

However, one person in the group was more rigid than the others.

Kaori Kanbara's eyes blazed, staring with intense focus at the bell in the young man's hand. She looked like she couldn't believe what was happening.

The boy rang the bell, cool and clear, once more. The sound brought Shoko back to her senses, and she rounded on him.

"Excuse me, young man..."

But she didn't have time to ask him what he was doing in her home before a scream drowned her out.

"Eeeyaaaaaagh!"

It was ear-splitting. Deafening.

Kaori, who had been stock still with her eyes trained on the young man, slammed her head on the table. Her teacup cracked. The whipped cream served with the cake splattered on her forehead and hair.

Shocked and terrified, the other women cried out "Kaori!" But Kaori put her hands over her head and pulled at her hair, like a toddler throwing a tantrum.

It was so startling that one of the housewives beside her rushed to help. She placed a hand on Kaori's shoulder, then pulled it back with a shriek, as one might after touching a hot stove.

"You shouldn't touch her," cautioned the young man with the bell. He was very calm.

And the surprises didn't end there.

"*Hyip!*"

A dog barked.

Shoko reeled. Animals like dogs and cats had always set her on edge. She was just about to demand the dog be taken outside when she saw the woman holding it enter from the room behind the young man. The two people looked similar in age, but the woman didn't seem nearly so calm, staring wide-eyed around the room in apparent fright.

The dog jumped out of her arms. The little brown thing was quite bold, and there was a red collar around its neck.

It rushed forward and jumped onto the table, weaving its way around the scattered silverware and headed straight toward Kaori.

"*Hyip! Hyip!*" it barked.

"*Gyap!*" It got even louder.

Shoko was sure it would attack Kaori, who was still slumped over on the table, and she looked away. But instead, the puppy focused on Kaori's hand. It leaned its little face near her fingers.

"*Hyip! Hyip! Hyip!*"

It seemed to be trying to send a message. Its bark resembled a call or summons, a desperate calling of someone's name, not an attack.

Kaori was still in agony. The flip phone slipped out of her fingers and fell onto the floor. Perhaps the screen picked up a fresh crack from the drop. Kaori's unkempt hair was strewn everywhere. She refused to lift her head. The agonized rocking slowed.

The only sounds in the quiet living room were the puppy's barks and Kaori's labored breaths. She was gasping for breath, struggling even. The dog licked her hands and hair concernedly.

"Ritsu Mikishima," the young man said.

Whom was he talking to? His eyes were fixed on Kaori Kanbara, still collapsed on the table. He called out to her.

"Ritsu. Come back to us, Ritsu."

He rang the bell again.

The stunned tea party could do no more than watch as Kaori's cheek twitched at the mention of the name Ritsu. She had one side of her face pressed to the table, and her upturned eye was shot wide. Whipped cream dirtied her hair.

"*Hyip!*" the dog barked again, then promptly began to whine, sidling up to Kaori's cheek. "*Heww, heww, heww,*" it mewled through its nose.

Kaori's open eyes caught sight of the dog. At last, they found focus again, and they leaked tears.

"H...atch..."

"Who...who is that?" Mio asked.

"Ritsu Mikishima, the wife who went missing in that complex," Kaname replied matter-of-factly.

The women held their silence, wide-eyed and alarmed, wreathing their agonized tea party companion.

Unperturbed by their presence, Kaname explained, "Half a year ago, two women died at Sawatari Apartments on the same day. One was Hiromi Sawatari, the wife of the designer who handled the complex's renovation. The official report is that her son pushed her off her veranda."

He paused, then continued without looking at Mio.

"The other was Keiko Kashiwazaki."

This name was unfamiliar to her.

"Late at night, after Hiromi Sawatari's death, she fell from the hallway of the south building and passed away. That same night, a wife went missing from an apartment with a direct view of the fall. The woman lived in Unit 515, which is where this dog came from. Just before she disappeared, Keiko Kashiwazaki was seen violently banging on her door and calling for her, according to eyewitnesses."

Kaname took a deep breath.

"The deceased, Keiko Kashiwazaki, lived in Unit 201 in the south building, and introduced herself to others as Kaori Kanbara."

"Ahhhhhh..."

There was a wail—not loud, but mournful. It came from the mouth of

"Ritsu Mikishima," the woman Hatch sniffed. The dog yapped adorably with great concern and care. *"Hyip."*

"Hyip!"

She'd heard it that day, too.

And then she remembered.

I am…Ritsu.

Ritsu Mikishima.

My husband is Yuuki Mikishima. My son is Kanato Mikishima.

The barking dog is my pet, Hatch.

That night, I saw Kaori Kanbara climb over the handrail and fall.

Yuuki and Kanato went out to get dinner, and while I was home alone, she rang the doorbell over and over and over. Kaori Kanbara was there…

"Oh, Ritsuuu."

"Let's go and see the dead."

Bam-bam-bam, bam-bam-bam, bam-bam-bam, bam-bam-bam, ding-dong, bam-bam-bam, bam-bam-bam, ding-dong, bam-bam, "Riiitsuuu," *bam-bam-bam-bam,* "you can't say you didn't know her this tiiime," *ding-donnng…*

"Hyip!" Hatch barked at the door. *"Hyip! Hyip!"*

He's barking frantically. I'm frightened, so frightened, and I clutch the little dog for comfort.

"Ohhh, Riiitsuuu…"

The voice called for her from beyond the door.

I hold my head. The air feels thin. I can't breathe.

"We need to tell Kanato, too. Asahi's mother's dead, after all. He'll be very sad, and he'll want to say good-bye. I can tell him about it. Let's go, Ritsu. Shall I go to him?"

Stop…

She only recognized the wail at the mention of her son's name as being her own when the pain in her exhausted lungs started. She was going to open the door. Open it and jump out, into the hallway...

Pressure squeezed her chest.

Kaori wasn't there. Then she looked to the side with a gasp.

"Boo!" Kaori shouted, leaping out from behind the door. Ritsu shrieked and jumped away, using every reflex and muscle to evade.

Kaori launched herself onto the hallway handrail at full force. Her body tilted, hard.

"Ah," a voice gasped—whether Ritsu's or Kaori's, she couldn't tell.

Ritsu collapsed to the floor. Her legs felt weightless. And then...

Bang. The sound of something bursting.

The sound of a fall.

Yuuki had described it as a *wham.* The noise instantly grew dim. She was engulfed in silence.

Well, that's that.

Kaori Kanbara had fallen right before her eyes.

Ritsu took the shock of that impact in with her entire being. She couldn't will her muscles to work, and she didn't want to peer down. She wished to close her eyes, but even that was impossible. And yet her vision was growing darker.

Flap-flap, fwup-fwup. Something was billowing in her ears. Through fading wits, Ritsu realized what the sound was—blue sheets.

The movers' tarps that covered Sawatari Apartments beat in the wind, all at once. A gigantic creature breathing in and out.

Her consciousness was rapidly fading.

The last thing she heard before falling into darkness was Hatch barking, *"Hyip!"*

*   *   *

She could hear Hatch again, loud and clear.

A bell rang, too.

Riiing, riiing, riiing.

The fog had shrouded her mind for what felt like ages.

She tried to think of something, to remember who she was, and the fog instantly felt much, much heavier. It was like the fog took physical form and became cotton. When she tried to resist it, even slightly, it grew heavy as though it had absorbed water, clinging to her mind and body.

But…

The ringing of the bell burned the fog.

Flames erupted from the center of the mist. The core of the cotton that she believed was empty crackled like bamboo splitting apart. The burning vapor charred her body from the inside. She screamed at the agony coursing through her, and as she did, she realized, *Oh, the fog and cotton were always such a dark color.*

It was shadow.

Ring, ring.

The fog dispersed with the ringing and the terrible, searing pain. Darkness was purged.

"Ritsu Mikishima," a voice called. She'd never heard it before, but it sounded very familiar and nostalgic. "Ritsu. Come back to us, Ritsu."

"Here," she mumbled.

At last, her lips moved of her own will, quivering imperceptibly.

Ritsu struggled as hard as she could to move. She called out, "H…atch…"

I am Ritsu Mikishima.

Not Kaori Kanbara. Ritsu Mikishima.

"The family replenishes itself."

Kaname didn't face Mio, or wait for her to respond or urge him onward.

"When they go down a member, they take over and absorb someone involved with them at the time and force that victim to fulfill the same family role. They find someone of similar age to play the role of mother, child, or whoever, to maintain the family. That's how they keep spreading darkness and death."

His words didn't make sense to Mio right away. She tried to chew on them, to ingest them, but her mind refused to follow. Kaname didn't wait for her to catch up.

"In order to fill the hole left by the dead Kaori Kanbara at Sawatari Apartments, the family picked her to be the *new* Kaori Kanbara."

Hatch stared concernedly at the collapsed woman's face, refusing to leave her side. Perhaps he was protecting her. Even if Mio didn't understand everything that was happening, the sight of the dog's tender care plucked at her heartstrings.

"Ritsu. It's all right," Kaname said. He'd finally stopped ringing the bell. After releasing a deep breath, he placed his palm over the inner corner of the woman's eye.

A single tear ran down her face. Gently, so gently, he told her, "You can sleep now."

Her lips convulsed into movement. Mio thought she imagined it, but it sounded like the woman whispered "Okay."

"Excuse me," said an extremely perturbed voice.

Time had stopped when Kaname and Mio appeared, but the other women were still sitting around the table in the center of the room. All except for one, who was on her feet and looking extremely irritated. She was a pretty woman with eye-catching features, wearing a flower-print skirt.

"Who are you people? What are you doing in my home? And what happened to Mrs. Kanbara? What is all this nonsense about going missing and being pushed and all of that?"

Her voice shook, making it impossible to distinguish anger from fear. Presumably, she owned this apartment. Mio had no idea how to respond, so she left it to Kaname.

"Your lives have been saved," he said, but, unlike moments ago with Ritsu, his voice was emotionless and cold. That statement alone wouldn't clear up anything for the women, yet they recoiled. Their eyes were wide and fixed upon Kaname.

They must understand what he means, Mio realized.

She knew because it had happened to her. When Itta Kanbara wore her down, she understood that something was slowly going crazy in her life. She definitely had the premonition that something terrible would soon befall her. These women undoubtedly sensed the same thing.

"I have a request for all of you," Kaname announced. "Tell me what you know about *this* Mrs. Kanbara's current family and residence."

◆

When the door opened, it was immediately apparent that something hideous and nasty escaped through the crack.

It didn't feel like a living presence. At most, it was a chill, like a burst of white slipping free when the freezer door was opened. Something bad, something unbearably horrible, seeped outside. Whatever the presence was, this entire place brimmed with it.

Mio had asked Kaname to take her along so she could see this event to its end, yet now she wanted to be anywhere but inside that apartment.

Kaname entered without a word. The apartment carried a musty odor in addition to the chilling presence. Maybe it was more than just mold. Despite it being a clear day outside, it seemed as though rain had fallen inside this home.

What was this desolate sensation?

According to the people at the tea party on a higher floor of the building, Kaori Kanbara had moved into Unit 302 two months earlier. It hadn't been that long, but the place looked as if it had been ransacked.

The unit's pretty sparse, so why is it so messy? Mio wondered—and then she realized the answer.

There were a few pieces of furniture and other items in the apartment, but their placement had no guiding design or reason. A frying pan, vanilla extract, and an empty flour container sat on top of the living room table. A large stuffed animal, the sort you could win from a crane game, stuck out of a cardboard box sitting on the couch. Elementary-school-age learning implements were scattered across the floor rather than placed on the shelf. Clothes—women's, men's, and children's—were placed on hangers and piled up in a corner of the room. The curtains were pulled firmly shut, leaving the whole place extremely dark.

It was a chaotic mess, yet it felt bizarrely uninhabited. It was impossible to imagine people living here, turning the lights on, and having conversations and meals in this environment.

According to what the women had said earlier, the Kanbara family had two children.

A big brother around college age, and a little brother in elementary school. No one knew where the older brother went to school. Rumors said he was a shut-in. The little brother attended the nearby elementary school. After hearing that tidbit, Kaname placed a phone call. It was the first time Mio had seen him contact someone using his phone.

"I'm going to need backup," he'd told his contact on the other end. Mio was stunned, but it quickly made sense to her. There were others like Kaname. He'd told the other person the name of the elementary school and that of the apartment complex. And with firm resolution, he'd said to his associate, "I'm going to end it right here."

After the call, he'd told Mio, "Let's go. The sooner, the better."

"Sooner? What do you mean?" she'd asked.

Kaname's lips had pursed. "They'll notice us. As shameful as it is to admit, they've escaped me at the very last moment on a number of occasions before."

Mio hadn't known what that meant, but she followed Kaname to this apartment.

Unit 302. The Kanbaras'.

A sliding wooden door stood on the far side of the living room. There would be a tatami room beyond it.

Kaname didn't hesitate. He headed straight for the door as though drawn by some invisible force. He already had that bell-like object in his hand.

I'm scared.

The sheer tension of the moment vibrated through the air. Mio wanted to run away, but she made sure to keep a step behind Kaname. However, she was fighting to stay on her feet, to keep from clinging to his back out of terror.

Kaname slid open the door. Immediately, the smell of mold and rain intensified. There was something else mixed into the odor, though— something cloying, like the smell of candy.

Mio screamed when she saw what was inside.

It was a person.

There was absolutely no sense of any life in this place, but now, seemingly out of nowhere, someone was here. A low bed had been placed in the far corner of the room, and someone sat up in it, utterly still. Initially, it seemed more like a mannequin than a person. The face was covered by long, scraggly hair, and it stared unmoving into vacant space. Mio found herself clutching the sleeve of Kaname's uniform shirt; her pulse quickened. Inside her head, a voice repeated, *Oh no, oh no, oh no... Is that...?*

"...Hanaka."

Mio hardly managed to choke out the name. Her mind couldn't catch up to what it perceived—the word simply dropped from her mouth. Sudden, powerful, aching pain gathered in her chest. She took one step at a time, watching carefully, waiting to see if the person would move.

"Hanaka...!"

A moment ago, Mio had been frozen with fear and nervousness, but now she released Kaname's shirt, gripped by an imperative to examine the face of this person sitting on the bed.

The features she could discern through the long hair over the face were quite changed from what she remembered. However, they were undoubtedly Hanaka's. She didn't react to Mio. She was blinking, but that was all; her mind seemed elsewhere. Her eyes weren't focused, either, and Mio worried she might be blind.

Her hair was long, enough so that she might not have cut it once since disappearing. Rapunzel popped into Mio's mind. She couldn't help but see the fairy-tale girl in Hanaka. A girl trapped in a high tower, unable to leave or do anything but grow her hair.

Her locks were black. At least, they should have been. Mio knew that, and perhaps that's what was so eerie. For in the darkness of that room, there seemed to be white, glowing hairs on Hanaka's head. It felt like she'd lost all vitality and somehow aged decades.

Hanaka didn't react to her. Mio had no idea what to say to her shockingly changed friend.

And there were so many things to say.

Have you been like this the entire time? Nearly two years, since the day you disappeared? While I graduated high school, went to college, and started a new chapter of my life?

"You'll be taking college entrance exams soon. That's great," Hanaka's mother had said. Mio was on the verge of tears now.

Hanaka was dressed in pajamas with a blue-and-yellow checkered pattern. But something about them struck Mio as wrong. Eventually, she realized the button order differed from what she was accustomed to. The left and right sides were reversed. Hanaka was wearing men's pajamas.

Mio couldn't begin to imagine the meaning behind this. She turned to Kaname as she felt the tears coming.

"Kaname. It's Hanaka…"

He nodded and rang the bell in his hand. Hanaka's expressionless face suddenly contorted and scrunched, as though threatening to crack apart.

Many things happened in the blink of an eye.

Hanaka screamed, bolting and leaping up where she had been utterly still before. She held her head and clawed at her chest. The sound of her shriek shocked Mio into action.

"Hanaka!" she cried, holding the girl's body down on the bed. It felt hard and light, as though made of nothing but skin and bone. Mio's heart sank. She recognized the voice, it belonged to a friend from high school, and she embraced Hanaka.

However, Hanaka's body was searing hot, and Mio instantly regretted the contact.

The same had been true of Itta Kanbara. His body had scorched like a heated iron. Mio recalled how Kaname had instructed her not to touch him.

And now he shouted, "Get away!" Mio didn't need to be told twice.

But her body and Hanaka's were stuck together like opposing magnetic poles, and she couldn't break free.

Oh no, Mio lamented. *I'm sorry, Kaname. I always do this…*

He warned me, and I was so intent on not being a problem, but I always do this. I'm supposed to keep up, yet I made a mistake instead.

You're too nice. You're a model student. Why do you go to those lengths to be nice? You're only going to give him the wrong idea. If you can't even turn him down… I'm saying this for your own good.

"That's just one of those things you do, Mio."

She saw Itta Kanbara's face; she heard his voice. "I'm sorry, Senpai," she said. She couldn't help but apologize.

She'd suffered under him for only a few days, yet even so long after, she couldn't help but remember him and what he had done.

◆

The next thing she was aware of was the smell of alcohol. Not liquor, but the sharp stink of disinfectant that stung the back of the nose.

Her eyelids rose, slow and heavy, revealing a white ceiling. The white wall to her side wavered. The wallpaper bulged and flowed, as though carried on the breeze. After a moment, she recognized that it was a cloth curtain.

A white screen. The kind found in…

A hospital.

Mio blinked twice. At some point, she'd fallen asleep in a bed somewhere. She sat up and looked down at herself. She still had the same clothes on.

"You're awake?" The curtains parted with the question. Kaname Shiraishi's face appeared. She was relieved to see him, even more so because he was acting as he usually did.

"Kaname…"

Why was she here? What happened? The answers wouldn't come for a moment, but the sight of his face brought them back.

The tea party with all the housewives. Hatch rushing to the woman writhing in agony. The visit to the other apartment, Unit 302. What they saw behind the sliding door.

Hanaka on the bed, her eyes blank.

"I'm sorry, I—"

She paused to gasp. Behind Kaname, who'd pulled open the curtains to peer at her, beyond the bright fluorescent light, was another bed. When she saw its occupant, she sprang to her feet.

"Hanaka!"

It was Hanaka.

Mio only felt able to rush to her friend because Hanaka was sleeping peacefully now, quite unlike how she appeared in the apartment. Her abnormally long hair was still unkempt, and she looked gaunt, but her pale cheeks held a bit of color. She felt *alive*, much closer to the Hanaka Mio remembered. She wasn't wearing those pajamas anymore. They'd been traded for a hospital gown.

Mio looked to Kaname. He pointed under the bed she'd been sleeping in.

"Your shoes."

He was pointing at her sneakers. Mio suddenly realized she was barefoot. She put the sneakers on, thanked Kaname, and inspected their surroundings.

It was dark beyond the window. Night had come already.

An ambulance siren echoed in the distance.

"Where are we? The hospital?"

"Yeah. Katagiri General Hospital's helping us this time."

"You brought me here?"

"Yeah."

"Sorry. I guess I didn't help very much after all…"

"Nah, it's fine," he grunted.

Mio made up her mind to tell him. She gazed at the sleeping Hanaka, so much more peaceful than before, and said, "Thank you."

"Huh?"

"You helped me see Hanaka again, like you promised. You saved her."

"Nah," Kaname grunted again evasively. He didn't seem bashful or embarrassed, just unsure of how to have an actual conversation.

"Is Hanaka going to be all right?"

"She is. I know so."

"Have you contacted her parents?"

"I did. But I'm having them wait a bit before they see her. There's still something left to do tonight."

"'Left to do'?" Mio repeated. That was quite vague, but Kaname didn't elaborate.

Hanaka's parents undoubtedly wished to see their daughter as soon as possible. Mio felt bad for them, knowing Hanaka's condition and how worried they were for her. However, they had to do as Kaname said for now.

I knew it would end up like this. I've already seen several unthinkable things happen today.

From the window, Mio saw the lights of the city. She examined the neon signs and the other sights viewable from the hospital room and realized she didn't know where they were.

Was it close to the complex where they'd found Hanaka? Or was it by Sawatari Apartments? Mio wasn't familiar with the name Katagiri General Hospital.

The room had two beds: one by the window, where Hanaka slept, and the one where Mio had awoken.

She looked down at Hanaka's face, and sadness built in her chest.

"When she wakes up, will I be able to talk with her like before?"

"Yeah. Maybe not right away."

"Will she remember everything? Like, what she was doing?" Mio asked. Her breaths turned short. "What was she doing there?"

"I can only imagine, but I believe she was doing *that* the whole time."

Mio's eyes widened. *That*, meaning sitting in the dark room smelling of rain and mold and a whiff of sugar, all alone, peering into empty space without moving...

"She was inside like that, all alone? For almost two years?"

"Probably."

"But that's just..." Mio paused to collect herself. "That's just awful. In the last two years, I graduated high school and started college. And Hanaka's done nothing but stay locked in that room, wasting away? It's just horrible. There's no way to make that better."

"You sure about that?"

Mio eyed Kaname with surprise. As usual, it was very hard to read the look in his eyes.

"She can make up for two or three years, can't she?" he asked.

"'Make up for'...?"

Mio thought it ghastly that he could talk about this stuff right in front of the victim. Maybe that was just the way of things. Nothing would come of arguing with him. He was always out of step with the rest of the world anyway.

But Mio couldn't let this be the end. It wasn't someone else's problem to deal with. If not for her good fortune, she could've easily been the one in Hanaka's position. Itta Kanbara had first set his sights on her. She'd made it out fine because Kaname had saved her, and if not for that, she would have suffered Hanaka's fate.

"Why did Kanbara-senpai take Hanaka there?"

"I think Hanaka was the replacement Itta Kanbara."

"'Replacement'?"

"Remember what I said? The family replenishes its lost members. They turned Ritsu Mikishima into Kaori Kanbara to make her the new wife and mother. So, being the closest in age, I'm guessing they turned Hanaka into the family's new 'eldest son.'"

"'Eldest son'...?"

There were two children in the family. An older son about college age, and a young son in elementary school...

"This is only conjecture, but I believe that Hanaka may have been a kind of emergency replacement for the Kanbara family. I inflicted too much damage, and they lost their older son earlier than expected, so they had to take her instead. They wanted a son, but because this one was of a different gender, she was unable to adequately fill the role of Itta Kanbara. So there was no choice but to let her become a shut-in and stay inside."

"All of this stuff about taking over and replacing family members. What does it mean?"

"Ah..."

Kaname inhaled. His answers were always a bit short and gruff, but if you asked, he would tell you. Mio just had to wait a little longer than expected.

"Do you remember the *old* Itta Kanbara? The one who died in the mountains of Mie Prefecture?"

"You mean my senpai from the track team?"

"Yes."

He'd treated Mio terribly, and she'd escaped only because Kaname saved her in the nick of time. Still, hearing him say *"died"* left a terrible weight in Mio's chest. She didn't care for him anymore, yet hearing his name and remembering his face brought the feeling to mind whether she liked it or not.

"I failed," Kaname stated. "I wanted to start with Itta Kanbara and track down the whole family to wipe them out, but I wounded him more than was necessary. On top of that, I didn't foresee the family fleeing so quickly. I was naive, and that made things worse for you and Hanaka."

He approached Hanaka's bed and gazed at her sleeping face. The siren still wailed outside.

"I didn't notice that Kanbara went after someone besides you, Miss Harano. I suspect Itta Kanbara perished while on the run after I wounded him. He took Hanaka when he realized his death was close at hand, to make her his replacement."

"What was the cause of Senpai's death?" Mio questioned, her pulse hastening. She'd only heard that he'd died in Mie. Even hearing *"perished"* from Kaname's lips didn't make it seem any more real.

Kaname stared at her without saying anything, then took out his smartphone. After a few taps, he showed her a news article on the screen.

Victim of suicide by hanging found in Mie mountains identified.

Mio gasped.

"He killed himself?"

"Yep."

Mio skimmed the article. It was dated about a month after the body was found.

On the seventh of last month, the body located in the mountains of Mie Prefecture was identified as Yukiya Yasuda, who went missing in Hokkaido seven years ago as an elementary school student...

Her eyes locked on the unfamiliar name: Yukiya Yasuda.

There was no photo of him in the article. But Mio could easily imagine a younger version of the senpai she had known. It was difficult to breathe.

"This is Senpai? This person named Yukiya Yasuda?"

"Yes. The *nth*-generation Itta Kanbara, older son of the Kanbara family."

"But why suicide?"

"Being part of that family, going outside your original humanity and spreading death and darkness around you, can be very tiring," Kaname explained, his eyes fixed on Hanaka's face. His words seemed to echo the gauntness of Hanaka's cheeks. "The closer you drag others to death, the closer to death you become. So even as they pull others down into darkness, they are always on the hunt for those who can become them."

"Why?"

"I can't really answer that, other than to say it's just how they are," Kaname replied uncertainly. He shook his head. "That's how exhausting it is to be a member of the Kanbara family, and maybe it's an indication of how badly they wish to escape it. You may not want to hear this after everything Itta Kanbara did to you, but the way he cornered you, spread his darkness around you, and insulted you wasn't something he could control. It wasn't his own will. As they are forced to play the family role, they get closer to their own deaths."

Kaname looked at the bag of IV fluid strung up over Hanaka's bed. "Take Kaori Kanbara, for example. I banished the darkness from Ritsu Mikishima today. Before her, Keiko Kashiwazaki was Kaori Kanbara, until she fell from the hallway at Sawatari Apartments. She probably jumped on her own, and did so to make Ritsu her replacement."

"So the people who become a part of the family were originally just ordinary people?" Mio stared at the name *Yukiya Yasuda* on the phone screen. She chose the words *ordinary people* very carefully.

After a short, hesitant silence, Kaname admitted, "I think the Itta Kanbara you met was originally a normal boy. From what I heard, the Itta Kanbara *before* him joined the baseball team near his home in Hokkaido, and that was how he worked his way in. Yasuda was the team captain, a very bright and sociable boy. However, he began to set harsher rules for the team, steadily worsening things. A year later, over a dozen people involved with the team were dead, including coaches and former members. Ultimately, Yukiya Yasuda vanished."

Mio recalled the desolate apartment where they'd found Hanaka. It was impossible to imagine a family spending time together and chatting there. What kind of life did he and his family have in such a place?

And that gave Mio another thought.

After Hanaka and Kanbara vanished, the teacher and other adults who went to the Kanbara home had said it was totally trashed, turned upside down. However, they'd also mentioned it didn't look like anyone had even lived there. Everyone believed it was messy because the Kanbaras had run out in the middle of the night, but perhaps it had resembled the apartment Mio had seen today.

"He played baseball," said Mio, her voice trembling. She didn't know why she felt like crying.

Yukiya Yasuda. Just a normal boy.

Suddenly, she wanted to hear about him. Kanbara-senpai had been very athletic and talented at track. The pain in her heart was becoming unbearable.

"Yeah," Kaname muttered. "Keiko Kashiwazaki—the previous Kaori Kanbara—killed her mother in Akita Prefecture and was wanted by the police. The authorities think she intended it to be a murder-suicide, and she was pushed to it because she couldn't bear the pain of keeping the old woman alive."

"Wha…?"

"Apparently, she was the kind of person who always put herself last, no matter how bad her problems got. It was like she always got the short end in life. According to a newspaper article from the time of the incident, she was constantly stressed from timidly watching to see what other people thought first. Before she vanished, the Kanbara family showed up in her town. The family at the time had a mother who said, 'Me too, I'm the same,' always agreeing with her target. I heard she told Keiko Kashiwazaki, 'Me too. I killed my mother, too, so you're just fine. Strangling her? That's nothing. Everyone does it. You're fine. Me too.'"

Goose bumps formed on Mio's arms. "So the family just continues like that forever? Constantly changing members and sucking up normal people?" Fury swirled in her heart. "They use people like disposable pawns. That's horrible."

Despite Mio's righteous anger, when she voiced her thoughts, the words felt trite. She bit her lip.

"What *is* the Kanbara family? Two children, a mother…"

"And a father," Kaname finished firmly. "A father, a mother, and two children. Four in all. The current members are all they have."

"Current?"

"The family has lasted indefinitely. They appear at some point, and sometimes they have children. They grow older like normal families do, passing through generations. If the Kanbara family children bring in wives and have kids of their own, those babies will grow, too. They'll get older, start school, go to middle school, then high school, find others to drag down, and spread their darkness. They make other people go insane and kill them."

Mio didn't immediately understand everything Kaname said. It wasn't particularly confusing, but she had difficulty accepting it.

The phrase *"sometimes they have children"* crawled into her ears. Kids born from manipulation, a need to replenish the family. *"Bring in wives"* also felt eerily lurid. The older son, Itta Kanbara, could have brought her in.

Mio thought back to an earlier remark.

Kanbara-senpai, when he was still Yukiya Yasuda, had met the Kanbara family through his baseball team. The family got older.

"When you say they appear at some point..."

"They've existed for ages. Those who inherit the Kanbara family. They have identities and histories of their own, and they go all the way back. They've been among us the entire time, spreading their darkness."

"So when they change people, they can still operate under that other identity?"

"When the people around them start to realize that it doesn't make sense, the Kanbara family members just force their way through. When their ages are off, or genders aren't right, they simply bend the logic and say, 'This is how we are,' somehow making it acceptable through sheer force of will. It distorts reality for everyone around them, and makes people accept it as normal. That's what makes them so difficult to deal with."

Kaname stopped for a breath, then continued, "Because their distortion helps them blend in with their surroundings, it's tough to find them again after we lose them." His eyes narrowed, and his voice dropped to a whisper. "We should probably leave now, Miss Harano."

"Huh?"

"This afternoon, around the time that we freed Ritsu and Hanaka at that apartment complex, my companions pulled Niko Kanbara out of the school he attends."

The name Niko Kanbara was new to Mio, but based on context, she could sense he was probably the second son of the Kanbara family.

Kaname confirmed it for her. "The younger child of the Kanbaras. A boy fills the role currently, but it might have originally been a girl. That's only going on the assumption that 'Niko' sounds like a girl's name. It could be the reverse of what happened with Hanaka. What was originally the younger sister turned into a younger brother, forced to assimilate into the family."

He was almost muttering to himself, and his lips formed a brief smile that vanished promptly.

"Niko Kanbara is asleep in another room at this hospital. And so is Ritsu. We've got three of them here right now. So I think he'll come to get them."

Ambulances were still wailing outside the hospital. They had been more distant before—the noise was coming closer. Kaname looked Mio right in the eyes.

"It's the first time he's lost three at once, so I'm sure he will. We're waiting for him now."

"Waiting for whom?"

"Father."

There were equal parts force and nervousness in Kaname's voice. Mio was stunned.

"If we do this the normal way, he'll probably escape again," he explained. "So we're going to set a trap."

"Is he the root of all of this?"

When Mio said "root," she thought of the phrase *root of all evil*. The source that continually replenished the family, brought in new members, and kept it going for ages.

"Is the father doing all of it? Why is he so focused on a 'family' in the first place? He could just do all of this stuff on his own!"

So he was the one who put Hanaka and Senpai through all of that, ruling over them?

Kaname's lips parted like he was going to reply.

But a massive sound ripped through the air and ground before he could.

A heavy booming erupted from below. The floor trembled and shook. Mio could sense the trembling in the air past the windows. It seemed like a large earthquake, but something wasn't quite right. What was the difference…?

A smartphone vibrated.

It wasn't Mio's. It was the phone she'd been using to read the article. She hadn't returned it to Kaname yet.

The online article with Yukiya Yasuda's name in it was gone, replaced by a black incoming call screen with the name *Yumeko* displayed.

"Kaname, is this…?"

The quake persisted. It was so tremendous that Mio couldn't tell if it was still going, if it had already ended, if things had truly been shaking to begin with, or if this was something else entirely. Mio felt like she'd stepped off a ship after a long time at sea, when you couldn't trust your senses to function normally yet.

Kaname snatched the phone out of Mio's hand and answered the call. "It's Kaname. Yes… That's right." After a moment, his expression hardened.

He turned on the TV next to the bed where Mio had slept, then promptly reached for the remote. For a moment, Mio was afraid that he'd rouse Hanaka.

The ten o'clock news appeared on the screen. There was a video of a burning building.

"I'm here at the scene of the disaster, but we've got to be careful.

"It's just a sea of fire around here.

"The explosion was so loud that it's left me unable to hear for the moment.

"I can't contact the rest of the crew."

Zzkkshsk—

The audio cut out, and the image from the on-site camera turned diagonally and froze.

Suddenly, the feed returned to the studio. A grave-looking newscaster was in the center of the screen. He sounded shaken.

"If you're just tuning in, at seven o'clock this evening, an employee at Yotsumiya Foods in Yokohama locked himself in the third floor of the office building that was the company headquarters. He's a member of the second sales section, and as we understand it, he was in possession of some kind of explosive. In phone calls to the police, he claimed he attempted to rekindle a romance with an ex-girlfriend and threatened to kill his boss and coworkers if she did not take him back. Police were hard at work negotiating with the man until moments ago, when there appears to have been an explosion on the third floor. We cannot yet confirm the safety of every member of our breaking news crew on-site..."

Kaname changed the channel. Another station was playing an emergency broadcast covering the event. Red flames licked at the night sky on the screen.

Sirens were audible.

Not just one, but many.

They might have been ambulances, fire trucks, or police cars; it was impossible to tell. A plethora of sirens spread throughout the night, echoing and resonating with each other.

"I see it," Kaname said to the person on the other end of the phone. "That's right. Yotsumiya Foods is Father's company."

Mio went stiff and stared at Kaname, but he wasn't looking in her direction. He was peering out the window, where one part of the sky was faintly brighter. For some reason, the roaring flames on the television and the light outside the window didn't connect as one phenomenon in Mio's mind. The burning structure's windows were entirely shattered. In the picture, passersby and TV crew members on the street were huddled and prone, holding their heads.

Kaname ended the call and turned his attention to Mio.

"I'm sorry, Miss Harano, but will you go back to your place at Sawatari Apartments? Once you're there, do not leave again tonight for any reason. Whatever happens, don't worry. I'll arrange a ride for you."

"Is this the work of the Kanbaras' father?"

He nodded. The sirens outside got louder and sharper. It was clear that they were getting closer.

"Our plans got messed up. The hospital was supposed to help us out, but it's going to be overrun soon with new emergency patients. So you should really—"

He likely meant to finish with "go back home."

But the words were drowned out.

Bang! There was a loud sound nearby, and Mio's vision instantly went dark. She wasn't sure what happened at first, but when she felt something light tap her head, she shut her eyes instinctually.

The fluorescent lights had burst. Kaname moved quickly, enveloping Mio's body in his arms. He lifted her and moved her out of the way to protect her from debris.

The light had gone out all at once. Too much of it, in fact.

No illumination filtered through the window anymore.

Someone screamed. Someone else started talking in a panic. People conversed nervously.

The incident hadn't been isolated to their room. Some unseen impact had shattered all the fluorescents in the hospital.

There was a muffled hum, and the dull orange glow of emergency lights came to life, revealing Mio and Kaname. The system had switched on in the other rooms, too. The approach to the hospital outside was tinted orange now.

The sirens abruptly stopped.

"He's here," Kaname muttered under his breath, his arm still around Mio's back.

◆

Kaname led Mio by the hand through the panicked hospital, weaving past the people filling the hallways. Several nurses and doctors rushed around under the emergency lights, inquiring if patients were okay.

White beams from flashlights scanned through the orange haze.

Kaname pulled Mio along behind him without a shred of hesitation. With his free hand, he placed a call on his phone.

"Hello? Let's switch rooms. May I ask you to take care of Hanaka Sawada?"

Hanaka.

Now that they'd moved out of the darkened hospital room, Mio suddenly worried that leaving her alone had been a bad idea. Mio wanted to tell Kaname they couldn't abandon her, but between the chaos of the explosion on the news and the power outage, she couldn't find the right moment.

Kaname maintained his pace once he finished talking on the phone. "It's all right," he said.

Mio looked up at him. His pale, expressionless face remained focused on the way ahead.

"I'm fairly sure Hanaka will be all right. Even if he comes to take them back, she's low on the priority list. It's questionable whether she can fill the role of older son again."

"Aren't you worried that you might become the elder son?" Mio asked. After all the talk of replenishing family members and finding replacements, she couldn't help but worry. She didn't know Kaname's exact age, but it was definitely close to Hanaka's and Mio's. He might fit as the older son.

"Huh?" Kaname blurted out, so stunned he turned his head toward Mio. He must have realized that she was concerned for his safety. However, he quickly faced forward again. "I'm fine. Thanks for your concern, but that won't happen. It would be truly ridiculous if I became his son."

His palm was warm in hers. She realized, upon reflection, that despite his thin emotional range and eerie mannerisms, Kaname was firmly on *this* side of the divide.

He's alive.

How exactly was he able to confront this family of darkness and purify their ill effects? Was it some kind of duty? If they survived this, she wanted to ask him about everything.

Kaname hurried to a different wing with Mio in tow. It was a large hospital. They made their way through a maze of halls, climbing stairs, passing immobilized elevators, and pushing through numerous automatic sliding doors.

When Kaname finally came to a stop in front of a particular room, Mio noticed several other people gathered there.

"Kaname," one of them said, a man in his fifties. Another woman also called his name. She looked to be in her midforties and wore a white nurse's outfit. There were a few more, and all of them seemed quite calm despite the emergency.

"I'll wait inside," Kaname said. "If Father comes, let me know."

The people shared a look. "Be careful," they replied, some placing hands on his shoulders. They all made way so Kaname and Mio could enter.

He told them, "I'm leaving Ritsu Mikishima and Hanaka Sawada in your hands."

The others nodded.

There was no number or patient name outside the room to identify it, and it was smaller than the one they'd left Hanaka in. There was just one bed, which held an unattended, sleeping child.

The child's features were very youthful, and he had smooth, clipped bangs. A pair of thick-lensed glasses rested beside the pillow. A school bag had been left on a nearby chair, confirming this boy was in elementary school.

Kaname finally released Mio's hand. He'd been squeezing it for so long that it throbbed. The awkwardness of holding hands, even during an emergency, left Mio unable to speak for a moment. After a deep breath, she asked, "Is this...the younger son?"

"Yes. Niko Kanbara. If he's going to come and take anyone back, it's probably this one."

"Why?"

"Excluding the father, this one has served the family the longest and most effectively. He was well suited to being Niko Kanbara, and he created many victims as a result. He was quite a talent."

The term *"talent"* made Mio's blood run cold.

A family charmed by darkness, replenishing its members from the general population. Some were better suited to their roles than others...

Without warning, there was a loud *boom!*

The floor shook again. Mio screamed and cowered, and she noticed fresh flames through the window. These were closer—much closer. Perhaps they were coming from the hospital itself. Maybe the room they'd been in earlier, where Hanaka slept...

Kaname's phone rang.

A burst sounded at the same time. Mio heard screams. It wasn't apparent what was happening, but something was coming.

Despite the distant clamor, the space inside the room remained shockingly quiet. It was like the world outside the door was completely disconnected.

Mio heard a *ktok*.

The uproar and shouting were still audible. Sirens blared endlessly.

However, this noise rang clearer, distinguishing itself from all others. The footstep bored into Mio's ears.

"I'm scared..."

The room had turned abnormally cold.

It felt nothing at all like a hospital anymore. Mio shivered and suddenly felt like she could no longer be certain where she was.

She'd tried to say she was cold. That's what she'd *wanted* to say. Mio couldn't explain why the words that had come out were "*I'm scared.*"

But she wasn't alone.

"Don't be scared," said Kaname from beside her.

She hadn't realized that he was so close. Their shoulders nearly touched. His back was to the sleeping child. He was there, and his voice was clear and present.

Ktok, went the sound.

Ktok, ktok.

Leather shoes, walking down the hallway, firm and careful.

Mio shuddered despite herself. She envisioned a freezing cold snake coiling around her back, and although she'd never touched one in her life, she felt the scales on her skin. It was unbearable. She wanted to claw at her back and flee. Somehow, Kaname's hand prodded her right where she felt the serpent, even though it was all in her mind.

"It's not scary. The family does surpass the bounds of your imagination. However, they can only use words and actions. They're bound by the same rules we are. They're not all-powerful, even when it seems they might be."

Ktok, ktok.

Ktok, ktok.

The footsteps drew nearer, quarter notes in a steady beat.

Mio couldn't move.

Kaname kept his hand on her back.

"The blackout was probably just a high-voltage pulse sent to the entire building from the electrical substation, which shattered the fluorescents. That would have flipped the hospital's breakers, nothing more."

Ktok, ktok.

"Consider this…"

Ktok, ktok.

Ktok, ktok.

"If he happens to stop at his 'family members" rooms, it's only because he figured out where they'd be before the blackout. He's not using some kind of psychic phenomenon to sense them or anything like that."

Ktok.

Ktok.

The strides themselves were getting longer, and the sound of the footfalls was growing duller. What had been a regular rhythm was noticeably changing pace, drawing Mio's attention and gnawing at her mind.

She couldn't stop imagining hundreds of *things* getting into her sleeves. Things that rustled like needles and were textured like armor…

She wanted to scream.

Centipede legs, crawling all over her skin beneath her clothes. The snake writhing on her back was now two. She couldn't move.

Thousands of earthworms entered her body through her feet…

Kaname's hand went from her back to her sleeve. He grabbed both of her wrists, closing off the sleeves, squeezing hard enough that it hurt.

"If you feel anything unpleasant, it's a result of your fear. You are the cause of those sensations. You're fine; there's nothing scary here."

Ktok. The footsteps stopped.

At some point, the horrible freezing cold inside the room had eased.

The door opened. It wasn't an especially heavy door, yet it made a spectacular sound as it came open.

A man wearing glasses peeked through the crack.

He was dressed in a shabby old suit. His lenses caught the light, making it hard to see the color of his eyes, or the look in them. There was an unsettlingly powerful menace coming off his thin frame.

Had Kaname's companions outside not tried to stop this man? Did the trap they'd set fail? A siren blared like lightning outside. The noise split the atmosphere in the room.

Kaname exhaled, as if to say, "Finally, we meet." Then he spoke to the unfamiliar man.

"It's been a long time...Dad."

Lightning flashed.

There was no rain, and no storm clouds covered the sky, but a bolt illuminated all of existence. A short while later, its thunder reached the hospital, roaring and close.

The sound was like that of living trees cracking apart. Flames rose somewhere past the window. Perhaps a nearby tree had been struck. Mio didn't know. Her eyes were trained on the man's face, not the blaze.

The man's face slowly warped at Kaname's words, and the expression behind his glasses became clear.

Despite the menace that triggered Mio's fight-or-flight response so powerfully...

He looks like a normal person.

Just a normal man, about my dad's age.

Like someone's nice, normal father.

On the news, field reporters occasionally flagged down passersby to ask for opinions. A tipsy man might wait by a train station until someone with a microphone caught him. "Sir, may I have a moment?" the reporter would ask. "Sir, aren't you afraid your wife will scold you for this?" *Sir, sir, sir.* It was a term applied to any middle-aged man. And here was one of them—someone's normal-looking father.

Mio's eyelids widened a bit.

At last, her body could move again. She glanced at Kaname and sucked in a sharp breath.

She'd never seen this expression from him before. Since their recent reunion, his resting face had been closer to a smiling one than back in high school. That was gone now, though. His features were screwed up, like he was about to cry from rage.

The bell rang.

It wasn't Kaname. His hands were supporting Mio's shoulders. He stared straight ahead, at the father of the family.

The fury in his eyes was an indescribable mixture of searing anger and grief. And all of it was focused upon the man who'd just entered.

They started coming to Mio's mind, one after the other.

All of the things Kaname had said.

The things he'd mentioned about the father.

"It's the first time he's lost three at once, so I'm sure he will. We're waiting for him now."

"Waiting for whom?" Mio had asked.

"Father."

And that wasn't all.

"That's right. Yotsumiya Foods is Father's company."

"I'll wait inside. If Father comes, let me know."

Father.

Father.

When the man finally, abruptly appeared, Kaname addressed him directly.

"It's been a long time…Dad."

Noises sounded in Mio's head.

The bell's ringing grew louder and deeper. There was more than one, in fact. Many, many bells, and their sounds overlapped, shattered, and scattered; an entire mass of formerly unified sound splintered and broke apart.

Concerned, Mio had asked Kaname. *"Aren't you worried that you might become the elder son?"* He'd looked shocked until he regained his poise.

"*I'm fine. Thanks for your concern, but that won't happen. It would be truly ridiculous if I became his son.*"

Oh...

The flash of the lightning strike died out, leaving the man standing in the doorway looking rather shocked. It was clear, even from behind the glasses, that he was staring at Kaname. His mouth opened and closed like a goldfish's, as though pulled by an invisible thread.

"Kaname," he said.

Kaname's face scrunched up. He looked ready to cry.

Their faces were very similar. Heavy, puffy lids. Hooked noses. Sloping eyebrows.

Because they were father and son.

Actual father and son.

"Dad." Kaname took one hand off Mio's shoulder and arched his back, seemingly resonating with the chimes coming from outside the room. He reared back like he was taking an enormous breath, then straightened up, bell in his hand.

Ding!

Mio heard the rustle of wind passing through bamboo, the sound she'd always heard outside her family home.

"Dad!" Kaname cried. "Come back!"

"Eeyyaaaaaaahhh!!"

There was a scream.

The wind billowed, whipping up the flames outside, which grew and stretched to reach for the sky. They struggled, anguished, as though in the throes of death...

The fresh scent of bamboo filled the hospital room, accompanied by the sharp, charred stink of something burning.

The hospital's garden was on fire.

Sirens blared.

Ambulances brought in victims from the food company office bombing. However, the hospital that was their destination had suffered a blackout and fire of its own. All of those ambulances had to find alternate destinations in a hurry. The sirens continued.

The noises closing in on the hospital now belonged to fire engines.

With the blackout preventing the hospital PA from functioning, someone had to get the emergency megaphone out instead.

"Warning! Please do not leave the hospital premises! Lightning struck a tree outside the hospital and started a fire. I repeat, do not go outside. The building is safe. There was a boiler explosion earlier, but that fire has already been extinguished. There is no further danger of explosions. Please do not panic! The fire outside will also be put out soon!"

The messenger repeated himself, urging people to stay inside and remain calm. Windows were opened, and patients leaned out to see the burning tree. Some had their phones out to take pictures of the incident. The crowd was a captive audience to the fire department's attempt to hose down the ignited tree, which had been split by lightning.

The announcement wasn't a hollow one, the firefighters were indeed getting the job done. The blaze was steadily dying out.

It'll be over soon, Mio thought.

She turned away from the window and back to the hospital room. Kaname hadn't budged from his father's side.

Not the Kanbara "father," but his own.

A pair of glasses was next to the pillow; lenses cracked and frames warped. The charred stench still hung in the air. Or maybe that was from the fire outside.

Kaname's father's suit was the one oddity that proved difficult to explain. He'd only screamed. That was how it had appeared anyway. Yet the jacket was covered in soot like it had been engulfed in invisible flames.

* * *

Kaname had stared pensively at the father who screamed and crumpled to the ground.

Eventually, satisfied that the other man was totally immobile, he rushed to his side to pick him up. The man's downcast face wasn't frightening anymore. The indescribable sense of menace that it had carried when he'd first opened the door had vanished. Now he truly looked like an ordinary person, nothing more.

"Kaname."

Someone entered. It was the people who'd stood outside the room earlier, the ones who'd warned him to be careful. They checked in on Kaname and asked Mio if she was all right.

Kaname, who knelt at his father's side, asked them, "Is everyone okay?"

His tone was urgent. He looked to them, pleading.

"We didn't let anyone get away? The mother and older brother are still here?"

"They are. It's okay," replied the oldest man in the group. Kaname's body promptly slumped. He let out a long, heavy breath.

"Oh, I'm so glad."

Just like with Hanaka, a room had been arranged for Kaname's father in the hospital. Kaname's companions left their fellow with his father, heading elsewhere in the still-chaotic hospital.

Mio ended up at Kaname's side. She didn't think it was appropriate for a relative stranger like her to remain present, but she wanted to know the whole story. And, although it was presumptuous, she felt it was wrong to leave Kaname alone right now.

Someone ought to be with him.

"Is he your father?" she asked, breaking the long silence. At last, Kaname tore his gaze away from the man's face.

"May I ask what's going on here?" Mio said. "Am I supposed to believe that you were previously absorbed into the Kanbara family and later escaped?"

Maybe Kaname was Itta Kanbara before Senpai. Or perhaps he was the true first son, from back when they were originally related by blood…

Kaname's expression softened. He finally looked his age, in that state of half boyhood, half manhood. She hoped that his face would remain that way forever. The thought made her heart sting.

"No. This man is my real father, Minoru Shiraishi. Before he was absorbed by the Kanbara family, he was a doctor who worked in psychosomatic medicine."

"A doctor…"

"He went to college with the director of this hospital. That's how we got all this help. And it made a real mess of the place," Kaname admitted. He took a moment to remind himself to apologize for that later. A rather lifeless smile showed on his face for a moment, but he composed himself as he prepared to reveal everything to Mio.

"The Kanbara family came around when I was just starting elementary school. It began when the father, Jin Kanbara, visited my father's hospital for an examination."

The air in the room was getting thinner. Kaname's father, Minoru Shiraishi, looked pained in his sleep.

"Jin Kanbara told him he was having trouble sleeping. And while my father helped him, trying to get to the bottom of his issues, his wife started coming to the hospital, asking for medical help, too. Half a year later, my grandparents, older sister, and mother were dead. I saw many people around me die or vanish. Although maybe not as many as this time."

Earlier, Kaname and Mio had briefly turned on the news again. The explosion at Yotsumiya Foods had claimed at least eleven lives so far. The number of injured was not yet known. The perpetrator, a member of the second sales department named Toshiya Suzui, was already confirmed dead.

The details on the news proved unbearable, and Mio had promptly turned it off.

The thought that the man lying on the bed, Minoru Shiraishi, had been involved in that blast made her throat seize up.

"They can only use words and actions, not some kind of psychic phenomenon, or anything like that," Kaname had explained. Still, that lightning bolt out of nowhere didn't seem like a freak accident. It was very clear to Mio that the family and Kaname surpassed the bounds of ordinary reason.

What about the fire in the boiler room? Was that something the father had caused on his own? Or had he whispered commands to someone else, pressured them, and manipulated them into doing it?

"I was the only one left that year," Kaname mumbled. He touched his father's hand, which dangled limply in a burnt sleeve. "I was in danger, too, when Yumeko and the others saved me. They've been my parents ever since. They taught me everything, made me stronger, and raised me."

"Who are they?"

"Those who drive away darkness. They detect the presence of people like that family, things that spread darkness, and protect others from them. Some of them were born to families that have upheld that duty for a while, but these days there are many who've joined because they've lost family members, fiancés, and the like. People like me who want their families back."

The light in Kaname's eyes dimmed mournfully.

"My father was amazing," he whispered. "That family replenishes itself. The father and mother can be replaced. And new members inherit their roles while incorporating parts of their innate essence. After taking over my father, who was a counseling doctor, Jin Kanbara became a very troublesome figure. Once my dad was the father of the Kanbara family, the damage worsened exponentially. It's why I was so determined to stop him."

Kaname's father was still asleep. His son wore a pained look. Kaname had said he lost his grandparents, older sister, and mother. His father was his only remaining blood relative.

"It took a long time, but he's finally back. I'm going to start things over with Dad."

"I'm so sorry!" Mio cried, bowing her head. Out of the corner of her eye, she saw that Kaname regarded her with surprise. She couldn't bring herself to lift her head, but bit her lip to summon the courage to continue. "Earlier, while thinking of Hanaka, I said something very insensitive to you."

Remembering it made the inside of Mio's head boil. She was racked with shame.

"I said there was no way to make up for losing two whole years…"

"That's just awful. In the last two years, I graduated high school and started college. And Hanaka's done nothing but stay locked in that room, wasting away? It's just horrible. There's no way to make that better."

Kaname had replied, *"You sure about that? She can make up for two or three years, can't she?"*

Mio had been shocked that he'd acted like two or three years was nothing, but now she understood. And it was far too late to do anything about it.

Assuming Kaname was Mio's age, if he lost his father at the start of elementary school, then that was a total of twelve years. His father had been gone all that time, yet Kaname would take him back so they could start over. The thought of so much time rendered Mio speechless.

Kaname grunted and slowly shook his head. "Why are you apologizing to me?"

"Because…"

"It might take a while, but we'll get back to normal. And I bet Hanaka will, too."

Mio didn't know what to say. Her vision went cloudy from tears. Through the blur, she could see Kaname's hand firmly clasped around his father's.

Mio fixated on that image and said, "But there's one thing I don't understand."

"What?"

"Your dad was the Kanbara family's father. He was a normal person until he was taken and forced to play the role."

"Right."

"Then who's the cause of all of this?"

That question had been stuck in Mio's head all night. An ominous thought occurred to her, and it sent an unpleasant trickle of sweat down her back.

"Maybe…that boy was the center of the Kanbara family?"

Kaname did say that if the father came back for anyone, it would be him—the child in the room during the confrontation. Niko Kanbara, the younger son.

The baby-faced boy with straight bangs. That sleeping face with pure, unblemished skin.

He was the only one Mio knew nothing about, a total mystery. She hadn't seen him awake or heard him speak.

What if this actually wasn't over yet? A chill stole over Mio. What would become of Niko after everything else wrapped up? Were Kaname's companions really watching over him?

"Is it the boy? Is he the one who kept replenishing the family and forced them to do all those things?" The panic was clear on Mio's face.

"Oh, right," said Kaname. Then, as casually as she could possibly imagine, he added, "Nah, he's not."

"Huh?"

"He's not. He was absorbed into the family four years ago, that's all. One of the women you saw earlier is his real mother. She's always regretted pressuring him so hard for failing his elementary school entrance exams. That created an opportunity for the Kanbara family to slip in. When she saw that her son was back, she clung to him, crying and apologizing. 'All I want is for you to be alive. You don't have to be good or special or the best—just alive.' Before he was Niko Kanbara, his real name was Taiga Miyaue."

"Then you're saying..."

"There *is* no center or root of evil," Kaname stated.

The sirens outside returned, as though suddenly remembering they were supposed to be on. Even at this hour, there were ambulances and police cars on the road. People were still suffering.

"There's no single person at the center of that family who rules the others. No one is the core or the root; the family gives them strength. If they lose one member, they replace them, and if another one goes, they replenish again. It's continued that way forever because, as best I can tell, it's the family that maintains the bonds that tie them together. No one person controls the bunch. If anything, it's the family structure itself that rules over them."

Mio recalled the apartment that felt uninhabited.

Cluttered rooms with no rhyme or reason to them. The smell of mold, rain, and sweets. She couldn't have imagined them existing there, functioning as a proper family would.

A shiver overtook her.

She imagined coming home to a place where each family member was present but simply stored in a box dubbed "home." They did nothing more than exist with empty eyes, the way Hanaka had sat on the bed, like it was her duty.

"That's why you need to exorcise them all at once. Otherwise it never ends. If a single one of them remains, it will replenish the others. I've been trying to get them all, to keep them from running off and making a new home. It's never gone as well as it did this time."

"So you're saying the vessel of the Kanbara family itself is cursed?"

Kaname stared at Mio with a questioning, wondering look. Hesitantly, he replied, "If you want to describe what that family did as a curse, then I suppose so."

"You told me they just showed up at some point and have existed ever since. So even though the Kanbara family is just a collection of unrelated people, the family itself persists, despite the lack of any one person's intent? They're all normal people, and none of them does it for a particular reason? They just…exist?"

"That's right. They just exist."

Mio put a hand to her chest. Her pulse was racing, and her breaths came fast and shallowly. There was no point or goal. *They just exist.* A group of people who spread darkness, harassed others with that darkness. They spanned eras and generations, absorbing the personalities and natures of various people—a clan of darkness, self-updating and self-maintaining.

Kaname bobbed his head. "They're not driven by any individual's will in particular. If you had to call it anything, it's the will of the family. The family controls them for the express purpose of maintaining form as a family."

"And there's no way to get out?"

The family exchanged its members for new ones. The members then spread darkness and malice around them, and that evil corroded and killed others. The damage expanded from the family, infecting others who continued the chain.

Kaname shook his head. "There's no way to be free of them aside from not making contact in the first place. Once you have, it's extremely difficult to totally protect yourself."

"But now it's finally over?" Mio asked. The question made her feel as though she'd borne witness to a historic moment, something that had never happened before.

A hollow family without a core that existed indefinitely, and the current of darkness they'd created had ended today. All the members had been driven out. At last, the cursed family had been dismantled…

Kaname nodded, although he didn't exactly look thrilled about it.

"Yes, it's over. The Kanbara family is, at least."

"'At least'?"

"Yeah."

"So you're saying…"

Mio was shocked by what she heard. Kaname's phone buzzed, and he answered. That drew his hand away from his father's, and soon, his expression was grave again. It stiffened as he listened to the call.

"Of the…family, you mean?"

Mio's ears started ringing from shock. She failed to make out the family name Kaname repeated.

Outside, sirens continued to wail.

EPILOGUE

Everything went crazy after she moved here.

Something crawled in my chest. I don't know why I thought about her so much.

"Listen, listen, listen! Hey, do you think I did something wrong? Can you read this text I got? I'm not the crazy one, right? It's him!"

At first, I was happy about it.

I wasn't close enough with anyone in class to have a best friend, so having an actual person to talk grades, gossip, and whatever else with was heartening. And she really listened to my problems, too.

But over time, her issues began to engulf everything.

"He totally likes me, doesn't he?"

"That teacher thinks I'm such an honor student, right?"

"She just treats me that way because she's jealous, huh?"

"The reason I'm isolated in class is totally because I'm special, and I have talents that ordinary people don't understand, you know?"

Calls, letters, texts, every little comment required a response, no matter how pointless. Day after day after day. I wanted to escape, to be free of them, but I couldn't ignore her.

"Oh yeah, everyone's jealous of you. They're just frustrated because you've got this and that," I would say to cheer her up, but that only made the remarks more frequent.

Look at me, look at me, look at me.

Compliment me.

Praise me.

Listen, listen, listen...

I thought I could control it.

I thought I could pay her some harmless compliments and say, "Uh-huh" enough to satisfy her. Why has the content of her chatting lost importance? It's the talking itself she cares for.

When I don't repeatedly praise her, it becomes a larger and larger problem in her mind.

"Why aren't you writing back?"

"Do you hate me now?"

"I thought you were my best friend."

"That's really heartless of you, after I spent so much time being your friend..."

Whine, whine, whine. Between her sentences, when she stopped to breathe, I didn't hear actual griping, just the sound of it.

Whine, whine...

"I'll kill myself, you know. Murderer," she whispered through the phone.

Not to her actual boyfriend, or to her best friend, or even a regular one.

I'm rapidly becoming the person she hates the most.

◆

Everything went nuts after he showed up.

I'm so worthless, aren't I?

I mean, I can't keep you safe.

I promised I would, and I can't.

You should give up on me and find someone better for you.

That's just how I am. I know I don't have any confidence, but you need to be with me.

I would absolutely die for you.

But what's worth it about a guy like me?

I don't even love you.

Each word a manipulation, each text message incomplete. I prayed for any response at all, even if it was just mindless, violent anger, but nothing, nothing, nothing.

What if he was in an accident? What if something happened? I waited and worried. And then he'd finally answer.

It's your fault.

You spoiled me, and you ruined me.

But that didn't tell me what to do. I was immobilized, tied down by the word "love." The phrase *"let's ruin it all together"* shook me to my core.

Let's die together.

*　*　*

There was no enemy, no obstacle, no anyone in my way, yet he gave me an invitation to escape.

◆

We all went crazy after that teacher showed up.

"There's no bullying in our class."

Maybe something was already going on with him when he made that declaration. As a matter of fact, kids were shunned by others regularly, and it was common to pester those you hated during school. We just assumed he didn't count that stuff.

But no matter what happened, the teacher repeated those words. *"There's no bullying in our class."*

Nobody decided on the goal of *Togetherness* written on the sheet of card stock paper hung on the wall, but there it was. Lunch cliques dissolved, and we all ate as a group to reinforce *"friendliness."* Whenever something happened, we pretended it hadn't. Not only was there no bullying, there was no fighting, either. One day, I, the class representative, was called up to the teacher's desk, and he showed me what was on his computer monitor.

A paper titled *The Tale of Group Togetherness.*

It outlined how he'd brought together a class that couldn't behave, and it was written like a novel. The teacher clapped me on the shoulder.

"It's up to all of you how this story ends. I'm submitting this to the research board. It's on you to make it right. Fix this class's story."

I didn't know what to say. My tongue was stuck to the roof of my mouth, and I couldn't speak. How had it come to this…?

◆

Everything changed after that message arrived.

What you're writing here is about my work, isn't it? Well, I'm stunned. This is very sad. Do you even realize how hurtful you're being?

I kept a social media account that I used to write movie reviews occasionally. Not long before, I had written my thoughts on a number of films without giving the titles. However, anyone was free to comment. There was no evidence that one was actually from someone involved in filmmaking, so I ignored it.

Then I started getting multiple direct messages. They were so frequent and high in volume that they became impossible to ignore, try as I might.

Why don't you make your own, if that's what you think?

If you can't even understand that your words affect other people, then you shouldn't be writing smug reviews in the first place.

I poured my life into that novel.

When I saw the word *novel*, I thought, *Aha*. My reviews were solely about movies. This person was just confused. That got me to finally write back.

Excuse me, but I think you're mistaken. I'm writing my thoughts on movies. Not a single one of my posts was about books.

But it didn't matter.

Don't lie to me.

Don't make excuses.

You won't get off that easy.

I found your old site and this picture on it. How about I spread this around?

It was an old selfie taken with a friend, but it wasn't posted on this account. Stunned, I could only watch helplessly as more messages came in.

And you live at _____, right? May I dig a little deeper? You really deserve to be punished for this.

Alarmed, I finally blocked him. However, I soon got another message from a new, unfamiliar account.

I'm the person who was just talking to you. There's no escape. You must face your punishment.

What did they mean, *punishment?* I hadn't done anything to deserve this. Why was this happening to me?

It all started on the day he said that crap.

The part-timers all seemed to agree that the manager was pushy and insensitive at times. But none of us knew how long we'd be working here, so we let it slide. It wasn't worth getting worked up about. We continued living our lives without calling it out.

But then...

"Hey, doesn't the manager really piss you off?"

Once it was out in the open, the unspoken understanding shattered. After that, things changed.

Someone saying it out loud meant we couldn't return to how things were before that person admitted it. Still, we didn't mean for *that* to happen...

We didn't mean to get together and do what we did to him...

It throws everything off.

When that underclassman's in the clubroom, it throws everything off.

At first, I thought she was great. A new team assistant with an upbeat attitude and a killer smile. Everyone fell in love with her, and it seemed like all the others were competing for her. That's why I was stunned when I heard the truth. She accepted every invitation to go on a date and every request to be someone's girlfriend.

When did things get like this?

◆

When he comes over, everything at home goes haywire.

◆

When that person...

◆

When...

yami-hara
An abbreviation of "yami-harassment."

yami-harassment
A compound of *yami* ("darkness") and *harassment*; unwelcome conduct toward a person stemming from darkness in one's own mind or heart. Applies to any action that threatens or violates the dignity of another person, regardless of intent or awareness.

yami-hara family
An individual or group that spreads darkness. They can appear anywhere and around anyone.

yami-hara
A compound of *yami* ("darkness") and *harai* ("exorcism"). To escape those who spread darkness. To exorcise their darkness. Also, the people who make it their duty to exorcise darkness.

※ This is a work of fiction.

Any resemblance to actual persons or
groups is purely coincidental.

But *yami-hara* can appear to anyone.
Please be careful.